It took every ounce of self-restraint Velth possessed to remain in place. The lizard that lived at the base of his brain insisted he run for the airlock. The trained Starfleet officer in him refused that imperative.

"Any chance you guys have fixed the transporters in the last two hours?" Velth asked.

"No, Velth," came Conlon's voice. She sounded every bit as stressed as Kim. *"Don't worry about the gear. Just start back toward the airlock, okay?"*

She didn't have to tell him twice. Velth rose and began his journey by retracing his steps to the array. As he did so, he began a cursory visual scan of the area around him while moving as briskly as his magnetic boots would permit. Nothing directly ahead or within ninety degrees of either side appeared to be amiss.

Fantastic, they're coming up behind me, Velth deduced. Turning slowly, he searched the darkness for whatever had spooked Kim and Conlon and activated his suit's proximity alert.

Even with his suit's sensor magnification set to maximum, it took a few seconds to pick them out among the visual spectacle of newborn stars and the distant lights that according to Kim were most likely alien vessels. At first glance, he saw two but soon enough, he could clearly discern five distinct figures. They were shaped like rectangles with no obvious extremities. Only bits and pieces of them were clearly visible as they approached.

Whatever their external suit, skin, or ships was constructed of, only portions of it reflected the distant light of the stars at any given moment. It was almost perfect camouflage but was also reminiscent of the material affixed to the hull he had just studied.

A bolt of adrenaline coursed through him as his sensors confirmed that his unwelcome visitors were less than a thousand kilometers from his position and were closing fast.

How the hell did that happen?

TO LOSE THE EARTH

KIRSTEN BEYER

Based on *Star Trek*®
created by
Gene Roddenberry
and
Star Trek: Voyager
created by
Rick Berman & Michael Piller & Jeri Taylor

GALLERY BOOKS
New York   London   Toronto   Sydney   New Delhi

Gallery Books
An Imprint of Simon & Schuster, Inc.
1230 Avenue of the Americas
New York, NY 10020

First Gallery Books trade paperback edition October 2020

For information about special discounts for bulk purchases, please contact Simon & Schuster Special Sales at 1-866-506-1949 or business@simonandschuster.com.

The Simon & Schuster Speakers Bureau can bring authors to your live event. For more information or to book an event, contact the Simon & Schuster Speakers Bureau at 1-866-248-3049 or visit our website at www.simonspeakers.com.

Manufactured in the United States of America

10 9 8 7 6 5 4 3

Library of Congress Cataloging-in-Publication Data

Names: Beyer, Kirsten, author.
Title: To lose the earth / Kirsten Beyer ; based on Star Trek® created by Gene Roddenberry
    and Star Trek, Voyager created by Rick Berman & Michael Piller & Jeri Taylor.
Other titles: At head of title: Star Trek Voyager
Description: New York : Gallery Books, [2020] | Series: Star trek : Voyager
Identifiers: LCCN 2020028894 (print) | LCCN 2020028895 (ebook) | ISBN
    9781501138836 (trade paperback) | ISBN 9781501138850 (ebook)
Subjects: LCSH: Star trek, Voyager (Television program)—Fiction. | GSAFD:
    Science fiction.
Classification: LCC PS3602.E934 T6 2020 (print) | LCC PS3602.E934 (ebook)
    | DDC 813/.6—dc23
LC record available at https://lccn.loc.gov/2020028894
LC ebook record available at https://lccn.loc.gov/2020028895

ISBN 978-1-5011-3883-6
ISBN 978-1-5011-3885-0 (ebook)

For John Van Citters.
He knows what he did.

"*To lose the earth you know, for greater knowing; to lose the life you have, for greater life; to leave the friends you love, for greater loving; to find a land more kind than home, more large than earth.*"

—Thomas Wolfe

HISTORIAN'S NOTE

Admiral Kathryn Janeway leads the Full Circle Fleet—*Voyager*, *Vesta*, *Galen*, and *Demeter*—on a mission of exploration in the Delta Quadrant. Many things have changed since a lone, lost *Starship Voyager* was trying to find her way home. The fleet is charged with discovering what has changed in the Delta Quadrant since *Voyager* was last here and the ultimate power in the quadrant, the Borg, departed.

This story takes place in September 2382, immediately following the events of the novel *Star Trek: Voyager—Architects of Infinity*.

Prologue

You almost died today.

So did your mom and I. A few hours ago, if you told me we would all still be here and I'd have time to sit for a few minutes and tell you about it, I don't think I would have believed it. This day started as the worst I've ever had in my life, and given the fact that I live and work in space, where a lot of things can and often do go very wrong, that's saying a lot.

Um . . . I'm your dad. Harry. Harry Kim. But you should probably call me Dad. When I was seven I spent two weeks calling my dad Pops because one of my friends at school asked me why my dad was so much older than his. I didn't understand anything then about my parents other than how much they loved me, but I was embarrassed by anything that made me different from the other kids. Kids can be really cruel to each other. You probably already know that but in case you don't, fair warning. We all face different challenges and everybody's situation is unique, but when you're seven, and for a lot of years after that, all you want to do is be just like everyone else, so the "Why is your dad so old?" thing really bothered me. I decided to pretend like it didn't bother me—another thing kids do—and somehow in my little kid brain just acknowledging the problem seemed to make it better. Like, I knew my dad was older than a lot of the other dads but I was cool with it. He was my Pops.

It didn't last long. My dad finally asked me why I didn't call him "Dad" anymore and my face started to feel really warm in that not good way that tells you you've done or said something dumb and I blurted out something about how it was not okay that he had waited so long to have me.

The look on his face, the sudden sadness—nothing rocks a kid's world like seeing one of your parents cry—and I swear, he was about to do just that. Then he told me that people don't always get to decide when to have a child. Children come when they are ready. He and my mom had waited . . . for me.

I'm not as old now as my dad was when I was born, but in case you ever wonder why I'm so old, it's because before I met your mom, I didn't know anyone I wanted to share my life with and make a family. And when you came along, I didn't want anything more than you and your mom and our little family.

But I didn't sit down to record this log to tell you all of that. All I wanted to tell you, really, is that you're the reason I'm still alive right now. And that's something that has never happened to me before. I face death a lot. It's part of the job. Most of the time the spark inside me, the white-hot thing at the center of my soul that stays lit even when everything else is going dark, is fueled by the simple terror of ceasing to exist. Once in a while, it is kindled by the fear in the eyes of the people I've come to think of as my family, the crew I work with day in and day out. But the thing I know now that I didn't know when this day started is that because you exist, because you are now part of my universe, what used to be a spark is now roughly the size of a newborn star.

Also, don't call me Pops. Anything else you like . . . Dad, Daddy, Father—no, that's weird—but you know, whatever, we can talk about it. Or, yeah, call me Pops. I don't know. You're only a few weeks old. Maybe I shouldn't start making decisions for you like that. We've got a long way to go before you call me anything. I'm not going to micromanage stuff like that for you. And if I ever start to, just tell me to knock it off. I don't want to be that dad. Mostly, I just want you to know that you have already changed my life. You are roughly the size of a pea and what I felt today when I thought you might die was something I never imagined was possible.

You might be wondering how you did that. You don't have hands yet, or feet, or a face. You don't even have a name yet. I'm going to wait and talk more to your mom before we decide that. There are so many things I need to talk to your mom about right now, but that's not possible. I managed to make sure we would all survive for the first thirty-six hours of this disaster and right now she's doing everything she can to make sure we live a lot longer than that. My whole job right now consists of staying awake, which is hard to do after thirty-six straight hours of terror and watching our main power relays in case they start to overload when your mom gets our fusion reactor running again. So I'm just going to talk to you a little longer if that's okay.

So yeah. Today. Here's what happened . . .

1

Lieutenant Harry Kim had never been so cold.

He didn't think he was dead. Pressing against the deck beneath him, he lifted his body and came to his knees. The darkness around him was near absolute. The faintest of orange lights emanated from somewhere behind him, as did a low murmur of pain from he knew not whom. The right side of his head burned with the pricks of countless tiny needles. Lifting a hand to it, he was rewarded with the shock of intense agony consistent with raw flesh meeting anything solid. A slick of blood now coated his fingers.

Where the hell am I?

Behind him, the murmurs became louder, approaching frantic cries.

"Harry? No! Please, no! Harry, help me!"

The thud of something solid hitting the deck was followed by the weight of a body meeting his back. Ice-cold hands groped over his shoulders. Someone was using him to stand up.

"Harry?"

The voice was Nancy Conlon's.

"Harry, get up!"

He wanted to oblige her. Some distant instinct insisted that he follow her command. But somehow whatever was troubling her seemed very far away.

"*God damn it, Harry. Get up! The baby is dying!*"

A jolt of pure adrenaline brought a moment's clarity. His baby, his daughter, she was there with him. And something was terribly wrong.

A memory that could have happened a thousand years ago slammed into the forefront of his consciousness—he and Nancy standing in open space beneath countless stars, holding each other in an embrace that was as close to holy as he had ever known. Beside them, in a gestational incubator, their daughter, only a few weeks old, floated in fluid that would sustain her while she developed over the next several months.

The sheer joy of the moment returned to him, warmth rising from the center of his chest to the top of his head. Something important had just happened between them. Something unexpected and impossible existed between him and Nancy. For the first time since he had learned of her illness, he believed that they were finally in this fight together. Three had become one.

Now Nancy's breath was random and panicked. She had moved away from him and was pounding on the solid metal door that separated the small space they occupied from the rest of the ship.

What ship?

The Galen.

"Nancy?"

"We have to get out of here," Conlon screamed as she continued pounding her hands raw. "Help us, please somebody anybody please help!"

Rising on unsteady feet, he ignored a wave of nausea washing through him. Tripping past Nancy, he checked his fall by placing both hands on the bulkhead beside the door. Where the flat of his hands met the solid tritanium plating, searing heat shocked his flesh.

But it wasn't heat.

It was cold.

A few new thoughts suddenly occurred to him. No room on a starship should ever be this cold. Environmental systems were offline and had clearly been offline for some time. That was bad. The door sensors were also offline, suggesting that main power might have been cut from this area of the ship. *Also very bad.*

On the plus side, he and Nancy were still alive. So there was enough residual oxygen present to sustain life. He had no idea how long that would last. Given the other catastrophic indicators, it was a good bet that the answer to that question was *not very long*, but in assessing any survival situation, it was important to focus on the positives as well as the negatives.

Spent and nearly hyperventilating, Nancy turned her back to the door and sunk to the deck. Her eyes were glued to the incubator where the baby floated. Power indicators on the side were already in the red.

"Main power is offline. We need power cells, backup batteries, anything," she said, shifting past panic and trying desperately to simply work the problem.

The problem?

The baby was dying.

Nancy had moved across the small room and was searching the few cabinets for anything that might help. "Hypos, dermal regenerators, no, no, come on! Where are the emergency supplies?" she shouted.

Suddenly, literally nothing else mattered to Harry Kim. For weeks this child, his daughter, had lived in a wasteland in his mind, alive, but not meant to live, present, but not yet real. Nancy had all but decided to terminate the pregnancy for reasons that essentially boiled down to her unwillingness to bring into the world a child she would likely not live long enough to raise.

But before she could act on that choice, she had suffered a brain hemorrhage. The life of the embryo had been in danger, so it had been transported into a gestational incubator. To all intents and purposes, his daughter had been born less than a week ago.

And everything had changed. Despite the fact that her continued development was far from assured within the incubator, odds were good that she would survive. And Kim was going to do everything in his power to see that she had that chance. It didn't matter that she was currently little more than a tiny mass of cells. In his mind, she was already snuggled in his lap as he read to her stories of *Timmy and the Targ.*

Of course, that wasn't going to happen if he didn't find a way to restore power to the incubator.

First things first.

"It's going to be okay," Kim said.

Nancy started to weep softly.

"Please, no," she murmured. "I can't . . ."

Bracing himself for the pain this time, Kim again placed his hands on the side of the bulkhead next to the door. He fumbled in the darkness until he found the panel he sought. Digging into its edges with numb fingers, he pried the panel from its housing and found the manual release lever. It took every ounce of determination at his disposal to wrap his hands around the lever and pull. His rational brain told him that he could not endure the pain of holding a bar-shaped block of ice any longer.

Fortunately for Kim, he was well beyond rational already.

With a groan, the lever began to move, and finally, the door. When enough space existed for him to pass his hands through it, Kim released the lever and attacked the door itself.

Strength born of desperation coursed through him. A gasp escaped Nancy's lips and moments later she was beside him, tugging at the door with all her might.

Don't let go, Harry thought.

Finally, enough space was created to allow Kim to step beyond it, inching sideways through the opening.

"Power cells," Conlon cried out. "As many as you can find."

"I'll be right back," Kim assured her. "Stay here."

Emergency lights along the corridor were out—*another terrible sign*—but at the end of the hall, which opened into the *Galen*'s main medical bay, flickering orange and red motes beckoned.

As soon as Kim passed into the main bay, illuminated intermittently by a few panels that seemed to have a little life left in them and randomly distributed SIMs beacons, his estimation of his current predicament downgraded from *bad* to *we're all going to die, aren't we?*

The biobeds were filled and the area around them was standing room only for many in desperate need of medical attention. Harry didn't remember how many organic crew members the *Galen* had, but it seemed likely that at least half of them were all occupying this relatively small space. Several of them were wrapped in silver emergency blankets but no one seemed to be tending to their injuries.

Where is the Doctor?

He assumed he wasn't the only person there who wanted an answer to that question, but like so many others, it would have to wait.

Weaving through the dazed and terrified officers, Kim made his way to the bay's supply cabinets and jerked them open. The first two contained medical stocks. It was in a small cabinet near the floor that he discovered a stack of emergency power cells.

Grabbing a handful, along with a couple of SIMs beacons, he rushed back to the private room he had just escaped. Nancy was still there, her hands hovering over the incubator as if she were willing it to remain functional for just a few more minutes.

"I got them," Kim said. "The power cells, I mean."

"Hurry," Conlon pleaded.

Hands trembling, Kim managed to find the power input and attach the first emergency cell as Conlon activated the small handheld lights and positioned them to cast their illumination on his work area. The incubator's panel responded almost instantly to the new power source, moving out of the red into a yellow status.

"Power partially restored," Kim said.

"Yeah, but it's not going to last more than a few hours," Conlon reminded him.

"Can you string these together to extend the time?" Kim asked as he passed her the other six cells he had acquired.

"Yes, yes," Conlon said, and went to work immediately opening their control interfaces and exposing their internal leads.

"What happened?" Kim finally thought to ask.

Conlon looked at him, her face racked with fear.

"I have no idea," she replied.

Lieutenant Reginald Barclay refused to panic, not that there weren't ample reasons.

His ears were ringing and he was pretty sure that the liquid substance he was wiping from his right eye every few minutes was blood, but none of that mattered. Twenty-seven minutes earlier, the *Galen* had suffered a catastrophic loss of power, and while he fervently hoped that he was only moments away from at least a partial emergency reset that would bring some percentage of the medical bay's systems back online, every second that passed fed his fear that even if he succeeded, this might be the least of the problems now before him.

The current power problem would have been significantly more challenging had Barclay not been one of the engineers responsible for designing the *Galen* and her unique holographic systems.

Normally, a starship's fusion reactors provided emergency power, but even in the event of their destruction, discrete emergency backups existed to provide short-term energy supplies. The *Galen* had more of those than most starships, multiple redundant cells attached to the main grid to supplement the ship's unusual holographic needs. Fully a third of the ship's crew complement was holographic and had they been powered as most holodecks were, by their own separate grid, the loss of that grid would have been disastrous. It had been Barclay's notion to desegregate *Galen*'s hologrid, linking it to *Galen*'s main power supplies, a design innovation many, including Lewis Zimmerman, had fought against. But Barclay had held his ground and if he succeeded now in figuring out why the ship's systems were not accessing the emergency power cells, his foresight was going to be responsible for saving this terrible day. Or at least buying others the time they would need to do that.

Around him, chaos reigned. People were dead and dying. He knew this. But the first rule of triage was prioritizing the most urgent issues. Two of the bay's human medics were attending to the incoming patients. They needed the Doctor, the ship's CMO who was a hologram.

Often, the Doctor's program was routed through his personal mobile emitter. It was the first thing Barclay had checked when he realized the Doctor wasn't present. He had found it in the Doctor's office, right next to his workstation, in a small container created specifically to protect it when it was not in use. Unfortunately, just before whatever the hell had caused the power loss, the Doctor's program had been routed through the main emitters. The primary hologrid would have to be restored to bring the Doctor back online, and that required power—power that did not currently exist.

In the Doctor's absence, the medics could make do a little longer. Without power to their diagnostic panels and medical tools, however, never mind functioning environmental systems, no one was going to live much longer.

Barclay waved his tricorder over the innards of the bay's core sequencer for what felt like the hundredth time. It confirmed what he already knew: the power cells were fully charged. But the main circuits refused to switch from the dead primary systems to the backup modules.

"You're going to have to force the relay integration manually," a voice said over his shoulder.

Looking up and wiping away yet another annoying trickle from his eye, Barclay saw Harry Kim standing over him.

"That will take . . ." Barclay began.

"The rest of our lives," Kim finished for him as he bent down and began methodically pulling relays from their sockets and manually adjusting their interfaces.

Working together for what felt like hours but was actually a little over five minutes, they managed to manually reset the power relays. They were rewarded for their efforts by spontaneous cheers when the medical bay's lighting was suddenly restored to roughly fifty percent of normal.

More important, the Doctor appeared as if from the ether.

"What in the world . . . ?" he began.

Kim wasted no time. "Where is your mobile emitter?"

"In my office," the Doctor replied. "But I haven't been wearing it unless—"

"Get it and put it on and don't take it off again," Kim ordered as Barclay immediately accessed the main hologrid and shut down all holograms other than the Doctor that had been running prior to the unanticipated shutdown. *No reason to use an ounce of power that isn't absolutely necessary*, Barclay reasoned.

The Doctor seemed ready to protest but as his eyes flew over the scene before him, he simply nodded and rushed toward his private office, already overflowing with waiting patients.

"How long will those cells last?" Kim demanded.

Barclay did a little quick math in his head and his heart sank as he replied, "Thirty-six hours on the outside."

"Better than nothing," Kim said.

"I need a little help here," the voice of Ranson Velth, *Galen*'s tactical and security chief, called.

You and everybody else on this ship, Barclay thought.

Slung over Velth's shoulder was the lanky frame of *Galen*'s chief engineer, Cress Benoit. Velth managed to find a spot on the deck near the door where he lowered Benoit down and positioned him upright so that the Doctor could examine him. Barclay noted that the left side of Benoit's face and torso was a mass of burns. Unconsciousness was probably a blessing for the young lieutenant.

As the Doctor began to run a medical tricorder over Benoit's body and quickly called for a hypo of hyronalin, Barclay followed Kim to the door, where Velth was struggling to catch his breath.

"Did you come from main engineering?" Kim asked.

Velth nodded.

"Report," Kim ordered.

Despite the fact that Kim wasn't part of *Galen*'s chain of command—he was currently serving as *Voyager*'s chief of security and tactical officer—both Kim's tone and demeanor seemed to have a steadying influence on Velth. They were the same rank and position on their respective ships, which technically gave Velth command over Kim, but in the heat of this moment no one with any sense was going to argue protocol.

"It's not good," Velth replied. "The warp core is cold. Primary and backup fusion reactors are down. Our dilithium and benamite crystals are dust. And the antimatter pods are empty."

"So literally nothing is working right now?" Kim confirmed.

Velth nodded, grim. "I didn't see any other survivors on my way. I found Lieutenant Bamps, one of my security officers . . . he didn't make it."

"I'm sorry for your loss," Kim said earnestly. "But right now, we need to focus on those we can save."

"Agreed," Velth said.

Kim nodded and continued. "I don't understand. Antimatter doesn't vanish. It impacts normal matter and the result is instant immolation unless the reaction is processed through a stabilizing element."

"Usually," Velth agreed, glancing around the room. "This is the only area of the ship I've seen that has any power flowing to it."

Barclay watched as Kim considered the issues, then said, "We'll work on the backup systems first. Do you have any idea what the status is of the main computer?"

"It'll take me at least half an hour to get to the bridge, a little less if I head for the computer core. I didn't see any structural damage between here and engineering, but there are six decks worth of Jefferies tubes to navigate between here and the bridge," Velth replied.

"There's no time for that." Turning to Barclay, Kim said, "Reg, Nancy is in the third room to the right back there. I need her."

The Doctor was programmed to respond quickly and efficiently to emergency medical situations. It had once been his primary function. Years of continuous operation later, as well as significant expansion of his holomatrix and subroutines, both his program and range of responses to stimuli had become much more complex. As he moved swiftly from patient to patient, attempting to bring order to something well beyond chaos, one of his subroutines was busy calculating the effect on *Galen*'s functional capacity given the number of injured organic crew members before him. His assessment of *Galen*'s survival potential without them fell well below twenty percent.

He was attempting to stabilize an ensign who was bleeding internally when Lieutenant Kim was suddenly at his side.

"Doc, I need your help," Kim said.

"Are you about to suffer a massive hemorrhage in your intestinal lining leading to sepsis?" the Doctor asked.

"No."

"Then I'm afraid you'll have to wait."

"I can't," Kim said evenly. "I need you to turn this patient over to one of the medics and come with me," he added.

A dozen curt responses occurred to the Doctor, but he ignored all of them. He had no idea what had brought the ship to its current state. The last thing he remembered was standing in a fully functional medical bay discussing minor system upgrades with Reg before everything around him had shifted to a hellscape of wounded and dying people. It was an unusual occurrence but not without precedent. His program had not shut down without warning in a long time, but it did happen. Because he only experienced and stored data accumulated while he was functioning, he had no awareness of how long it had taken for the ship's circumstances to so radically change.

More important, there was something in Kim's voice that brooked no refusal. Signaling to the nearest medic and offering a set of quick instructions, he followed Kim just outside the open door of the medical bay, where Lieutenants Velth, Conlon, and Barclay now stood waiting for him.

Kim seemed to be the undisputed leader of the small group and was addressing Velth and Conlon. "Both of you need to get back to main engineering. Don't stop to help anyone on your way. Your job is to restore emergency power as quickly as possible, prioritizing environmental and computer systems."

Kim turned to the Doctor. "Reg has managed to shunt a little emergency power to the bridge's holoemitters. I need you to transfer yourself there and assess the situation."

The request made sense. Without turbolifts or transporters, it would take precious time that was clearly nonexistent for any other officer to perform this function.

"Understood," the Doctor said, and initiated the transfer.

Less than a second later, the Doctor materialized on the bridge of the *Galen*.

The ambient darkness wasn't a problem. His visual subroutines adjusted automatically to the absence of light, rendering the bridge in monochromatic values that allowed him enhanced differentiation. He studied the scene before him and as he did so, his previous calculations of survivability declined further.

There was no power present in any of the bridge computer systems. The main viewscreen was dark, so it was impossible to tell where the ship was or if they were still anywhere near the rest of the fleet. The temperature was nine point four degrees Celsius. Oxygen levels were thirty percent below nominal. Two of the bridge crew members, Ensigns Michael Drur and Lynne Selah, who handled operations and science respectively, were conscious and responded almost immediately to his appearance.

"Doctor, we need help here," Drur shouted, beckoning him to the small well between the captain's chair and the flight control panels.

The Doctor almost tripped on the prone body of Ensign Lawry, *Galen*'s pilot, who had been thrown several meters from his station. By what, the Doctor had no idea. Drur and Selah were kneeling over the body of their captain, Commander Clarissa Glenn. A quick scan indicated that she had suffered head trauma. A long gash running over her scalp would probably have bled out already were it not for the near freezing temperature. The Doctor assumed that there would be cranial swelling to go along with the external damage.

"I need you to get her to sickbay as soon as possible," the Doctor advised.

"Do we have turbolifts?" Selah asked.

"No. You'll have to carry her. Do what you can to keep her head stable on the way."

"Aye, sir," Drur responded as if this request were not just this side of impossible.

"I'll send someone for Lawry as soon as I can," the Doctor promised before transferring back to sickbay.

Lieutenant Velth was moving throughout the wounded, offering encouragement and requesting reports from those who were able about the status of the ship in their previous duty assignments. Lieutenant Kim was focused, for the moment, on a young woman with tight ginger braids running down her back who had apparently been in the mess hall when disaster struck.

"The ship just changed its shape," she was saying as the Doctor approached. "One minute it was a sphere, and the next it elongated and started flashing these blinding lights."

"White light?" Kim asked.

"All along the spectrum," she replied. "I thought I should get back to engineering but then this wave of something hit me and the next thing I knew . . ."

"It's okay, Ensign . . ."

"Unhai," she added helpfully.

"What was your duty assignment?" Kim asked.

"I'm a slipstream specialist," she replied. "Not that it's much use now, I guess."

"I want you to work with Ensign Finley collecting emergency supplies."

"Sir, without power . . ."

"We are going to restore power to all critical systems," Kim assured her.

"Aye, sir," she said, probably feeling more doubt than she was showing.

As she hurried to follow Kim's orders, the Doctor took her place.

"How bad is it?" Kim asked.

"There is no power to any of the bridge systems," the Doctor said. "Commander Glenn is seriously injured. If she survives transit here, I'll have a better sense of whether or not I'll be able to help her. Our pilot is also unconscious. Someone needs to bring him here on the off chance we're going anywhere any time soon."

Kim accepted this stoically. He seemed determined not to allow the obvious hopelessness of their current predicament to even enter his thoughts. This wasn't surprising. Seven years in the Delta Quadrant the first time around had taught all of *Voyager*'s senior officers that long odds were business as usual and panic was never an option.

Finally Kim said, "For now, we're going to consider sickbay our center of operations. We have limited power, enough to last about thirty hours. But we'll have to restore at least partial environmental systems well before that. We've already got a team going deck by deck collecting all emergency food, water, blankets, and lights."

"What about search parties for other injured crew?" the Doctor asked.

Kim shook his head. "That's our second priority. I know that sounds heartless, but . . ."

"I understand," the Doctor said, then asked, "What happened?"

"I have no idea. It sounds like we came under attack from some sort of shape-shifting ship. I don't know." He sighed heavily. "If we all survive the next thirty hours, maybe we'll be able to figure it out."

"What about the rest of the fleet? Surely they will come to our aid," the Doctor insisted.

Kim shook his head. "Ensign Unhai confirmed that when she woke up in the mess hall after we were attacked, none of our sister ships were visible through the ports. The rest of the fleet is gone."

"Without help . . ." the Doctor began.

"I know," Kim said. "No one is coming to save us. If we're going to live, we're going to have to save ourselves."

2

The first time Harry Kim died had been shocking. Not *presumed* dead. Not *transported-to-a-distant-planet-inhabited-by-aliens-that-were-awfully-quick-to-send-their-elderly-population-to-the-next-emanation-through-a-subspace-vacuole* dead.

The first time Harry Kim had *died* he'd been ejected into open space while trying to repair a hull breach.

Commander B'Elanna Torres had been there. Hers had been the voice that announced to Kathryn Janeway that Ensign Kim was dead. Then, as now, Chakotay had been standing beside Janeway on *Voyager*'s bridge. Then, as now, Janeway had felt the news first as a lurch in the pit of her stomach, a faint buzzing in her head, and a sensation of sudden, extreme warmth on the back of her neck.

And then, as now, Janeway found it nearly impossible to believe. Not long after learning of Kim's death, Janeway had found herself leaving sickbay with a copy of him from an alternate universe that was indistinguishable from the original. He had been created by a freak warp core accident that duplicated *Voyager* and her entire crew.

She had no cause to hope for something like that to repeat itself. Still, hope refused to relent.

The words "What was he doing on the *Galen*?" almost escaped her lips, but they died there as a tiny memory pushed its way to the front of her mind.

Nancy Conlon was stationed indefinitely on the Galen.

Harry Kim.

Nancy Conlon.

The Doctor.

Reg Barclay.

Clarissa Glenn.

Ranson Velth.

Cress Benoit.

Had it been a year since Janeway had asked to read the names of the fleet's deceased during the memorial service honoring the hundreds who had died in their encounter with the Omega Continuum?

Was it possible that another of her fleet's ships and her entire crew had just been lost?

Janeway turned to Chakotay. She could see that the same names now running through her mind were also on his. Without thinking she placed a hand on his arm—not seeking comfort; offering it.

The entire bridge crew sat in stunned silence. A miasma of chirps and beeps, sounds so familiar on any starship bridge they were usually ignored, stood out in stark relief against the deafening silence of this moment.

"Send the logs from the attack to astrometrics," Janeway ordered Lieutenant Lasren at ops. "Captain," she said sharply, pulling Chakotay from his internal recitation of the dead, "with me."

Five minutes later, she, Chakotay, and Seven stood before the lab's massive display screen as events none of them remembered played out before them in all their fascinating horror.

Only a few days prior, the Full Circle Fleet had made orbit over an extraordinary planet, christened by the most unimaginative of stellar cartographers as DK-1116.

The name didn't begin to do its extravagant mysteries justice.

At some point in the Delta Quadrant's distant past, several alien races had used DK-1116 as a sort of scientific research station. Their purpose had been to conduct experiments on a unique substance that had either been left there by or was part of a species known as the Edrehmaia.

The planet had once orbited a pair of binary stars. Before dozens of away teams had barely begun to scratch the surface of the planet's strangeness, the environmental protections created by the ancient alien species to preserve the Edrehmaia's planet in its inert configuration had been unintentionally disrupted. An unimaginable buildup of stored energy deep below the surface had been released and its entire force aimed at the smaller of the two stars in the pair.

What had happened next was a spectacle both unfathomable and awe inspiring. The planet had successfully forced the smaller B star from its orbit around its mate and sent it careening off into space, destination unknown.

The fleet's efforts to analyze this unexpected development had been cut short by the arrival of an alien vessel. Its black surface and sphere shape had evoked memories of the Borg, a race of cybernetic beings that had once been the bane of the existence of every sentient race they encountered. But the Borg were no more, and the first thing the log they were reviewing indicated was that initial scans of the sphere showed traces of several unusual alloys, including the substance associated with the Edrehmaia that the fleet's crew had taken to calling *Sevenofninonium.*

"What the hell is that?" Chakotay's voice could be heard asking over the display screen.

"Unknown, sir," Lieutenant Gaines Aubrey reported from tactical. *"Sensors didn't pick it up incoming. We started reading some sort of displacement field, and then it was just suddenly there."*

A few minutes of speculation by the bridge crew followed along with Chakotay's order to take the ship to yellow alert.

"You think it's the Edrehmaia?" Chakotay finally asked.

"I think it could be," Admiral Kathryn Janeway replied.

Janeway watched as the part of this experience no one remembered began. They had all been rendered unconscious from this point forward.

Massive waves of energy began to ripple outward from the surface of the sphere. The admiral was unsure if they were intended to disable the ships in its vicinity, but regardless, that had been their effect. As the waves had begun to roll over *Voyager,* her shields fell instantly and an electromagnetic pulse had coursed through the ship, knocking out several primary systems. A momentary loss of artificial gravity, quickly rectified by emergency backup systems, had been responsible for multiple serious injuries, but the total loss of consciousness of all living beings aboard the vessels seemed to be a side effect of the pulse. It had temporarily disrupted every organic as well as technological system it encountered.

Thankfully, sensors had been restored long before the crew had recovered. The rest of the incident played out like a nightmare.

The configuration of the sphere began to shift, elongating until it settled into a rectangular shape. It seemed possible that the energy waves that had done so much damage might have simply been a necessary side effect of this transformation. Janeway suspected this because for several minutes following the shift, the alien vessel had begun to transmit a great deal of information toward the fleet using photonic waves. Lights along the entire visible and invisible spectrum flowed over the surface of the ship. It was eerie and beautiful in its way, but this hardly seemed to be the point. Data at rates of exaquads per millisecond flooded the ship's sensors as the blinding lights cascaded over the data screen. Janeway was anxious to examine the data, but that could wait until she had committed every moment of this dire event to memory.

The lights finally ceased. For several seconds, the alien vessel maintained its position. *Waiting for a response, perhaps?* Janeway wondered but said nothing.

Finally, a single, blindingly bright pulse of energy had been emitted from one end of the alien ship directly toward the *Galen*. The small special-missions ship was the fleet's dedicated medical vessel, staffed largely by experimental holograms, including the Doctor.

Janeway held it together as best she could. She was not the only person in the room for whom the next moments were unbearable to witness.

Galen's shields had been restored, likely automatically, and for a few moments, they held against the onslaught of energy her crew had yet to analyze but was apparently several orders of magnitude beyond any normal directed-energy weapon. Eventually, they gave way and in a massive explosion, *Galen* vanished.

U.S.S. DEMETER

"Anything, Atlee?"

Commander Liam O'Donnell's XO, Lieutenant Commander Atlee Fife, did not pull his gaze from the sensor scan he was reading as he replied, "No, sir."

"Any response from Lieutenant Patel?"

"No, sir," Fife replied.

O'Donnell considered asking Fife for the odds that either of these answers would change in the next few hours and decided against it. Fife, like every other member of the Full Circle Fleet, was undoubtedly still processing the sudden traumatic loss of their sister ship, the *Galen*, at the hands of an unknown alien vessel. Given the chance, Fife would most certainly add the word *hostile* to any description of the alien vessel. Since Fife was responsible for, among other things, *Demeter*'s security and tactics, and was naturally inclined to view the unknown with suspicion even before it killed dozens of innocent people without warning, O'Donnell understood this proclivity. That it was reductive and ultimately not terribly useful if one's goal was to *understand* the unknown was a problem, just not one O'Donnell was going to force Fife to confront right this second.

They need time to move beyond their grief.

O'Donnell didn't.

He needed answers.

Life had ceased to be a mystery to Commander Liam O'Donnell in his early twenties. The traits of life, as it was understood by biologists, were reasonably simple and clear. Living things were composed of cells or cell-like units, they could transform energy to maintain homeostasis, they could grow, adapt, respond to stimuli, and reproduce. These were the essential physiological functions attributed to life-forms at the most basic level. When these functions ceased, death was said to have occurred.

In O'Donnell's experience, death was a little more complicated. So vivid had been his sense of connection to his beloved wife, Alana, even decades after she had passed away following the miscarriage of their child, that he could have argued successfully that in every essential way, she remained alive within him. When he had finally accepted her death, that sense had solidified, even as its indicators—constant conversations between them that had taken place entirely in his mind—had ceased to occur.

What he and his fellow officers had discovered on the surface of DK-1116 had been something new: a significant number of organisms that appeared lifelike but scanned as dead until damaged, at which point they regenerated themselves. Admiral Janeway had suggested the classification *zombie*. It remained as accurate now as any other description O'Donnell could conjure.

O'Donnell understood that all the evidence currently at their disposal suggested incontrovertibly that several Starfleet officers had just been killed and a unique experimental vessel destroyed. But as absolutely nothing he had encountered since Captain Chakotay had first reported the existence of *DK-1116* fell within the normal bounds of reality as he had heretofore understood it, he had a hard time believing that what they knew at this moment was all that was to be known on the subject.

He doubted that *Galen*'s crew had been transformed by the powerful beam of light that impacted it. He didn't believe that the beam had somehow imbued them with its ability to exist between life and death. But he did believe that ever since the fleet had made orbit around the planet that wasn't a planet and discovered the life that wasn't life, trusting old ideas of what was possible was a mistake. *Something* had clearly happened, but he wasn't ready yet to say exactly what. Until he knew more, he wasn't even inclined to theorize. All he could do was collect data and hope that it would lead him in a more fruitful direction than grief, toward actual understanding of the miracle that had been wrought here millennia ago by the Edrehmaia.

O'Donnell could have spent the rest of his life attempting to understand how this miracle worked. He was a genetic botanist and had spent most of his career creating impossible things to help revive and sustain living communities. He sensed that the answers to most of the questions now plaguing him could be found beneath the surface of the planet, or among the asteroids that had been displaced when the system's B star had been freed from its orbit. The answers lay in a substance that had almost killed one of *Voyager*'s ensigns a few days prior and, if he was right, also aboard the alien vessel that had apparently destroyed the *Galen* only a few hours ago.

As the alien vessel was gone and had left behind no obvious warp trail or means to pursue it, that left the asteroids and what was left of DK-1116. As soon as Fife had confirmed that *Demeter* had sustained no serious damage during the fleet's encounter with the aliens, O'Donnell had ordered him to begin scanning the planet and asteroids for any traces of the Edrehmaia substance, a viscous black liquid that according to Lieutenant Patel and Seven's reports was unlike anything he or Starfleet had ever encountered.

O'Donnell had been scheduled to meet with Seven and Patel several hours ago. That meeting had been postponed by the tragedy that he firmly believed was not yet really a tragedy. His humanity demanded that he allow those around him time to recover from their shock and pain. His gut told him that this was a colossal waste of time and that every second would be much better spent searching for the truth.

A year ago, he wouldn't have spared a thought for the feelings of his crew. He would have pushed them mercilessly to get back to their assigned duties. But unexpected loss had become a recurring theme among these men and women, and O'Donnell feared that to push them too hard was to risk breaking them.

They need time, he reminded himself.

Time he feared *Galen*'s crew, wherever they were now, might not have.

U.S.S. VESTA

Captain Regina Farkas was pissed. From the first moment she had stood on the surface of DK-1116, her gut had told her that something was wrong. She couldn't put her finger on it. Its strange plants and odd structures could have belonged to any random alien world. Exploring worlds like it was the first and most important part of Starfleet's mission statement, something she had always embraced without reservation. On paper, the fleet's extended exploratory mission had seemed to promise a welcome respite from the hazards they had faced more or less constantly since they had arrived in the Delta Quadrant a little over a year earlier.

Even before their sensor scans of life-forms that weren't alive had begun to register, Farkas had begun to feel deep misgivings about the planet. She had chosen to swallow her instinctive fear and focus on her duties. It hadn't taken long, however, for her to begin to voice her concerns to the rest of the command staff and lobby for a quick return to the safety of their ships.

When the fleet had first been dispatched to determine whether or not the Borg were really and truly gone, transformed by an extremely powerful alien race known as the Caeliar, they had been nine ships. One had been wantonly destroyed by an immature race of extremophiles who called themselves the Children of the Storm. Farkas still had nightmares about that moment—small "ships" composed of super-hot chemicals that sustained the aliens surrounding the *Planck*. Farkas had been on an open comm line with its commanding officer, Captain T'Mar, when the ships merged and unleashed their destructive power on the *Planck*, vaporizing it in seconds.

Horrific as that moment had been, it had only been the prelude to the fleet's encounter with an accident of evolution, an entire continuum of omega particles destined to one day end the universe. That mission had cost them four more ships and hundreds of lives, many of whom had been hers to protect aboard her first command with the fleet, the *Quirinal*.

And now, the *Galen* and her crew had been added to the list of casualties.

Not forty-eight hours ago, Farkas sat on the surface of DK-1116 along with Admiral Janeway, Captain Chakotay, Commander O'Donnell, and *Galen*'s captain, Commander Clarissa Glenn. Farkas had actually chastised Glenn for suggesting that her instinctive concerns stemmed from some latent version of post-traumatic stress.

Farkas wished she could go back now and extract the dismissiveness from her remarks in response to Glenn. She hadn't known the commander all that well, but well enough to be certain that the kind and patient woman with the heart of an explorer had deserved better than a quick scan and a killing blow by an unknown alien vessel. Further, odds were pretty good that Glenn had a point about the old demons Farkas was still battling. The seasoned captain hated to admit her weaknesses, but facing them squarely was the only way to make sure they didn't end up running the show. Glenn had tried to give her that chance and Farkas had snapped.

Not your finest moment, Regina.

On any other day, Farkas would have unloaded these unpleasant thoughts on her oldest and dearest friend, Doctor Sal. As it had been less than twenty-four hours since she had temporarily removed Sal from her post as CMO, she knew better than to attempt to seek comfort there.

Which left one option.

She usually made it a habit to have her thoughts well organized before she presented them to her superior officers, but in this case, she decided to make an exception. The moment Admiral Janeway's face appeared on the screen of her ready room's terminal, she withheld nothing.

"What's your status, Captain Farkas?" Janeway asked crisply. In fairness, the dark circles under the admiral's eyes and deep worry lines creasing her brow suggested that Janeway felt this new loss as

keenly as Farkas did. Unfortunately for them both, Regina had misplaced her ability to empathize.

"My status? I have a little over seven hundred crew members, many of whom started this journey aboard the *Quirinal*, who are once again reeling from a disaster that should have been preventable."

Admiral Kathryn Janeway was a complicated woman. Farkas had nursed deep reservations when she learned that Janeway had been given command of the fleet only a short time after having been resurrected from the dead by a member of the Q Continuum. Over time, watching Janeway in action, Farkas had come to respect both her abilities and her humanity. She was a born leader who did nothing by half measures and was as devoted to the service as anyone Farkas had ever known. Farkas had been particularly impressed with Janeway's leadership during the fleet's mission to establish relations with one of the Delta Quadrant's only civilizations that rivaled the Federation in size and technology, the Confederacy of the Worlds of the First Quadrant.

But none of that changed the fact that this fleet, much like the first ship Janeway had led through the Delta Quadrant, had been forced to absorb trials and losses that should have sent most of them to an early retirement. And she had treated their discovery of DK-1116 like a holiday, even over Farkas's protestations.

Janeway's initial response was measured. *"I'm not sure what your take on the sensor logs might be, but my analysis is that it is currently too soon to determine exactly what happened to the* Galen. *Multiple departments are reviewing the logs and I'm still waiting on their final reports. Difficult though it might be, I would reserve judgment and resist the urge to despair until we have more information at our disposal."*

"Well, my crew is already wondering where we're planning to hold our next memorial service."

"Captain . . ."

"No, Admiral. We may not have known what we were dealing with when we entered this system, but well before the planet revealed its true nature and pushed a star out of orbit, you had a crew member seriously injured by an alien substance that then proceeded to eat a shuttle before our eyes. I appreciated the fact that you ordered *Vesta*, *Demeter*, and *Galen* out of harm's way before the planet was scheduled to explode and you remained behind to rescue the last of our stranded crew members, but that run through the asteroid belt was a nail-biter and odds were less than even that any of us were going to survive.

"I hate to say it, but I now find myself wondering whether or not your ability to effectively gauge the risks associated with our directives is properly calibrated."

Janeway's jaw clenched before she responded. *"As this fleet's commanding officer, I accept full responsibility for my orders and their consequences."*

"As well you should. My only question is: Has this experience taught you anything?"

"Captain, I don't have a problem with those I command freely expressing their concerns. I welcome it. But there is a line and you are very close to crossing it."

"Were our positions reversed, Admiral, I wouldn't hesitate to tell me exactly where I could put my concerns," Farkas replied. "You are my commanding officer. I am duty bound by the oath I swore when I accepted my commission to follow you wherever you choose to lead me and to serve you and my crew to the very best of my abilities. But I wish to make myself perfectly clear. Death in the line of duty is a tragedy we all find ways to reconcile. Carelessness is a character flaw and one with which I have never had much patience."

"Thank you for your candor, Captain," Janeway replied. *"Consider your concerns duly noted and stand by to receive further orders. Janeway out."*

Farkas wasn't sure what she had expected from the admiral. Janeway's rank meant that she was never required to justify herself or her choices to those beneath her in the chain of command. But that didn't mean it wasn't a good idea, both in terms of morale and, more important, in earning the devotion that brought every crew member's best to the surface when it was most needed.

She had said her piece. And now, she felt worse than before she and the admiral had spoken.

"God *damn* it," she said aloud to her empty ready room.

She was seriously considering hitting her rack for a few hours when her operations officer alerted her to a new incoming transmission. She half hoped it was the admiral reaching out again.

It wasn't.

Instead, Farkas found herself staring into the face of a man who identified himself as an agent of the Department of Temporal Investigations named Marion Dulmur.

3

GALEN

"**H**ow are we doing, Chief?"

Not that long ago, maybe a week and a half prior, Lieutenant Nancy Conlon would have given anything to hear these words; for the sum total of her existence to be reduced to an engineering issue. In this one aspect of her life, she had achieved a level of mastery. When faced with even the most challenging problem with a warp drive, power regulation, computer processing, and the complex relationships between the systems necessary to keep a starship operational, she was distilled to the essence of her best possible self.

Far too many personal issues had come between her and this better version of herself in the last few months. She had processed the traumas, accepted that her medical issues were likely terminal, and made peace with the choices surrounding her unexpected pregnancy. She had worked diligently to remove every obstacle standing between her and resuming her duties as *Voyager*'s chief engineer. Before an artery in her brain had ruptured, requiring major surgery, the induction of a coma to allow for her brain to heal, and the emergency transport of her child into a gestational incubator, she had decided that the rest of her life, however long or short, would be devoted to one thing only: solving the most mundane or complex engineering challenges her job could throw at her.

Had she known then what she knew now, she might have reconsidered her wish list.

Staring at her handiwork of the last thirty hours, she was certain of this much: when she reactivated the *Galen*'s primary fusion reactor, there was a better than average chance that the ship would explode. She was laser focused on the circuit bypass she had just created and the hastily constructed interface indicating that sufficient power now existed in the series of interconnected emergency battery packs to power up the reactor.

"We're ready," Conlon replied to the officer who had asked the question.

"You're sure?"

Conlon glanced toward Lieutenant Ranson Velth. She hadn't known him at all when they had entered the *Galen*'s cold, dead engineering room and she had begun the process of getting acquainted with the heart of a ship that wasn't her own. She would have felt a lot better about the cobbled together system she had just created if the ship's chief engineer, Cress Benoit, were available to review her work and offer the kind of insights unique to any ship and the officer who knew her best. But Cress Benoit had never regained consciousness. He was counted among the deceased and none of his engineering staff had the experience to take his place. The twenty-two survivors of the catastrophe—which had transformed *Galen* from a fully functional starship to a carcass of its former self—were now huddled on decks five and six, both of which were part of *Galen*'s vast medical bay, wrapped in emergency blankets, changing out power cells in portable heaters and SIMs beacons, venting backup oxygen tanks to supplement the dwindling breathable atmosphere, and monitoring carbon dioxide filters. Harry Kim was alone on the bridge, waiting for her to flip the switch that would either extend their lives or put an end to what had become a truly terrifying existence.

"I'm sure that there is nothing else I can possibly do to prepare the reactor," Conlon replied. "We're only going to get one shot at this and the more time I spend thinking about all of the things that could go wrong, the worse I feel."

"You want to walk through it, junction by relay, one more time?" Velth asked.

He was trying to be helpful. He had been nothing but helpful up to this point. She knew next to nothing about him apart from the fact that in a crisis, he was the best possible companion: supportive, attentive, quick witted, and eager to be of use, despite the fact that he had to be every bit as exhausted as she was.

"I really don't," Conlon said. "Starfleet didn't design this system with our particular crisis in mind. Normally when there is a catastrophic failure of the warp reactor, safeties and emergency backup systems protect the fusion reactor. You don't usually lose both at the same time without losing the entire ship. We are in uncharted territory, Lieutenant Velth, and while I think I have accounted for every eventuality, the basic problem hasn't changed. We are about to cold-start a nuclear reactor. Outside a lab or testing facility designed for that purpose, it's a terrible idea. But it's all we've got."

"Then let's do it," Velth said.

"Any last words?" Conlon asked.

Velth took a moment to think about it. "I hope this works."

"Yeah, me too," Conlon said.

"Not just because I'm curious to know if we're still going to be alive in thirty seconds, but because I really want to find whoever did this to us and make them sorry they did it."

Conlon turned to face Velth. She had clearly heard the first part of his statement but had difficulty understanding the second. It sounded like he'd said *"because I really want to ground sleeves and truck leaves crippled."*

Obviously the absurd amount of stress she was under coupled with a lack of sleep was taking its toll. "I'm sorry, what did you say?"

"I know seeking revenge isn't very Starfleet of me, but don't judge me too harshly," he said, somewhat chastened. "A lot of people I care about are suffering right now, and a few more it was my job to protect are already dead. I'm going to allow myself a little healthy anger about that and make sure that when the time comes, I take it out on the right people."

Conlon nodded in relief. *Must find time to sleep soon*, she decided before replying, "Assuming this works, I might just help you do that."

"Okay, then."

Conlon took a deep breath. "Okay."

Her hand was surprisingly steady as she reached for the initiation switch.

There was tired, there was exhausted, and then there was whatever this slightly sick to your stomach, famished but couldn't possibly eat a bite, light-headed but strangely focused feeling that seemed like it was all Harry Kim had ever known.

Alone on the bridge of the *Starship Galen*, staring at a dead viewscreen, wondering how much longer it would take for Nancy to attempt her reset of the fusion reactor and whether or not he would ever see her, or Tom, or B'Elanna, Captain Chakotay, Admiral Janeway, his parents, or his daughter again, Kim found it hard to believe it had come to this. If he closed his eyes, he could almost imagine that he was back on *Voyager*'s bridge during a lonely gamma shift. He wished he had his clarinet with him. He'd passed many an hour during those seemingly endless shifts allowing the dim lighting and pinpricks of stars before him to conjure new pieces of music from the instrument he had reluctantly picked up for the first time when he was eleven. The simple act of releasing his thoughts into a series of tones always made him feel connected to the universe in a way that felt transcendent. Whatever his concerns might be, they settled into the back of his mind as he attempted to do nothing more or less than live in and give voice to a singular moment. Invariably when he finished, solutions to difficult problems or, at the very least, possible new strategies would emerge.

He wondered if Nancy had ever played a musical instrument, or if his daughter might one day try to play. He hoped so.

A sudden rush of stale air, accompanied by a series of clicks, beeps, and whirs, brought him to his feet. His heart pounded fervently in his chest and pure adrenaline jolted his extremities. Turning to the operations station, Kim watched expectantly as the display screen began to glow faintly. Moments later, a series of commands appeared indicating that the station had initiated its start-up procedures.

"She did it," he said aloud. "Way to go, Nancy!"

He moved quickly from station to station, confirming that the primary systems were responding to the sudden influx of power coursing through them without overloading. Any minute now, communications would be restored shipwide. His first duty, however, was to route what power they had to the ship's most critical system, feeding much-needed life support to sickbay and engineering, and activating sensors.

Before the main computer could begin generating data about the ship's location, the bridge's viewscreen surged to life. Kim stepped closer to it, beyond the well that contained the captain's chair and flight control station, and tried to process the sight that now met his eyes.

He had no idea where the ship was in relation to where it had been just before the attack Ensign Unhai had described. But wherever they were, it was an astonishing sight, and one with which he was actually quite familiar.

Just before the Borg had decided to instigate an all-out assault on the Alpha Quadrant, *Voyager* had been dispatched for a long-term study of star formation within the Yaris Nebula. Staring at the images before him now, Kim could easily believe they had returned to that stellar nursery.

Vibrant pink, blue, green, and orange streams of plasma floated before him, dotted throughout with young stars. "The edge of a nebula?" he asked the empty bridge. In the distance a series of flashing lights caught his attention. "Those are too close together to be stars."

He was suddenly conscious of a hint of panic in the form of sudden tightness around his chest.

Unhai had said that the vessel that attacked them emitted something similar. He scanned the viewscreen and began to count, struggling to distinguish these distant ships from the multitudes of stars among them.

When he reached twenty, he stopped counting.

The ship that attacked them was like nothing Unhai had ever seen before and it had changed its shape right before the attack began. Kim didn't like to speculate based upon little or no evidence, but he had personally observed matter found on an asteroid near DK-1116 that had also shown impressive malleability of form while in the process of—*transforming? ingesting?*—one of *Voyager*'s shuttles. According to the last reports he had read from the away teams that had explored the surface, a great deal of a similar substance had been found beneath the surface of the planet. Whatever the substance was, it had been created by a species called the Edrehmaia. If the attack on *Galen* was connected to the events that had taken place in and around DK-1116 over the last few days, it seemed possible that the Edrehmaia were the ones who had brought them here, and *here* appeared to be their place of origin, or at the very least, some sort of rendezvous point. The only good news was that most of the potential Edrehmaia ships he could make out through the viewscreen were holding position thousands of kilometers distant from the *Galen*.

But *where* exactly were they?

Kim returned to the ops station and ordered a long-range positioning scan. To his mingled relief and dismay, he was soon rewarded with his answer.

"Engineering to Kim."

He was conscious of another celebratory flutter of his heart at the sound of functioning communications equipment.

"Nancy?"

"We're still a long way from full power, but so far, the reactor is stable."

"That's great. Good job."

There was a slight pause before Conlon said, *"Good job? Harry, we just overcame the first and most dangerous problem we were facing. That's better than 'good,' right?"*

Kim continued to scan the astrometric display the sensors were generating. "I'm sorry. Yes, of course. It's great."

Another pause.

"What's wrong, Harry?"

"Are you alone?"

"Yes. I sent Velth to check the nearest relay junctions. I won't be able to run any diagnostics for a bit, so I've ordered him to perform manual scans to check for any overloads."

"Long-range sensors just came up."

"It's bad, isn't it?"

"We're alive, so it could be worse."

"Where are we?"

Kim shook his head. *Voyager* had once been transported seventy thousand light-years from its position into the far reaches of the Delta Quadrant in a matter of minutes. That fact alone meant he couldn't rule out what the sensors were telling him, much as he wished he could.

"I'm going to run the scan again."

"Harry, where are we?"

"We're still in the Delta Quadrant, forty-seven thousand light-years from our previous position, near the outermost edge of the Milky Way."

Another long pause.

"That's not possible."

"Yeah, I'm going to run the scan again."

"Harry, if you're right . . ."

"I know. Stand by."

Kim waited anxiously for the results of the new scan to populate the screen before him.

"Come on, come on . . ."

A short trill sounded. Kim's heart sank.

The results were the same.

Lieutenant Ranson Velth had never had much patience for briefings. Commander Glenn, who was still unconscious in sickbay but had mercifully survived the trip there despite suffering severe head trauma, tended to keep them short. He liked that in a commanding officer. Her senior staff meetings weren't terribly democratic affairs. Reports were concise, Glenn's orders were clear and definitive. They rarely lasted more than fifteen minutes.

Staring at the faces of the officers now huddled together on the bridge, sipping something the folks who prepared emergency rations had the temerity to call coffee and munching on a bar that tasted like spiced tree bark, Velth realized that briefings were a thing of the past. From this point forward, much of his day would consist of multiple meetings with those assembled as they moved step by step toward their mutual goal of restoring the *Galen* to something resembling full functionality.

With the exception of the Doctor, all present were lieutenants. Each of them had assumed responsibility for one of the ship's primary departments: Kim for operations, Conlon for engineering, Barclay for maintaining critical holographic systems and life support, and Velth for security. If he ever found it necessary to stand his former post on the bridge again, he would also be responsible for tactical. The Doctor, who was the most critical holographic system they had, was, naturally, in charge of sickbay.

Kim was emerging as their de facto commanding officer in Glenn's absence. Velth had no problem with that as long as Kim continued to defer to the experience of *Galen*'s actual crew members and to allow everyone present to offer meaningful suggestions as to how best to proceed.

As their mutual survival was the priority, and would likely continue to be for several more days until full power was restored to all systems and repairs were underway, Velth was inclined to accept Kim's choice to temporarily fill Glenn's boots as the purview of the officer with the most command experience present rather than a coup. If Glenn recovered, Velth would make damn sure she got her seat back. He doubted Kim would fight that. So far, he seemed reasonable, capable, and determined as hell, all qualities Velth could respect.

Conlon, whom he liked tremendously, and not just because her cold start of the fusion reactor had spared him a slow death by freezing, was in the process of offering a depressing analysis of their propulsion systems. Like everyone else present, she struggled to remain focused and from time to time drifted away into her own thoughts. He'd caught her staring off into the distance a handful of times since the briefing had begun until their engineering issues had become the subject of discussion.

"The warp core is a dead stick," she advised Kim.

"I know the odds aren't great, but we might find some dilithium out here," Kim said.

"Even if we did, we'd still have to figure out a way to create and safely contain antimatter," she noted.

"You're not even contemplating that, are you?" Barclay asked, aghast.

Reg Barclay was a puzzle to Velth. They had served together for a year already and undertaken a handful of away missions together. The man was brilliant. Most Starfleet engineers were, but this guy had ridiculous game. Barclay had once confided to Velth that he had served on the *Enterprise*. Wouldn't have surprised Velth a bit. The flagship had its pick of Starfleet's finest.

Barclay had been assigned to the *Galen* to oversee their holographic personnel, all of whom, along with the ship, he had helped to design. What surprised Velth were Barclay's ongoing anxiety issues. For someone who could slip seamlessly between eminently practical and mind-numbingly esoteric engineering issues, he lacked all but the most basic of social skills. When interacting with those who knew him well, like the Doctor, Kim, and Velth, he maintained his focus and composure. With Conlon he was no less perspicacious but was often hesitant, borderline embarrassed, and bedeviled by a stammer.

"I admit, I have no idea how we might accomplish it," Conlon said, "but that doesn't change the fact that we're forty-seven thousand light-years from the fleet's last known location and we're not going to get anywhere near them or within range of any of our communications buoys on impulse alone."

"We h-ha-have to find a way to bring the fleet to us," Barclay insisted. "They h-ha—will bring us the antimatter reserves we need."

"Which means our communications relay needs to be the next priority," Kim said.

"What about the slipstream drive?" the Doctor asked. "That doesn't require antimatter, does it?"

"No," Conlon replied, looking momentarily dazed. Velth reminded himself that she couldn't have slept for more than half an hour since this mess had begun. "But it does require benamite crystals, and all that's left of ours are piles of dust."

"Can't they be recrystallized?" Kim asked.

"In theory," Conlon allowed. "But B'Elanna's revolutionary matrix wasn't designed to reconstitute crystals that had been completely pulverized, only ones showing normal wear and minimal microfractures."

Kim nodded. Velth suspected he had known this, but it seemed important to him that everyone present be on the same page.

"Internal diagnostics show the communications array has alignment problems, likely caused by whatever they used to bring us here," Kim continued.

They, Velth thought. The *Edrehmaia*, or so they had apparently been christened by the species that preceded them on DK-1116. Aliens powerful enough to bring a starship halfway across the quadrant weren't unheard of, but they were extremely rare. Scans showed thousands of anomalous readings within a million kilometers of *Galen*. Without a lot more information, it was impossible to tell if they were ships or life-forms or advanced and intelligent technology. All Velth knew for sure was that he'd be hard-pressed not to take a shot at one of them should they venture too close to the ship. For now, they had kept their distance, which, in many ways, Velth found more concerning than anything they had done. *Why did they bring us here? What do they want?* Much like the planet they had found that started them down this path, the Edrehmaia were a question with no ready answer.

"Someone is going to have to get out there and manually adjust the array," Kim noted.

"That will take hours," Conlon said.

"Possibly more," Kim offered.

"I'll do it," Conlon said, as if that settled the matter.

Kim shot Conlon a quick look that seemed to say, *The hell you will.*

"Benoit and two of his three organic engineers were killed during the attack, and the third, Ensign Unhai, is a slipstream specialist," Conlon reminded him.

"Unhai could certainly handle a routine . . ." Kim began.

"I'll do it," Velth said quickly.

"I'd rather have an actual engineer take point on this, Velth," Kim said.

"Unhai is a year out of the Academy," Velth retorted with a grim chuckle. "She's spent the entirety of her brief career mastering our fantastic new drive system, but the one time Benoit asked her to fix a malfunctioning replicator, everything it produced for the next few days tasted like salmon that had been out in the sun too long. Get those benamite crystals restored and there will be no shortage of work she's qualified and capable of doing, but until then . . ." Velth shook his head.

Kim clearly considered Velth's words carefully, then turned back to Conlon. "All the EV suits have visual transmission capabilities. With internal comms working again, you could talk him through the repairs," he suggested.

"It would be quicker and easier if I just do it myself," Conlon said stubbornly.

"It would be," Kim agreed. "And I am not insensitive to the need to move quickly."

Velth knew these two were in a relationship. Up until now it hadn't hindered the work before them. He also knew she'd been a permanent resident of *Galen*'s sickbay for the last few weeks but had no idea what condition she had that required treatment on the fleet's dedicated medical vessel. He hoped it wasn't too serious. Conlon was one of the best and most experienced engineers Velth had ever known. Most of her service was with the Starfleet Corps of Engineers, a division renowned as miracle workers. After the last couple of days, Velth felt confident they had come by that moniker honestly. Velth had liked Benoit. He was bright and dedicated and curious and played a mean hand of poker.

But he wasn't Conlon.

"You're the only chief engineer we've got right now, Lieutenant Conlon," Velth interjected. "And Lieutenant Barclay"—Velth nodded toward Reg—"while also clearly qualified, needs to make sure the Doctor stays online. We *can't* lose either one of you. I'm going," he added in a tone that brooked no further refusal.

Kim nodded, clearly grateful he hadn't been the one to have to say it. "While you're out there, I need you to check a few other sections of the hull," Kim continued. "There are areas that show internal microfractures. The exterior readings indicate the presence of unidentifiable composites. I need to know what they are and, if possible, what purpose they serve."

"You think whoever brought us here mended our ship after we arrived?" Velth asked.

"I have no idea," Kim said. "We could have picked them up in transit. They might be space born life-forms that are native to this area and have taken an interest in us. I can't tell if the fractures were there first or the materials. I need a full visual inspection and tricorder scans."

"Happy to help," Velth said, though the thought of unidentifiable materials residing on the hull and possibly in the process of eating through it was enough to put him completely off the rest of his ration bar. "I'll get suited up right away."

"When was the last time you slept?" Kim asked pointedly.

"Yesterday, I think," Velth replied. "I got about four hours."

"Four in the last fifty-six?"

"I'm fine," Velth insisted.

"Hit your rack for six hours and then you can go," Kim said. It came out as an order. Velth chose to hear it as a friendly suggestion.

"I couldn't sleep right now if I wanted to," Velth admitted.

"Let me be clear," Kim said. "For the foreseeable future, this is our home. We're not going to solve this problem and get out of here in days or weeks. At best, it is going to be months before we get this ship in any condition to set a course and depart this nebula. All of us have to get on something resembling a normal schedule. This is still an emergency situation, but that's not going to change any time soon and if we don't rest, we'll get sloppy and even a small mistake right now could kill us."

"Well, when you put it that way . . ." Velth said.

"Are we going to talk about th-the-them?" Barclay asked.

"The Edrehmaia?" the Doctor attempted to clarify.

Kim shook his head. "There has been no change in the status of those currently occupying this area of space since we arrived. I'm actually hoping they keep ignoring us, at least for a while."

"Hope isn't much of a plan," Velth said.

"No, it isn't," Kim replied sharply. "But right now, it's all we've got."

As the group broke up, Conlon made a beeline for Kim. She waited until the bridge was nearly clear before saying softly, "We need to talk."

Kim turned to her and, for a moment, the calm, determined face he wore for the benefit of everyone else on the ship slipped a little. He was beyond exhausted and she honestly had no idea how he'd held himself together this long.

Years of practice was the best she could come up with.

Kim sighed and the mask went back up. It was heartbreaking in a way. They had known each other for a while now. Their capacity to be honest with each other, especially in the most difficult of circumstances, was the only thing that had seen them through. No matter how desperate things were, she couldn't bear to lose that.

Softening her tone a little, she went on, "I understand your concerns for me. But it will take Velth twice as long, if not more, to do the repairs you just handed him."

"Damn it, Nancy, don't you think I know that?" Kim said, then caught himself immediately.

She could have taken offense. She chose not to.

"I'm sorry, I didn't mean to snap," he offered quickly. "There's a good reason Starfleet frowns on officers who report directly to one another in the chain of command also being . . ."

"Involved?" Conlon said with a soft smirk.

"I'm trying to consider all of this objectively," he continued. "I know that's my job. But when it comes to you, it's really difficult."

"Putting in for a transfer is a little tough right now," she said.

"And pretending that you aren't the last person on this ship I'm willing to sacrifice is damn near impossible," he admitted.

"I know my limits," Conlon said. "And I'd like to think you just shot me down in front of the crew because you need your chief engineer. But I'm going to have to insist that you give me the same respect I'm showing you right now. Don't shut me down because you're afraid to lose me. And if you think you're about to, stop and take a beat."

Kim took her hands as his eyes locked with hers. "I will," he said. As she thanked him, the warm smile spreading across his face suddenly dimmed.

"What did you just say?" Kim asked.

"Thank you?"

Kim shook his head. "That's weird. I thought . . ."

"What?"

"It came out more like *Shershoo*."

A dull ache centered in Conlon's chest began to burn. She had already begun to question her auditory processing abilities. Several times during the briefing she had lost track momentarily of what her fellow officers were saying or simply found her attention drifting. She had chalked it up to fatigue, but the other specter, continued degeneration of her brain brought about by her DNA's inability to repair itself, was also a good candidate to explain her new symptoms. If *speaking clearly* was going to be added to the list, her ability to assist Harry and everyone else on board was going to diminish considerably. The thought of spending the next few days or weeks as a prisoner of sickbay while everyone else worked to solve their many problems wasn't just unpleasant, it was terrifying.

Worse, Harry could probably see it.

A soft hand fell on Conlon's shoulder.

"May I have a word, Lieutenant," the Doctor asked.

"Of course."

Kim continued to stand awkwardly as the Doctor waited for him to step away. Finally, he asked, "Is it all right if I stay?"

Conlon hesitated. If she insisted Kim allow them to speak alone he would want to know the reason why. She quickly decided that would create more problems than it might solve and nodded. "It's a little late to worry about waiving my right to privacy. Go ahead, Doctor."

"Very well," the Doctor said. "I need you to report to sickbay right away."

A twinge of nausea rippled through Conlon's gut.

"Is something wrong?" she asked.

"I don't know," the Doctor said. "Under normal circumstances, I would have done at least two full biometric scans on you in the last few days. It wasn't that long ago you came out of a coma. I need to make sure that your DNA hasn't been behaving too inappropriately while you were busy saving all of our lives."

"I feel okay," she said. "A little fatigued, but that's to be expected, isn't it?"

"Stress exacerbates your condition, Lieutenant," the Doctor said firmly. "Were it not for our—I was going to say *unique circumstances*, but who am I kidding, this is the Delta Quadrant—you wouldn't even be on duty right now. As it stands, I'm going to need you to check in at least once every twenty-four hours to make sure there are no new issues we haven't anticipated."

Conlon looked toward Harry. He was doing a fair job of maintaining his composure, but it didn't take a telepath to know what he needed her to say next.

"I need to check on the reactor," Conlon said. "But as soon as the diagnostics are done, I promise I'll stop by sickbay."

"Very well," the Doctor agreed before transferring himself back to the medical bay.

"It would be so helpful if I could do that right now," Conlon said as she turned toward the turbolift. Kim reached for her hand as she did so. She stopped and forced a smile to her lips, hoping it looked reassuring.

"I'm going to be fine," she insisted.

She wished she hadn't been able to see so clearly in Kim's eyes the doubt that followed that statement.

4

Marion Dulmur's face was nothing if not forgettable. Eyewitness identification was notoriously unreliable, but even so, Captain Farkas was briefly astonished by the lack of distinguishing features on the face before her. It was as if a computer had been asked to render "random white male" and succeeded beyond all expectation.

Farkas did suspect that this might be essential in his line of work.

"Thank you for accepting my transmission, Captain," Dulmur said. "I'm sure you have your hands full out there and I understand that your time is at a premium."

"You said you're with the Department of Temporal Investigations," Farkas acknowledged. "That means, like it or not, I don't have a lot of choice when it comes to accepting your calls, Agent."

"Director," Dulmur corrected her gently.

"Congratulations," Farkas replied.

Dulmur obviously chose to ignore the copious amount of snark conveyed in that single word. "I'll get right to it, then. Are you aware, Captain, that your commanding officer, Admiral Kathryn Janeway, recently received a directive from our offices to return to Krenim space and attempt to open normalized diplomatic relations with them?"

"I am not," Farkas replied. "Nor is there any particular reason why I would be until the admiral chooses to issue orders that concern me related to that directive."

Dulmur's stare did not waver. He paused, perhaps long enough to wonder if he was witnessing garden-variety courtesy or something a little more defensive, then pressed on. "The directive was issued by my former partner, Agent Gariff Lucsly. We are both unofficially concerned that the admiral might not be inclined to give his orders their due consideration."

A chill ran up Farkas's spine. "I'm still waiting to hear the part of this story that has anything to do with me, Director," she said evenly.

One corner of Dulmur's mouth lifted slightly, conveying faint amusement. *Oh, good. He's human after all,* Farkas thought.

"You might not be aware, Captain Farkas, but your current commanding officer has, in the past, demonstrated a somewhat troubling tendency to ignore both the letter and spirit of our regulations concerning temporal manipulation."

A chuckle burst from Farkas's gut. Was Dulmur naïve enough to believe that she would have accepted this commission without acquainting herself with her commanding officer's record in full, or was he trying to determine whether she shared Janeway's predilections? Farkas certainly had her own issues with the admiral right now, but she'd be damned if an officious bureaucrat was going to school her on her duties as a Starfleet officer.

"Permit me to be blunt, Director," Farkas began.

"That doesn't seem to be a challenge for you, Captain," Dulmur interjected.

"Fair point," Farkas conceded. "While I understand and respect your position and the DTI's mandate, I have also witnessed firsthand how incredibly complicated and delicate matters of temporal manipulation can be out here on the front lines. I don't doubt that the admiral's past experiences in this matter have given her all the insight required to judge your agent's recommendation on its merits and determine how to properly address it."

Dulmur's chin dipped slightly and his voice dropped a little as he said, "I wish I could agree with that assessment, Captain."

"If that's the problem here, I suggest you take it up with the admiral's superiors, Director Dulmur."

"It is certainly one of the many options open to me, Captain, but I was hoping we might find a way together to head off such unpleasantness."

Farkas paused. She knew that to ask more was to wade into an area that was beyond her purview. But Dulmur didn't strike her as an idiot. If he was reaching out to her, well outside the normal chain of command, he had a reason. She just wasn't sure she wanted to hear it.

"I assume this has something to do with our efforts to untangle the mess that the Krenim, Rilnar, and Zahl made of Sormana?" Farkas ventured. These included the discovery of a temporally displaced version of Kathryn Janeway and a number of unresolved questions surrounding the actions of the father of their daughter, a Krenim agent named Dayne. Farkas had never been so happy as when Sormana was put in her rear sensor feed. She had been one of many voices counseling patience from the admiral in relation to Dayne, the *denzit*; the child, Mollah; and the entire Krenim Imperium. If Janeway's gut told her to leave the situation be, Farkas wasn't going to object to that for a second.

"It does in the sense that the chain of events reported to the DTI by the admiral put the Krenim on the DTI's radar and warranted further investigation of their actions."

"Happy to help," Farkas quipped.

"But it's more than that."

Of course it is.

"I am not in a position to disclose to you the nature of the indicators that have arisen as a result of our analysis of the Krenim," Dulmur continued. "What I am saying, officer to officer, is that our concerns are incredibly well founded and Agent Lucsly's directive was not issued out of an abundance of caution or a desire to annoy the admiral."

"Why would the admiral suspect that?" Farkas asked.

"Lucsly and Admiral Janeway didn't begin on the best of terms. It is my belief that they are both committed, body and soul, to doing right by their people and the Federation. My fear is that personal considerations might drive the admiral's choices—ones for which I wouldn't blame her in the least. I was present during her debrief by the DTI when her ship first returned to the Alpha Quadrant. Lucsly defends temporal equilibrium with the passion of a zealot. And you and I are better for it. But Janeway doesn't know him like I do, and any number of reasonable responses to that first meeting on her part could lead all of us in a dangerous direction."

"So exactly what are you asking of me?" Farkas demanded.

"Misunderstandings can complicate any humanoid interaction. I'm not suggesting that you march into the admiral's office and demand that she comply with Lucsly's orders. I would just like to establish and keep open a line of communication with you so that in the event the admiral opts to ignore the directive, you and I might work together to find a way to at least make sure that if further evidence presents itself relating to the DTI's concerns, you would feel comfortable reporting it without violating your duty to obey your commanding officer."

Finally, merciful clarity.

Farkas inhaled deeply. "You and I don't know each other at all, *Mister* Dulmur," she began. "So allow me to help you out here. What you are asking might sound to you like political expediency. From another point of view, it could also be interpreted as contemplating, hell, *conspiring* to commit mutiny."

Dulmur started to interrupt but she rolled right over him.

"I am all for keeping lines of communication open, but the proper channel in this case exists only between your Agent Lucsly and Admiral Kathryn Janeway. Neither of them tripped over something and landed in their current positions. Both understand their responsibilities and take them seriously. Any disagreement between them as to the best course of action is *between them*, and the only recourse available to you or me lies in taking the matter to their superior officers.

"I'm not your girl here, Director. I don't play games and I don't lie by commission or omission to those whom I have sworn honorable service."

Dulmur nodded slowly. "It was not my intention to suggest otherwise."

"Then you shouldn't have," Farkas said simply. "As I said, the admiral has not chosen to include me in this issue and until she does, I will take no action to undermine her authority or decisions. You might have a problem here, but I am not the solution. Have I made myself perfectly clear?"

"You have, Captain. Before I sign off, permit me to add further clarity to the situation for you. Agent Lucsly has briefed all of his superiors on the evidence and rationale behind the directive he issued. That includes both the Director of the DTI, Laarin Andos, and the C-in-C of Starfleet Command, Admiral Akaar. They fully expect the admiral to comply with the directive in question, and outright refusal on her part will likely lead to the suspension of her command. You are the most likely replacement should that occur. Bottom line, *someone* is going to be tasked with establishing normalized relations with the Krenim Imperium. Were the admiral my friend and my commanding officer, I would want her to be aware of those facts. You may certainly disagree. But that's where we are right now. Do you have any questions?"

"Not a one," Farkas replied.

"Very good. It has been a pleasure speaking with you, Captain. Thank you for your time."

VOYAGER

"Resume the log," Captain Chakotay ordered.

Admiral Kathryn Janeway, commander of the Full Circle Fleet and the only officer present who outranked *Voyager*'s captain, lifted her fingers from the table ever so slightly. Seven registered the gesture to belay Chakotay's order and refrained from initiating playback. Since they had gathered in *Voyager*'s briefing room, the officers present had already watched four times the entire series of events leading up to the apparent destruction of the *Galen*.

"I presume that vessel does not correspond with anything in the fleet's database?" Janeway asked of the room. In addition to Seven,

Chakotay, Commanders Paris and Torres, Counselor Hugh Cambridge, and science officer Lieutenant Devi Patel were all assembled around the briefing room's table.

Captain Chakotay seemed to barely register the question. Commander Torres, the fleet's chief engineer, was the first to reply, "No, Admiral. There are minimal markers that suggest Borg origin, but we've never encountered a vessel capable of completely altering its entire configuration like that. Honestly, are we even sure it is a vessel?"

In the hours that had passed between the event itself and the commencement of this meeting, Seven had begun her own cursory review of the logs and made a few notable observations. The time had not been sufficient, however, for her to thoroughly analyze them. She did not doubt that as they spoke, every single officer on duty was busy scrutinizing the logs, nanosecond by nanosecond, and that additional data would be at the senior staff's disposal shortly.

Still, Seven offered, "While the ship's database would not have characterized the substance that attacked Ensign Gwyn on a nearby asteroid and subsequently began to transform the shuttle *Van Cise* as a *vessel*, there are significant similarities between it and the ship in question."

"Meaning we have no idea what we're dealing with at all here," Torres said.

Janeway's gaze settled on the former Borg mission specialist. "We're not far from former Borg space," she said, her low voice resonating in the range of gravel that typically indicated extreme exhaustion. "Did they ever encounter a ship like this?"

Seven shook her head. "No, Admiral. Nor did they record observing anything similar to the unusual living alloy that attacked the shuttle."

"Don't you mean *ate* the shuttle?" Commander Paris asked.

"Casual observation certainly suggested that," Seven replied evenly. She could well imagine the torment Paris and Torres were suffering. Lieutenant Harry Kim was more like a brother than a fellow officer to them, and Lieutenant Conlon had been close to

Commander Torres as well. For her part, Seven had barely begun to reconcile herself to the apparent loss of *Galen*'s CMO, the Emergency Medical Hologram known as the Doctor. She simply could not imagine her continued existence without him and therefore refused to acknowledge the reality until a final verdict on the events portrayed in the logs had been rendered.

"At this time it is impossible to accurately characterize the alloy based upon the data our sensors were able to collect," Seven continued. "Whether we were witnessing metabolism or a form of subatomic transformation remains an open question."

"In this case, I'm not sure there's much of a distinction," Lieutenant Patel piped up. Among those assembled, she and Seven were the only individuals who had closely observed the substance in question, Seven on an asteroid and Patel in a chamber below the surface of the planet DK-1116. Patel had barely survived her encounter, risking her life in an attempt to make certain that the data she and her team had collected on their away mission to one of several biodomes present on the surface was recovered by the fleet. At the time her choice might have appeared to be a youthful indiscretion or an extreme attempt to attract the attention of her commanding officers. While Seven could not speak to the emotional motivations of the lieutenant, she had already concluded that Patel's choice to sacrifice herself in favor of transmitting the data had been a defensible calculation. That data was already proving invaluable in their analysis of the strange new world the fleet had chosen to study only a few days prior.

Patel continued, "The Edrehmaia substance is something we have never imagined as a possibility. We don't know if it is naturally occurring or a product of centuries of genetic manipulation. While we have not been able to sample it, we know that it can integrate both simple matter as well as human and alien DNA into itself and create new forms with them. But more important, it is the most efficient energy storage and release system I've ever seen. I wouldn't be surprised if its structure is based on quantum scales."

"That's quite an intuitive leap," Janeway noted.

"Perhaps," Patel agreed. "I'm simply searching for a theoretical framework that incorporates all of the evidence we currently have at our disposal."

"Fascinating as these hypotheses may be," Captain Chakotay interjected, "can they help us understand what just happened or why of all the ships present, it chose to destroy the *Galen*?"

There was an edge to Chakotay's question that did not go unnoticed by the group. Seven suddenly remembered that this entire endeavor, altering course to examine DK-1116 and the combined exploration and shore leave in which the crew engaged while there, had been Chakotay's idea. *He's blaming himself for this*, she realized.

"It is strange," Janeway said. "*Galen* was the smallest ship in the fleet and her defensive capabilities were the weakest. That said, the energy present in that beam could likely have done the same to *Vesta* had she been the target."

"Or *Voyager*," Paris added somberly.

"From a tactical perspective, it makes no sense," Seven agreed. "Therefore we should consider other ways in which *Galen* was unique."

"I don't care why they did it," Chakotay said. "I just want to know where to find them."

Seven turned her head to briefly study Chakotay's face. His eyes were haunted and there was no trace of the wise, gentle spirit that had helped to bring Seven through some of her own darkest times.

"Really?" Counselor Cambridge, who had been silently observing the entire group, finally said. "Without even the most basic understanding of what they are and what drove them to us?"

"What they are, Counselor, are murderers," Chakotay retorted.

"Are you sure?" Cambridge asked, clearly unafraid to test Chakotay's nonexistent patience.

"Do you need to watch it again?" Chakotay asked.

"I think you might," Cambridge said. "The energy waves that came off that ship just before it altered its configuration were powerful enough to disrupt our ship's shields and power systems, however briefly. More to the point, they rendered everyone aboard each of our ships unconscious for eight to eleven minutes. They incapacitated us without breaking a sweat well *before* they fired upon the *Galen.* We're no match for them and you know it."

Chakotay accepted this silently, but not graciously, if Seven could judge by the expression of disgust on his face.

"That's not all they did," Janeway interjected quickly, clearly hoping to steer the conversation down more productive paths. "Those lights, all along the visible and invisible spectrum, what were they trying to communicate with them?"

"Data at the rate of exaquads per second were carried on those photonic waves," Seven said. "Analysis has begun but it could be days before we can translate, let alone interpret it."

"Even if opening communication was their goal, they didn't give us a chance to respond before they attacked," Paris noted.

"You're assuming that was an attack," Patel said.

"What else would you call it, Lieutenant?" Chakotay asked.

Patel, to her credit, refused to allow the bite behind those words to faze her.

"It might have been another method of data transmission," she suggested. "They might not have intended to destroy our ship."

"You're saying something that advanced might not have known its own strength?" Janeway asked.

"I'm saying, Admiral, that there are far too many unknowns present for us to intuit, let alone assign motive to, the actions of those on board that ship."

"How many were there?" Torres asked of Seven.

"Life signs?" Seven asked.

"Did our sensors pick up anything?"

"Just as with the scan taken on the planet's surface of organisms we believe were created by or with the substance, life-sign readings were inconclusive," Seven replied.

"It bears remembering that we chose to come to this world and to explore its mysteries," Patel said. "As best we can tell, it had remained intact for over four thousand years, and in two days we disrupted safe-guards put in place by species that clearly understood it better than we did and activated some dormant mechanism with unimaginable consequences. *We did that.* And we can't blame them if it got their attention and they decided to investigate us and our handiwork."

Chakotay was clearly ready to respond, but Janeway silenced him with a look.

"While I can't take issue with the facts as you have stated them, Lieutenant," Janeway began, "I wouldn't go so far as to place all of the responsibility for what transpired at our feet. Any species advanced enough to construct this planet, and if Seven is right, to have created this entire star system long before that, must be aware that the majority of spacefaring races out here could not have anticipated the results of our exploration attempt. And yet, they chose to leave DK-1116 as they did, to abandon it."

"That is pure speculation," Seven said.

Before Patel could respond, a small voice spoke from the back of the room.

"They're not dead."

The entire assembly turned to face the voice's owner, *Voyager's* helmsman, Ensign Aytar Gwyn.

"At least one of them isn't."

Admiral Janeway stared in disbelief at Gwyn.

"I beg your pardon, Ensign?"

Gwyn's eyes were red and glistening, and her cheeks were ruddy. In the brief time Seven had known her, Gwyn had never been one for emotional displays. She was young, but well trained, and performed her duties as *Voyager's* alpha shift pilot better than anyone, short of Tom Paris. She also tended toward the forthright end of the spectrum, sometimes to the point of indecorousness. Seven found her refreshing. Standing at the door to the briefing room, fretting nervously, clasping and unclasping her hands before her, she was as far from composed as Seven had ever seen her.

Before Gwyn could answer the admiral, Counselor Cambridge

rose from his seat. "Forgive me, Admiral, but as you are well aware, the last several days have been quite difficult for Ensign Gwyn. Permit me to speak with her privately?"

Janeway seemed inclined to refuse this request, one that was more than reasonable under the circumstances.

"I'm not crazy," Gwyn insisted. "I know how it sounds, but . . ."

At this protestation, Janeway nodded to Cambridge. "Of course, Counselor."

As Cambridge departed, ushering Gwyn from the briefing room before him, Seven wondered why the counselor had been so quick to silence Gwyn. While it was unlikely in the extreme that the ensign had any special knowledge of the fate of the *Galen*, there had been something in her insistence that gave Seven pause. Her assertion was hard to believe, but Seven was absolutely certain that true or not, *Gwyn believed what she was saying.*

Within a few minutes, Cambridge had settled Gwyn in his office. The petite ensign sat cross-legged on a small sofa. Her head down, she stared intently at her hands, folding them together and releasing them repeatedly. Cambridge moved to sit opposite her, perching on the edge of a deep leather chair in which he normally sat during counseling sessions.

"Ensign?"

Gwyn lifted her face to his. Her distress was obvious but whether she had lost touch with reality or simply feared that everyone around her believed that she had was difficult to tell. Her short, spiked hair was multitoned, sandy-brown roots giving way to a fading pink color. One of these days he was going to find out why she found it necessary to alter its color on a regular basis. He suspected boredom, but there might be more to it than that.

"I'm not crazy," she asserted.

"No one said you were, Ensign," Cambridge offered gently.

"I saw the logs like everyone else. I know what it looks like. But

I'm telling you, they weren't destroyed. I'm not imagining this or making it up."

"Very well. I, too, have seen the logs, and while I am no expert, I found nothing to suggest that anyone aboard the *Galen* could have survived that encounter." He paused for a moment before asking, "Upon what do you base your belief that my eyes have deceived me?"

Gwyn crossed her arms over her chest in understandable protectiveness. "It's just a feeling."

Cambridge nodded. "What kind of feeling?"

Gwyn seemed confused by the question.

"Let me put it another way. What do you see in those logs that the rest of us are missing?"

She shook her head. "Nothing."

"But you *feel* certain that the *Galen*'s crew is still alive?"

Gwyn's next words were chosen incredibly carefully. "I feel certain that one person aboard that ship is still alive and if they are, the others could be as well."

"Who?" Cambridge asked.

Gwyn hesitated to respond.

"Am I correct in assuming that if this fleet were yours to command, you would order it immediately to begin a search for the *Galen*?" he asked kindly.

Gwyn nodded.

"Do you have any sense of how close they might be or where we might find them?"

"No."

"And do you understand that in that process, every other member of this fleet would be endangering themselves on your orders?"

"We do that every day," Gwyn said a little too defensively.

"That's true, but you would be asking us to engage in activity that might lead us into the path of that alien vessel again. Do you believe another such encounter would end well for us?"

"I don't know, and I don't care," Gwyn said. "They're helpless. They need us. We have to find them."

"Why won't you tell me who this one person you feel certain survived is?" Cambridge asked.

Softly, Gwyn replied, "You won't believe me."

"Try me."

Gwyn took a few short, quick breaths and finally answered, "Harry Kim and Nancy Conlon's daughter."

Cambridge took a moment to collect himself before saying, "I see."

He wasn't disappointed. On the contrary, he had suspected since Gwyn first spoke up in the briefing room that this was the case. Now he needed to find out if there was any way this impossible assertion could also be true.

Shortly after Cambridge and Gwyn departed the briefing room, the meeting ended with the admiral's orders to each officer present that they advise her immediately should any new information regarding the attack become available. Captain Chakotay knew that it was her intention to return to the *Vesta* and that for some undisclosed reason, she wasn't looking forward to that. Despite his recommendation that she invite Farkas and O'Donnell to the briefing, Janeway had pointedly chosen to limit the initial group to *Voyager* personnel. Chakotay didn't know why. He only knew that it was unusual. Speculating beyond that was not something for which he currently had the presence of mind.

He understood on some level that he wasn't thinking or perceiving reality around him with the clarity he considered "normal." As he responded automatically to the questions posed by his fellow officers, he could hear how argumentative and defensive he sounded, but he couldn't seem to care. He knew that he probably *should*; it was simply not possible.

He could not stop seeing the *Galen* being destroyed in his mind. Even as he tried to focus on the present, his conscious thoughts returned stubbornly to the moment, or rather the *latest moment* that had brought painful change to his life. Reason was lost to the maelstrom that accompanied the emotional blow, an internal explosion happening over and over again.

He had experienced shock before. He had survived psychological agony so acute as to render him nearly nonfunctional. He remembered those experiences, even as the distance between them and this moment had mercifully lessened their impact. He understood the inchoate rage living just beneath the surface of the shock and its intense desire to be given free rein to spend itself by lashing out at everyone within arm's length. He also knew in some distant, almost disconnected part of himself that this feeling would pass, others more painful would follow, and that eventually he would have to begin the task of reintegration, of creating himself anew with spaces left forever empty within him where those he had loved and just lost had once lived.

But he was clearly not yet ready to do that work, nor could he imagine himself ever being quite ready.

The last of his officers had filed out but Commander Tom Paris remained seated at the briefing room table, slouched in his seat, staring forward, his gaze fixed on something a thousand light-years distant.

Chakotay reached for words that might bring Paris from this stupor, then thought better of it. Tom was undoubtedly in the same place he was. Words could wait.

As he willed his feet to step toward the door, Paris's voice struck him like a shot.

"You can't do this again, *Captain.*"

Chakotay could count on one hand the number of times Paris had addressed him by his rank rather than his name in private conversation over the last year. The clearly intentional emphasis hit the nerve Paris had been aiming toward and stopped Chakotay in his tracks. He turned on his first officer ready to justify his next words with every weapon that rank afforded him, but when Paris lifted his face to Chakotay's, something—perhaps the sheer tonnage of loss between them—made him think twice.

Paris clearly saw this as progress, and an opening to continue. Rising to his feet, he said, "There's something you should know."

"Something about how badly Kathryn's death once broke me and how there is no time right now for a repeat performance?" Chakotay asked. The words were harsh but he managed to modulate his tone toward the compassionate end of the spectrum. Both stood on the precipice of saying a thousand things they would later wish to take back, and Chakotay had no desire to be the first to step over the edge.

"No," Paris replied. "I mean, you're not wrong, but the last time we had that exact conversation you nearly punched me, and I don't like making the same mistake twice."

"Then what?" Chakotay demanded.

"Harry Kim was a father."

The words registered but somehow remained incomprehensible. "Of course Harry Kim had a father," Chakotay replied.

"No. Harry Kim *became* a father," Paris said, enunciating each word slowly and clearly. "Five days ago, just before we reached orbit, Nancy Conlon suffered a hemorrhage in her brain and required emergency surgery. She was a few weeks pregnant at the time and something went wrong. The embryo was in danger, so they transported it to a fetal incubator. For the last five days of his life, Harry Kim *was* a father."

All of this was news to Chakotay. Although Counselor Cambridge had reported regularly to Chakotay about Conlon's progress, the details of her illness and apparently her pregnancy had remained private.

"Why didn't he tell me?" Chakotay asked. "Why didn't he tell any of us?"

Paris shook his head. "It was early. Nancy didn't even know yet. She was still in a coma when he confided in me and insisted I keep it between us. He wouldn't even let me tell B'Elanna."

This revelation ignited a cascade of new, troubling feelings but Chakotay couldn't help but fixate on Tom's face. Painful as this obviously was, there was a deep sense of peace radiating from the commander that Chakotay found inscrutable.

"How is this okay?" Chakotay demanded. "How does the waste of another completely innocent life somehow make this acceptable?"

Paris shrugged. "I don't know. Harry changed after he met Nancy. He found some stability, some reserve of strength from which he drew even when everything kept going to hell all around us. And he wanted that child as much as I've ever known him to want anything. The baby was only a few weeks old and he was already thinking about how to make her life perfect. I don't like believing that he's dead any more than you do, but I'm so damned happy that he got to experience at least a little of that before he died. I honestly never thought he would."

Chakotay tried to find the comfort Paris obviously felt, but it was a struggle. It was all so damned unfair.

He caught himself before the words left his lips. *Unfair?* Of course it was unfair. Life was unfair. There was no basis for comparison by which every moment of each life couldn't be judged as such. It was the cry of a childish mind and belied the experience and hard-won wisdom that had seen Chakotay through his darkest days.

"We still don't know what happened to them," Paris continued. "And I'm not at all convinced that there are any more miracles left for us. We've used up more than our fair share over the years. But the people on this ship and in this fleet who we are meant to lead follow our examples closely. Ensign Gwyn almost threw her career away on a hunch a few days ago. Devi Patel decided to *end her life* so that we would receive the data she collected from that damned planet. They did those things because on some level they knew that in their places, *we would have done the same.*

"We owe it to them now to deal with our personal grief on our own time and as best we can. We have one another to hold on to no matter which way this goes. And I wouldn't be doing my job if I didn't remind you that your anger is pointless and serves nothing but your own ego."

"All of this is my fault," Chakotay said, his eyes burning brightly.

"At least that's what the anger and pain that have refused to be silent ever since Waters reported *Galen*'s loss have been reminding me. If I hadn't insisted on exploring this world, none of this would have happened."

"That's bullshit and you know it," Paris countered.

"It is and I do, but that doesn't make the feeling any less potent," Chakotay replied.

"Try focusing on the good that was Harry's life, Nancy's life, the Doctor's existence . . . how much they gave us and how full these last months have been. There are worse ways to live and definitely worse times to die."

Having said what needed to be said, Paris headed toward the door. Chakotay called to him just before he reached it.

"Thank you, *Commander*."

"Anytime, Chakotay."

Counselor Cambridge had ordered Ensign Gwyn to return to her quarters and rest until the start of her next duty shift. His next move was to contact the only person in the fleet who could confirm what Gwyn had told him.

It took only moments for the weathered face of Doctor El'nor Sal to appear on the viewscreen in his office.

"You rang?" Sal greeted him.

Vesta's chief medical officer was well into her eighties and one of the most delightfully complex individuals Cambridge had ever met. This woman brooked no one's nonsense and demanded far more of herself than was probably healthy. Cambridge liked her, but she had lost perspective in her quest to heal Nancy Conlon and, as a result, had been relieved of duty by her commanding officer, Captain Regina Farkas. An unfortunate side effect of Sal's quest to heal Conlon had included an experimental procedure on Ensign Gwyn that had caused significant short-term trauma. The potential long-term effects upon the ensign remained an open question. But as Cambridge stared into the doctor's gray eyes, he couldn't help but notice that something in them, a ferocious intensity, had faded.

"Are you quite all right, Doctor?" Cambridge asked.

Sal sighed and took a long sip from a clear glass of pale blue liquid. Her next words betrayed a slight slur. *"Seeing as how I've been relieved of duty for the foreseeable future and apparently the patient whose case cost me my reputation and my oldest friend has just been killed, I thought I might drink a little."* She wavered slightly as she spoke, a gentle side-to-side rocking of which she was probably unaware. *"As soon as you're done helping everybody over there through the first stages of grief, you're welcome to join me."*

"I'm assuming you're talking about the real stuff?" Cambridge asked.

"What do you take me for, a barbarian?" Sal replied.

Cambridge hadn't asked because he was remotely interested in joining the good doctor. He had asked because he needed to know exactly what he was seeing.

"Doctor, I need you to focus for a moment."

Sal chuckled. *"For you, anything. Oh, wait, you're an ass."*

"You're not wrong, but can we set that aside for a moment? I need to know something about Ensign Gwyn."

"Ensign Gwyn? Lovely girl. Sorry about unintentionally activating that recessive gene. Do you think she'll forgive me? Hang on, I did that to save someone else's life, didn't I?"

"Doctor, am I going to have to order you to sickbay for an antiintoxicant or can you possibly get a tighter grip on your horses?"

Sal seemed to seriously consider the question. *"Go ahead."*

"Ensign Gwyn. A few days ago, you unintentionally initiated the *finiis'ral* in her, a biological imperative unique to Kriosians that should have required her to bond with another individual, a process that would have permanently altered her mental state to force her to become that individual's perfect mate."

"I did. Didn't . . . didn't mean to, though. That antiproton therapy . . . what the hell was she doing on that damned asteroid anyway?"

"Stay with me, El'nor. We were all worried that if she didn't complete the *finiis'ral* she would die."

"I know. It's horrible. I'd really like to understand what evolution was thinking when it selected for that trait."

"Be that as it may, the process apparently reversed itself. Do you remember?"

"No, it didn't," Sal insisted. *"She completed the* finial, finn . . . fizzer . . ."

Had Cambridge possessed the ability to reach his arms through the data screen and slap Sal, he would have done it. "The *finiis'ral?*"

"Yep. That one."

"But how?" Cambridge demanded. "You had a theory, but there wasn't time for you to explain."

"She bonded with the baby. I didn't tell you that?"

"How is that possible?"

"Dunno."

"In your studies of the Kriosians, did you ever encounter another instance of such a bonding?"

"Nope."

"Then how can you be certain that—"

"There's no science to explain it," Sal said gruffly, cutting him off. *"At least none the Kriosians are willing to share with the rest of the class."*

"In a normal bonding, can the connection between a Kriosian and their perfect mate span great distances?"

Sal's forehead fell into deep wrinkles as she pondered his question. Finally she released a long, slow sigh. *"In theory, yes. All of them are low- to mid-level telepaths and the bonding is both a physical and mental connection. I'm not sure where Gwyn falls on the psi-scale, but wait a minute. Why are you asking me this?"*

"Because Ensign Gwyn believes that the baby is still alive."

"Wasn't the baby on board the Galen *when . . ."* Sal trailed off as the potential ramifications of this hit her. *"Shit,"* she finally said.

"I'm going to send a medic to your quarters to get you back on your feet, Doctor. You're going to need to make a full report to the admiral within the next hour regarding Gwyn's condition."

"That's going to be some trick, seeing as I can't remember where I left my boots," Sal opined.

"We'll talk soon, Doctor," Cambridge said, signing off. He then dispatched the necessary orders to *Vesta's* medical staff.

He knew that Gwyn's feelings were a pretty flimsy strand upon which to base an argument that everything they currently believed about the *Galen's* fate was false. He also knew that Admiral Janeway and Captain Chakotay would grasp for anything remotely hope-shaped at a moment like this and move heaven, Earth, and every astronomical body in between to prove her right.

5

"*R*emove the switch plate carefully," Conlon said in the same tinny voice with which Lieutenant Velth had become all too well acquainted during the last two hours.

"How about I just rip out the entire housing, Chief?" Velth asked—kidding—as he gingerly began to tug at the plate's edge.

"*If you have a spare one in your pocket, sure thing,*" Conlon teased right back. "*If you don't . . . well, how badly do you ever want to talk to the rest of the fleet again? Maybe I should have asked before you went out there.*"

Velth silently thanked whoever had developed the EV suit's engineering gloves. Someone had clearly given thought to the manual dexterity required by engineers toiling in the vacuum of space. They maintained his body temperature perfectly and felt much like a second skin. Work like this would be damn near impossible without them.

"Almost got it," he said.

"*Carefully. Like an egg,*" Conlon added.

Velth held the edge of the plate as delicately as he could, applying just enough pressure to ease it out. When it slipped free undamaged, he released a breath he hadn't realized he was holding.

"Got it."

"*Show me,*" Conlon requested.

This was the lieutenant's cue to lift the plate to his own eye level. The EV suit's imager transmitted what he saw directly to Conlon on the bridge.

"*Rotate one hundred and eighty degrees, please,*" Conlon ordered. He did so, gently. After a moment she said, "*There it is.*"

Velth studied the back of the plate. To his untrained eye, nothing seemed out of sorts.

"There *what* is?" he asked.

"The primary relay is fused."

"That sounds bad."

"It's fixable. Set the plate down on your mag panel. Then go to your case and find me a sixteen-beta-four head. Attach it to your decoupler and target component DX9RQ."

Velth did as he had been ordered. "Are you sure that a reasonably well-trained monkey couldn't handle this?" he asked.

"We have monkeys on board?" Conlon retorted. *"See, that would have been helpful information to have a few hours ago. Monkeys would have been done by now."*

It took Velth another twenty minutes to replace the fused relay. Returning the component to its housing was completed without incident.

"Stand back, Lieutenant," Conlon ordered as Velth finished stowing the tools he'd used to perform the meticulous repairs.

"How far?" Velth asked.

"Give it at least five meters of clearance."

"Why?"

"I'm about to restore power to the array and in the event you're not as good at following instructions as you appear to be . . ."

"Boom?"

"You're in space, so you won't hear it, but you'll definitely feel it."

"Will it be the last thing I feel?"

"Just stand the hell back."

"Copy that, Chief."

Thirty seconds later, Velth was treated to the sight of a functioning communications array unfolding like a sunflower turning toward a light source. Velth released a deep sigh of satisfaction.

"Looks great from out here," he said.

"In here too. Nice work, Velth," Conlon said with palpable relief.

"Can I come home now?"

"Not just yet."

Oh, right, Velth remembered. "The microfractures?"

"Face the comm array and proceed forward toward two o'clock, about ten meters."

"What exactly am I looking for?"

"Anything that looks like it shouldn't be there," Conlon replied.

"Okey-dokey."

Velth was approximately two meters away when he spotted it.

"What the . . . ?"

"I need you to get a little closer, Velth."

He wished he didn't have to.

He hadn't seen most of the really weird things some of the teams who'd studied the biodomes on DK-1116 had reported: strange vegetation, objects that read as nonliving but regenerated when sampled. His work had consisted largely of helping Commander Paris prep a lakeside area in one of the larger biodomes for crew recreation activities. He had, however, been on *Galen*'s bridge watching when *Voyager* had destroyed one of its shuttles that had made contact with a black, sludgy substance and been almost entirely consumed by it. Fascinating as the shuttle's immolation had been to witness, he'd felt significantly better when it had been blown to bits than he had while watching it approach the fleet's position. The only thing he clearly recalled of that moment was thinking that the stuff in the process of eating the shuttle sure looked hungry.

Whatever was now affixed to *Galen*'s hull easily checked both the "really weird" and "possibly hungry" boxes.

The patch was roughly oval shaped, though its edges were irregular. It was definitely attached to the hull and had a fluid quality to it. Though primarily black, faint vivid flashes of color all along the visible spectrum emanated frequently from the substance. Velth couldn't shake the sense that it was alive, despite the fact that his suit's sensors, which automatically fed data to a display in his helmet, were not detecting anything remotely close to a life-form when angled directly toward it. It was moving, but not growing, and Velth felt almost certain that were he to disturb it, it might take offense and turn its attention toward him.

Velth took a half step closer and bent on one knee to give Conlon the best view he could comfortably provide.

"Are you receiving my sensor feed, Chief?"

"Yeah," Conlon replied. *"It's a little confusing."*

"Any idea when we picked it up?"

"No. But it does appear to be repairing some damage to the area."

"How?"

"Hard to say. There's evidence of molecular adhesion and biochemical changes that are definitely reinforcing the fractures."

"So, it's friendly?" Velth asked dubiously.

"I wouldn't go that far," Conlon said. *"Friends might have asked before they attached a foreign substance to our ship. That said, internal sensors show similar readings at more than a dozen places on the hull. I'm guessing the fractures happened in transit and these were put in place to make sure the ship didn't rip itself apart before we had a chance to do our own repairs."*

"There are a lot of assumptions in that statement, Chief," Velth noted.

"I'm trying to maintain a positive attitude in the face of adversity."

"That's adorable. I'm more of a realist, myself."

A long silence followed. Velth maintained his position, assuming Conlon was busying herself collecting all the data his sensors could give her. After almost a minute had passed, a soft ping caught his attention. "Is that my sensor grid saying 'Hello'?" he asked.

"Hold on. There's a lot of weird radioactive particles out there. Could just be a random . . ."

Velth's stomach tightened a notch as the voice keeping him relatively calm trailed off.

"Chief? Conlon?"

"Lieutenant Velth, it's Harry." The stress in Kim's voice was easy to hear.

"Do we have a problem?"

"It is possible we have attracted a little attention," Kim said.

"What kind of attention?" Velth asked as a wide array of frightening possibilities began to occur to him.

"Stand by," Kim ordered.

It took every ounce of self-restraint Velth possessed to remain in place. The lizard that lived at the base of his brain insisted he run for the airlock. The trained Starfleet officer in him refused that imperative.

"Any chance you guys have fixed the transporters in the last two hours?" Velth asked.

"No, Velth," came Conlon's voice. She sounded every bit as stressed as Kim. *"Don't worry about the gear. Just start back toward the airlock, okay?"*

She didn't have to tell him twice. Velth rose and began his journey by retracing his steps to the array. As he did so, he began a cursory visual scan of the area around him while moving as briskly as his magnetic boots would permit. Nothing directly ahead or within ninety degrees of either side appeared to be amiss.

Fantastic, they're coming up behind me, Velth deduced. Turning slowly, he searched the darkness for whatever had spooked Kim and Conlon, and activated his suit's proximity alert.

Even with his suit's sensor magnification set to maximum, it took a few seconds to pick them out among the visual spectacle of newborn stars and the distant lights that according to Kim were most likely alien vessels. At first glance, he saw two but soon enough, he could clearly discern five distinct figures. They were shaped like rectangles with no obvious extremities. Only bits and pieces of them were clearly visible as they approached.

Whatever their external suit, skin, or ships were constructed of, only portions of it reflected the distant light of the stars at any given moment. It was almost perfect camouflage but was also reminiscent of the material affixed to the hull he had just studied.

A bolt of adrenaline coursed through him as his sensors confirmed that his unwelcome visitors were less than a thousand kilometers from his position and were closing fast.

How the hell did that happen? he wondered, then remembered

that the ship that had approached the fleet and apparently been responsible for dragging them tens of thousands of light-years away
from it hadn't even been detected on long-range sensors. No one had
a clue it existed until it was almost on top of them.

Velth's next step was to check his belt for his phaser, and to
visually confirm that the physical tether connecting him to the
airlock was still in place. Often during routine spacewalks, this
extra precaution was not utilized. In *Galen's* current predicament,
Kim had insisted and assigned one of the bridge officers, Ensign
Selah, to monitor Velth's physical connection to the ship during
the entirety of his extravehicular activities. Taking the tether gently
in one hand to make sure it didn't get tangled and clutching his
phaser in the other, he continued back toward the airlock. A quick
glance over his right shoulder confirmed that his new friends were
still coming.

"*Velth, it's Harry again.*"

"Nice to hear your voice, sir."

"*Change of plans,*" were the next entirely unacceptable words that
Velth heard. His gut flipped as he wondered how much he was going
to hate whatever Kim said next.

"If you're even considering asking me to stay put and attempt
first contact, Lieutenant . . ." Velth began.

"*Stop walking, now,*" Kim said urgently.

Velth did as he was told. Seconds later, the reason became clear.
He could now see that the five distinct figures moving toward him
had adjusted their position to compensate for his movement. Kim
had to be tracking their speed. If he had calculated that they would
reach Velth's position before he could make it safely back to the airlock, they had to be moving awfully fast.

"Tell me you have a better plan than me just opening fire right
now and taking my chances," Velth said.

"*Take hold of the tether with both hands and prepare to release your
mag locks. We're going to reel you in. We need you to give a little push as
soon as you're free. We're going to release some extra tether line to make*

sure you clear the edge of the hull. As soon as your alignment is right, it will only take a few seconds to bring you in."

Okay, it was a plan. Just not a great one.

"Wait for my order to release, understood?"

"Copy that," Velth replied. Of course, the first part of the plan required pocketing his phaser—another action his primitive brain cautioned against. Still, Kim's firm command and years of training won the day. The bigger issue was really the rest of the plan.

"Sir, are you sure that the tether will hold?" Velth asked, not certain he really wanted to hear the answer. It was meant to serve as a backup in the event he unexpectedly lost contact with the hull. But the return procedure was usually executed incredibly slowly. He anticipated that part of Kim's plan was to push the safety limits of the rig in order to make sure he got to the airlock before the aliens reached him.

"We believe it will," Kim replied. *"You set?"*

Velth no longer had to turn his head to see the aliens. They were coming at him now, directly ahead. "Do it," he said.

"On my mark. Three . . . two . . . one . . ."

"Mark," Velth said simultaneously with Kim as he released his boots from the safe haven of the hull and pushed off.

It took a moment for his body to register the sensation of floating free and less than that for his stomach to begin to protest. He continued to move steadily away from the ship, heading straight toward the aliens.

Lieutenant Kim had shifted the visual feed of Velth's progress to the main viewscreen. He was moving away from the hull on a more or less straight trajectory while Ensign Selah fed more tether line to him. When he had enough distance, she would halt the feed. The tension would then reverse his momentum, bringing him into alignment with the airlock. Only then would Selah reel him in.

According to his scanners, there were five distinct alien contacts closing on Velth's position. They had first been detected a little over a thousand kilometers out and even with their course adjustment had closed almost two hundred kilometers in the three minutes since sensors had first detected them.

"We should have given him a propulsion pack," Conlon offered nervously.

She wasn't wrong. But it was too little too late now.

"He's going to make it," Kim insisted.

"Their speed is increasing," Conlon noted.

"How?" Kim asked. "Scans indicate no apparent means of propulsion."

"Didn't the Children of the Storm navigate their vessels by thought?" Conlon asked.

Kim wasn't sure. They might have. After reading O'Donnell's reports of *Demeter*'s encounter with those beings, Kim's honest appraisal had simply been gratitude that *Voyager* had been spared most of that first contact.

"Doesn't matter. He's almost at the clearance point. He'll be back on the ship in two minutes." Hoping to confirm this estimate, Kim called to Selah, with whom he had maintained an open comm line throughout Velth's EV mission. "Selah, how's it going?"

"Twenty more seconds should do it," she replied. *"He's almost reached the optimum distance and angle to initiate retrieval."*

"Velth, you still okay, buddy?" Kim asked.

His breath was coming too quickly now, likely a combination of anxiety and exertion. *"Oh, you know . . . just looking forward to feeling something solid beneath my feet again."*

"Try to relax," Kim requested, knowing how hard that would be. "Your heart rate is climbing pretty fast."

"Is that an order, sir? Because with all due respect . . ."

"We're about to halt the tether feed. You're going to feel a jolt. It's not a problem. In five, four, three, two . . ."

A grunt followed by several quick breaths came in response.

"Okay, it's okay," Velth said, clearly panicking a bit at the abrupt directional shift. *"I've still got the tether."*

"We've got you, Velth," Kim said. "Nothing to worry about."

"Harry?" Nancy said urgently.

Kim checked the aliens' approach and immediately understood her concern.

Somehow in the last twenty seconds, the aliens had made up four hundred kilometers. The tension in Velth's line was drawing him back toward the ship in a gentle arc, but at this rate, they would be right on top of him before Selah could begin reeling him in.

And there wasn't a damned thing Kim could do about it.

Velth watched as the airlock drifted into view. He understood that he was the object in motion, but his brain insisted that the opposite was true. The illusion was disorienting, so Velth chose to focus on the taut line connecting him to the ship, anchored to his suit like an umbilical cord and in roughly the same position as his original had been. He tried to mentally prepare himself for another jolt when Selah reactivated the rig to bring him home. Best guess, he was forty meters from the airlock. The outer door was open and the tether rig was clearly visible, attached to the airlock's inner door. Through a small port above the rig, he caught glimpses of Ensign Selah operating the control panel.

Get a move on, he pleaded silently. He hadn't been able to track the movement of the aliens for what felt like forever but in reality had likely been less than three minutes. In his mind, they were right behind him, moving ever closer. He told himself his fears weren't real. And even if they were, there was always the chance that they weren't interested in him at all. Perhaps they had simply returned to check their patch job on *Galen's* hull. Maybe they had been waiting to initiate contact until they received confirmation that those on board had survived the trip.

Or maybe they never expected us to survive and have come to finish the job, he thought grimly.

"Hey, Kim, how far are our unexpected guests from the ship now?" Velth asked.

There was a pause that could have indicated Kim was calculating the exact answer to his question, but much darker thoughts reared their heads as the silence grew longer.

Finally Kim said, *"I'm not going to lie to you, Velth. They're a little less than two hundred meters from your position."*

Oh, come on, Velth thought. There was no way they were moving more than three hundred kilometers per minute without a ship. Kim had to be wrong.

Problem was, when it came to math, guys like Kim were very rarely wrong.

"Hold tight, Lieutenant. You're going to feel a sharp tug on the line." Ensign Selah sounded every bit as tense as Velth felt. He checked his grip once again, willing himself to hold on, even if the damn thing detached from his suit.

"Just do it, Ensign," Velth ordered.

He didn't dare turn his head. He didn't have to. He could *feel* them coming now. A slight sense of pressure—impossible to actually feel in the vacuum of space—began to assault him.

A vivid memory quite suddenly asserted itself. It consisted of five-year-old Ranson Velth and a ski slope in the Swiss Alps.

Velth couldn't remember a time he hadn't known how to ski. He believed to this day he had been able to ski before he'd been able to walk, although his mother had sworn this wasn't the case. Both of his parents had been teachers, his mother at Oxford and his father in Okinawa. But their family homes had always been in snow-covered mountains.

The ski run that now rebuilt itself in his imagination wasn't near his family home. It was part of a resort in Adelboden-Lenk, not far from Zurich. While most of that trip had been devoted to the runs down Engstligenalp, the purpose of that particular family outing had been to visit the Engstligen Falls. One of the longest waterfalls in Switzerland, they never froze, even in the deepest winter, and were stunning to behold, even for a child who would much rather have been flying down a mountain as fast as humanly possible.

Nothing else could touch that feeling: the freedom, the speed, the utter bliss of near weightlessness despite the presence of gravity. More than anything, Velth adored the fearlessness with which he took each run. This was key to the joy of it, until the day he learned that fearlessness was a lie.

The morning after their family hike to the falls, while navigating a relatively gentle intermediate slope alone, young Ranson had found himself overtaken by a pack of older children. He wasn't even aware of them until they were suddenly swooping by him, much too close for safety, laughing and shouting to one another. It was the first time Ranson could remember feeling insecure on his skis. He wanted to stop and simply allow the group to pass, but was terrified that if he did so, one of them might plow right into him. He settled for screaming at them in quick bursts of incoherent rage as they passed.

He had to keep going, so he did, until one of the boys clipped the back of his ski and sent him tumbling down the slope. Their laughter was carried back to him on the brisk wind.

He had fallen on his skis a hundred times. That was part of learning how to ski. Falling safely was a hard-won skill. What stayed with him long after the day had turned to night and he had been tucked into bed was the speed with which a lovely perfect moment had been transformed into terror. He didn't know that could happen until the day it did.

He was pulled from the memory by a fierce tug at his waist. Even this momentary distraction had been sufficient to loosen his grip on the tether. It slipped through his fingers and an alarm suddenly began to blare within his helmet.

"*Warning, microbreaches detected at tether anchor point,*" his suit's computer reported.

"Activate emergency seals," Velth said, hoping that the computer was already doing so.

The good news was that even though his suit had torn, he was now moving briskly toward the open airlock. Selah's face was centered in the port. She looked like she was shouting, but she must have closed her comm channel, because he couldn't hear her at all.

"Warning, oxygen/nitrogen-mix depletion detected."

"Have you sealed my damn suit yet?" Velth shouted. "Because we both know where my oxygen is going."

A new thought occurred as he drifted ever closer to the airlock. He couldn't hear Nancy or Kim either. But they would never have closed their channels, even if Selah had been taken out of the communication loop.

It didn't matter. He was less than ten meters from the airlock.

He was going to make it.

A sharp burst of static punched through his suit's comm system. *"Velth . . . on't . . . repeat . . . elth . . ."* The transmission quickly dissolved into white noise. It was Kim, like Selah, shouting about something. Had their comm line failed, or was it perhaps being jammed?

Five meters to go.

He lifted his arms in preparation to grab the sides of the airlock. His heart rate was off the charts. Sweat was pouring into his eyes. A gentle buzzing sensation in his head made it difficult to concentrate, but something still grounded firmly in reality was trying to advise him that on the other side of that airlock everyone working their asses off to bring him safely home was in the middle of some sort of meltdown.

That was probably a bad thing.

The nice thing about oxygen deprivation was that it cushioned all the blows, at least at first.

He was two meters from the airlock when his sense of forward motion suddenly stopped.

He looked down and realized that the tether was no longer in his hands.

It shouldn't have mattered. He had sufficient velocity and was on the right trajectory to enter the airlock. In zero-g, unless something came along to change your course, you kept moving along that course. That's how space worked.

Why isn't space working? How do you break space?

It was an idle thought. He was suddenly conscious of how very tired he was. Sleep sounded fantastic right about now.

I'm passing out, he realized. That thought should have bothered him a great deal more than it did.

A burst of adrenaline suddenly shot through him.

Don't die, not like this, it insisted.

He lifted his arms again, reaching desperately for the edge of the airlock. It was like swimming against the strongest current imaginable and did not alter his position in the slightest.

More pressure from somewhere behind him.

Damn it all.

Suddenly he was turning. His entire body moved against his will and the airlock drifted out of view.

It was replaced by the sight of a rectangular-shaped monster, maybe four meters high and two meters wide. Bursts of blinding colored lights flashed over it from top to bottom. Velth wasn't sure why, but those bursts seemed both intelligent and angry.

Suddenly he was five years old again and bliss had been replaced by terror.

He barely had enough breath left to scream, but he did his best.

6

VESTA

Although it had taken most of her professional life, Admiral Kathryn Janeway had become a firm believer in both the chain of command and the art of delegating authority. She had only realized this after frequently failing to honor the first and to even attempt the second throughout most of her time as a Starfleet captain. She didn't judge herself too harshly. Her longest command had been aboard *Voyager* and the circumstances had been unique. Those seven years lost in the Delta Quadrant hadn't lent themselves to lessons in mentorship. They had been a daily struggle for survival, and she had taken the possibility of failure so personally, she had often been blind to her crew's need to develop their own leadership skills.

It had taken death (hers), resurrection (also hers), and assuming command of the Full Circle Fleet for her to confront the reality that there was much to be gained in allowing those beneath her to face their own struggles and learn from their own mistakes, rather than taking both upon herself.

As the fleet's commanding officer, ultimate responsibility was always hers. Her people's successes and failures would be credited to her account by those to whom she reported. But each of her fleet captains had demonstrated repeatedly in the past year that they neither required nor had any patience for micromanagement. She had consciously chosen not to make a habit of second-guessing their command decisions and had come to truly enjoy working with them as a group. Their individual points of view were each quite different, and between them all, she always found refreshing new perspectives on whatever problem they were facing as a fleet.

The *Galen*'s possible destruction, however, was beginning to test her newfound sense of reserve.

"What do you mean, Captain Farkas relieved you of duty?" she demanded of Doctor Sal.

El'nor Sal tossed a glance bordering on contemptuous toward Counselor Cambridge, who had brought Sal to Janeway's quarters to share their findings regarding Ensign Gwyn's remarkable belief that the crew of the *Galen* might still be alive.

"You're her chief medical officer," Janeway added.

"Not anymore," Sal said with a shrug.

"Are you certain she did not intend this to be a temporary state of affairs?" Janeway asked.

"You'd have to ask her, Admiral," Sal replied. "For my part, I am content to stand relieved and would appreciate it if you would add my name to the list of those scheduled to return to the Alpha Quadrant the next time one of our ships makes a run in that direction."

"I'm sure I don't need to remind you that our fleet has just lost its dedicated medical vessel," Janeway countered. "While each ship that remains has its own medical staff, we are going to be a bit short-handed for the foreseeable future. I am not content to lose one of our most experienced doctors over what appears to be a simple disciplinary matter. Especially as you were the lead physician treating Ensign Gwyn."

"Regina didn't file a report with you about this?" Sal asked.

Janeway didn't have to look at her queue of reports to know that Farkas's latest was likely there. She'd barely had a moment to rest since DK-1116 had begun to devolve toward disaster, let alone catch up on her reading.

"Perhaps we should set the protocol issues aside for the moment," Counselor Cambridge suggested.

Janeway inhaled deeply and released the breath in a long, slow count of five. On a good day, she could make ten. Today was clearly not going to be a good day. Apart from trying to make sense of Ensign Gwyn's report, she was also struggling to wrap her brain around the fact that apparently Lieutenants Kim and Conlon had recently become parents.

"For the moment," Janeway agreed. Turning back to Sal she asked, "How certain can you possibly be that Ensign Gwyn completed this *bonding* with an embryo?"

Sal shook her head. "Not as certain as you would probably like. Not certain enough to unequivocally support you ordering the fleet to seek out creatures that could easily do to us what they did to the *Galen*. I've lived long enough to know that fear can be healthy. The biggest mistakes I've ever made were when I consciously chose to ignore mine."

"But it is possible?" Janeway asked of both Sal and Cambridge.

"It seems so," Cambridge replied. "I've never encountered a bonded Kriosian, so I, too, am shooting in the dark here. That said, Gwyn's assertion rings true to me, and it does explain her miraculous recovery from a state that, while synthetically created, certainly appeared to be serious and terminal at the time."

"Go through it once more," Janeway requested.

"Ensign Gwyn—" Cambridge began.

"Not you," Janeway said. "Doctor Sal, please."

Sal reached up to rub the back of her neck. "Starting where?" she asked.

"Close enough to the beginning so that I have all relevant facts," Janeway suggested. "Bearing in mind, of course, that time is very much of the essence if Ensign Gwyn is right."

Sal nodded in understanding. "Thirty years ago . . ."

At this, Janeway stepped back and rested on the edge of her desk. "Is it possible to bottom-line anything that didn't happen in the last few days?" she asked.

"All right," Sal continued. "Suffice it to say, the people of Krios were not completely honest with their fellow Federation members when they joined our union. There is always the possibility that those who negotiated their entrance into the Federation were aware of the facts I am about to provide, but our official history has certainly forgotten it."

"Bottom line, Doctor?"

"Bottom line, while the Kriosians have always maintained that a very small portion of their population contain the genetic tendency toward empathic metamorphism, the biological fact seems to be that most Kriosians carry the necessary gene, even if it is a recessive variation."

This was news to Janeway, who could count on one hand the number of full Kriosians she had met in her years of service. Her understanding was that Ensign Gwyn shared half her genetic heritage with that species.

"Apart from the ethical dubiousness of rewriting their history, why is this important?" Janeway asked.

"For most people, it is a curiosity, nothing more," Sal allowed. "But for me, and for Nancy Conlon, it recently became a matter of life and death."

"How so?"

"Metamorphic cells are the most malleable that exist, eclipsing even embryonic stem cells in their capacity to rewrite damaged genetic code. Lieutenant Conlon's condition is such that it is likely only these cells would be capable of curing the defect in her DNA's ability to repair itself, which has been the cause of her most troubling symptoms since the diagnosis was first made. We were unable to use Lieutenant Conlon's embryonic stem cells, as we did not receive permission until they were too developed to be of use to us. The only other option I could see was to gain access to a group of metamorphic cells."

"Did Ensign Gwyn possess these cells?" Janeway asked, beginning to see what might have driven Farkas to bench her CMO.

"In theory. I tested her blood cells and found the appropriate genetic sequence. I then replicated a series of hormonal injections intended to activate those sequences."

"Ensign Gwyn agreed to the procedure?" Janeway asked, surprised.

"She agreed to allow me to use her cells to help one of my patients. I didn't feel comfortable going into too much detail out of concern for Lieutenant Conlon's privacy."

At this, Cambridge shot Sal a look of clear derision.

"It would have worked," Sal bellowed in response.

"We're going to discuss the ethical boundaries you may have already run roughshod over in due course, Doctor. For now, please continue."

"Between the time I administered the injections and could retrieve the activated cell cultures, Ensign Gwyn was sent on an away mission. During that mission she was attacked by something that breached her EV suit and exposed her to a great deal of exotic radiation. Upon her return, she was immediately given a course of antiproton therapy by your old EMH."

"So, what you're saying is that had it not been for the unfortunate radiation incident, your therapy protocol would not have actually activated Gwyn's metamorphic cells," Janeway surmised.

"The point of the procedure was to isolate a small number of metamorphic cells," Sal said, nodding. "The radiation exposure kicked the process initiated by the hormonal injections into overdrive, producing billions of additional metamorphic cells, and once that happened, Ensign Gwyn began to experience the *finiis'ral*."

"Got it in one this time," Cambridge teased.

"Shut up," Sal retorted.

Janeway favored them both with an impatient glare.

"We were still in the process of attempting to find a cure for the *finiis'ral* that did not include Gwyn bonding with any of the available crewmen, thereby permanently suppressing her own personality, needs, and desires in favor of her mate's, when the condition appeared to reverse itself," Sal finished.

"Did you run any tests to determine how that had happened?" Janeway demanded.

Here, at least, Sal had the grace to appear appropriately chagrined.

"It was a little difficult. The fleet had been ordered to leave orbit and Gwyn had left sickbay and stolen a shuttle. I asked her to report to *Vesta* once she returned, but before she could do so, I had been removed from my position."

"Then what, may I ask, leads you to believe that she successfully bonded with the embryo?" Janeway asked. "As the condition was brought on by external synthetic factors, isn't it also possible that it subsided on its own as her body's natural balance reasserted itself?"

"Anything is possible, Admiral, but in addition to Ensign Gwyn confirming this fact, there is circumstantial evidence provided by Ensign Icheb that supports the embryonic bonding," Cambridge noted.

"What the hell does Icheb have to do with any of this?" Janeway demanded.

At this, Sal deferred to Cambridge. "Long story incredibly short," Cambridge said, "Icheb has a particular genetic mutation that made it biologically impossible for Gwyn to bond with him. His presence was comforting to her. She asked and he agreed to remain with her during the worst of the *finiis'ral*."

Janeway shook her head. Farkas's decision to discipline Sal seemed increasingly well founded. The admiral was only receiving word of this debacle in the broadest possible strokes and she didn't have enough fingers left to count the number of ways in which Sal had transgressed against multiple crew members, starting with the fact that she had performed these procedures without the knowledge and oversight of her superior officer. "Very well. Go on," Janeway said.

"Icheb reported that Gwyn's condition had remained unchanged until she entered the room containing the gestational incubator but once she returned, she seemed different—more *herself*," Cambridge finished.

"Isn't that still quite a leap?" Janeway asked.

"It is, unless you've been asking yourself as long as I have how an entire population of female empathic metamorphs were able to throw off the chains keeping them shackled to a strictly enforced societal structure that had been in place for thousands of years in a matter of a few generations," Sal said. Off Janeway's furrowed brow, she continued, "By the time the Federation encountered the Kriosians, the number of true metamorphs on their world was quite small. But only a few centuries prior, most Kriosians were full empathic metamorphs. Normal genetic variation doesn't do that. Something cataclysmic happened without decimating their population, which also shouldn't have happened. My belief is that the women of Krios realized that they could bond with embryos, still largely unformed in utero, thus relieving them of the need to lose their identity to a mate. I also imagine that this choice would have actually created stronger intergenerational bonds among Kriosians, thereby stabilizing their society even in the midst of what must have been a huge upheaval."

Much as Janeway hesitated to accept this at face value, without a shred of scientific evidence to back it up, she also had to admit it was a compelling theory.

"Damn," she finally said softly.

"Indeed," Cambridge agreed.

"Very well," Janeway continued, "I will need a full physical and psychological evaluation of Ensign Gwyn before I can thoroughly evaluate whether or not to act upon her beliefs."

"I can handle the psychological part, but the physical might be a bit more challenging," Cambridge said.

"Why?"

"Because the ensign has requested Doctor Sal and *only* Doctor Sal tend to her medical issues."

"She is uncomfortable with Doctor Sharak?" Janeway asked.

"In the first blush of her condition, she believed she was meant to bond with him," Cambridge explained. "She is embarrassed, although I am certain Doctor Sharak did and would continue to behave in an entirely professional manner toward her at all times."

The situation was far too delicate to ignore Gwyn's preferences in the matter. But that was going to mean an even more uncomfortable conversation with Captain Farkas than their last had been.

"I will speak to Captain Farkas. For the moment, I am lifting her restrictions on your duties, Doctor Sal, in Ensign Gwyn's case only, but allow me to make myself absolutely clear. Should there be the faintest whiff of ethical impropriety in your treatment of the ensign, you will be reported and charged accordingly."

"I would like to say, in my defense—" Sal began.

"All due respect, Doctor, don't push me right now," Janeway cut her off. "Counselor, I want you to be present for all of Gwyn's medical evaluations."

"Yes, Admiral."

"Dismissed."

DEMETER

"You wished to see me, Captain?" Commander Fife asked upon entering *Demeter*'s main lab.

Liam O'Donnell, a man who probably had fewer years ahead of him than he did behind him, lifted his head from the display and turned toward his XO. His eyes were lit with an intensity Fife had rarely seen but knew well. Every now and again, his captain decided to bend the universe ever so slightly in a new and personally satisfying direction. Sometimes this was done through the creation of a new life-form. More often, as Fife could personally attest, it was by challenging those around him to think differently—usually bigger.

For a moment, the weight that had been bearing down upon Fife since he had witnessed the destruction of the *Galen* lifted. In the brief silence before O'Donnell answered, Fife believed he was about to be told that their recent tragic loss had been a mistake, a sensor glitch, perhaps a mass hallucination. Nothing less, he assumed, could so radically lift the spirits of anyone currently serving the fleet.

"Take a look at this, Atlee," O'Donnell said, beckoning him toward his station.

Fife stepped forward and peered at the display. It was a sensor scan of the planet DK-1116, similar in many ways to the hundreds he had reviewed in the past week. It took a moment for Fife to register the specific readings that might have been responsible for his captain's enthusiasm, and another to contain his disappointment.

"Do you see it?" O'Donnell asked.

Fife did. Almost a kilometer beneath the surface a large, visibly reinforced structure of several thousand square meters was clearly visible. "It appears that there is an intact underground facility present, much like the one in which Lieutenant Vincent and his team nearly died while studying it a few days ago," he replied.

"Which we should be able to access with our transporters," O'Donnell continued.

"Why would you want to?" Fife asked.

O'Donnell's face fell.

"Our people have successfully, albeit accidentally, unraveled the mystery of the planet and its purpose," Fife said in response to O'Donnell's unasked but obvious question. "This world was designed to absorb and store vast amounts of radiant energy, which, when released, pushed one of the system's stars out of its orbit. What more do you wish to know that might require a visit to this structure?"

"How the hell the Edrehmaia substance manages to store that energy, among many, many other things," O'Donnell replied.

"Forgive me, Captain, but our only contacts with that substance have been disastrous."

"You've read Vincent's report?"

"And Patel's," Fife added. "The so-called station they entered and became trapped within appeared to be a library of the experiments conducted by several species within the connected biodomes. It also contained experimental subjects and access to a deeper cavern that appears to have been adapted from the planet's original design by Species 001—whoever they were—to facilitate their experiments. That cavern contained vast quantities of the Edrehmaia substance as well as several pieces of technology that appeared to maintain the surface biodomes."

"I should have known you'd be able to pass a test on the material," O'Donnell noted with a grin.

"I will admit to a certain morbid curiosity on the subject, once the *Galen* was destroyed," Fife allowed. "I hoped their analysis might contain some clue that could help me make sense of it all."

"And did you find one?"

"I believe so, sir," Fife replied. "As best I can tell, we have found ourselves in the center of a confluence of several poor decisions made by multiple species less advanced than these Edrehmaia. Unfortunately, *we* were the ones with the misfortune to attract their attention. The result was the loss of several dozen crew members and our dedicated medical vessel."

"Poor decisions?"

"Yes, sir."

"You consider our predecessors' curiosity about the Edrehmaia substance and their choice to construct the stations and the biodomes in order to study it a *poor decision*? How the hell else would they, or anyone, learn from what the Edrehmaia left behind?"

It had been some time since Fife had found himself on the opposing side of an argument with O'Donnell. As these scenarios usually ended badly for him, he chose his next words carefully.

"Curiosity in the face of advanced technology is not a sin," Fife began. "However, there must be times when the concurrent risks outweigh the potential benefits of satisfying that curiosity. When we found these biodomes, they had been abandoned for thousands of years. Clearly whoever constructed them did not find what they were seeking. Patel's report of her conversation with an interlocutor constructed from her DNA indicated as much. Their work was left unfinished. While I am as awed by the work of Starfleet's Corps of Engineers as anyone, I doubt even *they* could have constructed the systems we found on that planet in another thousand years. The technology is simply beyond our current understanding of the universe. Our questions will not be answered by additional blundering around in the darkness of our own impotence. Indeed, it is likely that further attempts to *understand* the Edrehmaia and their technology might cause them to return again and destroy the rest of the fleet." Fife met his captain's eyes without flinching. "I am not certain what you are contemplating, but if it includes attempting to enter that station, you will do so over my strenuous objections."

O'Donnell sat back, considering his XO. He absently began to scratch the back of his head where tufts of dark hair met the edge of his balding pate.

"Had Zephram Cochrane been your superior officer, would you have objected to him strapping himself to a modified nuclear warhead and flinging himself into space to test the possibility of warp flight?" O'Donnell finally asked.

Fife did him the courtesy of seriously considering the question.

"Probably," he finally agreed.

"Then can we agree that your tolerance for risk might be set a little low?"

"Not in this case."

"I see," O'Donnell said.

Fife waited as the seconds built to an uncomfortable silence. "You're going down there again anyway, aren't you?" he asked.

"Yes," O'Donnell replied. "And to be clear, I'm not insensitive to the risks."

"But you just can't help yourself?"

"We're talking about constructing life at the quantum level," O'Donnell replied. "We're talking about interplays of matter and energy heretofore unimagined by humanity. I couldn't live with myself if I didn't at least attempt to analyze it further."

"Of course you could," Fife said without a trace of sarcasm.

Fife had never been adept at conveying his emotions. His vocabulary in this regard was simply limited by both lack of experience and desire. But that statement was as close as he had ventured toward admitting how much he had come to care for and rely upon his captain.

The corners of O'Donnell's lips tugged gently upward, a sign that he understood the concern, even though he would never acknowledge it directly. "We will only have this one chance, Atlee, to view the universe through the eyes of gods."

Fife was taken aback. O'Donnell was many things, but he had never been confused with a religious man.

"Intelligent life exists on a continuum," O'Donnell continued. "I didn't know, until we discovered this world, how far humanity had yet to go or how mortified I could be by our ignorance. It's simply intolerable. I am awed by the accomplishments of the Edrehmaia and I am completely unworthy of standing in their presence. But with every fiber of my being, I *wish* to be. I do not, for one moment, credit their skill to supernatural causes. Every bit of magic we have seen in our travels, including the abilities of species like the Q, is based upon natural laws. It *must* be, even if we have not yet grasped the pertinent calculations. It turns out humanity has spent too much time in the children's section of the universal library, and I'm not content to allow that state of affairs to continue indefinitely. Why are we here, Atlee, if not to transcend ourselves? And how are we to do so if we shrink from the work transcendence demands?"

As Fife had never before contemplated a state of being beyond that which he currently enjoyed, he could only respond with a quizzical stare.

"You could die," he said. "And you could get the rest of us killed in the pursuit."

"I won't ask anyone who isn't up to the challenge to accompany me," O'Donnell said, his petulant side rearing its head. "I will leave *Demeter* in your capable hands and trust that if we attract any unwanted attention, you will preserve the lives of those we command. But *I am* going."

Fife nodded briskly. "Please advise me when you are ready to depart."

"Thank you, Atlee."

Fife left the lab feeling considerably worse than he had when he entered, an accomplishment he hadn't imagined possible.

VOYAGER

When Lieutenant Commander B'Elanna Torres entered the astrometrics lab, she found Ensign Icheb and Lieutenant Phinnegan Bryce standing before the large display screen instead of the lab's usual occupant, Seven of Nine.

Icheb turned immediately to greet her. "Commander, thank you for joining us."

"You said it was urgent," she acknowledged. Nothing else could have pulled Torres from her quarters in the middle of gamma shift. Her son, Michael, was still only a few months old and her daughter, Miral, although four, regularly had trouble sleeping through the night. What little sleep she managed to get Torres guarded fiercely.

This night, however, she and Tom had spent nestled in each other's arms in their living room, attempting to process their losses: Harry Kim, Nancy Conlon, a *child* Torres had known nothing about and did not fault Tom at all for not having previously mentioned at Harry's insistence, the Doctor, and so many others. Their grief was raw, truly unfathomable. The loss of so many they considered family was still a stubborn shock. At some point they were going to have to tell Miral, but neither of them could think how to begin that conversation. They needed to pass through the worst of it themselves before they inflicted the truth upon their daughter, who had loved Harry like an uncle and had recently grown close to Conlon as well. The call from Icheb had been something of a relief, but Torres had felt as if she were plowing through deep snow with every step between her quarters and astrometrics.

"Sorry to wake you," Bryce said.

"It's okay. I wasn't sleeping."

As fleet chief, both Bryce and Icheb fell under her department's supervision. Despite the fact that Lieutenant Bryce was *Vesta's* chief engineer, he seemed to spend every moment of his off hours aboard *Voyager*. The young man was incredibly capable—nothing else would have accounted for his position or the faith Captain Farkas had placed in him since his field promotion to chief following the critical injury of her first CE, Preston Ganley. And Icheb was the definition of devotion to duty. He had graduated early from the Academy and been assigned to the fleet by Starfleet's C-in-C, Admiral Akaar. But Torres knew that their constant proximity to each other had a deeper cause, and although she encouraged it in theory, she worried that their relatively new attachment could spell trouble if they didn't learn quickly how to balance their personal lives with their professional ones.

Of course, she couldn't imagine having spent this night without Tom's comforting presence, and she wouldn't be surprised if Icheb found the same in Bryce's.

"You wanted me to see something?" Torres asked.

"We do," Icheb replied.

"We've been studying the *Galen*'s last moments and have detected a few irregularities," Bryce added. Torres was certain that many of their fellow fleet officers were probably doing the same but probably few as tenaciously as Icheb and Bryce.

"The visual sensor display at the moment of *Galen*'s apparent destruction is a little confusing," Icheb continued.

"As are the logs immediately following the event," Bryce interjected.

Torres's heart began to burn anew in her chest as she lifted her eyes to the massive image. It had been hard enough to watch on a standard-sized display. Magnified in this way, it felt much larger than life—truly overwhelming. Tears began to sting her eyes, but she forced herself to focus on the data streaming along the side of the screen, registering the atomic information scanned just after the ship appeared to explode. It helped, but just barely.

Icheb reversed the image, stopping it a few seconds before the first flares of the explosion would be visible in the aft section of the small ship.

"Note here, the sensor data," Icheb said. "Every atom of the ship is accounted for by the sensors as you would expect, along with a surge in tetryonic particles that were initially read as a by-product of the electromagnetic wave that impacted the ship several minutes prior."

Torres was familiar with this much. She had scanned the logs several times herself.

"There are *also* trillions of particles the sensors cannot identify," Bryce continued.

"There was a ton of exotic radiation surrounding the alien vessel," Torres noted.

"Yes, but if you force the sensors to delineate the proximity of those unidentifiable particles, the far greater mass is found in and around *Galen*," Bryce pointed out.

"Suggesting what?"

"The potential presence of a different kind of waveform," Icheb replied.

"The one that destroyed the ship," Torres assumed.

"Maybe," Bryce said.

"*Maybe?*"

Icheb then advanced the display by ten microseconds. Torres blinked to clear her eyes. For a moment, *Galen* appeared suddenly almost transparent.

"Is that a rendering error?" she asked.

"The ship was clearly visible on the sensor logs until we ran it through a microspectral scan augmented by an anti-tetryonic algorithm," Icheb said.

"What the hell is that and why would you run it?" she asked. Torres was as savvy an engineer as any and it had never occurred to her to create, let alone run, an algorithm identifying an anti-particle that was only theoretical.

"I had an idea," Bryce said with a shrug. "I didn't want to bother anyone else with it. I know how close you all were to *Galen*'s crew. I'd only met Benoit a few times and he seemed like a capable and good guy, but I think, well, I'm almost sure that my perspective on this whole thing is a little more objective than yours could ever be. When I ran it by Icheb, he insisted we work on it together."

"What theory?"

"Our standard scans are blunt instruments. Most of the time they are more than adequate, but every now and again they miss important information," Bryce began.

"You've been in Starfleet how long, Bryce?"

"I'm three years out of the Academy, ma'am."

Ma'am?

"Stick with *Commander*, Lieutenant," Torres suggested none too gently. "And these blunt instruments are the product of millions of hours by the most capable scientists Starfleet has ever produced."

"I agree completely, Commander," Bryce said quickly. "I am in radical, violent agreement with that assessment."

"But?"

"Our sensors aren't optimized to function in the presence of quantum variances and theoretical particles, like the ones present here. They're just . . . well, *not*. They default to known parameters and fill in any missing information according to what *should* be there, even if sensors can't detect it. But in this case, a good sixty to seventy percent of what we are looking at is *unknown*."

Torres considered this, detached herself from the personal umbrage she took to Bryce's assessment of her sensors, and was finally forced to agree.

"Okay. So, you created an anti-tetryonic algorithm. And this is what it came up with? It's clearly missing data. The ship is almost invisible."

"Now watch this," Icheb said.

Another handful of microseconds elapsed, during which the *Galen* appeared to vanish completely while a simultaneous conflagration ignited where its aft section had just been.

"What is that?" Torres asked, stepping closer to the display.

"*Galen*'s antimatter containment pods," Bryce answered. "Or, more accurately, the *absence* of the containment pods. That's just antimatter impacting normal space and doing what it does."

Torres's heart began to pound, and the heat that had been burning her heart began to move up her spine, spreading rapidly over her head.

"Where did the pods go?"

"Presumably wherever the rest of the ship went," Bryce offered. "For whatever reason, they just couldn't take the antimatter with them."

"Run it again," she ordered.

They did. When she had seen it three more times, and confirmed the atomic scans, she was convinced that Icheb and Bryce had just performed a miracle—*resurrection*.

Galen hadn't been destroyed. It had been transported. The question was *where*.

7

"**D**amn it," Harry Kim shouted as Ranson Velth was spirited away from the airlock by a pack of unknown life-forms, to where, he knew not.

"Their speed is increasing," Conlon said. "They're almost a hundred kilometers distant from the airlock now."

Kim started toward the turbolift. "I'm going after him."

"What?"

Power hadn't been restored to the lifts yet, but Kim slid through the gap between the turbolift doors before Nancy caught up with him. He had already opened the panel to the maintenance shaft he would have to descend to access the rest of the ship when she reached him.

"Get back here," she demanded.

"I can save him, Nancy. I have to try."

"No, you don't."

"Don't argue with me about this. We can't lose him."

"He's already gone," Conlon insisted.

"No, he isn't."

Conlon stepped back, giving his rage a little room to vent itself. For nearly three days, without complaint or rest, Harry Kim had become the rock-solid center of those left aboard the *Galen*. Conlon hadn't seen him raise his voice, let alone lose his temper, even once.

It was past time, and she knew it, even if he didn't.

"It's not your fault, Harry," Conlon said softly.

Kim stood, one hand resting on the edge of the open shaft access panel, his head bowed and his breath coming in deep, quick spasms.

"I sent him out there," Kim finally said.

"He volunteered. Because there was no other way to get the

comm relay fixed. Because that's what all of us are trained to do—whatever the hell it takes to survive and preserve the lives of those with whom we serve."

Kim turned his head to look at her. "Does *Galen* have any shuttles?"

Conlon frowned. Whatever Kim had just asked, it probably wasn't "Does Grandma needle munckle?" *You're tired, that's all*, she told herself. "Say again?"

"Shuttles? Do we have any?" Kim repeated.

"A small medical shuttle. Seats two, I think, with a little room in the back for supplies and a single biobed. Its systems were drained along with everything else and I haven't even looked at restoring power to it. I need to make sure the rest of us are going to be able to keep breathing indefinitely before I even add it to the list of priorities."

"How soon do you think you could . . . ?"

Now it was Conlon's turn to raise her voice.

"You're not going out there, Harry. Velth is gone. His suit was breached even before the aliens got to him and his oxygen was already in the red. Velth is dead, Harry, and you know it. Stop pretending you're about to pull some crazy miracle rescue scenario out of your ass. He's gone. Accept it."

Her words hit him like a gut punch. His legs seemed to give out and he landed on the deck of the lift, a small, weary bit of humanity broken under the weight of unimaginable stress.

Conlon slipped through the doors and came to rest on her knees beside him. Reaching out, she took his hands and held them as the emotions he'd been shoving down as deep as he could found release. He rested there, weeping and rocking, until, finally spent, he grew quiet.

It had been a long time since she had been close to him in this way. She was struck by how strange it felt.

Kim's love for her had never really been a question. He'd spoken of it and, more important, shown it in so many ways large and small that there had been no room left to doubt its permanence. But circumstances had forced her to set that aside so that she could consider the choices before her about the baby and her illness rationally, logically, unclouded by emotion. She hadn't wanted his feelings for her to be the most important factor in her calculations. That place had to be reserved for *her* feelings.

She told herself later that she had been driven to that point by fear. Fear told her that she would end her journey alone and to pretend otherwise was courting unnecessary pain. Fear told her that he would grow tired of her and her problems long before the end, that he would never want or love the child they had created together, and that what she felt was irrelevant.

Fear was a powerful thing. It led people down paths that felt true, even if they were lies.

Loving was always a risk, but she had known since the day she had first asked him for a date, a *real date*, that there was something special about him. That exploring that relationship was important. That given enough time, whatever it was she felt for him could become love. She'd never had that before and Harry had seemed to be the safest possible person with whom to go looking for it.

But almost as soon as that journey had begun, fate had intervened, throwing one crisis after another at her until she'd barely had time to breathe, let alone consider her future dispassionately. Harry had become her lifeline, the one solid place she could always go to find comfort. As long as that remained true, it didn't matter how much time she had left or exactly how her body was finding new ways to fail her right now. *This*, her connection to Harry, was essential to her continued survival.

She didn't know if that was love, but it was close enough.

He finally lifted his head and shifted his position so that they could sit side by side, his hand firmly holding hers.

"I'm sorry," he said.

"Don't be. You've taken responsibility for everything. And you're not usually one for procrastinating when it comes to your emotions.

It's one of my favorite things about you. You stay present for the good and the bad. I never need to wonder what you're feeling. I just have to look at your face to see it." She squeezed his hand gently. "But that stopped the minute we woke up in the middle of this nightmare. You've been holding everything in, afraid that if you let yourself feel how awful all of this is, you'll break, and you'll scare everyone who is looking to you for leadership. All the things you feel, Harry, you don't need to hide them or hold them in. They are your greatest strength, and everyone who knows you at all knows that."

"We needed him," Kim said.

"We did. I only met him a couple of days ago, but I wouldn't have gotten through them without him. He knew when to talk, when to make a dumb joke, and when to listen. And he wasn't afraid to look stupid. If I asked him to do even the smallest thing and he didn't understand, he made damn sure he did before he touched anything. He was a great security chief."

"Out of curiosity, what makes one a *great* security chief?" Kim asked.

"You looking for pointers?"

"Maybe."

"Good security chiefs make you feel like they will jump in front of a phaser for you. Great ones make you want to do the same for them. And yes, you are also one of the great ones."

"Do you know if he had any family?"

"He said he had a sister and a couple of nephews, maybe? Nobody else in Starfleet, though."

Kim nodded. "I wish I'd had a chance to work with him and the other security teams on DK-1116. I wish I knew more about him beyond the fact that he traded his life for our chance to communicate with the fleet again. If we ever get out of here, it will be to his credit."

"I wish I didn't know how terrified he was at the end," Conlon said flatly.

Kim nodded and both sat for a long miserable moment in silence.

"You need to inform the crew—officially, I mean. Rumors move at maximum warp on a ship this small, and it's going to frighten people if they don't get the facts from you."

Kim nodded. "Are these working yet?" he asked, gesturing to his combadge.

"Should be."

"What am I . . . I mean, how do I . . . ?"

"Just tell them the truth. They need to hear it and he deserves that much."

The Doctor had only served with Commander Clarissa Glenn for a little over a year. In that time, she had proven herself to be a competent physician and an extremely patient commanding officer. Their crew was young and eager but lacked the tempering he had come to associate with the more experienced officers that held senior positions among the rest of the fleet. Glenn led them with a firm hand, always conscious of their relative inexperience while still demanding that they meet her expectations and exceed their own. She did not merely issue orders or make demands. She offered instruction when necessary, encouragement when appropriate, and made time to get to know those she led as individuals.

The *Galen* had been the brainchild of his creator, Lewis Zimmerman, and Lieutenant Barclay. Together they had proposed the construction of the small vessel meant to serve as a supplemental medical resource for fleets like Project Full Circle, whose mission parameters took them well beyond the Federation's medical infrastructure. It was also meant to be a test bed for the next generation of holographic personnel. Although these supplemental officers had yet to see much action, both the Doctor and Barclay were anxious to test their abilities. In time, the Doctor hoped that others like him might show signs of exceeding their original programming and

Glenn had embraced that potential more readily than many in her position might. To her credit, she made no distinction between the Doctor and her organic crew, accepting that he was a unique individual and always giving him her full support and a friendly ear when needed.

They had journeyed together to Starbase 185 when Starfleet had recovered a former Borg drone known as Axum and been the first to help him acclimate to his new life following his transformation by the Caeliar. Glenn had impressed the Doctor as she worked patiently and diligently to help Axum begin the long journey of psychological healing that lay ahead of him, and she had thrown herself willingly between their patient and a number of unfamiliar officers whose intentions toward him had, in retrospect, been dubious at best.

The Doctor liked his new commanding officer very much and had been deeply concerned when she arrived in sickbay with a serious concussion and small hemorrhages in her cranial cavity following their unexpected assault by the Edrehmaia. Fortunately, Glenn was an officer who prided herself on maintaining excellent health, both physical and mental, and she had responded extremely well to his treatment of her injuries. He had been slowly reducing the cortical inhibitors he had used to place her in a temporary coma over the last several hours, and when her eyes fluttered open, he greeted her with a warm smile.

"Welcome back, Captain."

She took a moment to acclimate but, as soon as she realized where she was, quickly overcame the quite normal urge to panic and said simply, "Report, Doctor."

"There was an incident involving our ship and an alien vessel. We have become separated from the rest of the fleet. Several of our major systems suffered great damage in the process, but our crew has been working diligently to restore power and critical functions, and for now we are quite safe."

Glenn took a moment to absorb this, then said, "Okay. Now give me the bad news."

The Doctor chuckled appreciatively. "How are you feeling?"

"Like someone has been using my head for xylophone practice," she replied.

"That's to be expected. You were injured while on the bridge and it took quite a while to get you here and begin treatment. You will make a full recovery, but it will be a few days until we can get you back on your feet."

Glenn didn't push him or dismiss his estimate out of hand as many captains in her position might have. They shared an implicit trust of each other's abilities, and she knew that his medical recommendations were realistic.

"Any chance I could get some water?"

Before the Doctor could reply, a chirp sounded from the comm system followed by the voice of Lieutenant Kim.

"Attention all hands, this is Lieutenant Kim. Harry Kim." He paused for a few seconds before continuing. *"A few hours ago, Lieutenant Ranson Velth accepted an EV mission to repair the ship's communications array. Lieutenant Conlon and I were monitoring his progress and in constant communication with him for the duration. Ensign Selah held position at the airlock to ensure his safe retrieval. Lieutenant Velth successfully completed the necessary repairs, but before he could return to the airlock, he was approached and surrounded by what we believe to be members of the alien species who brought us here."*

Kim's voice wavered a bit as he continued. *"Ensign Selah is to be commended for her efforts to retrieve Velth under extraordinarily difficult circumstances. The aliens severed Velth's tether line before he reached the airlock and proceeded to take him with them when they departed. Once they had surrounded him, our communications were jammed. We don't know why, but I promise you, that is one of many mysteries we are going to solve.*

"Given Velth's oxygen levels and damage sustained to his EV suit, it is our belief that Lieutenant Velth could not have survived for long once we lost contact. He is presumed dead. I wish I could offer the hope that

we might retrieve him, but I'm not going to lie to any of you. We don't have the means right now, and I am not willing to risk further loss of life in an effort to recover his remains. We don't know enough about the beings who brought us here to speculate on their motives. They've left us in peace until now. As our power reserves increase, we will prioritize restoration of our defensive systems as well as our weapons. If they come for us again, we will be ready to defend ourselves.

"I offer my sincere condolences to those of you who served with Lieutenant Velth. He was a good man and an outstanding Starfleet officer who sacrificed himself in the line of duty to ensure our continued survival. His loss is unacceptable. He will be greatly missed."

As soon as Kim signed off, the Doctor took a moment to recall his memories of Lieutenant Velth and store them in a segregated buffer. Velth's loss was tremendous and, in the Doctor's estimation, significantly reduced their odds of continued survival.

He suddenly felt Glenn's icy hand grasp his. When he looked back at her, she was sobbing fitfully. He placed his free hand over hers and offered the simple comfort of mutual loss as she allowed herself to begin to mourn her friend and fellow officer.

When she had recovered enough to speak, she said simply, "Please bring Lieutenant Kim to me as soon as possible."

"Of course, Captain."

In the year that Clarissa Glenn had served the Full Circle Fleet, hundreds of bright and dedicated men and women among their ranks had lost their lives.

Until now, none of them had been *hers.*

At two memorial services, she had been among the survivors, willing herself into a state of contemplative meditation in an attempt to exert control over the centers of her brain that were processing the painful stimuli generated by the words spoken as all present stood in witness of their collective loss. She could not control the stimuli or the events that precipitated them. But with years of practice she had developed the skills to disrupt what her brain did with those inputs. Focusing on her breath, she could counter the neurons telling her respiratory system to increase its rate as well as the hormonal cocktail that produced sensations of fear, the body's first response to anticipated pain.

The human body was a magnificent and efficient system in many ways. The brain performed these tasks in order to protect itself from potential threats, relying upon past experiences to prepare itself for immediate dangers that could result in temporary or permanent damage. This was a good thing. When processed properly, the emotions that accompanied any situation were warnings meant to ensure survival. But powerful emotions triggered during moments of intense trauma could leave permanent marks upon the entire system, manufacturing inappropriately intense responses to very small stimuli, creating chronic stress long after any real risk of danger had passed.

Glenn knew this. She could pass, in fact *had* passed, multiple tests and examinations covering this information.

Nothing that she knew changed the nature or lessened the despair of this moment.

She had dreamed since she was young of leading explorers into space. But early in her training she had decided that the experiences she was likely to face while doing so required a deeper understanding of her body and how it processed complex emotions. Everyone who chose the command path developed their own tools for reckoning with the challenges inherent in encountering new alien species, defending their vessels against attack, and the long, often dull hours in between when it was necessary to maintain a state of alert relaxation in order to stand ready to face the unexpected. This had been the genesis of her eventual decision to become a doctor before becoming a commanding officer. Knowledge was her weapon of choice and thus far it had served her well.

But when it came to the sudden loss of almost a third of her crew, for reasons she was having great difficulty isolating and organizing, all of that information and practice was failing her, particularly, she suspected, because Ranson Velth was now included among the list of those lost.

They had first met the day the Full Circle Fleet had gathered for their initial mission briefing with then Admiral Willem Batiste. She had, of course, reviewed Velth's file when she had selected him to be her chief of security, but the cold facts of his life on paper prior to joining her crew had failed to capture the depth of compassion and the absolute loyalty that had defined him and that she had come to rely upon in the past year.

She would mourn each and every crew member she had lost, but only now was she faced with the grim reality that Velth had been one of the few, along with the Doctor, who had become essential to her in a personal way. They had been peers.

They had been friends.

The others seemed so young, which was odd to say when she wasn't more than a decade older than most of them. Each had specialties and areas of expertise that had been critical to their assignments. As she had reviewed their weekly performance reports—compiled by Velth—she had been pleased with their progress, especially as they had faced several truly grim challenges while serving with the fleet.

But each time she had undertaken an away mission, Velth had been by her side. He had become her de facto first officer, patiently guiding the fresh-faced ensigns on the bridge, helping them to acclimate to their holographic counterparts, and allowing her to revel in the experience of her first command because he was always there, at her back, standing between her crew and whatever darkness they confronted.

It had only been a few days since she had studied a biodome on the surface of DK-1116 with the other fleet captains, marveling at the mysteries present and embracing them with the wondrous joy and curiosity that had compelled her to devote her life to Starfleet. She well remembered Captain Farkas's fears and how she had privately diagnosed them as a mild form of post-traumatic stress, honestly earned by *Vesta*'s captain. Farkas's losses while serving with the fleet had been massive.

Then, Glenn had been an observer. Now, although the numbers were vastly different, she felt a new, deep kinship and compassion for Farkas, along with a vast quantity of regret that she had not taken the captain's concerns more seriously.

Glenn could not have prepared herself more thoroughly to face the challenges of this mission. Still, she realized that she had begun this mission with the naïvete of a child.

Childhood was over.

"Commander Glenn?" Kim said as the doors to her room slid open.

"Come in, Lieutenant."

Kim did as she had asked but came only as far as the foot of her biobed. They were roughly the same age. According to his file, she was only a year and a few months older than he. But while he had spent seven years as an ensign, she had completed not only medical school, but also her command training, putting her on the short list to lead the *Galen*. She didn't make a habit of comparing herself to others. Everyone's path was their own and people moved over them at whatever pace best suited their skills and temperament. But when she considered all that this man had done in the last few days to save her people and her ship, she truly wondered why he hadn't risen more quickly through Starfleet's ranks. There hadn't been many opportunities for advancement in position during *Voyager*'s maiden trek, but field promotions were common in circumstances as unusual as theirs had been. If she ever saw Admiral Janeway again, Glenn resolved to ask her why she had found so little cause to consider the future career prospects of those who served under her.

Glenn suddenly wondered whether the admiral had truly believed she would bring her crew home and if she would come to question her own ability to do that in the weeks and months ahead.

She didn't want to believe that she now found herself in the same circumstance that Captain Kathryn Janeway had more than a decade earlier: stranded, thousands of light-years from Federation space, her ship damaged and understaffed, at the mercy of hostile aliens. But the comparison was hard to ignore. Much as she was tempted to simply thank Kim, whom she did not know at all, dismiss him, and relocate command of the ship to sickbay until she was fit to return to the bridge, everything but her pride counseled her to take seriously the reality that between the two of them, Lieutenant Kim had, by far, more experience than she did in their particular extreme circumstances.

She had asked the Doctor to elevate her upper body on the biobed so that she could meet Kim at eye level. Searching his eyes now, she saw how guarded he was. *Mistrust?* It hadn't occurred to her until now that she might bear some specific responsibility for what had transpired. She did not remember the attack or much that preceded it, but it was possible that she had miscalculated at a critical moment once it began. Was knowledge he possessed coloring his estimation of her?

Defensiveness cut through the miasma, providing a burst of adrenaline and newfound focus. "The Doctor has briefed me on our current circumstances as best he can. It seems that in my absence, you have effectively assumed command of my ship."

Kim nodded. "It wasn't anything formal, Captain. I just knew we needed to get power restored and Lieutenant Conlon was the only engineer available for that task. I made a plan, and no one questioned following it."

"Formal or not, I am assured that my crew now continues to follow your orders. I am curious to know why you chose not to defer to Lieutenant Velth, who was the ranking officer when you regained consciousness."

"He didn't ask, Captain. Frankly, we worked together. I suggested he help Conlon restart the fusion reactor, and once that was done, he, Conlon, Barclay, and I met to figure out our next priorities."

"But you ordered him on the EV mission that claimed his life, did you not?"

Kim straightened his shoulders a bit. He appeared to be ready-ing himself to accept a blow. The ruddiness that surged into his cheeks suggested embarrassment, but when he spoke again, strug-gling to keep his voice even, she recognized that he, too, was griev-ing Velth's loss. "He volunteered without question to be Conlon's eyes and hands when she outlined the scope of the work. Without another capable chief engineer on board, none of us felt that we should risk her. Without Conlon, we really are in trouble, Captain. Nonetheless, I do take full responsibility for the events that led to Velth's death and am willing to accept any disciplinary action you feel appropriate."

Glenn had internalized Kim's initial appearance, assuming as most people did that it had something to do with her. She chided herself, understanding now that *he* was every bit as frightened as she was. The playing field was level, but it couldn't stay that way.

"I understand the challenges you all faced, and I commend you for rising to them as best you could. But as I am sure you are aware, starships function best when the chain of command is observed. I intend to resume command of my ship effective immediately. Is that going to be a problem?"

"Of course not, Captain," Kim replied.

Compassion followed quickly on the heels of insight.

"When was the last time you slept, Lieutenant?"

Kim smiled faintly.

"Something funny?"

"No, Captain. It's just, I asked Velth the same thing yesterday and ordered him to hit his rack for a few hours, over his objections."

Now it was Glenn's turn to smile. "Sounds like Ranson."

"He was a good man."

"He was much more than that, Lieutenant. He was also a de-voted brother and somewhat reluctant uncle to two rowdy boys, a world-class skier, whose favorite poet was Robinson Jeffers and favorite band was the Beatles. He hated yoga, despite my many attempts at conversion, and never hesitated to get his hands dirty. He treated our emergency security holograms as he would any fellow officer, despite the fact that not one of them so much as cracked a smile at his jokes. My helmsman, Ensign Ben Lawry, worshipped him, and Ensign Selah has been nursing a crush on him since the day we launched."

"I didn't know any of that, although Nancy, *Lieutenant Conlon*"—he corrected himself automatically—"did tell me that his jokes were pretty dumb," Kim admitted with a regretful smile.

"Of course you didn't. You couldn't. But I don't have that luxury. He was my friend." At this, Glenn's stress response spiked, threatening to overwhelm her. She took a moment, a few deep breaths, and continued, determined to shift to the safer ground of practical matters. "What is our current status? Is the communications array functioning?"

"Yes, Captain."

"Have we attempted to contact the rest of the fleet?"

"We are over forty-seven thousand light-years from our previous position and twenty from our nearest comm relay. Unless the fleet moves much closer to us or that particular relay, we will not be able to contact them for a very long time."

"Then we should make restoring power to our engines our primary concern."

"Due respect, Captain, we don't have any antimatter, dilithium, or benamite. All of them were lost or destroyed during our transport here."

"Transport?"

Kim shrugged. "I don't know what else to call it. Sensors weren't functioning, so I can't confirm that theory, but it's the only one that accounts for all of the evidence at hand."

"And apart from killing Velth, the aliens haven't attempted to make contact with us?"

"There's a case to be made that they didn't kill Velth intentionally. They might have been curious and unaware that their actions would harm him."

"They attacked us."

"They brought us from our former position, where we had engaged technology they might classify as proprietary, and while we suffered tremendous damage when they did that, it is still not clear that they intended to harm us."

"Upon what do you base that speculation, Lieutenant? Other alien species had been experimenting with that technology long before we arrived. Why are you so determined to give them the benefit of the doubt here?"

Kim sighed. "Because any other supposition means we are probably all going to die sooner rather than later."

This simple statement of fact sent a fresh streak of pain through Glenn's head. She could feel herself slipping into an adversarial position with Kim. That could be a positive thing. Captains were only as good as the officers that served under them, and she made it a point to encourage her crew to speak freely in her presence. That said, she was conscious of her insecurity where Kim was concerned, and an almost reflexive, uncharacteristic need to assert her authority. She was going to have to temper that for them to develop a productive working relationship. "Why do you believe that to be true, Lieutenant?" she asked more gently.

"We're talking about a species advanced enough to create a planetoid designed to store enough energy over time to move a star out of its orbit and powerful enough to transport our ship over forty thousand light-years," Kim replied. "If they decide they want us dead, we're going to die, so I have to believe they don't, and we should do everything in our power to avoid changing their minds."

There was something refreshing in his bluntness. It nurtured trust. But that didn't entirely change her calculus. "I want us ready to defend ourselves the next time they approach this vessel," Glenn said.

"I do too, but I believe our first priority, beyond restoring as much power as possible, has to be establishing communication with them."

Glenn shook her head. "Every action these aliens have taken thus far has been hostile, Lieutenant. They assaulted us. They moved us against our will, almost destroying our ship in the process. And they took a member of my crew from us."

"They also left material on our ship that even now is helping to seal fractured areas of the hull," Kim said.

"So, you believe this is some great misunderstanding?"

"I don't know what to believe. And until we have more information, I'm not going to decide to approach them with hostility. Forgive me, Captain, but while I understand and share your anger, I've never found acting from a place of anger, especially in first-contact situations, to be a good plan."

As a rule, Glenn didn't either. But she had rarely felt as out of control as she did at this moment. It was an unnerving and frightening sensation.

"If I order you to fire on them if they approach the ship again, will you do it?" Glenn asked.

"It's your ship, Captain, and I will serve at your pleasure for as long as you are willing to have me do so. I will follow any order you choose to give. But I'm not in the habit of following orders with which I disagree without at least making my superiors aware of that fact at the appropriate time and place."

Glenn sat back, suddenly light-headed. The Doctor had advised her that she wouldn't be ready to return to duty for several days. She was beginning to understand the physical limitations that made that recommendation practical.

"Duly noted," Glenn said. "How do you suggest we proceed?"

"Every time the Edrehmaia approach us, they emit photonic signals on a wide spectrum. Assessing whether or not those signals might be a form of communication is my next priority."

"So we can ask them why the hell they did this?"

"Assuming we can restore any power at all to our engines, I was thinking we might ask them to let us go."

Glenn was struck by a new thought. "If their intentions toward us are as benign as you hope, why don't we ask them to send us back?"

Kim considered it. "We barely survived the trip here. I'm not sure I would risk returning the way we came. We'd do better to focus on restoring our slipstream drive."

"Without benamite?"

"We are working now on recrystallizing what was lost."

"Do you have any reason to believe that will work?"

Kim shook his head. "I honestly don't know. I've seen Nancy perform miracles before and I'm hoping she has a few more for us up her sleeve."

"Lieutenant Conlon?"

The question Glenn had forgotten until now to ask was suddenly on the tip of her tongue. Fleet personnel often moved among their sister ships but those who transported to *Galen* were usually injured or visiting the injured. *Why had Kim been aboard her ship at all?*

"You were here visiting the lieutenant at the time of the attack, weren't you?"

"Yes."

"You and she are . . ." Glenn began.

Kim's cheeks again began to redden.

"I think we're past the point of standing on formality," she said. "If you and I are going to work together, we're going to have to learn to trust each other. In my experience, that begins with honesty."

Taking a deep breath, he said, "Nancy Conlon and I are intimately involved. Our daughter, who is only a few weeks old, is residing in a gestational incubator a few doors down. I will leave it to her to brief you on her personal medical condition, but you must have been aware that she was transferred here weeks ago in order to treat a serious illness."

"I was. I approved the transfer. But as I am not her treating physician, I was not informed of the specifics of her case. I assume you know more than I do and are comfortable with her performing the duties of our chief engineer?"

"Honestly, I'd rather have her here devoting herself entirely to getting well. But under the circumstances . . ."

"None of us are going to be able to have what we want for the foreseeable future, are we, Lieutenant?"

"No, Captain."

Naming the unpleasant reality that faced her when she had begun to process her new circumstances and found herself unequipped to do so had a calming effect. Nothing about this situation was okay or was likely to be so for a long time. But at least she had someone beside her now who was willing to face that reality along with her, and, if possible, conquer it.

That knowledge helped.

8

"We have to go after them," Chakotay said.

Admiral Janeway, who did not disagree, rose from her workstation where she and Chakotay had been reviewing Bryce and Icheb's data. Much as she, too, wanted to simply ignore the many inconvenient facts that stood between her fleet and their lost vessel, she could not afford to make a choice based purely on her emotional attachment to *Galen*'s crew.

"Devil's advocate?" she asked.

Chakotay's eyes narrowed as he clearly struggled to comprehend why she would bother.

"Even if Bryce and Icheb are right and this was an advanced transport of some kind, we still don't know that the ship survived the process."

"Ensign Gwyn seems to think they did."

"Doctor Sal and Counselor Cambridge have not yet completed their evaluation of Gwyn."

"Kathryn, if there is even the slightest hope that they are alive, we have to make the attempt."

"Fine. Do you know where they are?"

"Not yet, but *Voyager* is already running long-range scans. If you would release the data to *Vesta* and *Demeter*, the search would go a lot quicker."

"I'm not ready to raise everyone's hopes just yet," Janeway countered. "I want to hear Sal's report first. And let's say they are within scanning range. What if the ship that took them is also in range? They knocked us out without breaking a sweat."

"We'll fight them."

"We'll lose."

"You don't know that."

She didn't. But she also couldn't help but think of Farkas's recent words, questioning her ability to accurately calculate risk. Her heart was with Chakotay, ready to rush headlong into whatever danger might exist, damn the odds, and find her people. Her head was another matter.

"Right now, I have no idea how to prevent it and neither do you," Janeway said. "I'm not risking more lives until I know we are ready to face them and for that, we need a lot more information."

"We're already analyzing their first attack against us."

"We only learned they were transported because Bryce and Icheb decided to scan for theoretical particles," Janeway insisted bitterly. "That's the tip of the iceberg of the things we don't know about the Edrehmaia. I understand why, Chakotay, but you're not thinking this through clearly."

"I'm not leaving them behind," he insisted.

"Neither. Am. I."

Chakotay knew a Janeway-shaped immovable force and he seemed to realize that he was standing right in front of one. "There might be another way," he suggested.

"I'm listening."

"We could try activating DK-1116 again. They might come back."

Janeway considered the notion. It seemed just this side of impossible, but then, most of their missions started in that general territory.

"I don't think we've got another thousand years to wait while that system recharges. More important, I want to know how to talk to them before we provoke them in any way."

"Lasren is already on it. He has broken down the photonic emissions the vessel displayed before it disabled us and is working on a new translation matrix."

"Good. Keep at it."

"Any other hurdles you want to throw in front of us?"

"Please don't pretend that I'm just giving you a hard time about nothing, Chakotay."

"We're talking about thirty-four lives that could be in desperate straits right now. Who knows how much time they have left?" Chakotay demanded.

"Thirty-three," Janeway corrected him.

Doubt flickered across his face. "Forgive me, but I was also counting the baby, Harry and Nancy's child."

Janeway felt herself flushing. She knew about the baby, of course, but her awareness of its existence was still so new, she wasn't yet accustomed to counting it among their potential losses.

"Listen to me," she said, taking his hands in hers. "I promise you that the moment we have a solid lead to follow, we will set course, and if they are still alive, we will find them."

Chakotay nodded but his eyes still registered wariness.

"I need you to trust me," she continued. "I need you at my side, not at cross purposes. These Edrehmaia, whatever they are, fill me with the same gut-level terror that used to be reserved for the Borg. And right now, I don't begin to know how to answer the thousand questions we have about them, what they want, what they're capable of, and why they chose to do this. Get me those answers, please," she said firmly.

Chakotay lifted a hand to caress her cheek. "I'm sorry," he said.

"You never have to apologize to me for wanting to protect our people," she said gently. "But my guess is that we're only going to get one shot at this. It has to be our best."

"Agreed," Chakotay said.

"Lasren is working the communications angle. I've had a request from Commander O'Donnell to return to the surface and investigate a cavern that might still be intact. He wants Seven and Patel to join him."

"Why does he want to do that?"

She shrugged. "If it's anything like the first . . ." She trailed off.

"I'll adjust their duty assignments accordingly and issue their new orders right away," Chakotay said.

"Can we maintain a transporter lock on them the entire time? No more seat-of-our-pants rescue operations if we can help it," the admiral requested.

"I will personally see to their security. I'd also consider sending *Vesta* out to do some scans of the asteroid field. Something out there adjusted the telemetry of that star and I'd really like to know more about it."

"Then we have the beginnings of a plan," she said.

"I'll keep you posted," Chakotay said.

She lifted her face to his and kissed him lightly. "Back to work."

Doctor El'nor Sal stood over Ensign Gwyn. Counselor Cambridge was seated nearby, swinging his gangly legs from the edge of the biobed and clearly wondering what previous mistakes in his life had led him to this moment. Much as she resented his presence, Sal also enjoyed the torment this assignment was obviously causing. Life was short. One needed to find amusements wherever possible, and for now, this would have to suffice.

"Well, Ensign," Sal began as she set aside the padd containing the results of her scans, "I am happy to report that your physical examinations all fall within normal limits. Your cortisol levels are a little high, but stress will do that to you and, for now, the readings aren't cause for concern."

Gwyn sat up. "What about the rest of it?" she asked.

Sal glanced toward Cambridge. "There are no visible signs of neurological damage. Almost everything I've seen conforms to your baseline scans when you joined the fleet."

"Almost?" Cambridge asked, sliding off the bed and approaching Sal from the opposite side of Gwyn.

"A significant finding of excess synaptic activity in your amygdala and temporal lobe suggests that new emotional connections are being processed."

"Do those findings correspond to anything in our database?" Cambridge asked.

Sal nodded. "Many years ago, Doctor Beverly Crusher of the *Enterprise* found herself in the presence of an empathic meta-morph. She had been brought aboard to seal a political alliance through marriage, and according to Crusher's logs, there was some concern on her captain's part that there might be an element of coercion involved. Crusher was not permitted, of course, to examine the metamorph, who was apparently undergoing the *finiis'ral* while on the *Enterprise*. But because Beverly Crusher was and remains one of the most indefatigable officers ever to grace Starfleet Medical, she managed to use the ship's internal sensors to take several inconspicuous scans of the young woman throughout her stay. They aren't as detailed as the ones I have just completed, but they do correlate in terms of neurological activity with what I'm seeing here."

"Does that prove anything?" Gwyn asked.

"It suggests to me that your account of bonding with the embryo is valid," Sal said.

The relief on Gwyn's face was palpable. "See?" she said, jerking her head toward Cambridge.

Cambridge nodded. "I do," he said. "And while this complicates our future, I am prepared to report to the admiral that your suspicions are now grounded in science and evidence, and should therefore be given significant consideration." After a moment he added, "Has your sense of connection to the embryo changed at all in the last several hours?"

Gwyn closed her eyes, clearly looking inside for the answers she sought. After a moment she shook her head. "She's still there."

"Very well, Ensign. You may return to your quarters," Cambridge said, dismissing her.

"Do us a favor, though?" Sal asked. "If anything does change . . . ?"

"I'll let you know. I promise," Gwyn said.

When she had gone, Cambridge followed Sal into her private office.

"I wonder if you can tell me, based upon your previous work

with the Kriosians, how well Gwyn is likely to hold up under the strain of being separated from the child?" he asked.

Sal sat back in her chair, crossing her arms. "I've never seen this before, so it's hard to tell. Bonding with the embryo meant she didn't have to sacrifice her sense of self to become another's perfect mate. However, the point of the bonding is connection, and I imagine this separation will be quite painful."

"But there will always be some distance between her and this child. It isn't as if she's going to move into the Kims' family quarters should we manage to find them."

"That's a bridge we won't have to cross for some time. For now, you need to keep her sane and focused on the things that she can control."

"I can't return her to duty."

"Then bury her in paperwork. And continue regular counseling."

"Didn't Icheb say that she wanted to talk to her mother?"

"I don't know. Did he?"

"I wonder if they're close."

"There are walls a mile wide around that kid. I don't know who she's close to, but I'd be amazed if it was her mother."

"Still something to consider, I suppose."

"You do that. I'm done practicing medicine for the foreseeable future. None of your patients will be at further risk of harm from me."

"El'nor," Cambridge said, "you're much too wise to allow a single lapse in judgment under obscenely unique circumstances to end your career."

"I'm afraid that isn't my call to make, Counselor."

"No, it's mine," the voice of Captain Farkas said.

Sal hadn't heard the captain enter her office. She turned abruptly and felt a twinge of nerves in her stomach.

Cambridge stepped toward Farkas immediately. "Regina," he greeted her.

"Counselor, would you excuse us, please?" Farkas asked.

Sal, who would have been delighted to have spent the last few hours without a chaperone, suddenly found herself wishing Cambridge would find cause for defiance—not that he usually needed persuading to make himself disagreeable.

The counselor, however, had mastered the art of reading a room. "Of course, Captain." With a cheeky nod to Sal, he departed, leaving the two women, once the closest of friends, alone.

"I was ordered by Admiral Janeway to examine Gwyn," Sal began, deciding to get a jump on the protestations part of this conversation.

"I know," Farkas said, crossing past Sal and perching herself on the edge of the doctor's workstation. She carried herself with a heavy, pensive air, one Sal had seen often enough. She was tempted to suggest Regina vent elsewhere whatever frustrations she might feel at this usurpation of her command prerogatives but was also curious to see how this was going to play out.

"What is it?" Sal found herself asking reflexively, as if the distance between them had never opened.

Farkas lifted storm-filled eyes to El'nor's. "I haven't formally reinstated you yet, so this conversation is as far from the official record as it is possible to get, yes?"

It had gone without saying for their entire careers that confidences between them were absolute. That Farkas felt the need to ask was painful. But then, so little of life wasn't.

"I'm still pissed as hell at you, Regina. But if the day ever came that you didn't feel you could talk to me about anything, I don't think I'd know what to do with myself."

Tangible relief graced Farkas's face. "I think we have a problem."

"Is this the *royal* we or am I included in that reference?" Sal asked.

"Could be all of us."

"Why is there never a single dull moment in this stupid quadrant?" Sal wondered.

Farkas released a ragged breath. "I wish I knew," she replied. "The DTI wants our fleet to return to Krenim space and attempt to make friends."

"Then I can only assume that the DTI hasn't met the Krenim," Sal said.

"With them, I guess you never know."

"Why is this our problem? Has the admiral agreed? She's never struck me as one with much patience for fools' errands."

"I didn't get this from her. One of the agency's directors reached out to me personally."

That was a surprise. Farkas's misgivings made more sense in this context. "Must be a slow day in the Alpha Quadrant if they're suborning mutiny all the way out here."

"That's what I thought at first," Farkas said. "But *hints* were dropped. I think they're really worried about something."

"Did they tell you what?"

"Of course not. They don't do clarity. They're spooks. Temporal lockboxes."

"What exactly did they ask you to do?"

Farkas shook her head. "My sense was that the agent was looking for a friendly ear out here. Someone to report on the admiral's decisions and keep an eye out for any disturbing anomalies."

Sal laughed aloud. "That doesn't sound at all dubious. He wants you to spy for him? Did he at least show you the secret handshake or offer to share his decoder ring?"

Farkas cracked a smile. "Come to think of it, *that* would have been tempting."

"So I guess nobody told him that Captain Regina Frances Farkas is constitutionally incapable of straying from the straightest available path. Or that she takes more pleasure in making her superior officers' ears bleed when they step outside the lines than going over their heads and tattling."

"Was any part of that a compliment?"

"It's objective reality. I'm not judging you. Just holding up your mirror." Studying the worried lines of Farkas's face, she added, "Why don't you like what you're seeing right now?"

"Because after I told him where he could shove his request, he made it clear that if Janeway doesn't step up, *I'm* next in line for that honor."

"Oh. *Damn*."

"So, I've got a couple of options. I could pretend the conversation never happened. I could report it to the admiral and make sure she knows she's under a microscope right now. Or, I suppose I could resign."

"Are you talking to me because you're wondering what the view is like from the cheap seats?" Sal asked.

"Damn it, El'nor, I didn't relieve you because I doubt your skill or dedication. You needed to take a beat and reevaluate your actions. You lost critical perspective and endangered your patient. Pissed or not, you know I was right, and I know for damn sure you'll never try a stunt like that again."

Sal wasn't sure Farkas was correct about the last part. "I still don't know what I could have done differently," she said honestly.

"You could have come to *me*," Farkas said, her voice rising. "I'm not just here for the witty repartee and nightcaps. I'm your best friend and your captain and I have to believe that together we would have found a solution that didn't include almost killing that poor ensign."

Sal felt her chin dropping toward her chest as she grasped the full magnitude of her error. On some level she had suspected that Farkas's actual problem hadn't been the outcome. Now, she knew. It wasn't that she'd failed. It was that lack of trust that galled Regina.

And for that, Sal couldn't fault her.

"But now the boot is on the other foot," Sal realized.

Farkas nodded somberly. "I can't betray the admiral. But I also can't say she's got my full confidence right now, and if she screws this one up . . ."

"The hammer falls on you."

"Yeah."

Sal moved to sit beside Farkas on the edge of her desk. "Command is such a lonely business," she said loftily.

"Oh, go to hell. If you're not going to take this seriously . . ."

"I wasn't finished," Sal interjected. "What does your gut say?"

"My gut is keeping its thoughts to itself right now."

"It picked a hell of a time to take a break. I'd take your gut's readings over my fanciest microspectrometer any day. It's the internal organ I credit with keeping both of us alive this long."

"I'm going to leave orders in my will to have those words engraved on my urn," Farkas said.

"That day might not be too far off, come to think of it," Sal said.

"Is that your expert opinion as my physician?"

"No. It's my expert opinion as the officer who just concluded that there is strong evidence to suggest that the *Galen* might still be out there somewhere." She allowed Farkas to digest this before adding, "I probably wasn't supposed to tell you that. You can't put me on report, though, because I'm still not on duty."

Farkas sighed deeply. "If we're going after that ship, you may consider yourself fully reinstated."

"Doesn't really help, though, does it?" Sal asked. "Our dance cards are probably going to be too full for the foreseeable future for us to backtrack into Krenim space."

"Actually, it does," Farkas said, suddenly rising.

"What are you going to do?"

Farkas chuckled. "My duty, of course."

As she headed for the door, Sal lobbed one last "I'm still pissed at you."

"Get in line," Farkas tossed back as she departed.

When Aytar Gwyn burst into a senior staff briefing to announce that the crew of the *Galen* was still alive, Lieutenant Devi Patel had transitioned quickly from shock to concern. Little Gwyn ever did *surprised* Patel. The ensign's spirit was both fierce and independent. Patel remembered thinking the first day Gwyn had reported to the bridge still pulling on one of her boots that the ensign didn't appear to *need* anyone's approval. Paris had dressed her down and Gwyn had shrugged it off. Were it not for her exceptional piloting skills, Patel doubted Gwyn would have lasted this long.

But part of Gwyn's ability to maintain her individuality and attitude was predicated upon a certain shallowness of feeling. Gwyn probably could access normal quantities of compassion and empathy; she just rarely chose to do so, in Patel's experience.

Despite this, Patel considered Gwyn to be a friend. Both fell into a category of officers assigned to important alpha shift duties who nonetheless felt somehow "second string" to those among them who had shared *Voyager's* seven-year maiden trek. For a long time, this had bothered Patel. To this day, it didn't seem to trouble Gwyn at all.

But something in Gwyn had clearly changed. A few days prior, Gwyn had risked her life and her career to save Patel's, and she had done it in the most flagrant manner possible: stealing a shuttle and disobeying direct orders from the admiral and Captain Chakotay to return to *Voyager*. The fact that Gwyn had also saved Commanders Paris and Torres must have bought her a little leniency.

But the part Patel couldn't align with every other thing she knew of Aytar Gwyn was why. *What on earth had moved Gwyn so about Patel's fate that could have caused her to act as she did?* Short of her parents—who didn't count *because* they were her parents—no one Patel had ever known had seemed to care enough for her to cross a crowded room, let alone fly a shuttle into the atmosphere of a world that was in the process of tearing itself apart.

The act, itself, spoke of untold emotional depths present in Gwyn that Patel had never glimpsed. She doubted that any of the dozen crewmen with whom Gwyn had chosen to briefly share her bunk in the last year had seen it either, given that none of those relationships had lasted longer than a few days.

And whatever had driven Gwyn to that act still seemed to be running the show. The flushed, harried, almost desperate young woman who had rushed in unannounced upon their staff briefing was clearly not in control of her emotions. Normally, Gwyn wielded control, both at the helm of a starship and in her personal life, with the skill of a surgeon. Its absence was entirely out of character and, thus, cause for concern.

Patel had new orders. She was due to report to *Demeter* along with Seven to undertake an away mission back to the surface of DK-1116 with Commander Liam O'Donnell. But she couldn't leave the ship again, *especially* on another mission that could easily claim her life, without knowing that Gwyn was okay.

The chime Patel had activated at Gwyn's door received no response. Patel was stepping back from the door sensor when it finally slid open.

"Oh, hey, Devi," Gwyn said.

Patel had secretly envied Gwyn's easy confidence and ability to fit in by standing out for the better part of a year. But now, there was an air of anxiety clinging to her and a sense of distance even though they stood less than a meter from each other.

"Did you want to come in?" Gwyn asked.

"I do," Patel replied, and immediately followed Gwyn into her cabin.

The lights were set low and a single candle burned on the table beside Gwyn's bunk. The bed looked rumpled, as if the ensign had been lying on top of it.

"Did I wake you?" Patel asked.

"No, I was just . . ." But Gwyn didn't finish that sentence. Instead she asked, "How are you feeling? You're back on regular duty, right?"

"Yeah. I'm fine. Good. I'm sorry I haven't had a chance yet to thank you for what you did," Patel finished, flustered.

Gwyn crossed back to her bunk and sat down cross-legged on top of it. "Yeah, that was a thing, wasn't it?"

"A thing? You saved my life, Aytar."

"You were doing something incredibly stupid. Someone had to stop you, and everybody else was a little busy at the time."

Gwyn shrugged, a move with which Patel was familiar. But the calculus could not have been that simple. "You could have lost your commission," Patel said.

"Compared to you losing your life?"

"I didn't want you to risk anything for me."

"So, you're not grateful?"

"No, I am, it's just . . ."

Somehow their conversation wasn't going at all as it had the fifty times Patel had rehearsed it in her head.

"Why did you do it?" Gwyn asked.

Returning to that moment in the cavern when she had placed her combadge on her tricorder and stepped away from the transport area was painful. Most of the time it could be kept at bay, a hazy, half-remembered dream where only certain moments were clear. But forcing it to the forefront of her consciousness now, and knowing what it had forced Gwyn to do, brought back the taste of iron in her mouth and the light-headed, almost out-of-body sensation Patel remembered vividly. Pushing past it she replied, "It's not that I wanted to die. I *had* to make sure the data survived. If we left without the information we'd gathered, it would have made everything we went through meaningless. It would have been like it never happened. And what we found down there was important."

Gwyn stared up at her as if she were speaking a foreign language in the absence of a universal translator. "Like I said, incredibly stupid."

"I guess," Patel finally admitted, "I wasn't sure it really mattered if I survived. Who was going to miss me? It sounds dumb now, but at the time it all made perfect sense in my head."

"That's why we talk to each other, Devi. To test the stuff in our head and make sure it makes sense outside, too."

"Well, thank you."

"Don't do it again," Gwyn said.

"I won't. At least, not on purpose."

Gwyn tilted her head gently to the side, her brow furrowing. "Not quite the full-throated denial I was looking for there, Devi."

"I'm going back to the surface with Seven and O'Donnell."

Gwyn rose quickly. "What? Why?"

"Orders," Patel said. "You remember those, right? Your superior officer tells you to do something and you don't question it, you just do it."

"You can't. I mean, you shouldn't. That's just . . . what more does anyone need to know about this place? We have to get out of here and look for . . ." But Gwyn didn't finish that sentence either. Instead, her gaze shifted almost involuntarily to the candle beside her bed.

This was as close to an opening as Patel was likely to get. "What's wrong with you?" she asked, regretting the accusatory tone immediately. "How do you know they're still alive?" she added more gently.

Gwyn lifted her chin to face her. There was a haunted quality to her eyes. The distance was back. Pulling herself again into the present moment seemed to require some effort on Gwyn's part.

"I just know," she said.

"Because you don't want them to be dead?"

"No, because I just know they're not."

"If anybody else said that, I'd suggest therapy," Patel said. "I'm guessing you've already spent most of the last few days with Counselor Cambridge, however, so . . ."

"Have you ever loved anyone, Devi? I mean, really, totally, unconditionally, irrationally *loved* anyone?"

Had Gwyn ever seriously asked this question in the past, Patel would have laughed aloud. The answer was, *she hadn't*, and neither, she suspected, had Gwyn.

Until now?

"Who?" Patel asked. "Who are you in love with that was on that ship?"

Gwyn shook her head. "I can't . . ." she said on the faintest of breaths.

Patel stepped back. The pinging back and forth between raw emotional connection and forced distance was confusing, infuriating even.

"Okay," Patel said, trying to pretend it didn't matter. "Well, I'm sorry. Thank you again for saving my life. I promise I will do my best to make it unnecessary in the future. I'm going to go now."

"Devi," Gwyn said as Patel started for the door.

"What?" Patel replied sharply as she turned back.

"I'm not very good at this," Gwyn said in an abrupt moment of clarity. "I'm not used to needing people. It's hard for me when things matter."

Patel smiled sadly. "For what it's worth, I'm not used to people giving a shit about me. It's unnerving in a totally different way. When I get back, if you want to, we can compare notes."

Gwyn nodded. "Don't die."

"I won't. I promise. And, Gwyn, there are worse things in this universe than needing people. Sometimes, it can be kind of great. Especially when they need you back."

Gwyn smiled faintly but hardly looked convinced.

DEMETER

"So here's some of what we know," Commander Liam O'Donnell said as Seven and Patel pulled chairs closer to the table in the lab *Demeter*'s captain had repurposed for their briefing. A small holographic generator had been placed at the table's center and a series of three-dimensional images began to cycle through as O'Donnell spoke.

Seven and Patel had already spent considerable time analyzing the structure of DK-1116 both before and after it had been activated. Seven was interested to see how Commander O'Donnell's conclusions compared with theirs.

"Behold DK-1116," O'Donnell began. "I have taken the liberty of renaming this place in my head *Species 001's World of Wonders*, or SWOW, but don't worry, I don't expect that to catch on. I find it more precise than its current astrometric designation, but—"

"*Commander*," Seven interrupted him wearily.

"Right, time rushing inexorably forward and all that," O'Donnell conceded. "At some point prior to four thousand, eight hundred years ago, the Edrehmaia brought a baby star into this system, where it was captured by the orbit of a larger, older star. Thus, a new binary system was born. The Edrehmaia then created SWOW, with the intention of using it to recapture that baby star and send it on its way at some future date." Here O'Donnell paused for effect. "And then, something miraculous happened."

"Permit me to guess," Seven said. "Species 001 discovered . . ." But here she faltered.

O'Donnell's face broke into a wide smile. "Come on, Seven. You can do it."

"Species 001 discovered *this planet*," Seven continued, "and created a containment system designed to prevent the planet from releasing the vast quantities of energy it was storing to move that star so that they could study the Edrehmaia's technology."

Here, Patel picked up the tale. "Shortly thereafter, a number of other species, at least a hundred and ninety-six of them, were either invited here or independently discovered the . . . uh . . . *planet*, and biodomes were created for each of them to experiment with an incredibly powerful substance left by the Edrehmaia. It was combined with biological life-forms as well as other elements in an effort to understand its nature and whether or not it could be made to work in concert with their own biology and technology."

O'Donnell had been considering Patel intently from the moment she began to speak. When she finished, he said, "How much time have you spent studying those experiments, Lieutenant?"

"Hardly any," Patel replied. "While trapped in Station Four data storage, my team was able to download details of many of those species' experiments, but I haven't had a chance to begin to review that data."

"It's truly fascinating," O'Donnell said. "You really should make the time. I'm certain that you would find them as extraordinary as I have."

"It is worth noting," Seven interjected, "that while their experiments resulted in the creation of a number of unique life-forms and elements, and the technology created to sustain the biodomes is remarkable, *our* interactions with the Edrehmaia substance to date have produced catastrophic results. Ensign Gwyn was seriously injured when it made physical contact with her EV suit. When it touched our shuttle, it proceeded to mutate and transform it. And the biodome regulation system was so delicate that within hours of our arrival, our mere presence there disrupted it thoroughly."

"Haven't you figured that one out yet?" O'Donnell asked.

Seven favored him with a withering gaze. "The, for want of a better term, 'power conduits' running throughout the entire planet were designed as a closed circuit. The purified water brought to the surface once the biodomes were complete was strategically placed to disrupt those circuits. Once we entered that water, it lost its purified state and ceased to effectively disrupt the system."

"Which we could not have known or even suspected when we began to study the surface," O'Donnell said.

"I do wonder, though, given how advanced Species 001 had to be, why they wouldn't have left some warning for those who came after them. It's not that hard to put up a 'No Swimming' sign," Patel noted.

O'Donnell shook his head. "We may never know. The system remained intact for thousands of years and was surely a beacon to any curious and sufficiently advanced species passing through. It occurs to me that Species 001 may have departed in a hurry, perhaps planning to return."

"It is also likely that those one hundred and ninety-six species might have represented all known sufficiently advanced spacefaring races able to access the planet at the time and it was deemed unlikely anyone else would come along and investigate," Seven suggested.

"I don't know," Patel said. "Everything about this place feels intentional. And this territory was once claimed by the Borg. What are the odds they never discovered it?"

"Apparently a hundred percent," Seven said.

"I mean, that they never *would have* discovered it," Patel corrected herself.

"Our knowledge of the Borg's activities throughout the Delta Quadrant is incomplete," Seven said. "And having once been Borg and privy to every thought of the Collective, I do find that disturbing. But we have come across more than one of the Borg's blind spots during this mission. It is my belief that any data irreconcilable with the Collective's core mission of assimilation in pursuit of perfection was regularly purged and this world, this entire system, could have fallen into that category."

"Fascinating as this speculation is," O'Donnell said, "our mission is not merely to indulge in hypotheticals."

"What exactly is our mission, Commander?" Patel asked.

"Clearly it is possible to safely experiment with the Edrehmaia substance. That substance, as you both know, is among the most complex kinds of matter Starfleet has yet discovered and it is my belief that like those who came before us, it is now incumbent upon us to pick up that mantle and continue their work."

"Our scans show no evidence of the Edrehmaia substance still present on the planet," Patel said.

"But Seven stumbled across some in the asteroid field. I'm sure that wasn't the last of it," O'Donnell reminded her.

"The issue is safely containing it for study," Seven insisted.

"Do you have any idea how we might accomplish that?" Patel asked.

"I believe we should start by asking them," O'Donnell replied.

"Ask whom?" Patel queried.

"You were able to create an interlocutor at the station you studied," O'Donnell said pointedly. "And while your report indicates that you did get a great deal of information from it, there were many unasked questions one could now pose to such a creation."

"Yes, but we broke the planet," Patel said. "We disrupted the containment system and the planet released its energy. There are no power readings within the intact cavern you discovered. I don't believe we will be able to reactivate it."

"Perhaps not," O'Donnell agreed. "But you were studying one of the data storage and retrieval stations. It was located approximately three kilometers beneath the surface. There were six other similar stations present," he continued, pointing to the display to indicate them on the holographic map. "The only one left intact following the planet's activation was the seventh and final station, and it is located much deeper within the planet, here," he said, indicating a cavern situated, perhaps suggestively, well below the north polar region.

"You believe *this* was the first station constructed," Seven rightly guessed.

"I do. Which means it might be the only one in existence left by those who built it containing evidence of how the entire amazing system was created."

"The Edrehmaia?" Patel asked.

"No, Lieutenant. Species 001," O'Donnell replied.

Patel inhaled involuntarily at this revelation. She started to speak, but Seven cut her off.

"Don't say it," she pleaded.

"I have to," Patel said sheepishly.

Seven shook her head. "Fine."

"*SWOW*," Patel and O'Donnell said in unison.

9

After three days of advising Lieutenant Conlon every time the Doctor saw her that she needed to report to sickbay for a series of standard medical scans, she had finally made the time. He understood how busy she was. He did not begin to suspect that she might have cause to avoid the tests until he saw the results. The new panel of full-body scans, including genetic analysis, now sat on the padd before him and the tale they told was not heartening.

As the Doctor analyzed them, Lieutenant Barclay knocked on the partition separating his private office from the rest of *Galen*'s medical bay.

"Good news," Barclay said without preamble. "In a few hours, I'll be able to restore the rest of your medical staff."

"Thank you, Reg, that will be most helpful," the Doctor replied perfunctorily, still studying the test results.

"The fusion reactor is running at almost fifty percent of capacity," Barclay continued. "Honestly, I never thought we'd be having this conversation. I was sure that a cold restart sequence outside a starbase would be the end of us. Nancy Conlon is a miracle worker."

At this, the Doctor lifted his eyes to meet Barclay's. "I beg your pardon?"

"How do you think we were able to restore power?" Barclay asked.

"I don't know. I've got five critical patients and another three who will require constant treatment for the next week at least. I guess I didn't think to wonder. I just assumed the surviving crew members were doing what they always do in situations like this . . . making the impossible possible."

Barclay's response hit the Doctor like a punch. "Nancy Conlon is the only reason we are still alive, Doctor." Something in the Doctor's face seemed to give Barclay pause. "Are you all right? You look tired."

The Doctor wasn't tired. One of the few things he was incapable of feeling was weariness, although the complex subroutines that animated his holographic matrix could approach near-perfect simulated presentations of emotional responses, including fatigue. These amazing algorithms, and one odd temporary body swap with Seven of Nine several years prior, were all the Doctor had to use as a reference point for the emotional responses he thought of as his *feelings*. For many years he had equated those sensations with the emotions he believed colored the lives of his organic patients. But as long as his holo-processors were activated, his program could run indefinitely, without lags in efficiency or detectable errors. It was impossible for him to actually *be* tired.

Still, Barclay was not wrong.

Throughout the many years he had been active, the Doctor had surpassed his original programming in significant ways. He had expanded his areas of expertise to include artistic pursuits—singing, writing, and photography. He had formed intense personal relationships with many of his fellow crew. He had loved, despised, and lost. He had, in his way, mourned the death of Kathryn Janeway and several other patients with whom he had bonded. And recently, he had chosen to delete many of his most poignant and significant memories of his friendship with Seven in order to conquer an invading alien consciousness determined to wrest control of his matrix from him. This had been the unfortunate by-product of an ill-considered attempt by his creator, Lewis Zimmerman, to allow him to approximate the human capacity for healing from painful experiences by dulling the memories associated with those events.

His existence was precious to him. It had been remarkable. And despite his many challenges, he had never wished for it to do anything other than continue, as it had. Each moment was filled with the possibility that his life, as he knew it, would continue to evolve and no one, not even those who knew him best, could say how or where that evolution might end.

Registering Barclay's assessment of Conlon's significance to the ship's continued survival while staring at Conlon's test results filled him with both existential dread and something approaching despair. Apparently, this particular cocktail of subroutines read as "tired."

The Doctor's ethical programming did not allow him to breach a patient's confidentiality, but it did allow for considerable latitude in searching for potential cures. Having finally been fully briefed on Doctor Sal's intended treatment regimen and its dire consequences for Ensign Aytar Gwyn, he was well aware that the desire to cure a patient could blind even the best among his medical compatriots to potential conflicts. But no such conflict existed when he and Lieutenant Barclay had begun to consider ways to extend Conlon's life using technological means until medical science found a solution.

A few weeks ago, the Doctor had begun to investigate a radical solution intended to buy more time for the physicians working to solve Conlon's problem—the construction of a positronic matrix to house her consciousness. Barclay had balked at the notion, not only because researching the project had included conversations with a holographic version of Commander Data, one of only a few positronic androids that had ever been created. Barclay had personally designed that hologram to help him grieve Data's loss and was rightly offended when the Doctor attempted to utilize it for his own purposes. Reg had insisted that the Doctor's pursuit was folly, given that even Data had never successfully created another android like himself. But Barclay had offered a counterproposal, the creation of a holographic matrix to perform the same function—to become a temporary home for a human consciousness that could not be damaged by its DNA's inability to repair itself until Conlon's body could be healed. The Doctor had already successfully done this with a Vidiian physician, Denara Pel.

Even as he had prepared for the possibility, the Doctor still hoped it would not be necessary. He had believed that Doctor Sal, who had previously found a cure for a similar syndrome, would succeed in her efforts to repair Conlon's DNA. Now, that hope had vanished. He was going to have to find a way to cure Conlon if she was going to survive, and to do that, he would need time—time these test results told him he did not have.

"Reg," the Doctor began, "what would you say the odds of our survival would be without the presence of Lieutenant Conlon?"

Barclay appeared stunned by the thought. He moved to sit opposite the Doctor, his mind clearly working the question. Finally, he said, "Our immediate power issues have been resolved. As long as the fusion reactor holds, we can survive indefinitely. But Conlon is by far the most experienced engineer on board and, in her absence, I do not believe we will succeed in the next critical steps."

"Which are?"

"Off the top of my head, we will need to find a source of benamite, or something that can replace it, in order to bring our slipstream drive back online. Even if we could solve the problem of creating antimatter, which is a big ask and one I believe to be insurmountable under our present circumstances, restoring warp power will never get us back to our fleet. We need the slipstream drive if we are ever going to see them again. Torres could have done it. Possibly the young man running *Vesta*'s engineering section as well."

"Bryce?"

"Yes. But without Conlon . . ."

"We're screwed?"

"Yes, I believe so," Barclay agreed.

The Doctor nodded.

There had certainly been times in the past, while undertaking certain away missions, for example, when his survival depended upon the actions of one or more of his fellow officers. Searching his memory, however, he could not remember a single instance where a medical choice before him could mean the difference between not only his continued existence, but also the survival of his ship and crew.

"Do you recall our recent conversation about the possibility of utilizing a hologram to store Conlon's consciousness?" the Doctor asked.

Barclay remained perfectly still. He likely not only recalled the conversation but the vehemence with which Doctor Sharak, *Voyager's* CMO, had objected to the prospect. "I do."

"When we had that discussion, our systems were in perfect working order and we were still connected to the rest of our fleet."

"True."

"Given our current situation, is it still your belief that such a thing would be possible?"

Barclay exhaled through his lips, causing them to beat rapidly against each other and producing a sound much like one of Tom Paris's antique engines starting. "Possible? Yes. But—and this is a big *but*—it would require me to reallocate our holographic resources considerably."

"How so?"

"A matrix that size would require all of the processing power currently allocated for the rest of our emergency holographic personnel. None of them have been reactivated yet, but the crew is hoping we can bring them back online quickly, if only to allow for more regular rest periods. Activating the hologram you are proposing would mean sacrificing our backup engineering, medical, and security officers."

"Could you select a few key holograms to initiate and still create the new matrix?"

Barclay shook his head. "I'd have to see the final specs on the new hologram. Honestly, without the additional power generated by our warp drive, I doubt it. I would need to bring the new hologram online first in order to accurately gauge its power requirements."

The Doctor considered the calculus. It wasn't often he found himself trading in lives, organic or holographic. The last time math like this had been necessary—being forced to choose between saving the lives of two patients, one he considered a friend and one he did not know well—it almost destroyed his program. Only now did he realize how well that experience had prepared him for this moment.

"I want you to begin working on the new holomatrix right away. Do not reactivate the rest of our emergency holographic personnel in the meantime."

"Commander Glenn ordered—"

"I will brief the captain personally."

Barclay nodded, then rose from his chair. "I understand."

"Thank you, Reg."

Kim hadn't slept particularly well. After almost an hour of forcing himself to remain still and at least try to rest, fitful sleep had finally descended. He found himself in a particularly vivid and disturbing dream. He no longer remembered the details, only that he and a group of nameless crewmen had battled for their lives, deck by deck. The certainty that failure meant death and the hopelessness that accompanied it lingered even after Kim had shaken himself awake and still clouded his thoughts as he made his way to the bridge.

It didn't take a counselor to unravel the dream's meaning. It was one of the more literal representations of his waking fears that his subconscious had offered up in some time. It was, however, singularly depressing to think he would be battling the same demons while waking and sleeping.

Entering the bridge, he found Ensign Michael Drur, *Galen's* alpha shift operations officer, already at work. He stood several inches taller than Kim, with salty hair that was clearly going prematurely white. Trepidatious light-blue eyes locked with Kim's as soon as he arrived.

"Good morning, Lieutenant," Drur greeted him. "I mean, I guess it's morning, right?"

"Works for me," Kim replied. "What have you got there?"

"Commander Glenn ordered me to start running the light transmissions of the aliens through our translation matrix," he said with a hint of defensiveness. As far as Kim was concerned, no one ever needed to apologize for doing their job.

"It's good to have you back on the bridge, Ensign," Kim encouraged him. "Have you found anything yet?"

Drur shook his head, clearly frustrated. "There's a lot of data here, sir. And the translator can't seem to lock into a workable paradigm."

Kim moved to stand beside Drur at his station. The ensign was running an analysis of every sensor log available with visible images of the aliens through the translation matrix simultaneously, beginning with the records from their initial encounter back in the binary system that contained DK-1116.

"Let me guess," Kim ventured. "Processing ceases at around two percent, right?"

Drur's face turned sharply to Kim's. "Yes, sir. How did you know that?"

Years of experience was the obnoxious answer, so Kim held it back. Volume of data was often a problem, but selection was equally important. "First things first. Have you added filters to these images to account for light along the invisible spectrum?"

Drur nodded. "I did, but that just made it worse. I figured I'd try to isolate the visible spectrum. There are exaquads of data present along those wavelengths alone."

"Understandable," Kim said. "But if you're trying to parse a new language, you need to start with a viable section of the whole thing. Fragments tend to confuse the translation algorithms." Kim quickly added the appropriate filters. The resulting image was fascinating. "It's like a damned star going supernova, isn't it?"

"That's . . . interesting," Drur said.

"In what way, Ensign?" Kim asked, hoping to coax Drur along. He could have completed this work alone in less than half the time it would take the ensign. But that wasn't the point. Not long ago, Ensign Gwyn had taken Kim to task for the way the more experienced fleet officers dismissed the input of the younger ones. Considering how likely it was that his new crew—*how had they become his in such a short time?*—was at the very beginning of creating a new life for themselves out here, Kim knew that this was one habit he was going to have to break.

"I guess it just occurs to me that these aliens . . ."

"The Edrehmaia," Kim offered.

"The Edrehmaia seem to have an almost proprietary interest in stars, don't they?"

It was a good observation. Kim filed it away for future consideration. "They really do. Now go ahead and run the same filters with the signals given off by the aliens that approached the ship yesterday."

"The ones that came for Velth," Drur said, not a question, just a miserable fact.

Conlon's words came back to him. *I wish I didn't know how terrified he was at the end.*

Kim wished the same. Velth's death was going to haunt him for the rest of his life. But avoiding the topic with his former crewmates would seem both callous and disrespectful.

"Were you close to the lieutenant?" Kim asked.

Drur shook his head. "He often had the conn in the captain's absence. He was . . . I don't know."

Glenn had spoken of Lawry's and Selah's admiration for Velth. Kim wondered why Drur didn't seem to share it. But he didn't want to push. Instead, he focused his attention on the new images populating the display before him. The sheer volume of photonic activity flooding the screen was massive.

"Is it possible that these emissions are just a by-product of the aliens' propulsion system?" Drur asked.

"Possible, sure," Kim said. "But they didn't begin emitting the signals until they came within a certain proximity of the fleet and Lieutenant Velth." Continuing to think out loud, he said, "They could be a simple code—rudimentary communication meant only for one another—but there was only one vessel present when the fleet first encountered them, so who else would they have thought they were talking to?" Kim knew he might be reaching, but every instinct he had told him that the photonic emissions were some sort of complex communication system—a language.

"You're saying that the act itself, the attempt to communicate, suggests that the aliens believed that those receiving the communication should have the ability to understand and respond?"

Kim nodded. "Xenocommunications can be an esoteric discipline. Lots of languages have common rules, patterns, repetitions, stress indicators, algorithmic variables that the universal translator eventually figures out how to parse. Language develops from the minds and bodies of the species that create them, and the similarities between humanoid species account for much of the ease with which modern comm systems operate."

"But the Edrehmaia aren't humanoid, are they?"

"I'm not even sure they are carbon based," Kim agreed.

"Could it be a computer language?" Drur asked.

Kim ordered the computer to isolate a segment of the full spectrum of emissions and applied a binary translation matrix as he replied, "If this is simply a computer language, the translator should be able to recognize those patterns. Like humanoid bodies, there are only so many ways to develop complex machines. At the root, there tend to be similarities."

As he suspected, the results were gibberish—the computer's way of saying it did not recognize the emissions as a language.

Drur was obviously growing more frustrated. "This isn't going to work," he said.

"It isn't working yet," Kim corrected him gently. "But knowing what the emissions aren't is still helpful."

"But the remaining set of what they could be is impossibly large," Drur noted.

Kim stepped back and began to pace the small bridge. Once again, he found himself missing his clarinet. The simple act of forcing part of his mind to concentrate on a task it had mastered tended to free up the rest of his mind and allow it to wander down darker roads and interesting tributaries.

He wasn't sure how long it would be until they could spare the power, but as soon as it was possible, Kim was going to replicate a new clarinet. He had a feeling he was going to need it in the days ahead.

Even without it, however, he could play, or rather, he could activate the part of his brain that he used while playing.

Glancing out at the main viewscreen and beholding the dazzling light display that was the baby star nursery, Kim selected a piece he hadn't played in years—the third movement of Claude Debussy's *Suite Bergamasque*, "Clair de lune." Originally composed for piano, it had been arranged for almost every orchestral instrument, including the clarinet. Kim's favorite was by Xi Cin, a twenty-third-century composer who had written out his arrangement in the hills above Guilin City as part of a celebration of the second century of lunar colonies.

Kim wasn't sure why this song rose to his mind. It might have been a subtle act of rebellion—a hymn to the moon from a place where no moons were visible. Appreciating the defiance of it, Kim inhaled and imagined himself playing the first few notes, those three tones—A-flat, A-flat an octave up, then down two and a half steps to F—until the haunting melody began to flow through him in all of its wondrous, melancholy beauty.

You're thinking too big.

Kim paused, once again enveloped in silence, wondering where the thought had come from and what it might mean.

"Lieutenant?"

"I'm sorry," Kim said. "I didn't mean to drift off. I was just thinking."

"Of course, sir," Drur said. "Sorry to interrupt."

"You don't have to apologize, Ensign." Seeing a faint smile creep across Drur's face, he wondered how accustomed this young man was to speaking his mind freely.

"It occurs to me that we might be thinking too big now."

"In what way, sir?"

Choosing not to question the inspiration, Kim returned to the ops panel. "Bring up the initial sensor log again and isolate the first photonic emission we detected from the alien ship."

Drur did so. The result was intriguing. "Now do the same for the initial signal from the smaller alien ships." *The aliens themselves?*

The result was the same.

"The first color transmitted along several sections of both entities was pure white light," Drur said. "The emission was sustained for less than one second, but it was there. Nothing along the invisible spectrum was contained in the very first emission."

"And white light isn't actually white. It contains a blending of all of the colors of the visible spectrum," Kim noted. "Now move on to the second emission," he suggested.

"Violet," Drur said once the process was complete, "plus some new waves along theta band."

"The amount of data contained in these two emissions taken together overloads the sensors easily, which is why the entire series of photonic emissions has the computer stymied. Run every translation algorithm we have against the first emission alone and see what happens."

"It's going to take a minute."

"We've got nothing but time," Kim said.

As Drur continued the operation, Kim began to pace once again. "Do your friends call you Michael?" he asked.

Again, that sharp, disquieting glance. "My friends?"

"The other bridge officers."

"They call me Ensign, or sometimes Drury."

"But that's not your name."

"I'm not really a people person," Drur said. "I keep to myself."

"Nothing wrong with that," Kim said.

"It can be taken the wrong way. As if I don't like people. I do. I just . . ."

Something about this young man was slowly beginning to break Kim's heart. He didn't know what the ensign's personal experiences had been in the last year, but he suspected they had been challenging. "Everybody is different," Kim offered, "but we all graduated from the same Academy. We all had to survive the same courses and instructors, and nobody gets a seat on the bridge of a starship that doesn't deserve it."

Drur nodded. After a long pause, he said, "Velth was the one who used to call me Dreary Drury. I guess the others thought it was funny, so it kind of stuck."

"My best friend, a guy named Tom Paris, spent the first year of our service together teasing me incessantly. I got used to it, but I never enjoyed it, if you know what I mean," Kim said.

"I think I do."

"He and his wife, B'Elanna, had a baby a few months ago. His name is Michael too. Personally, I like that name a lot."

"My mom used to call me Mike."

"Is that what you prefer?"

"I guess."

"Mike it is, then," Kim said as a shrill screech began to pierce the air around them.

"The hell?" Kim asked, rushing back to the ops station.

Drur's hands moved swiftly across the panel. "We've got something," he said.

"Can you turn it down?"

Drur did so.

"What is that?"

"That's the data from the first signal, isolated on a single band," Drur said, a true smile finally breaking on his face.

Kim smiled back. "You know what else it is?"

"No, sir."

"Progress," Kim said. "And you should call me Harry."

One thought ran ceaselessly through Nancy Conlon's mind as she stared at the tiny bean floating in the gestational incubator before her. *How am I going to do this?* Ready or not, she was a mother. Her daughter—*at some point I'm going to have to talk to Harry about names*—still had months of development ahead of her before she would be able to leave the incubator, but she was alive and healthy and growing, and soon enough would need to be held and fed and taught a million things. Even if Conlon managed to get the ship moving again, her days would likely be quite full. But this little one was going to need more time than regular duty shifts were likely to allow. For a moment she thought of B'Elanna Torres, carrying Michael through the ship in a sling while arranging lessons for her daughter, Miral. Torres made it look easy, but Conlon knew the strain that defined B'Elanna's existence since her children were born. It wasn't a bad thing. But it was a hard thing. It required everything a person had to give and then some.

And Conlon had no idea how she was going to manage all of it. In her darker moments, she wondered if she would even have to face that challenge.

When the Doctor entered the room and Conlon tore her eyes from the incubator to greet him, her unease intensified. "You're not walking in here with good news, are you, Doc?" she asked.

"No," he replied.

"I take it this means the degeneration continues, despite your recent surgical interventions?"

"Yes," the Doctor said simply.

"Neurological?"

"Yes. How did you know that?" the Doctor asked.

Conlon knew it was time to come clean, but to say it made it real in a way she would have preferred to deny a little longer. "There have been a few times in the last several days when I haven't heard things quite clearly."

"Because they are too soft?"

"No, it's more like the words don't make sense in my brain."

The Doctor nodded. "Auditory processing difficulties. Has your speech been affected?"

"Once or twice," Conlon admitted.

"I'm sorry. I wish I could say it was surprising, but given these results, it is to be expected."

Conlon bowed her head, absorbing the blow. When she lifted it again, her eyes were bright, but dry. There was no time now for self-pity. "How long do I have?"

"If we do nothing, a few months at best. I suspect you will find your neurological functions further impaired, perhaps seriously, within the next few weeks."

This new reality stiffened Conlon's spine. "Is there anything you can do?"

"There is a possibility I could buy you a little more time, but the treatment regimen, so to speak, is somewhat radical."

Conlon was intrigued. "When you say radical . . . ?"

"It is a procedure I have successfully completed once before but under our current limitations will be significantly more challenging than last time."

"What is it?" she asked.

"Would you like to sit down?"

"No. I'm done facing this particular demon on my knees or on my back. It wants me, it's going to find me on my feet," she replied.

"Good," the Doctor said. "The days ahead will be a struggle. But I'm glad you're prepared to fight." He paused, collecting his thoughts, then continued. "Essentially, I am proposing that we prepare a holographic matrix, transfer your consciousness into it, and place your body in a coma while I continue my efforts to repair your DNA."

"That's possible?" Conlon asked, dubious.

"As I said, it has temporarily but successfully been done once before."

"Can I review your files on the previous transfer?"

"Of course."

Conlon turned away, tried to take a few steps, but decided the room was much too small for pacing. She settled for placing her hand on the back of a chair resting near the incubator.

"How long would I have to live in a holographic body?" she finally asked.

"I don't know," the Doctor replied. "Doctor Sal's intended treatment regimen depended upon the existence of easily mutable cells to which I do not have access. I will be starting again from square one. I do have her work on Vega Nine to use as a guide, but it could take months to duplicate."

"And during that time, I would still be able to work?"

The Doctor nodded. "Yes. That is the one upside of our presence on the *Galen*. There are active holographic projectors throughout the entire ship. As long as the matrix remains stable, you would have free rein."

It was a lot to process. But one question quickly outpaced the others. "What would it . . . I mean, can you tell me how it *feels* to be a hologram?" she asked.

"I cannot tell you precisely what your experience of it would be. It would depend entirely upon the nature of the integration of your consciousness with the holomatrix. There would be obvious differences. You would no longer require rest or need to ingest nutrients, for example."

"We're going to be surviving on emergency rations for a long time, Doctor," Conlon said. "Not needing to eat is a net plus."

"Then you are open to the possibility?" the Doctor asked.

"There are no other options, right?"

"No."

"Then I'd be pretty stupid to dismiss this out of hand, wouldn't I?"

"I don't like calling my patients 'stupid,' but yes," the Doctor agreed.

"Who else would have to know about this?"

"Lieutenant Barclay is already working on the construction of the holomatrix. Lieutenant Kim was present a few days ago when the idea was initially discussed and, as you might expect, was very supportive of any available measures meant to extend your life. And I am obliged to inform our captain, Commander Glenn. But otherwise, no one, for now. It will, however, become obvious to your fellow crew members once the transfer is complete. More important, this isn't something I would suggest keeping secret. You will need a great deal of emotional support and your friends will be best able to provide that. You should prepare yourself to be as open and honest as possible."

Conlon nodded. "How soon do I have to decide?"

"We're not quite there yet. But depending upon how quickly your neurological degradation proceeds, it could reach a point where the transfer might not be possible."

Conlon inhaled deeply. "Okay," she said. "If you are asking for my permission to prepare for the transfer, you have it. Do what you need to do and let me know when you are ready."

"May I ask," the Doctor ventured, "why you are so amenable to the idea? It is a significant change, not without risk, and I would have thought you would require more time to consider it."

Conlon shrugged. "None of us have time anymore for fear-based decisions. We are incredibly vulnerable out here. Mine is no longer the only life on board that could easily be measured in weeks. I just watched a good man die trying to help us restore our communications array. To do less, to risk less than that, would make his choice meaningless."

"I understand," the Doctor said. "And thank you."

"For what?"

"For everything you have done to keep us alive and trusting me to help you keep doing it."

A shadow of a smile crossed Conlon's lips. "Don't give me too much credit. Right now, the thought of being able to attack my to-do list without needing rest is tempting. I was just trying to imagine how I would be able to do all the things that need to be done once this little one is ready to join us out here. This might be a permanent solution," she said, only half teasing.

"I wish to be clear, Lieutenant," the Doctor said. "This is a temporary measure, at best. I will work diligently to resolve your DNA's inability to repair itself. But should I fail . . ."

"I'll take as much time as you can give me, in any form."

The Doctor smiled uneasily. "Good. I'll let you know as soon as the matrix is ready."

"Do me a favor?" Conlon asked.

"If I can."

"This is my decision. I understand that it isn't meant to be a secret, but until it's done, I don't want to discuss it with anyone else. There are too many other things that require my attention. Can we keep this between us until then?"

"Of course."

10

Operations officer Lieutenant Kenth Lasren had burned through several duty shifts and cups of *raktajino* while attempting to translate the signals emitted from the Edrehmaia's vessel. But the pieces of this particular puzzle had remained a jumbled mess until he heard "the scream."

"You've heard this before?" Captain Chakotay asked.

"Yes, sir," Lasren replied. Both Chakotay and Commander Paris had moved close to his station on *Voyager*'s bridge. "When Devi, Omar, Vincent, and I were exploring the caverns we found beneath the surface, one of the chambers, the one filled with what appeared to be biological experiments with the Edrehmaia substance, well, for want of a better word, *screamed* at us before it allowed us access."

"And yet, you did not turn and run," Paris observed.

"I wanted to," Lasren admitted. "But now I'm glad we didn't. At the time, I didn't understand what was happening."

"And you do now?" Chakotay asked.

"I think so. The similarity in the sound our translator defaults to with these signals made me begin to search for commonalities in the types of data they might contain. These signals all carry dense amounts of information on their waveforms. Separating it from the photonic emissions was the first challenge. Part of the problem is the volume of information being transmitted. It is so far beyond anything we normally process that it has to be broken down into incredibly small sections before it can be translated, but given the nature of the communication, that makes sense now."

"To you. Not to us," Paris reminded him.

"The initial transmissions were damn near impossible to translate, but about three minutes after they approached us, they shifted to a considerably less complicated form. The Edrehmaia scanned us shortly after they arrived. Once they did, the signal resolved into incredibly long chains of five distinct and identifiable terms."

"Their language only has five words?" Chakotay asked.

"That's the first part of the problem. There are no words in these transmissions. The five terms I was first able to translate are molecules: adenine, cytosine, guanine, thymine, and hydrogen."

"DNA base pairs?" Paris asked.

"Perhaps they were searching for basic terms we share in common in order to begin to build a shared language," Chakotay said. "It's not that unusual and does suggest a desire to communicate with us."

"I actually believe that they were identifying both themselves and us," Lasren said.

Paris and Chakotay exchanged a confused glance.

"The terms in the first transmission I was able to decode are repeated a little over three billion times," Lasren continued. "They weren't simply sending data they expected us to be able to understand. With Doctor Sharak's permission, I ran the first transmission against the genetic profiles of the entire crew."

"Was there a match?" Paris asked.

"There was," Lasren said. "The first message they sent was Lieutenant Devi Patel's entire genome."

"That's . . . unexpected," Paris ventured.

"Maybe not," Lasren said. "She was aboard when they scanned the ship, so they could have correctly identified her presence among us. More significant, I think, is that Devi's DNA was used to grant us access to the station on DK-1116. There were numerous points that required her to place her hand on an interface, and each time, a sample of her blood was taken."

"Was there more to the message you were able to translate?" Chakotay asked.

"Yes, sir. After Devi's genome was sent in its entirety, another genome was transmitted. It included identifiable parts of her genome, along with billions of other base pairs that were different. They were included as if they were part of her genome but contained eighteen other molecules for which we have no reference. I think, although I can't be sure, that it might have been the genome of the interlocutor that was created when Devi interacted with the station's communication system."

"The interlocutor was a kind of synthetic hybrid of Devi and the Edrehmaia substance, wasn't it?" Chakotay asked.

"We believe so, sir," Lasren confirmed.

"I have questions," Paris said. "Do you believe that the message was sent to Devi? Was it directed at her because they somehow had a record of her? And if so, how in the hell did they, wherever they are, receive data that had only been entered into this planet's storage system just a few days ago?"

"If they're that close to us, long-range sensors should have detected them by now," Chakotay added.

"Not necessarily," Lasren said. "They are certainly technologically advanced enough to have some form of cloaking technology. They could be holding position next to us right now and we might not know it."

"There's another much more depressing possibility," Paris said. "If they have mastered quantum-entangled communications, they could be literally anywhere and still be monitoring any system to which they are connected in real time."

"I have to say, sir, that I believe that's the more likely option," Lasren noted.

"Why?" Chakotay asked.

"It's just a feeling, but it's based on the general level of complexity of their biology and their technology. Once I was able to translate the interlocutor's code, I used that algorithm as a basis for addressing the initial segments of the transmission again. It, too, was a series of base pairs and it contained forty-seven unique molecules, including the five that form the base of our DNA."

"So the entire transmission was essentially them introducing themselves to us and then identifying the one member of our crew on whom they have genetic data?" Chakotay summarized.

"Yes, sir."

"But nothing else?" Paris asked.

Lasren shook his head. "As languages go, this one comes with both advantages and disadvantages."

"It separates the men from the boys, that's for damn sure," Paris noted.

"Beg pardon?" Chakotay asked.

"In developmental terms," Paris clarified. "If you are not sufficiently advanced to recognize your own molecular biology, there is no way to establish communication. They're not going to bother even trying to talk to you."

"The obvious disadvantage in terms of striking up a conversation is processing power. It is incredibly cumbersome to introduce yourself and identify your target in a sentence that is billions of words long," Lasren said.

"But it is also very precise," Chakotay said. "There is a case to be made that if you were able to converse beyond these introductions and had sufficient computer processing to engage in such a discussion, there is zero margin for error."

"So, we can conclude from this transmission that the Edrehmaia are quite possibly the most pedantic species we have ever encountered," Paris said. "I'm not sure how much that helps us."

"It's a start, Tom," Chakotay said. "Send those unknown molecules to every ship in the fleet's biological science divisions and have them begin to prepare models. This is excellent work, Lieutenant. Well done."

"One thing, sir," Lasren said. "Devi mentioned that she was assigned to an away team that is going back to the surface. I wonder if that's a good idea."

"We are maintaining a transporter lock on the entire team," Chakotay said.

"Okay, but again, we are dealing with technology that we know almost nothing about other than the fact that she has been identified down to her component molecules by the Edrehmaia. They have some interest in her."

"Yeah, I see the problem," Paris said. "Should we bring her back?" he asked of Chakotay.

"I don't know that she would be any safer here than on the surface," Chakotay said. "But I will advise Commander O'Donnell at once."

"Thank you, sir," Lasren said.

"One more question," Paris said. "Let's assume for a minute that this first encounter was simply their way of introducing themselves, a ridiculously complicated way of saying, 'I am the Edrehmaia. You are Devi Patel.' How do you say anything else using the terms we know? How do you even say hello?"

"You don't, at least not yet," Lasren replied.

"There could be more to the message we haven't yet translated," Chakotay suggested.

"There isn't, but I think I know why," Lasren said.

"Why?" Chakotay asked.

"Because we didn't answer them," Lasren replied.

"You're late, Ensign," Counselor Cambridge noted as Gwyn entered his office.

"I lost track of time," Gwyn said.

"Really? Doing what?" Cambridge asked as he crossed from his desk and gestured for her to take a seat in one of the two chairs before his desk.

The truth was: nothing. With no regular duty shift to distract her, most of Gwyn's time of late had been spent in something approaching a meditative state, monitoring as best she could the continued existence of her child.

Well, not hers exactly.

"Have you ever read one of Ensign Gleez's duty logs?" she asked.

"Can't say that I have."

"I don't recommend it. I've never known anyone who can reduce the sheer joy of flying a starship to its most mundane component parts the way he can. 'Attitude adjustment .05 degrees. Helm response sluggish. Requested level-one diagnostic.' May as well leave the damn helm on autopilot for all the good he does you in the chair."

"In fairness, aren't we basically flying in circles right now, holding position above DK-1116?" Cambridge asked.

"Flying is an art, Counselor. It's communion. It's the seamless merging of mind and machine. The details matter, but there is so much more to it than that."

"You speak of it as if it's sacred."

"I guess it is. At least to me. I don't know what it is to poor Gleez."

"Do you feel ready to return to your regular duties?"

The silence that followed wore on before Gwyn said, "I suppose."

"How's your focus?" Cambridge asked. "By that I mean, how much of any given hour do you spend thinking about the baby, and how much on literally anything else."

The answer was next to none, but Gwyn didn't think that would get her back in her chair any time soon.

"A bit," she admitted. "She's still there, if that's what you're asking."

"It isn't. I am wondering how difficult you are finding it to compartmentalize the stress of separation."

"Um . . . not too difficult?"

"Are you asking me?"

"No. Not difficult. Okay, a little, but . . ."

"Are you sleeping?"

Not at all.

"A few hours here and there."

"Have you discussed your situation with any of the crew you consider friends?"

"They wouldn't understand."

"Some of them might. There are several species on board that have some measure of psionic abilities. Are you close with Lieutenant Lasren?"

"Kenth's a good guy," Gwyn admitted. "But he hasn't been around much. He's kind of glued to his station these days."

"While I understand your desire for privacy, it might help to get some insight into what has to be a very new experience for you," Cambridge suggested.

"I'll think about it."

Cambridge continued to stare at her in a way that made her feel he could read her mind. She knew he couldn't. He was human. Still, she was certain he wasn't buying what she was halfheartedly trying to sell.

"When you look at me like that, you remind me of my mother," Gwyn offered.

"When was the last time you spoke with your mother?" he asked.

Eight years ago, when I left home.

"It's been a while."

"Are you close?"

"We share some fairly profound differences of opinion when it comes to"—*everything*—"many of my life choices."

Cambridge chuckled at that. "Do you have any other Kriosian friends with whom you are in regular contact? I'm looking for anyone who might be able to offer you insight into your current predicament."

"Empathic metamorphs are segregated from the rest of society. I don't know anyone who knows one."

Except, perhaps, my leedi, Mayla Fui.

"I see."

No, I really don't think you do.

Cambridge leaned forward. "Have you ever participated in regular counseling sessions before?"

"Never needed to."

"There are limits to their efficacy, and those are set by the patient. Unless you decide that you want my help, there is very little I can do for you."

But you can't help me. No one can help me. I just need us to find her and the Galen *and then everything will be the way it is supposed to be.*

"Okay."

"Same time tomorrow, then?"

Gwyn sighed. "Sure."

SWOW (THE PLANET FORMERLY KNOWN AS DK-1116)

The first time away teams had been dispatched to the surface of this planet, Seven did not join them. She busied herself, instead, with attempting to determine how this unusual system had formed. To her utter disbelief, her models demonstrated that the most likely answer to that question was that the binary system had been formed when a rogue star had been sent careening through an existing system, destroyed several other planets in the process, and fallen into the main star's orbit. She had then left the ship to analyze the debris this event created, now organized in two asteroid belts, one surrounding the B star and one surrounding the entire system. It was during this mission within the nearer asteroid field that she had first encountered the Edrehmaia substance and nearly lost her pilot, Ensign Gwyn, in the process.

Of the three now present, Seven, Lieutenant Patel, and Commander O'Donnell, only Patel had seen one of the planet's subterranean stations up close. When the fleet had begun their explorations, all of the stations and biodomes had contained sufficient power to remain operational. One of the initial teams' advantages had been the stations' ability to regulate their atmosphere until it was suited to the precise needs of those occupying it. Patel's team had conducted their survey sans environmental suits. Seven's team was forced to perform theirs while wearing the bulky, uncomfortable

EV suits when scans showed no signs that a breathable atmosphere remained.

As soon as the team materialized at the entrance to the cavern they had designated "Station One," Seven checked her suit's oxygen levels. "We have approximately two hours to complete our initial survey," she advised the others.

"Then we'd best move quickly," O'Donnell said, his voice sounding tinny and distant when processed by her suit's comm array. *"We have a lot of ground to cover."*

Seven privately suspected that O'Donnell would have been content to keep the team working here for the rest of their lives, so determined was he to understand everything there was to learn of the Edrehmaia and the first species to experiment with their creation. She understood his fascination. Few scientific mysteries were as tempting. But she also respected the potential hazards. For the first time she wondered if anything beyond professional curiosity was driving O'Donnell.

As the entire team lit their SIMs beacons and began to examine the walls of the cavern, little more than a wide tunnel leading to a larger space barely visible ahead, O'Donnell asked, *"Anything look familiar, Lieutenant Patel?"*

"Station Four consisted of a central hub for data retrieval and analysis, a library containing detailed visual records of past experiments conducted on the surface by multiple alien species, and a smaller tunnel consisting of cells protected by force fields that held samples of biological test subjects."

"Was that where you found the interlocutor created from your DNA?" Seven asked.

"It was," Patel replied. *"There was also a vast cavern several hundred meters below where we found some of the technology controlling the biodomes and containing the raw materials used by the Edrehmaia. It was filled with the power conduits that were woven throughout the planet, composed almost entirely of the Edrehmaia substance and a number of unusual alloys."*

Lifting her tricorder to scan the walls, Patel continued, *"Many of the same minerals and metals found in the tunnels leading to Station Four are also present here."*

"I'm not picking up any power signatures," Seven noted.

"That's to be expected, isn't it?" O'Donnell asked. *"I assume Species 001 found a way to tap the planet's natural power source to sustain their stations. But all of that stored power was released a few days ago."*

"Do we believe that these caverns were natural formations, discovered and utilized by Species 001?" Seven asked.

"It's hard to know for sure," Patel replied. *"The planet itself was designed by the Edrehmaia. The larger caverns containing the conduits were probably pre-existing. But I suspect that most of this,"* she added, gesturing to the tunnel walls, *"was done by those who came later."*

The entrance tunnel where the team had materialized quickly gave way to a wide, long rectangular space where a solid floor made of a single, seamless piece of thick metal alloy was surrounded by squared-off walls embedded with nonfunctional screens and interfaces. Inches of dust covered every surface.

"This looks familiar," Commander O'Donnell said as they began to play their lights over the floor. *"We found one of these huge metal plates on the surface in the biodome we were studying a few days ago."*

"What was your analysis?" Seven asked.

"We couldn't make heads nor tails of it," O'Donnell replied. *"It was too big to have been transported to its position and didn't appear to have been constructed of smaller pieces."*

"Did you consider the possibility that smaller sections had grown together over time, eliminating any seams?" Patel asked.

"Given that it was metal, no," O'Donnell replied. *"But knowing what we do now about the Edrehmaia substance, we probably should have. I wish you'd been with us, Lieutenant."*

They continued forward until they reached a single transparent column centered on the floor, extending ten meters high, where it disappeared into the rough, rocky roof of the cavern.

"Huh," Patel grunted as she began playing her light along the walls on both sides of the column.

"Something you'd like to share, Lieutenant?" Seven asked.

"Station Four contained a similar structure, but it was activated by sensors and wasn't solid," she replied. *"I wonder . . . "* she continued as she approached the column and placed a hand on its surface.

"Careful," O'Donnell said too late as Patel's hand moved through the column, forcing her to catch herself before she tumbled to the floor.

Seven immediately raised her tricorder. Its unhelpful report on the column's composition was *"Unknown alloy. Atomic structure does not correspond to database records."*

Patel stepped back and again began to search the walls. Finally, she seemed to find what she was seeking, a small alcove five meters overhead, embedded in the wall across from the column. An extremely faint light emanated from a sphere embedded in the alcove.

"What is that?" O'Donnell asked.

"I believe it is a data storage device," Patel replied. *"There were dozens of these at the other station. Each one contained the records of the experiments of a single species and could be analyzed in detail within the station's library. But in order to retrieve them, you had to access the column of light."*

"Perhaps this is an earlier prototype of the same technology," Seven suggested.

"That's my thought as well," Patel agreed. *"I'm going to try something."* Steadying herself, Patel faced the column, then stepped inside. Cascades of faint light ran up and down the column once she was within it.

"Hello there," she said as she began to move her hands over the edges of the column. *"The interface appears to be operational. Let me see if I can find the appropriate designation."*

Seven again lifted her tricorder, this time searching for the power source activating the data interface. The only readings present came from the column itself.

"At least we know some of it still works," O'Donnell said. *"That's good news."*

"I would feel better if we understood why it was still working," Seven noted.

"Heads up," Patel warned as the sphere in the wall grew suddenly brighter and ejected from the alcove, flying directly toward Patel's hands. She caught it and exited the column. Roughly the size of a grapefruit, its black surface was mottled with lighter patches that now blazed with a greenish hue.

"Shall we see if they also have a library interface?" she asked cheerily, holding the small sphere before her.

"Yes, please," O'Donnell replied, stepping closer to study the sphere.

As Seven joined them, a tingling at the back of her neck raised the fine hairs there. She felt her head tilt slightly to the right as she searched for what felt like a memory. "There is something familiar about this device."

"How so?" Patel asked.

"Species 419, a humanoid-crustacean hybrid, regularly stored their genealogical records in something similar."

"So, of course, you assimilated them," O'Donnell said.

"*I* didn't," Seven said, a little testily. "Their entire planet was assimilated more than a thousand years prior to my joining the Collective. But we did retain knowledge of their technology."

"Crustaceans?" Patel asked.

"Once their exoskeletons were removed, they made excellent drones," Seven said.

"But when you think about that now . . . ?" Patel began.

"I prefer not to," Seven said, ending the discussion.

The team continued forward into the darkness, but apart from several low, rectangular metal-stone hybrid formations that appeared to be randomly placed on the floor, nothing else looked familiar to Patel.

"If the sphere contains data on Species 001, we might be able to use our own computers to access it," Seven suggested.

"We're definitely taking that back with us," O'Donnell agreed. *"I'm not getting any readings consistent with the Edrehmaia substance."*

"Confirming what our ship's sensors showed. It is also possible that Species 001 did not experiment with it in this location," Seven suggested.

"Let's not give up just yet," O'Donnell said. *"Watch your step here,"* he added as the floor began to slope downward. They had covered another fifteen meters when they realized they had descended into an oval depression. From here, the floor sloped upward again. It was as if they had suddenly found themselves at the bottom of an empty pool.

"Anyone else wondering who put this here and why?" O'Donnell asked.

Seven searched the surrounding area until she found the answer. "Over here," she said, moving forward.

Metallic debris littered the floor. Along the "walls" of the pool in two distinct areas opposite each other, roughly circular burns approximately two meters in diameter were visible.

"This chemical reaction happened very recently," O'Donnell noted.

Seven knelt to collect a piece of the debris, but Patel's voice halted her.

"Don't touch that," she warned as she scanned the surface with her tricorder.

"We should collect some for analysis," Seven said.

"I believe this was a test pool for their circuit-breaking technology," Patel said. *"This formation is covered with a fine coat of silicon, similar to what was used on the surface pools. There was water here at some point, but it has obviously evaporated. When it did, the two sections of conduit that had been divided by the pool forced their way through and connected to each other. All of the conduits contained the Edrehmaia substance, particles of* Sevenofninonium, *and other trace metals. I think this is what was left once the conduits released their stored power."*

Although Seven chaffed at the use of the fleet's initial designation for an isotope of the Edrehmaia substance, she let Patel's comment pass.

"Hang on a second," O'Donnell said as he knelt to examine the fragments with his tricorder. After a moment, he removed his phaser, targeted one of the larger fragments, and fired. The alloy began to glow, a bright, angry orangish-red color, but did not dematerialize.

"I think you got it," Seven said dryly.

O'Donnell ceased firing, then trained his light and tricorder on the fragment. After a few moments, the metal, which had been softened by the beam, began to morph gently into a defined square.

"It shouldn't be doing that, right?" O'Donnell asked.

"Step away from it," Seven said.

"I've got a better idea," O'Donnell said, removing a containment pod from his rucksack. He tapped his communicator. *"Atlee, are you there?"*

"Go ahead, Commander. I read you clearly."

"Can you get a sensor lock on a fragment of metal near my position that was just exposed to phaser fire?"

"A moment, please. Aye, sir. I've got it."

"I want you to try and transport it into the containment pod I am placing right next to it."

"Understood. Stand by."

Seven watched as the fragment dematerialized. When it had rematerialized within the containment pod, it did so as a liquid mass of metal. The liquid moved up the sides of the pod before solidifying.

"Now, I think we got it, Seven," O'Donnell said. *"Atlee, you still there?"*

"Aye, Commander."

"Erect a level-ten force field in my lab at workstation beta and transport this pod directly into it. Have a security team standing by and if anything unexpected happens, disengage transporters. Understood?"

"Can you define 'unexpected'?" Fife asked.

"Anything that appears to endanger you or the ship. I trust your instincts, Commander."

It took a few moments for Fife to comply with O'Donnell's orders. When the canister dematerialized, a weighted silence hung between the members of the away team. Finally, Fife's voice sounded over the comm. *"Transport complete, sir. Eighty-two point six one eight percent of the targeted mass came through. The rest was rejected by the ship's biofilters. Will that be sufficient?"*

Dejected, O'Donnell replied, *"It'll have to do for now. Thank you, Atlee."*

This much accomplished, the team ascended the far side of the pool and continued forward until they reached the edge of the solid metal platform that ran the length of the station. Where it terminated, the cavern once again took on a more natural, rough-hewn shape, the walls and ceiling curving around what appeared to be a flat, solid transparent wall. Behind it, a dense fog seemed to rest over whatever lay beyond it. Light bounced back when it was illuminated, revealing nothing.

Patel was the first to find another transparent column in the corner to the right of the wall. It, too, was filled with the odd white fog. Beside it, there was a circular indentation in the wall. She began to dig with her fingers and loose rock and dirt fell easily from it.

"Help me," she said.

O'Donnell reached her and quickly aided her in unearthing the feature's intended shape—another alcove.

Seven could not see Patel's smile of accomplishment through her helmet, but she could hear it in the lieutenant's voice as she said, *"This is the data interface. Watch the column,"* she added as she gently deposited the sphere into its new home.

Seconds later, the fog within the column began to swirl, resolving itself into an unsettling image.

The figure was a female humanoid, standing a little over two meters tall. Both of her legs had been amputated at the knee, as had her right arm, just below the shoulder. In place of her former limbs, braided metallic prosthetics were present. The hand contained five fingers that did not appear to have articulated joints.

Her torso, chest, and face had been surgically altered. Wide scars marred her pale flesh, centered by an inky black line, as if she had been sewn up with black thread. The flesh at the edges of the scars retained a reddish color, perhaps somehow still infected. The most prominent scar was a single line running from her forehead over what had been her right eye, down to the middle of her cheek. The left eye was open, the iris solid black. A series of small folds circled the underside of the eye, the only clue to part of her former alien identity.

A sharp burst of adrenaline activated Seven's fight-or-flight response. Her mouth was suddenly parched and her heart raced with light, irregular palpitations.

Patel was the first to speak.

"I think this was Species 001," she said.

That's not possible, Seven thought.

O'Donnell stepped to within a few feet of the column and studied the image within it. After a moment, he turned to Patel. *"Is there more?"* he asked.

"The library records in Station Four had a similar design. There were controls present that allowed you to view all of the data collected by an individual species. But I don't see anything that looks like the activation panel we used," Patel replied.

No, stop, Seven thought, but was unable to find her voice.

The fog behind the wall was now beginning to swirl as well. When it cleared, it revealed a vast, rocky plain of dark-red earth and jet-black rocks beneath a night sky. High above, distant stars cast the faintest of illumination on the scene.

A high-pitched tone sounded all around them, followed by a series of clicks and scratches. Seven felt suddenly light-headed as sweat began to pour down her face. She knew that sound well, a long-banished nightmare.

The scene began to move, as if the viewer were now walking through the barren landscape. A slow turn to the left, then the right, revealed nothing dissimilar as far as the eye could see.

Another series of mechanized grunts and rapid clicks echoed over the plain.

One of two, primary adjunct to submatrix six three nine assessing, Seven translated automatically.

"What are we looking at, Devi?" O'Donnell asked.

"I can't say for sure, but I would be willing to bet that this was the first recorded moments of Species 001 setting foot on the planet," she replied.

A quick overlay of unfamiliar symbols suddenly filled the scene, much like the data scrolling over Seven's faceplate.

Suddenly, a series of quick, loud lower tones, reminiscent of an alarm klaxon, began.

Two of two under attack. Assess and repair, assess and repair, Seven heard with absolute clarity.

The view shifted with disorienting jumps, the movement no longer steady and assured. It came to rest on a figure kneeling on the ground.

"What the . . . ?" Patel said.

The figure was clothed in black from the neck down. Black tubules were wound around its torso. Its head was covered with a black helmet, broken around a single eye, as well as the nose and mouth, revealing sickly, pale green flesh.

More jumpy motion as the individual recording this encounter moved quickly toward the kneeling figure. It appeared to have touched one of the black rocks and where it did, the rock had become liquid, running up its arm.

It tried to pull away, and then made the mistake of attempting to remove the viscous fluid with its other arm. Unfortunately, that arm did not terminate in a hand. Instead, it ended in a pair of black pincers. Seven watched, nauseated, as the victim attempted to sever its arm at the shoulder, but the fluid moved much too quickly for that.

Its face turned now toward the viewer, the victim's agonized screams could be assumed, but not heard, except as the constant alarm klaxon. Seven heard the warning shift to a new command— *termination indicated.*

Another arm was raised, now by the viewer, and from the mechanical appendage at its end, a bright green beam of light struck the victim's arm. This had the effect of slowing but not stopping the fluid's motion.

The view then shifted down to the ground. More bright flashes of warning visible only to the viewer as it realized it was standing in a pool of the liquid. Soon, it, too, began to be consumed.

Seven stumbled toward the alcove and grasped the sphere with both hands.

"*Seven?*" Patel said urgently, moving toward her, even as O'Donnell remained transfixed by the horrors still unfolding on the planet's surface thousands of years ago.

"No," Seven said as she removed it from its place, tossing it onto the deck, where it rolled a few meters before coming to rest. The scene on the wall and the figure in the column abruptly vanished. Only once they were gone did Seven allow her feet to give up supporting her, opting to rest on her knees instead.

No, no, no, no, she repeated to herself.

The next thing she knew, Patel and O'Donnell had come to rest beside her, urgently peering into her helmet.

"*We should get her back to the ship immediately,*" Patel was saying.

"*Give her a minute,*" O'Donnell said. "*It's okay, Seven. Just breathe. They're gone. They're not here anymore. Those were nothing but ghosts.*"

"Species 001," Seven began, unable to take a full breath.

"*I know,*" he said. "*It's amazing, isn't it? I'm actually surprised it didn't occur to any of us until now—Species this and species that.*"

"*Species 001 was . . .*" Patel said, but she, too, trailed off.

"*Was the Borg, yes,*" O'Donnell confirmed.

VESTA

Admiral Kathryn Janeway hadn't willingly donned an EV suit in years. But *this* she might just have to see in person.

When she had first accepted command of the Full Circle Fleet, she had received a briefing on the Borg invasion of the Alpha Quadrant and the subsequent actions of the Caeliar, the species that had unwittingly spawned and eventually absorbed the Collective into its gestalt. Once this had been complete, the Caeliar, now substantially larger than it had been before, departed the galaxy for parts unknown. The overriding mission statement of Janeway's fleet was to confirm that the Caeliar had spoken the truth and that they and the Borg were no longer present in the Milky Way Galaxy.

What Commander O'Donnell's team had discovered beneath the surface of DK-1116 was evidence that humanity's understanding of the Borg and its history remained woefully inadequate.

O'Donnell seemed to be no worse for wear a few hours after his away mission, but Seven sat stony and silent at the end of the briefing room's table beside Patel, who was equally staid. Captains Chakotay and Farkas, along with Counselor Cambridge, completed the group. Cambridge glanced toward Seven regularly, his concern obvious.

"It makes perfect sense," O'Donnell said, once he and Patel had completed their initial report. "We've always known this was once Borg space. They did find the planet and they did try to assimilate it. But they failed."

"The question is, Commander, what happened next?" Janeway said. "One of the most comforting things about the Borg was their somewhat binary world view. Anything they encountered was either added to their perfection through assimilation or destroyed. Either way, it ceased to exist."

"There must have been other options," Cambridge said. "We do know that they ignored species they believed unworthy of assimilation."

"Yes, I've read the logs about the Indign," Janeway said. "What I have never imagined is a version of the Borg that was capable of any other way of interacting with the universe. If you are right and Species 001 *was the Borg*, why didn't they simply abandon what they could not assimilate? The biodomes, the stations and their libraries, none of this resembles the Borg we know in any way."

"But these were ancient Borg, weren't they?" Farkas asked. "How do we know they didn't evolve into the form we came to know? Perhaps in their youth, they were a little more open to experimentation."

"Although these were not the Borg of our time," Seven finally said, "they were not that different. Their language, for example, was identifiable."

Both Patel and O'Donnell turned to stare openmouthed at Seven.

"What language?" O'Donnell asked.

"You have never heard the voice of the Collective when it wasn't processed through your universal translators," Seven said, staring straight ahead, her eyes haunted. "I have. Just not for a long time. It was disorienting."

"What were they saying?" Janeway asked gently.

"It was a standard assessment directive. Two Borg were dispatched to the surface to test the planet's viability for assimilation. Even in its untouched state prior to the erection of the biodomes, there are many elements and minerals present that would have been valued by the Borg."

"They obviously encountered some of the Edrehmaia substance on the surface," Patel said.

"And it didn't kill them?" Chakotay asked.

"It looked to me like the Edrehmaia substance did to the Borg exactly what the Borg usually do to their victims. It added *their* distinctiveness to its own," O'Donnell replied.

"You're saying the Borg you saw were transformed by the substance?" Farkas asked.

"Clearly they survived," Patel said. "There was evidence in the image of Species 001 that its Borg implants had been replaced by new prosthetics and their other wounds healed."

"Prosthetics that did resemble some of the larger formations we later found on the surface," O'Donnell noted.

"Whatever happened to them was beyond the Collective's ability to process," Seven said. "Undoubtedly, this dyad was severed from the rest of the Borg once they were attacked and the Edrehmaia substance was likely classified as something that could not be assimilated."

"So, two former Borg, this world's Adam and Eve, constructed everything we found?" Janeway asked. The notion was both fascinating and somehow impossible to imagine.

"I have trouble believing that any biological entity could survive contact with the Edrehmaia substance and remain intact," Patel offered. "I saw some of the attempts in Station Four. They were monstrosities that appeared to have been cobbled together at the genetic level."

"Those *monstrosities*, as you call them, were early attempts to create the interlocutors for those other species," O'Donnell suggested.

"How do you know that?" Patel demanded.

"You really need to read the logs your team discovered at Station Four," O'Donnell replied. "All of the species that came here engaged in biological as well as technological experiments."

"It does seem clear that the Borg who were sent to assess this planet did survive their contact with the Edrehmaia substance," Cambridge said. "Hell, they did better than that. Based upon what was left behind, one might even say that they thrived in their new state."

"But they didn't know what they had become," Patel said. "My interlocutor said that the purpose of the system, of Species 001, was the evaluation and propagation of the Edrehmaia. The former Borg clearly created some prototypes of the library technology that would eventually be replicated elsewhere below the surface. They might have simply been trying to figure out what had happened to them, and part of that was maintaining a scrupulous record of their work."

"What we found, the biodomes, the library, the experiments both on the surface and beneath, could have been the work of the species that came later, building upon what the Borg started, attempting to re-create it and unlock the potential of the Edrehmaia,"

O'Donnell said. "It could have been a collective effort, just not the kind the Borg are accustomed to."

"Or perhaps, the drones retained enough memories of their time with the Borg that they defaulted to working collectively with others," Seven suggested, "even in the absence of a neural link."

Farkas raised her hand from the far end of the table. Janeway looked up, bit back a smile, and said, "Something to add, Captain?"

"Fascinating as all of this is, I am just wondering what good it does us to keep poking around here. We have learned that certain individual Borg were capable of evolution, something that anyone who has met Seven would have no trouble believing. There seems to be no further evidence of Edrehmaia activity or the substance that has done so much to alter this corner of the quadrant, and nothing that might point us in the direction of our lost ship, if, as Lieutenant Bryce and Ensign Icheb believe, it was transported rather than destroyed. I love a good science project as much as the next girl, but where does this leave us?"

Janeway sat back, considering the question as well as the various priorities of those with whom she led this fleet. Farkas had been ready to cut and run within hours of arriving on the surface of the planet. O'Donnell's heels were firmly dug into scientific possibilities inherent in the Edrehmaia's technology, and Chakotay would set course this instant if he had any idea where the *Galen* might be found, heedless of the dangers inherent in any future confrontation.

Both Patel and Seven seemed troubled, in very different ways, by their discoveries. In Seven's case, it wasn't difficult to understand. However briefly, she had once again been touched by the species that had stripped her individuality from her, a species all of them had hoped they would never encounter again in any form. But the admiral didn't know Patel all that well, beyond her recent choice to sacrifice herself rather than the secrets the planet contained. Her connection to this world was, if anything, the most personal of anyone's present.

"Lieutenant Patel," Janeway said, "your first survey of the planet contained the most detailed information we have of both the Edrehmaia and those who came later to exploit their technology. Does this discovery change your perceptions in any meaningful way?"

Patel sat incredibly still, perhaps not terribly comfortable at finding herself the center of the room's attention. It was a sensation with which Janeway could relate. Many times as a junior officer, when called upon by those well above her in the chain of command, she had known both the excitement of feeling *heard* as well as awareness of the immense responsibility conferred upon her by the company in which she found herself. In their initial briefing, just following the attack, it seemed to Janeway that Patel had begun to find her voice. She had no difficulty speaking her mind when she commanded the subject matter. But now, something seemed to be holding her back.

"You should speak freely," Janeway added gently. "I am genuinely curious."

Patel turned to Seven. "What happened to those drones, is that the same thing that happened to Gwyn on the asteroid you were studying?"

"It was," Seven replied. "Although the substance did not touch her body. It had barely breached her suit when I fired on it."

Patel nodded, clearly dismayed. She then turned to O'Donnell. "I think our assumption that Species 001 was somehow the key to this world might have been a mistake. They were, in that what happened to them set off a scientific chain reaction, but when I looked at this planet before, I saw a miracle, an enormous leap forward in living technology handed down by a superior race, left for those who came after to integrate and build upon. I never really considered why it had been abandoned."

"Devi?" O'Donnell asked.

"Almost two hundred species invested an incredible amount of time and expertise in this world. Because we proceed, as a species and a Federation of worlds, in curiosity, in the pursuit of knowledge for its own sake, I think I unconsciously assigned the same values to those who were here before us."

"And now?" O'Donnell asked.

"Imagine living in the Delta Quadrant four thousand years ago. No matter how far your civilization has advanced, there is a Borg-shaped specter hanging over you. At any moment they might appear and lay waste to everything you have accomplished. That was the reality of the lives of countless beings within a thousand light-years of Borg space. The Edrehmaia could defeat the Borg with a touch. A substance they created, or for all we know is simply a product of their own biology, was, perhaps, the only viable weapon these people ever discovered that might end the threat posed by the Borg. No wonder they came here, built and maintained all of this. Fear brought them together and sustained their efforts. I wonder now if they abandoned it because they realized that no effort to domesti-cate the Edrehmaia's technology would succeed and went looking for other ways to attempt to conquer their fear."

"Depressing, but plausible," Cambridge said. "And for what it's worth, Admiral, I am inclined to agree with the lieutenant's assess-ment. Placed in that context, the existence of this inexplicable world suddenly becomes quite, well, *explicable*."

"I don't give a damn *why* a hundred ninety-six other species came here," O'Donnell said. "And I don't care why they left. The pursuit itself had value. They weren't wrong to explore the potentials of what the Edrehmaia left behind, and we would be foolish not to as well. Whatever they are, the Edrehmaia are evolutionarily beyond anything we have ever encountered, short of the Caeliar. They have lit a path we must walk if we are ever to hope to join them in what-ever their version of 'the great work' might be."

"Forgive me, Commander, but I didn't realize grappling with gods, or transcending our current state of being, was our purpose here," Cambridge noted.

"One does not grapple with gods," Chakotay said softly. "One traditionally prostrates themselves before them in supplication."

"Chakotay?" Janeway asked.

"If there were a way to continue to safely experiment with the Edrehmaia substance, to unlock its unusual atomic state and genetic possibilities, I would never suggest we ignore it. But that's not the only pressing issue before us. You have said, Admiral, that before we face the Edrehmaia again, we must understand them better. Species capable of building those biodomes and the power systems required to sustain them were clearly at or beyond Starfleet's current level of technological expertise. And they left this place intact. I don't know if they chose to leave or were chased away, but they didn't dismantle their work. Presumably, they could have. I'm starting to think that they wanted others to follow in their footsteps. I like to imagine that they felt what Commander O'Donnell feels when he looks at a substance capable of rewriting genetic code that has been evolving for billions of years. Perhaps they were ultimately humbled in the face of it. They might even have learned to integrate small portions of what they found into their own technology. But in the end, *that work* did not attract the attention of the Edrehmaia."

"No, *we* did that," Janeway said. "And only because we broke the containment artificially imposed on their technology and allowed it to fulfill its true purpose."

"Our progress in translating the Edrehmaia's communication suggests that they are capable of monitoring their work in real time. They came here within hours of the planet's activation and the freeing of that star," Chakotay continued.

"Quantum entanglement?" Janeway asked.

"Definitely a possibility," Chakotay replied.

"If they transported an entire vessel to places unknown, very little is beyond them," Farkas added.

"It also could indicate a certain amount of curiosity on their part," Janeway said. "They didn't come here and simply destroy us for meddling with their technology. For all we know, they didn't care what anyone was doing with their creation in the least. Our machinations, and those of the other species who came here, might not concern them at all. But when they arrived to, perhaps, check the progress of the star they brought here, and found us, they chose the smallest vessel with the fewest life-forms aboard, and took it away."

"For analysis?" Cambridge asked.

Janeway shrugged. "Maybe they detected something about us that attracted their interest."

"So, you're counseling prayer, Captain?" Farkas asked of Chakotay. "You believe if we supplicate ourselves, or find an acceptable offering, they might deign to give us our ship back?"

Chakotay shook his head. "We pose no threat to them. If they have taken our ship and analyzed it, they know that by now. And space is simply too big for a hard-target search. We need to reach them again, somehow, to establish communication. And for that, we need to find an example of their technology that is intact, like the planet was, and either use it, or break it. But this time, when they come back and try to speak with us, we need to be ready to answer them."

11

GALEN

PERSONAL LOG: LIEUTENANT HARRY KIM

Hey there. It's me again. Your dad.

Things are definitely looking up since the last time we talked. Your mom fixed the fusion reactor. Main power to most systems has been fully restored. You don't know what that means yet, but trust me, it's good news.

I've spent the last eighteen hours or so trying to solve a problem. It's kind of a math problem and, also, kind of art. You should definitely do both, okay? Math is one of those things you just have to have. At first it might seem hard, but once you get . . .

Holy shit, what was that?

Sorry. I was just sitting here recording this log and I heard, plain as day, this skittering sound, like a small animal, maybe a dog, and the sound it makes when its little nails tap the floor. When the floor isn't covered with synthetic fiber. When it's solid, like our deck plates. I used to have a dog. I called him Trout. I don't remember why. He was really my mom's dog. Followed her everywhere. Jumped in her lap any time she sat down. He liked playing with me, but he loved her. Dogs can be like that.

There are no dogs on this ship. I don't know what that sound was. I'm going to add it to my report tonight just in case ghost dogs are about to become a thing around here.

I wonder if you're going to want a pet. Dogs are great. Tough on starships, but not impossible. Not that you'll be living on a starship. I mean, maybe you will.

Sorry, my mind is wandering. I'm pretty tired.

But math. Art. Sometimes, especially with music, they're the same thing. Both are about solutions and how you get to them. Sometimes in math it's simple. One plus one is always two. Sometimes, like now, you know there is a solution but you just can't see it. That's when art helps. Art happens in the intuitive part of your brain. And spirit. We'll talk at some point about what that is. Not everyone believes in them. I do. I always have. Because I feel mine when I do things like play music. It's almost like it takes over and does the playing for me. It's cool. Trust me.

But this math problem is a little bigger. Very long story short, your body is made up of cells and the nature of those cells is determined by something called DNA. Your DNA came from your mom and me. You got half of each of us. But whether you will look more like me or her or love the same foods or want a dog isn't necessarily half me and half your mom. DNA blends in people in very interesting ways. You never quite know what you're going to get.

There are molecules . . . groups of atoms that determine what a thing is by how they combine . . . that are sometimes present in cellular DNA that are different from your mom's and mine. We're human, so our DNA is made up of four types of molecules connected by hydrogen atoms. Other species have different DNA but most of them use the same basic molecules in different combinations. A few rare ones use some additional molecules and those life-forms don't tend to look anything like you or me.

Okay, that was definitely a dog walking across the floor. Or my ears are hallucinating. Maybe I shouldn't rule anything out just yet. Impossible stuff tends to happen out here more often than you'd think.

Did you hear that? Right, no ears yet. Sorry. Never mind.

One of the things your mom and I like to do is travel around space in a starship so we can meet new people. New species. Usually it's great. Sometimes it's scary. But the whole thing with new people, aliens or not, is that you can't go in just looking at the ways you are different and decide you'll never get along. You have to look for the ways you are the same. They can be hard to find but they are almost always there. And once you find a little common ground, that's how you get to know each other better.

We just discovered a new alien species. We haven't been able to say hello yet, but they're out there, not far from our ship, and they have *already sent us some messages. The problem is that the messages don't tell me anything about who they are or what they want. They just tell me what their DNA contains. I know this because they've also clearly scanned us and have transmitted to us a complete record of the DNA of every person who is on this ship. Their DNA isn't exactly like ours, so it's impossible for me to tell how many of them are out there trying to introduce themselves. There's a chance it's only one. Could be a few hundred. Without knowing how their DNA works, it's hard to tell.*

But the important thing is that they have tried to identify themselves to us. And they are telling us that they understand something about who we are too, at least our DNA. It feels like they want to communicate with us, to get to know us better. I certainly want to know them better. For lots of reasons. The most important is that they brought us to a place that is very far away from the rest of our ships, and I am hoping that if we can find a way to work together, maybe we can get back to our friends more quickly.

But the desire to communicate isn't enough. That's where the math and art come in. The math is about finding common terms, words we both use that when strung together create meaning. The art part comes in when you are interpreting the meaning. Even if you speak the same language, sometimes meaning isn't clear. Experience helps us get to the meaning behind the words. But we only have a few words so far in this language we are trying to use and frankly, none of them are any good at conveying meaning.

So what do we do?

I really wish I knew.

We know they understand biology from a chemical perspective. We have certain molecules in common. Which means we also share an understanding of the mathematical concepts that underpin the physical universe. But how do you go from there to a language that can communicate more than those concepts? There is no math problem that can solve for love, for hunger, for laughter, for why? Even if they could give us the specifications for the technology they used to drag us across the quadrant, how do we ask them why they did it? How do we ask them who they are

*beyond the basic molecules that make up their anatomy? What does it
even mean to ask who are you?*

"*Lieutenant Kim, please report to the bridge immediately.*"

"Acknowledged. I'll be right there, Captain."

I have to go. I love you, little pea. I'll be back as soon as I can.

Commander Clarissa Glenn had spent the last several days
anticipating her first view of the Edrehmaia. Curiosity was part of
it. So was anger. Both needed to be set aside, and she knew it. The
past was the past. There was no changing it. She needed to proceed
forward now focused on the present moment, mindful of her fears
without allowing them to define her options.

Thus far, the only description reported was that they moved
through space in rectangular shapes, four meters high by two wide,
that transmitted messages encoded on the full spectrum of visible
and invisible light. Whether or not those "shapes" were vessels or the
aliens themselves was unclear. The photonic emissions had recently
been translated by Lieutenant Kim and Ensign Drur as identification messages: not everything she had hoped for, but a much better
start than opening fire. The longer they went without attacking, the
more cause Glenn had to hope that there were reasons for their actions, even if they were not presently understood.

It was good to be back on her bridge. It felt normal in a universe
where nothing was normal. It also felt right. Her fears that Lieutenant Kim might be in the process of a slow-motion coup attempt had
been entirely unfounded. He reported to her of their progress several times daily and cheerfully accepted her orders. If anything, he
seemed somewhat relieved to have her back in command. It was interesting to her that the moment Ensign Selah had reported unusual
sensor activity, Kim was the first person Glenn wanted by her side.

"The contact has now shifted to section B-17," Selah noted.

The "contact," whatever it was, had simply appeared suddenly
on their sensors, apparently moving across the ship's hull. Visual

confirmation was difficult to obtain because, unlike its predecessors, this one did not emit any light as it did whatever work it had come to do. It did, however, make a disconcerting scratching noise as it moved over the hull.

When Kim stepped off the turbolift—finally once again fully operational—he crossed immediately to stand beside Glenn. The bridge only held a single command chair. It had never seemed odd to her before, but Glenn suddenly found herself wishing she could offer Kim a seat beside her.

"Captain," he greeted her.

"We have a visitor," she said.

Kim paused as the scratching sound returned. "Not a dog, then."

"What?" Glenn asked.

"Nothing," Kim replied. "Is it just the one?"

"Sensors say yes, but we can't get absolute visual confirmation."

"Did you raise shields?" was Kim's next question.

Glenn shook her head. "I didn't want to do anything that might seem provocative," she replied. "For now, I am content to assume the best of these creatures, all evidence to the contrary."

Kim nodded, a tight smile communicating that he knew how much it had cost her to follow his lead. "I really hope I'm not wrong about that," he said under his breath.

"Now you tell me?" she teased gently.

"Has it said anything?"

At this, Drur piped up. "No, sir. No photonic emissions detected."

"What the hell is it doing?" Kim asked.

Ensign Selah turned from her science station and said, "Would you take a look at this, Lieutenant?"

"Sure," Kim said, moving toward her station. As soon as he saw the sensor feed of the points of contact, a puzzle piece clicked into place. "It's checking the patches, isn't it?"

"I think so," Selah replied. "It looks like the patch covering B-17 has increased in volume by a few hundred thousand cubic centimeters."

"You're talking about the unusual substance found on the hull?" Glenn asked. "The one Velth went to investigate?"

"Yep," Kim said. "We haven't confirmed it with another EV mission for obvious reasons, but we have been monitoring the patches using sensors and taking internal readings. They appear to be repairing hull fractures."

"Not just stabilizing them?"

"No, Captain. And I can't tell you how they are performing this miracle."

"Given what we saw on DK-1116, I'd say it's well within their capabilities," Glenn said. "So, what does this tell us about our new friends? Everyone, feel free to offer hypotheses."

"If nothing else, it suggests that the Edrehmaia were the ones who put the patches in place," Selah said.

"I'd go a little further than that," Glenn said. "It also might indicate an ongoing concern for our continued survival."

Kim crossed to Drur. "Hey, Mike, how are you doing?"

Mike? Glenn thought. When she saw the ensign's shoulders straighten a little and his almost buoyant "Hi, Harry" in response, she decided something had changed for the young operations ensign who rarely said more than a few sentences per duty shift, despite her best efforts over the last year to draw him out of his shell. *Well done, Mister Kim.*

The scratching sound came again as Kim said, "Have you made any progress adapting the comm array to respond to the Edrehmaia?"

"We can match the invisible spectrum emissions through the deflector array, but I had to isolate a third of our running lights to emit the visible signals," Drur replied.

Kim smiled broadly. "That's excellent. I think we should give it a try, don't you?"

"Mister Kim?" Glenn said.

"Sorry, Captain. Once we figured out how the aliens were communicating with us, I asked Drur to find a way to use our systems to respond as closely as we could in their language."

"And you're ready to try and speak to them?"

"It's worth a shot," Kim replied.

"What exactly are you planning to say?"

"I thought I might just try to say, 'Hello, I'm Harry Kim.'"

Glenn sat back in her chair. "Okay. Sounds harmless enough."

"I've broken down our genomes into discrete packets of data," Drur said.

"Great. Transmit mine, then list all subspace frequencies using their numerical bases. Once that's done, transmit my name in Federation Standard across all bands."

"Do we even know if they are monitoring subspace?" Glenn asked.

"We don't, but if they aren't, this is going to be a very short conversation," Kim replied. "We only have a few terms of their 'language' to work with. We're going to have to expand that by teaching them ours to establish communication with them. I'm hoping they will recognize our normal comm frequencies."

"Well, what are you waiting for, Ensign Drur?" Glenn asked with a smile.

"Ready?" Kim asked of Drur.

"Transmitting now," the ensign replied.

The only response to the initial transmission was that the sound of the alien moving across their hull ceased. After a few more moments, Kim said, "Send it again."

Drur did as he had been ordered.

"Sirs, sensors are tracking movement," Selah noted.

"Where is it going?" Glenn demanded.

The answer came seconds later as the main viewscreen suddenly lit up with a barrage of flashing lights. Both Kim and Drur studied the ops console as it translated the response.

"The alien has dislodged itself from the hull and is holding position directly ahead approximately a hundred kilometers from the ship," Selah reported.

"Do we have any idea what it's saying?" Glenn asked when no immediate response seemed to be forthcoming.

Kim shook his head. "It's a transmission we have received before. It appears to be part of the alien genome."

"But that could be significant, sir," Drur said. "This is the first contact we have had with a single Edrehmaia. This could be its individual genome."

"Any response on subspace?" Kim asked.

"No, sir," Drur replied, clearly unhappy with that result.

Kim thought for a moment. "Now send the captain's genome, followed by her name," Kim suggested.

Drur did and the same light show was repeated seconds later.

"Same transmission, sir."

"Okay, at least we have its attention," Kim said.

"So how do we take the next step?" Glenn asked. "All we are doing now is sharing information we both already know."

Kim began to pace the bridge. "The key to communication is a common language. With the Protectors, we were eventually able to create a language consisting of our sensor logs. They used images from our own experience to convey their thoughts and feelings. It wasn't an exact science, but it did the job well enough. I wonder what Doctor Sharak would make of this," he added.

"Why Sharak?" Glenn asked, intrigued.

"He was the first to make the connection between the data purges and the Protectors. Given that his language is metaphoric, it wasn't as much of a conceptual leap as it would have been for any of us."

"Okay, so what would we say is the basis for the Edrehmaia's language?" Glenn asked.

"Genetics," Selah suggested.

"Chemistry," Kim offered.

"Math," Drur said.

Glenn nodded. "Is it possible for you to translate our entire scientific database into their language and transmit it?" she asked.

Drur shrugged. "The algorithm is the same."

"It's worth a try," Kim said. "We need to add a few more words to our language."

"Do it, Ensign," Glenn ordered.

As he did so, Kim said, "I wonder if they will respond in kind."

"Can our translation matrix handle that much data?" Glenn asked.

"I doubt it."

"Let's not decide the worst will happen before it does," Glenn suggested.

"Transmission sent," Drur confirmed from ops.

"Given the sheer tonnage of data we're sending, it might be . . ." Glenn said, but as she did, a single flash of white light emanated from the Edrehmaia.

"Captain, in addition to the standard emission, I am receiving a response on all subspace bands."

"What is it?" Kim asked before Glenn had the chance.

"Two words, sir. DEFINE SET."

Glenn and Kim exchanged a puzzled glance.

"What does that mean?" Glenn asked.

"It could mean a lot of things," Kim replied. "But let's go with the most obvious. Drur, respond with each of our crew members' genomes and names."

"Shouldn't we include our standard friendship greeting?" Glenn asked.

"As soon as you can give me the mathematical equivalent of 'we come in peace,' sure," Kim said.

Another series of flashing lights all over the spectrum came a few moments later.

"Mike?" Glenn hazarded.

Drur was staring quizzically at his display. "The subspace response is longer. EVALUATION OF CURRENT INPUTS INDETERMINATE."

"Sounds like an arcane way of saying 'I don't understand,'" Glenn said. "What was the rest?"

"It's another genome, Captain. One of ours, almost."

"Almost?"

"It contains a few additional base pairs I can't identify, but which are included in the Edrehmaia's DNA."

"Can you run it through our database excluding the additions?" Kim asked.

"Already on it." When the process was complete, Drur said softly, "It's Velth's genome."

"Did you include his in the crew list?" Kim asked.

"No, sir. I assumed you only wanted to include our current, you know, *living* crew members."

"So, is it asking us a question or checking our math?" Glenn asked.

"Send our list again and, this time, include Velth in the set," Kim suggested.

There was no visible response. Instead, the alien simply vanished from the viewscreen.

When Lieutenant Reg Barclay found Nancy Conlon in main engineering, it felt as if he was entering the room on any other day he had spent in the Delta Quadrant. Every station had power. They were without most of their organic engineers, but it was still nice to feel that things were returning to something resembling a routine.

Conlon stood with Ensign Unhai at the slipstream operations panel. As he approached, Conlon said, "Try it again."

Barclay turned his attention toward a small rectangular module stationed just beside the slipstream generator. He recognized it at once, as it had been constructed shortly after the fleet's mission had begun. Within the unit, a small pile of dust sat on a flat panel. At Conlon's order, it vanished in a swirling transporter effect and was replaced by a small crystal.

"Well?" Conlon asked.

Unhai dutifully checked her data panel and replied, "Purity is sixty-seven percent."

Conlon sighed deeply. "That's better, but it won't do."

"We could try using a smaller sample," Unhai suggested.

"This unit was designed to recrystallize benamite that had minor fractures," Conlon replied. "Ours has been pulverized. I think we're going to have to start over from scratch. I'll get busy working on the new specifications. Please collect all of the test samples and return them to storage."

"Aye, Chief," Unhai said, and moved to retrieve the crystal.

"Good evening, Lieutenant," Reg greeted her.

"Hey, Reg. Something I can help you with?"

"I was wondering if you intended to end your shift any time soon?" he asked.

Conlon checked the chronometer. "I should have signed out an hour ago," she replied.

"If that is a yes, there is something I'd like to show you," Reg said.

Conlon stared at Reg blankly until his cheeks began to redden. When it dawned on him how his statement could be taken, or mistaken, he added quickly, "I have created a test m-meh-matrix that requires your review."

Conlon shook her head, worry lines creasing her brow. "I'm sorry. I didn't hear, that is, I couldn't process . . ."

Barclay tried again. "I understand. This way."

Conlon alerted the engineers to her departure and followed Barclay down the corridor to his holographic lab. When they entered, he gestured for her to take a seat next to his behind the workstation. Just beyond it stood a circular platform with a waist-high transparent barrier.

"There are a few parameters I have yet to enter into the primary matrix. I wanted to get your input before we do our first test run," Barclay said.

"That's very thoughtful of you, Reg."

"Okay, here we go."

Seconds later, a hologram appeared on the platform. Physically, it was a perfect rendering of Conlon in uniform. Barclay glanced over to check Conlon's response and saw her staring almost sadly at his creation.

"The physical presentation is really little more than a shell. We could alter any of the parameters quite easily."

"Could I be taller?" Conlon asked.

Barclay complied by adding four centimeters in height to the display.

"No, that's weird," Conlon said immediately.

"I honestly believe you will be most comfortable if the hologram is as close as we can come to the physical version of yourself with which you are familiar," Barclay said as he undid the fix.

"I agree, but just because, show me platinum-blond hair. I've always been curious but never had the nerve."

Barclay complied.

"Yeah, no," Conlon said.

"There are certain capabilities that you might find useful. For example, all holograms can control whether or not they exist in a solid or permeable form."

"I don't . . . what?" Conlon asked.

Barclay reached for a padd next to him and tossed it to the hologram. She caught it effortlessly, then threw it back. He then made a tweak to his panel and tossed the padd again. This time it went through the hologram, clattering onto the deck behind it.

"There might be times when it would be advantageous for you to be permeable. The Doctor has utilized this function frequently when his ship has come under attack."

Conlon nodded. "Do it."

"It's done," Barclay said, clearly pleased to have found a modification of which she approved.

"The one question the Doctor couldn't really answer for me is how it would feel to be a hologram," she said.

Barclay turned a compassionate face toward her. "The honest answer is that we won't know until the transfer is complete. You have sensory memories that the Doctor will never acquire. That might add levels of complexity to your experiences he will never know."

"Is there a chance the transfer will fail?" Conlon asked.

"There is always a chance," Barclay conceded. "But the better prepared you are, the smaller the chances of rejection become. When the Doctor transferred Danara Pel to her holographic body, she found the experience so compelling, she was reluctant to return to her own body."

"He also said it can't be permanent. Do you know why?"

Barclay sighed. "It has to do with a holomatrix's ability to store and retrieve data. We're not creating a new brain for you. We can't do that. Our main computer will function as this matrix's processor and it does not work the same way organic matter does. Over time, your new experiences as a hologram will supersede your memories. You will become more accustomed to 'thinking' and processing as a hologram."

"Meaning I will lose my humanity?"

"The Doctor is one of the most 'human' life-forms I have ever encountered," Barclay said quickly. "But his nature will never be ours. For a long time, it will be a matter of very small degrees of degradation. But eventually, your understanding of yourself will change. At that point, there would no longer be a consciousness to return to your physical body once it is healed."

"Will I feel it happening?"

"Not n-neh-necessarily," Barclay said with obvious effort.

Conlon rose and crossed to the hologram, staring up at herself. When she turned back to face him, her eyes were glistening.

"Maybe this is a bad idea," she said.

"It is your choice," Barclay said. "Personally, I believe the Doctor will be able to cure your physical body well before any serious loss is sustained."

"But he could still do that if he just places me in a coma."

"He could, but . . ."

"But you'd be left without a chief engineer."

Barclay nodded.

Conlon lifted both hands to her cheeks and held her head. Finally, she asked, "Can we do a test run? A partial transfer, just so I can get a sense of it?"

"I wouldn't suggest that," Barclay said. "What I can promise you is that if the transfer is unsuccessful, or you find your new state unbearable, we can terminate the procedure at any time."

"If I ask you to do that, how will you know it's me?" Conlon asked.

Barclay considered the question, then said, "Step back for a moment, please."

Conlon did as he had requested and suddenly, the hologram came to "life." She first turned to Conlon and said cheerfully, "Good evening, Lieutenant Conlon." She then directed her attention to Barclay. "Hello, Lieutenant Barclay. How may I be of service to you?"

Conlon stared at the hologram, holding herself with her arms crossed at her chest. "That's not me."

"No, it isn't," Barclay agreed. "And it won't be until the transfer happens. Trust me, I will always know the difference."

Conlon approached herself and said, "I am in the process of redesigning a benamite recrystallization chamber. Can you give me the specification of our current model?"

"Module X016.2 was activated on stardate . . ." she began, but immediately fritzed.

Conlon turned to Barclay. "Did I break it?"

"No, hang on," Barclay said, running a quick diagnostic. "The initial program includes our basic engineering database as well as modifications specific to *Galen* as a part of your primary reference library. This is meant to be a backup for your own knowledge base."

"Every test I take from now on will be open book?"

"Something like that," Barclay said. "It might come in handy. But there is a processing lag I don't understand."

Conlon moved back to his display and peered over his shoulder.

"I'm no holographic expert, but it looks like those partitions are too small," she noted.

"Let's try this again." Addressing the hologram he said, "Please continue with your recitation of the technical specification of Module X016.2."

The hologram opened its mouth to speak but only gibberish came out. The form again lost cohesion and, moments later, vanished.

Barclay looked again at his diagnostic and immediately recognized the problem. "Thank you for your time, Lieutenant," he said. "I believe my request was premature. There are a few issues that will require resolution before we can proceed."

"What issues?" Conlon asked.

"N-neh-no-nothing to worry about," Barclay stammered.

"Reg, we're talking about my life here. You have to tell me," Conlon insisted.

Barclay didn't want to tell her. He wanted to double-check his results and make sure he was right. Except that he already knew he was right. He had created the maximum possible space to allow for the integration of Conlon's consciousness into the matrix. It required all available space once designated for the thirty-three other holograms that had served on board.

But it wasn't going to be enough.

There was an answer, of course. Just not one he had ever anticipated proposing.

As these dispiriting thoughts ran through his mind, Conlon said, "It's okay, Reg. If we can't do it, we can't do it."

"Oh, we can do it," Barclay said. *We just might lose the Doctor in the process.*

"I don't understand," Commander Glenn said. "This ship was created to run dozens of holograms simultaneously, including Meegan. How is this suddenly a problem?"

The Doctor was curious as well, although he didn't doubt Barclay's conclusion. The trio sat in his private office off the main medical bay.

"Meegan was a special case," Barclay said. "We created a version of the Doctor's holographic emitter, extremely advanced technology acquired from the twenty-ninth century, in order to allow her holomatrix to expand along with her sentience. But that emitter was lost when her program was stolen by the Seriareen. The rest of our holograms were not designed to evolve in the same way. We optimized for quantity rather than this particular quality. I hoped that by purging all of our other holograms, there would be sufficient room in our computer to sustain Nancy's consciousness within the matrix, but I no longer believe it is going to work. Even in the absence of her consciousness, the empty partitions still require more processing space than we can accommodate."

"You built one mobile emitter and it seemed to function perfectly," Glenn said. "Build another."

"That module was created on Jupiter Station by Lewis Zimmerman," the Doctor said. "It contains a number of alloys we cannot replicate."

Glenn glanced between them. "So, you're telling me that my choices are to lose my chief engineer or my chief medical officer?"

"The Doctor's program can be run through the *Galen*'s main holomatrix generator," Barclay said quickly. "That was part of our original specifications for the vessel. We would not necessarily lose him."

"Unless we suffer a catastrophic power loss, which, given the fact that we are operating on our main fusion reactor with no source of supplemental warp plasma and are alone at the ass end of the quadrant tens of thousands of light-years from any help and at the mercy of an alien species, is not entirely outside the realm of possibility," Glenn countered.

Barclay shrugged. "I didn't say I was happy about this."

Glenn turned her attention to the Doctor. "What do you think?"

"Under any other circumstances, I would say that using my mobile emitter to sustain Lieutenant Conlon's consciousness in a holo-matrix would not be my first choice."

"But under these circumstances, it is?" Glenn asked.

"I have already begun replicating vectors similar to those created by Doctor Sal when she cured Vega Nine. I am hopeful that I will be able to cure the lieutenant within the next few weeks."

"Not to be discouraging, but you and an entire team of Starfleet's finest medical minds have been working on this issue for some time. I like your optimism, but this decision needs to be based on facts and evidence, not hope, Doctor," Glenn replied.

"The facts are quite clear, Captain. If we refuse to allow Lieutenant Barclay to modify my emitter for Conlon's use, we will be without a competent chief engineer until we rejoin the rest of our fleet. If we proceed, we will have access to both my program and hers."

"I'm not going to approve this unless you do, Doctor," Glenn advised.

When the Doctor had decided to pursue the creation of this hologram, he had weighed the consequences of inaction against his desire to continue to survive. It had been a statistical problem, an intellectual exercise, albeit one born of his intense desire to continue to exist. It had now become a more personal matter. In the first scenario, one where Conlon was lost, the odds of the ship surviving without her had been given great weight, but in the event she did not survive, the likelihood was that the entire ship, including the Doctor, would be destroyed. Now, the Doctor was forced to reckon with the possibility that the ship would continue, but his existence could end.

He did not relish this possibility. Indeed, it was somehow more disturbing to contemplate. But if nothing else, it incentivized successfully healing Nancy Conlon in a way nothing else could.

Rather than wallow in unknowns and probabilities, the Doctor reached for the only solution that honored both his identity and the needs of those he considered his friends.

"Computer," he called. "Transfer Chief Medical Officer's program to the main holographic emitter."

A light chirp confirmed completion of the operation. He then detached his mobile emitter from his arm and handed it to Barclay.

Glenn nodded somberly. "I appreciate your willingness to make this sacrifice, Doctor, but I also believe we must prioritize healing Nancy Conlon as soon as possible . . ."

"Bridge to Commander Glenn."

She tapped her combadge and replied, "Go ahead, Lieutenant Kim."

"Please report to the main airlock right away."

"On my way," she said, clearly concerned by this odd summons. "Gentlemen," she said curtly as she departed.

Lieutenant Kim and Ensign Selah met Commander Glenn as she approached the airlock. "Report," she ordered as soon as they were in sight.

"We have incoming," Selah said as she began to unlock the interior access to the airlock.

"Not long after you left the bridge, we detected two contacts approaching the ship," Kim added. "They sent a transmission as soon as they were in sight consisting of the precise coordinates of our airlock."

"Are we about to be boarded?" Glenn asked. "Because I'm going to have an issue with that."

"They also transmitted Velth's genome again," Kim said.

Glenn's heart paused momentarily, before beginning to race.

"You said there was no chance he survived."

"I didn't think there was," Kim confirmed.

"Do scanners detect any life signs?"

"No," Kim replied. "They might just be returning . . ."

"His body," Glenn finished for him. "I guess that speaks well of them, in a way."

"We identified him as a member of our set. They could have construed that as a request that they bring him back to us," Kim said.

"Sirs," Selah said, her voice tense.

Glenn stepped into the airlock and peered through the port. One of the approaching forms was consistent with the Edrehmaia. The other appeared to be an EV suit. "Both of you, step back," Glenn ordered.

"I really don't think you should face them alone," Kim said.

"Not your call, Lieutenant," Glenn replied.

Kim and Selah cleared the airlock and Glenn sealed the interior access. She then made haste to don the room's emergency EV suit. She had just clicked her helmet into place when the approaching party paused less than ten meters from the ship.

Velth's suit looked functional, but it was impossible to see if he was conscious through the faceplate of his helmet. Terrified, but determined, Glenn activated her magnetic boots, planting herself on the deck, and opened the airlock.

She was greeted by an almost blinding display of light from the alien. She could not translate it, but there was something almost joyful in it. Of course, that could have been her characteristic optimism talking. It had been a while since it made its presence known, and the feeling was one of heady relief.

The EV suit drifted toward her. Only now did she see that it was dotted with holes, all of which had been sealed with a solid black substance. More important, she finally saw the face of Ranson Velth.

As she welcomed him back, grasping his suit in a firm embrace and guiding him into the airlock, tears began to stream down her cheeks.

Velth's eyes were open.

12

ieutenant Commander B'Elanna Torres had faced and overcome enough challenges in her life that she found it impossible to believe that there was no way through this one, especially if it included bringing Harry, Nancy, the Doctor, Reg, and the rest of *Galen*'s crew home. Captain Chakotay's directive had been quite clear as to the first step. She, Lieutenants Bryce and Elkins, and Ensign Icheb must find a way to bring the Edrehmaia back to the fleet's current location so that true communication could be established between them.

Bryce and Icheb ran headlong into the thick of it, tackling the problem the way Miral had attacked her first electromagnetic building set. Lieutenant Garvin Elkins, *Demeter*'s chief engineer and the man who had essentially built her, sat silently, his gaze fixed stubbornly out the room's nearest port.

"They must still be monitoring the star," Bryce insisted. "You don't go to all the trouble of creating a planet that can store enough power to move a star without also developing the means to track that star's movement."

"But how? It has already traveled millions of kilometers beyond its point of origin," Icheb said. "If the technology they used to correct the star's course and prevent it from destroying the system when it departed was still active, our sensors would detect it."

This specific technological miracle had first been observed by *Voyager*'s sensors prior to the planet's release of energy that moved the star. Once the star had broken free, intense energy released in waves from the asteroid field ensured that it assumed a course that would take it out of the system without damaging any of the other bodies it contained. It had prevented *Voyager*'s destruction.

"We've extrapolated the location of the course-altering system based upon our initial sensor readings. All we have found are intact asteroids with the same rough metallurgic composition as every other rock out there," Torres said.

"Then where did the technology go?" Bryce asked. "It didn't vanish."

"Unless it did," Icheb suggested. "Some sort of self-destruct mechanism once it had performed its primary task, perhaps?"

"Wouldn't we have observed that, though?" Bryce countered.

"The current working theory"—*courtesy of Seven*, Torres did not add—"is that the technology was designed to remain inert until DK-1116 was activated, and once the process was complete, it returned to a state of technological hibernation."

"But it's still there. Why don't we suit up and do a physical inspection of the asteroids in question?" Bryce asked.

"That mission is already underway," Torres replied. "Tom and Lieutenant Patel are prepping an away team. But if long-range sensors aren't picking up any evidence of alien technology out there, there's no telling how long it might take us to find it."

"The star itself is useless to them," Elkins said, still staring out the port.

Torres, Bryce, and Icheb all turned their attention toward the engineer simultaneously. "Beg pardon?" Torres asked.

Elkins rose from his seat at the table and moved closer to the port, still clearly entranced by the view. "They're not tracking it, because they have no need of it," Elkins clarified. "That's why the system is no longer active."

"How can you possibly know that?" Torres asked.

Elkins turned to face the small group. "Because species that design systems like DK-1116 don't think in terms of anything that happens over the course of days, years, or decades. This was the work of centuries, most likely a test of their power storage and release capacity circa almost five thousand years ago." As this sunk in, he continued, "If we are ever to understand this species, we have to begin by trying to put ourselves in their position. We have to think like them."

"But we know so little about them," Bryce said. "How do you even begin . . . ?"

"Start simple," Elkins interjected. "What *do* we know?"

Bryce rose, crossing toward Elkins. "They created the power storage planet to move the star knowing it would take thousands of years for that system to collect enough radiant energy to perform its task. During that time, countless life-forms studied and even temporarily disrupted the system's circuits, and it doesn't seem to have concerned them in the least."

"Nothing our predecessors did while on the surface of DK-1116 moved the needle," Icheb said. "They created biodomes powered by tapping the planet's power sources, environments that could be altered to suit the biological requirements of many different sentient life-forms, as well as numerous lower life-forms, to maintain those environments. They discovered and devised synthetic elements, alloys, and botanical life-forms that were hybrids of more common matter combined with the genetically complex substance at the heart of the Edrehmaia's technology. All of this we find extraordinary but the Edrehmaia did not."

"Correct," Elkins said. "And their lack of interest in the fate of the star since it was released tells us that, too, is no longer relevant to them."

"But they did come back," Torres said. "If it wasn't to check on the progress of the star, why did they bother?"

"That's the real question," Elkins said.

"The first thing they did when they arrived was to transmit three genomes. The first, we believe, is theirs. The second and third were Devi Patel's and that of the interlocutor that was created by blending her DNA with the Edrehmaia substance," Torres said.

"So Devi Patel is important," Bryce offered.

"Or the interlocutor is," Icheb said.

"So, were they sending us instructions?" Torres asked. "Create more interlocutors?"

"And almost immediately after that, they took the *Galen*. If Patel and her interlocutor were the most interesting thing we had done, why not take *Voyager* so they could interact with Patel directly?" Bryce asked.

"It doesn't make any sense," Icheb said, clearly frustrated.

"Only because we aren't thinking like them yet," Elkins reminded him. "It is possible that the release of the star brought them here, but the first thing they bring up in conversation was the entity that was the bridge between our species and theirs. Their awareness of her predated the release of the star. By the time they got here, that interlocutor was long gone."

"That's further evidence that all Edrehmaia matter might share properties of quantum entanglement," Torres noted. "They became aware of the interlocutor when it was created, but that wasn't enough to make us of any interest to them."

"Hundreds of other species also created interlocutors," Icheb reminded them. "Why was ours different?

"We were the ones that broke containment," Bryce offered. "The Edrehmaia weren't responsible for the creation of the interlocutors. That was other species playing with their toys. But clearly, they detected it, as well as Lieutenant Patel's presence. They might have assumed she restored the planet to its original purpose intentionally and wondered if they had encountered a species that was their technological equal."

"I wonder if they're lonely," Icheb speculated.

"It wouldn't surprise me," Elkins said. "We've been out here exploring space for a few hundred years now and the number of species we would consider their peers can be counted on one hand."

"But I ask again, *why take the* Galen?" Bryce said.

"Because it was the smallest ship and it had the fewest life-forms aboard," Icheb suggested. "If they were curious about us and our abilities, *Galen* and her crew of thirty organic beings was the easiest target."

"If they were looking for their technological equals, I'm guessing that their ultimate analysis of the *Galen* has proven disappointing in that regard," Elkins said.

"They're still alive," Torres insisted.

"We think," Elkins said gently.

"Admiral Janeway and Captain Chakotay are convinced by the evidence they have seen. That's good enough for me," Torres said. "But let's say you're right. Let's assume that they have no use for the star. It was an ancient experiment that ran its course. They have studied *Galen* and determined our level of advancement to be irrelevant. That doesn't change our mission. How do we bring them back?"

"We prove them wrong," Elkins said simply. "We have to devise a technological miracle on par with theirs. We have to show them that we are worthy of their attention."

"Do you have any idea how to accomplish that?" Torres asked.

"No. But I think it's helpful that we're finally asking the right question," Elkins replied.

VESTA

Admiral Kathryn Janeway was en route to her private office, her aide, Lieutenant Decan, by her side. The list of issues requiring her attention was, as ever, absurd. Decan made himself utterly indispensable to her by always keeping the list manageable.

"Operations is awaiting your approval to transmit the week's logs to Command," Decan said.

That had to be near the end of the list, Janeway surmised. "Have I reviewed them yet?"

"No, hence the *awaiting*."

"Have you reviewed them?"

"Yes, Admiral."

"Do they contain anything that is likely to get the fleet recalled or my command staff relieved of their positions?"

"No, Admiral. The abridged notes I prepared for you contain

all of the highlights and will only require a few minutes of your time."

"Great. I'll carve them out of the next half hour before I join the engineers' briefing."

"We have received another *request* from Agent Lucsly of the Department of Temporal Investigations," Decan continued.

"How many is that now?"

"Four, Admiral."

"Oh, good. I'd hate for him to think I was ignoring him."

"But you are ignoring him."

"Yes, but it is very important to me that he not *feel* I am ignoring him or his request that we alter our mission objective immediately."

"Wouldn't a better way to ensure that be to actually respond to his request?"

"Possibly. But I still haven't found the most politic way to tell him where he can shove his request."

"I see."

"As soon as I do, he'll be the first to know," Janeway added with a wink.

They arrived at the door to her office as Decan said, "There is one more thing."

Janeway passed the sensor threshold and entered to find Commander O'Donnell standing before her desk. He turned as she crossed to him.

"Good morning, Admiral," he greeted her.

"Commander O'Donnell has requested a few moments of your time, Admiral," Decan said serenely.

Janeway refrained from replying that she could see that and said simply, "Thank you, Decan."

"Would you care for a fresh pot of coffee?"

Janeway raised an eyebrow in O'Donnell's direction. "Will you join me, Commander?"

"Never touch the stuff. Far too weak," O'Donnell replied evenly.

"Very well. Fresh coffee for me, and an Andiluvian *Jot Mott* for the Commander," Janeway said. "I hate to drink alone."

"Yes, Admiral," Decan said, departing without confirming O'Donnell's reaction.

Once Decan was gone, the admiral settled herself at her desk. "My mother hates coffee. The *Jot Mott* is her recipe. It's got plenty of caffeine but finishes without the bitterness. You might like it."

"I am always up for exploring the unknown," O'Donnell said, deadpan.

A hoarse chuckle escaped the admiral. "What do you need, Commander?" she asked, gesturing for him to sit opposite her.

"Species 112, the Borlath Clan, spent five years testing the molecular bonds between hydrogen atoms and six genetic bases for which we have no name," O'Donnell began. "They referred to them as AX-1, BT-5, NR-6, ZE-11, MC-19, and CY-32."

"Were their findings significant?" Janeway asked.

"They were attempting to confirm that the weakness of the bonds, something akin to what we call a van der Waals interaction, was essential to the ability of these proteins to shift their location during replication. As best I can tell from the records they left behind, they were unable to verify the hypothesis, but their work does demonstrate an almost incomprehensible malleability of the Edrehmaia base."

"It's extraordinary, isn't it?" Janeway mused. "The part I find most interesting was the ongoing fascination with the interaction with the base and various life-forms, as well as what seems now to be the inevitable results. Life, without life, if that makes sense."

"Right. The botanical *zombies*. I think I might have cracked that too," O'Donnell said. "Species 91, the, well, I'm sure I'm butchering the pronunciation, but the Tee-ich-esth came right out and said that their primary goal was the indefinite continuation of biological organisms."

"They were looking for the fountain of youth?" Janeway was astonished.

"When studying the material Lieutenant Patel and her team recovered from SWOW, it is remarkably easy to lose yourself for extended periods of time, following threads of experimentation that usually end in disappointment, but are, nonetheless, vivid windows into the varied ways in which sentient life-forms evolve."

"Wait, SWOW?" Janeway asked.

"Catchy, isn't it?" O'Donnell said, smiling broadly. "I suppose I should change it now to BWOW, but I honestly don't have the heart."

"Commander?"

"Species 001's World of Wonders," O'Donnell elucidated.

Janeway thought for a moment, then decided. "I don't hate it. But I won't be using it in our formal logs." Rising from her desk and moving to perch on the front of it, she continued, "I imagine the driving forces behind most sentient species' desire to explore space begin with acquiring resources and simple curiosity. I confess that mine have never included the possibility of eternal life. Are we not thinking big enough?"

"It's problematic, to be sure," O'Donnell said. "For much of my life, I hardly knew what to make of the time I'd been given. Knowledge, for its own sake, is less inspiring to me than knowledge that brings with it practical applications, especially those that can be used to better the lives of those with whom we share the universe. That said, these days I do wonder if there will be enough time left."

"To do what?"

"I don't honestly know," O'Donnell admitted. "I could spend the next several years doing nothing but reading Patel's files and it would bring me no closer, I fear, to understanding the most basic properties of the Edrehmaia. I wonder if at any time in their development they were more like us, or if they have ever even known what it is to grapple with hunger, pain, loss, or love. There is such purity in their creations. They seem beyond any parochial notions. They have harnessed the power to reshape the physical universe to some unknown purpose. But does their existence so far removed from our experience of being alive deny them community with the wider universe? Is that something they would ever think to miss?"

"Perhaps not," Janeway said. "I do know, however, that it is essential to my existence, I dare say, to *ours*. What good is knowledge if it cannot be shared?"

"Anxious as I am to find them, the closer we get, the more I wonder what of any significance I might even ask them."

"Why? When? How? I'd start with the basics," Janeway suggested.

Disappointment flashed across O'Donnell's face.

"So often out here, we encounter alien life that is quite similar to ours," Janeway continued. "Those that are truly unique, that clearly did not evolve as we did, are few and far between and often incapable of connection in any meaningful way beyond acknowledgment and a willingness to coexist peacefully. But we are not diminished by those encounters. They are an invitation to imagine beyond our limitations, and that is truly the work of a life and a lifetime."

"They humble me, Admiral. And I don't care much for that feeling."

Janeway smiled. "Yes, but I wonder how many lives have been extended by humility. There are things we cannot know until we are ready. And we, as we are, may never be. But we are not the end of humanity. I hope we aren't even its midpoint. Sometimes the best we can do is offer those who will come after us a glimpse into their own potential future. It's a gift, just one that we will never be permitted to unwrap."

The door chimed and Decan returned, setting a pot of fresh coffee and an empty mug along with a tall glass of something steaming on the low table in the admiral's informal seating area.

"Thank you, Decan," Janeway said as she crossed to pour herself a cup.

"Engineering . . ."

"Is waiting, I know," Janeway acknowledged, dismissing him

with a nod. When he had gone, she brought the steaming glass to O'Donnell for inspection. He sniffed it, then sipped it gingerly.

"Well?" she asked.

O'Donnell nodded gravely. "I don't hate it."

"Bear that in mind when you are still climbing the walls in the middle of gamma shift. There's at least two full pots worth of caffeine in there. Honestly, I think my mother meant it as a challenge, or a way to break my addiction, once and for all."

O'Donnell rose from his seat. "That explains more about you than I suspect you anticipated revealing." Shifting gears, he continued, "I do have one request to make, Admiral."

"Yes?"

"Before we depart this area of space, I intend, that is, I hope to safely contain at least some of the Edrehmaia substance for future experiments."

"I understand and share your curiosity, but I will not permit any of the substance to be stored aboard our vessels until I am satisfied that it can be safely contained."

"I have already begun analyzing the fragments that were used to contain the substance at Station One. As soon as I am done, may I have your permission to locate a source for extraction?"

"One step at a time, Commander."

"Understood, Admiral." After a moment he said, "Assuming we do find the Edrehmaia and are able to retrieve our lost ship, what's next?"

"There's still lots of Delta Quadrant to explore," she reminded him.

"Always," he agreed.

"You seem less than enthusiastic at the prospect."

O'Donnell lifted his shoulders, and they remained stuck as he replied, "For my part, I will hope for better things." As he crossed to the door, he added, "Thank you, Admiral."

He departed without a backward glance, leaving the admiral to ponder the curious man who had become one of this mission's most perplexing revelations.

VOYAGER

Lieutenant Devi Patel found *Voyager*'s pilot, Ensign Gwyn, seated in a corner of the mess hall across from Kenth Lasren and made a beeline toward them.

When the pair took notice of her arrival, Lasren seemed embarrassed. Gwyn dropped her chin quickly and wiped her cheeks with the back of her hand.

"I'm interrupting," Patel realized too late.

"No, it's fine," Gwyn said, starting to rise.

"Don't go, I need you," Patel said quickly.

Lasren exchanged a meaningful glance with Gwyn. It made Patel feel even more the odd man out. "It's up to you," he said.

Gwyn stared at Patel for a moment, then nodded faintly. Lasren pulled up an empty chair from the nearest table. Patel took it, saying, "Thank you."

Awkward silence hovered until Lasren, clearly anxious to build a bridge, said, "Aytar and I have been talking about empathy, specifically psionic empathy."

It was the last thing Patel expected to hear. "Why? Gwyn's never had that, has she?" It came out far more dismissive than Patel intended, and she noticed Gwyn recoil slightly.

"Everybody has empathy," Lasren said. "Except maybe sociopaths."

"I was talking about the psionic part," Patel added hastily. Wondering if this was connected to Gwyn's earlier question about loving someone, she suddenly realized she might have just inserted herself into a deeply personal conversation.

Lasren as a potential partner for Gwyn had never crossed Patel's radar. He seemed much too bright and sensitive to knowingly engage in meaningless hookups, but then, one never knew. Patel's interactions with him since the away mission had been entirely professional. There had been moments, especially when she awakened in sickbay to find him by her bedside, when she had wondered if something more might be possible between them. But she had been far too preoccupied by her duties since then to give the matter any thought. Faced with the prospect that she had misread simple professional concern for something else and missed entirely a new relationship developing between him and Gwyn, she found herself suddenly floundering in a miasma of insecurity she hadn't felt since the hours leading up to her away mission on SWOW.

A soft smile suddenly lit Lasren's face. Followed by a noticeable reddening of his cheeks. Gwyn did a quick double take between Lasren and Patel, then said, "Oh, come on. You two haven't . . . ?"

If anything, this made Patel's genuine confusion worse.

"Drop it," Lasren said with quiet intensity. Gwyn shook her head but at least for a moment seemed to have pulled herself from her own emotional quagmire.

"You said you needed me?" Gwyn asked, clearly trying to change the subject.

Patel, equally anxious to segue, said, "I want you to take the helm of the *Delta Flyer* for me. I've been assigned an away mission to explore the inner asteroid field; specifically, to search for the technology the Edrehmaia used to control the star's movement once it had escaped orbit."

"Why?" Gwyn asked seriously.

"Because it might be the only intact technology left now and you're the best pilot we have."

"And?"

"And what? We need to understand the Edrehmaia better before we face them again."

A deep sigh escaped Gwyn's lips. "Isn't that sort of like expecting an alien race to understand us by giving them one of our antigrav lifts?"

An unintentional chuckle escaped Lasren.

"They'd probably end up assuming we all weighed five hundred kilograms," Gwyn added darkly.

Patel could not conceal her confusion. "You have been pushing for us to find the *Galen* since before most of us even knew they had survived. How is understanding every single thing about the species that took them not at the very top of your to-do list?"

"It is," Gwyn replied. "But, those asteroids . . ."

"I don't think she knows the whole story, Aytar," Lasren interjected.

"I know you were injured in the only mission we've undertaken thus far to explore the asteroids," Patel said. "I'm sure it was terrible."

"The stuff you found under the surface, the so-called *Edrehmaia substance*, it attacked me," Gwyn said. "It didn't think or ask or say hello. I was slicing off a chunk of rock, exposed some of it, and it just grabbed me. It started moving up my arm and eating through my suit before Seven stunned it with a phaser. That's the only reason I survived. The shuttle we were in didn't.

"This is not an alien we establish first contact with. This is a force of nature, driven by its own agenda, that simply does whatever the hell it wants. I'm guessing the things that made it are exactly the same."

"They did try to communicate with us," Lasren said.

"They gave us the biological equivalent of name, rank, and serial number," Gwyn shot back. "And then they took one of our ships, just because they could. You and the rest of the senior staff are acting like this is some poor, misunderstood exotic life-form that just needs a hug or, worse, some kind of pet science project. It isn't. They're not. It's liquid death and it doesn't care who we are or what we want."

"So how would you suggest we deal with them?" Lasren asked. "Since our standard protocols don't seem to be working for you."

"We just need to know where they took our ship," Gwyn snapped back. "When we figure that out, we go in, transport as many of our people as we can to safety, and get the hell out."

"And pray that's the end of it?" Patel asked.

"Yes."

Patel sat back, wondering again what had happened to her friend in the last few weeks. Some of the trauma she understood. A great deal more she could not fathom. Finally, she said, "You're scared. I get that. And you're angry. I am too. Those *things* called me by name when they showed up, which is more than a little terrifying. But they didn't take me, and I have a feeling they could have if they'd wanted to. It's not a game, but it is a puzzle and we don't have enough pieces yet to formulate a plan. Part of that is anything their technology can tell us, which might include how to find them. And you should probably know that this mission includes safely extracting and studying some of the Edrehmaia substance."

"Don't go, Devi. Don't do it. I know you're feeling good right now. You're planning missions with the senior staff, feeling important, and that's something you wanted, but . . ."

"Shut up," Patel said. "Just shut the hell up."

"Devi," Lasren pleaded.

"This isn't about me, you idiot," Patel continued, her voice rising. "I don't know what happened to you. I don't even know who you are anymore. I don't feel important. I feel every bit as frightened and sad and worried about our lost ship as everyone else around here. Why are you so pissed at me?"

"Because if you hadn't decided to throw your life away, I wouldn't have had to—" But at this, Gwyn stopped short.

"To do what?"

Tears began to form again in Gwyn's eyes. She wiped them quickly and cast a plaintive look toward Lasren.

"Tell her," he said simply.

Gwyn shook her head. "You promised," she said, a soft accusation.

"I know. And I stand by that," Lasren said. "I'm not going to betray your confidence. But this is pointless. She can't help you if she doesn't know what you're trying to protect."

"I don't need her help. I don't want anyone's help."

Lasren glanced between them, at a loss. "Here's what I can tell you, Gwyn. This isn't going to get better. What you did, what you became, we're in uncharted waters here. And if we never find the *Galen* . . ."

"Don't say it," Gwyn protested.

"Someone has to. If we never find the *Galen*, you're going to have to figure out how to deal with that loss. Even if we do, you're never going to have the kind of life you're hoping for."

"I'm not hoping for anything. I don't need anything."

Patel watched this exchange, trying desperately to find some secure purchase. But none of it made any damn sense. It was both irritating and exhausting. And on some level, so *like* Gwyn, who until very recently never seemed to have a thought in the world that wasn't about herself. "I'm sorry," she said. "I'm sorry I was a part of whatever is happening to you now. I'm sorry if my choice forced you to do something you didn't want to. Most of all, I'm sorry you don't feel like you can trust me to understand." She rose from her chair. "But there's only so much I can take responsibility for and so many things I can apologize for. Excuse me."

With that, she left the mess hall. She was confused, hurt, and angry. Patel hadn't had that many friends when this mission began. Lasren and Gwyn were certainly among them. And she could see that Kenth was struggling to walk a difficult line.

Not long ago, she had decided that duty was all that mattered to her, not thinking of the long-term consequences, as she didn't expect to be around to suffer them. Gwyn had changed that. She had saved her life. But somehow that choice had broken something between them Patel doubted could ever be repaired.

Once duty had been all that mattered. Now she wondered if it might be all she had left.

13

"I have no idea how long I was out," Lieutenant Ranson Velth said through parched lips. He had been brought to a private room in the medical bay where only the Doctor, Commander Glenn, and Lieutenant Kim were present. The EMH was in the process of completing a full-body scan as Glenn and Kim questioned Velth gently. "And it was pretty confusing when I woke up, because I didn't seem to have any trouble breathing."

Velth's EV suit had been removed and placed behind a level-ten force field as soon as alien bio-matter had been detected that had fused with the suit. That matter had apparently been responsible for saving Velth's life. The small black "plugs," as Kim had christened them, were tiny photosynthesis powerhouses. They had functioned as oxygen generators, removing carbon dioxide Velth exhaled while simultaneously capturing and filtering out the excess carbon molecules. A larger patch of alien material had been found on his right arm that had been responsible for providing sufficient amounts of water to keep the lieutenant alive for the duration of his spacewalk. It had punctured the suit, somehow cauterized the breaches, and wrapped itself around Velth's arm, injecting the necessary fluid directly into his veins. Apart from an unusual tightness and constant itching sensation on the arm, Velth hadn't even been aware that the alien substance had become part of his body. He had been barely conscious when the "IV" was revealed, and as soon as he saw it, he became alert and distressed. Almost immediately upon being exposed to the atmosphere of the ship, it had withered and fallen from his body of its own accord. It, too, was now being studied using extreme safety precautions.

"They kept you alive," Glenn reminded him.

Velth nodded somberly. Despite the efforts of the Edrehmaia, he was severely dehydrated and 1.5 percent of his body weight had been lost. He had not ingested solid nutrients for almost six days.

"They did more than that. They gave me a guided tour of the area."

"How many of them are out there?" Kim asked.

"Thousands," Velth replied. "Maybe more. I know this will sound speciesist as hell, but they all look alike to me. Five of them were always nearby. John, Paul, George, and Ringo were almost impossible to tell apart. Eventually I settled for referring to them as the 'fab four.' But the fifth one, Pete, was a little different."

"Different how?" Kim asked.

"I kept thinking that the lights, the flashes, had some meaning, but I'll be damned if I ever figured it out. With the fab four, it was like a damned kaleidoscope whenever I looked at them, but after the first few days, Pete's flashes were only white. They came in short bursts, one, two, sometimes three times."

"Was there anything else unusual about Pete?" Kim asked.

"He stayed closer to me than the others, always at my right hand. I think he was my designated navigator. He seemed more curious about me than the others. Sometimes he would just sit there for hours at a time—or what felt like hours. The display on my suit was fried, so I really wasn't clear on the passage of time. He would flash a single time. Then wait awhile and do it again. I told him about the Beatles. I even sang a bunch of their songs to him. I think he liked it even though I have a terrible voice. 'Yellow Submarine' was his favorite. Whenever I sang, that's when the flashes would come in different patterns. But like I said, if he was trying to tell me something, I never understood it and without interfacing directly with my suit, I can't imagine that he could hear or understand me. It was comforting, though, in a way. Made me feel like he cared, you know?"

"Maybe he did," Kim said. "Clearly they took you with some intention. And they went to great lengths to make sure you could survive with them."

"Yes and no," Velth said. "I mean, there wasn't anything to eat, so I wasn't going to last forever out there. And I still don't know why they brought me back. I asked a thousand times for them to return me to the ship but either they didn't want to or didn't understand."

"What else did they show you?" Glenn asked.

"There are thousands of baby stars out there. And they're not forming naturally. The Edrehmaia are creating them and nursing them. I actually watched a group of a dozen or so circle up and hold hands."

"Hands?" Kim asked.

"I didn't like to think of them as tentacles, but that's probably more accurate. When they want to, they can extend long tendrils from their bodies and the ends of them can merge with other Edrehmaia. Their bodies would begin to glow in every possible color until they settled into the brightest white possible. When they did that out in the nursery, a faint spark would ignite in the center of their circle. Over time it would begin to develop into a new star." Velth paused and coughed before he could continue. "I think they require radiant energy in order to survive. They move in large groups and spend considerable amounts of time just sort of sunbathing near some of the more mature stars. Eventually, they release it. Of course, they might be doing more. But it isn't obvious from their movements."

"It's almost like DK-1116 was a primitive version of the Edrehmaia," Glenn said.

"Seven described the whole planet as the most efficient power collection and release mechanism ever devised," Kim agreed. "That does sound like what we're seeing here. And we're not so different. Some of our most advanced technology is created in our own image. Did there seem to be any purpose to the creation of the stars or are they basically just light farmers?"

"The first thing they did after I woke up, or maybe while I was sleeping, was take me out well beyond their nursery. It had to be dozens of light-years from here. Don't ask me how we covered that much space in so short a time because I don't know. I only know how far it was because from there, I could see the edge of the galaxy. Way in the distance, I could see this wide purple band, like a halo over everything."

"The galactic barrier?" Kim asked.

Velth nodded. "I think so. They were pretty quiet until we reached it. But as soon as we arrived, their bodies started flashing furiously. I don't know if they were mad or excited or what, but if that's how they speak to one another, it was suddenly like I was in the middle of a damned coffee klatch.

"And there is a stellar formation out there I don't remember ever seeing before on any of our charts. It's a single series of stars extending as far as the eye can see in pretty much a straight line. It begins with a young G-type star near the edge of their stellar nursery and each consecutive one in the line is smaller and younger."

Glenn bowed her head and seemed to laugh quietly to herself.

"Commander?" Kim said.

She shook her head as she raised it. "Something similar was visible from DK-1116," she said. "A bridge of stars. The scientific consensus is that they are the result of the natural pull between galaxies as they move apart from one another. A few random stars will maintain their positions relative to one another, creating the appearance of a link between them. In this case, it would extend from the Milky Way to Sagittarius Dwarf Elliptical, our next nearest galactic neighbor."

"Does it extend on both sides of the galactic barrier?" Kim asked.

"It didn't appear to. And you can't tell with the naked eye, but I believe there are Edrehmaia out there near each of the stars in that line."

"Did they build it or are they making use of a natural formation?" Kim asked.

"I think they created it," Velth said. "And there was one other thing. We were on our way back, near what I would call the center of their operations, and there was a construct. Its exterior looked like a single Edrehmaia, but it was spherical and a thousand times larger than an individual."

"A ship?" Kim asked. "The one that attacked us was spherical, at least initially."

"I don't think so. It was too big. It's completely black and the only light visible on it was reflected from the stars and the other Edrehmaia. It felt like one of them, just much, much bigger. But I can't confirm that."

"Did you go anywhere near it?"

"No," Velth said, shaking his head vigorously. "It scared the crap out of me. I don't know if they were responding to my fear or if they didn't want me near it. They gave it a pretty wide berth and there weren't any other individual Edrehmaia close to it."

"I understand you both have a lot of questions," the Doctor interjected, "but the lieutenant has been through an incredible ordeal. He needs rest and nutrients, and there are a few surface injuries that require attention."

"I'd kill any one of you for a cheeseburger right now," Velth noted.

Glenn smiled. "Replicators are back up. I'm sure we can arrange that."

"Not yet," the Doctor said, "unless you want it to come right back up again. The lieutenant will be restricted to clear liquids for a few days."

Glenn shrugged. "Doctor's orders."

Velth coughed again, a deep rasping sound.

"Rest, Ranson. Get your strength back. That's an order," Glenn said with a wide smile.

"It's good to have you back," Kim added. "I'm so sorry," he began.

"Don't worry about it, Harry. It wasn't your fault. I know you and Selah did everything you could. I kept wishing when I was out there that I could tell you that. I knew you'd feel like hell, and it wasn't necessary."

"I did. Thank you," Kim said.

Velth's face grew serious again. Hints of the terror that must have been his constant companion over the last several days were etched in new creases on his forehead and around his eyes. "Why did they bring me back?" he asked.

"We've finally figured out how to talk with them a little. Their vocabulary is extremely limited. We'll give you the full report once you are back on duty. But we think they identify all of us by our genomes. The first thing they asked us to do was to define a set. When we included you as part of our set, they brought you back," Kim said.

"All you had to do was ask?" Velth said, nonplussed.

"Pretty much," Kim said. "We're working on expanding our conversations, but it's slow going."

"I don't think they mean to keep us here," Velth said. "I didn't at any time sense even a hint of hostility from them. It was more like when I was a kid visiting my grandmother's house. She had this collection of small ceramic chickens. She used to name them. And every time I came to visit, she took me to those shelves and introduced me to each of the new ones. I know that's not a great analogy, but that's what it felt like. They wanted me to see them, to know them. I think if they could help us, they would."

"If you're right, we just have to figure out how to ask," Kim agreed.

Ensign Michael Drur had a theory. This was unusual for him. *Galen* had been his first starship post following graduation from the Academy and he had spent most of his first year of duty trying to keep his head down, do his job, and avoid attracting attention to himself by doing anything that might garner unwarranted notice, like having theories.

There were lots of different kinds of people at the Academy, but they all had one thing in common: they were the best of the best.

Many of them had done notable things, excelling as athletes, math-letes, musicians, artists, inventing things—hell, his roommate had published his memoirs of his childhood spent on Cygnia Minor creating new variants of their version of a tomato, which he claimed he had done out of sheer boredom. This was the essence of the problem. Boredom drove Cadet Vynott to greatness. If greatness lay anywhere within Drur, it was well hidden.

As a child, Drur hadn't dreamed of attending the Academy. He'd been reasonably proficient in math and one of his counselors had suggested he apply. His parents had been more enthusiastic about it than Mike, and so, to make them stop asking, he had completed the application and tests. To everyone's surprise he had been accepted. Upon arrival he had been told by his advisor that his test results indicated great potential for abstract mathematical constructs. One day, he would accomplish great things with this skill, he had been assured. Thus, his long, slow journey inward had begun. Put a problem in front of him and ask him to solve it, he was fine. Better than fine. Ask him to talk about how he had done it, that's when the challenges began.

Competence bred confidence, at least in Drur's peers. For him, it had been a source of satisfaction, even small bits of pride, but never a bridge upon which he could travel to reach everyone around him.

But he had accepted this about himself. He could stand in a crowded room, or on a fully staffed bridge, and feel completely at home in his loneliness. Knowing he was different and apart was almost his superpower. He didn't need to change it. He wasn't sure it was possible, even had he desired to do so. All he asked was an uneventful duty shift during which he could perform his assigned tasks flawlessly, and individual quarters where he could spend his off-duty hours. This would have been true had he accepted an assignment at a starbase or colony. He had no idea why he had been chosen for *Galen*, but at least out here, the constant change of scenery was interesting and gave him plenty to think about.

In the first few months of the fleet's journey, every member of the bridge crew and other departmental staff had made a point of trying to get to know him. Some had even seemed to recognize the agonizing torment their efforts created and acknowledged it by leaving him be. Those were his favorite fellow officers. His least favorite were those like Commander Glenn, who seemed to take his clear discomfort with interpersonal interactions as a challenge to be overcome—or worse, Velth, who clearly harbored a deep desire to shame Drur into opening up.

Even the light ribbing Velth had administered occasionally on the bridge had become tolerable. Only Drur knew that each time Velth failed to receive a response of any kind from him, the ensign celebrated this as a small victory. His walls remained intact. His ground was secure. No one else needed to know or understand how important that was to him.

Harry Kim had caught him off guard. Without warning he had somehow breached Drur's defenses, coming in completely under the radar. That was the only way Drur could explain the odd kinship he now felt for the lieutenant. Part of it had been the skill with which Kim had approached the initial communications problem with the Edrehmaia. Drur could learn from Kim, and that was valuable. The rest had been Kim's admission to being teased as a new officer. Kim did not share Drur's challenges in conversation or connection. He treated everyone as if they were a dear friend of long acquaintance and had almost immediately gained the respect and admiration of the rest of the crew. For Drur, Kim was the first officer in a long time—perhaps ever—whose approbation he desired, and with whom he felt no discomfort when they were working together.

Perhaps this desire to be of use to Kim was responsible for Drur's new theory. It was also possible that it was derived from the endless complexity of the problem they were both attempting to solve—building an entirely new language upon which their survival might depend. But testing his theory required a guinea pig and it wasn't until Velth's unexpected return to the ship an hour ago that an appropriate test subject had appeared.

Drur was alone on the bridge. He assumed the rest of the crew was busy tending to Velth or probably celebrating his return. He spent many of his current shifts alone lately. Lawry and Selah were only present when they relieved him at the conn or when Commander Glenn took the bridge. Much as Drur understood that this could not be a permanent home for *Galen* and that if they ever managed to get their engines operational again, life on the bridge would return to its old routine, he rather enjoyed the current state of affairs, likely a great deal more than the rest of *Galen's* crew. It was something of a pleasant respite.

The guinea pig in question was a single Edrehmaia that had approached the ship with Velth and remained behind after Kim and Selah had left the bridge to head to the airlock. It had been Drur who had decoded the transmission indicating the Edrehmaia's intended destination, and this minor victory had given him the courage to begin testing his theory as soon as he and the single alien had found themselves more or less alone.

Drur had begun by transmitting his genome and name to the Edrehmaia. The response had been immediate. The alien had sent back its own genome but nothing else over subspace channels, nor had it asked any new questions. Drur and Kim's initial breakthrough, when the Edrehmaia had asked them to "define set," had made it seem like they had begun to understand one another. But Drur's theory was that despite this, the aliens really had no idea what a language was in that they did not attach meaning to any of the things they transmitted. Their communication was limited to the constant exchange of factual information only.

In a way, they were very much like Michael Drur, or, at least, he imagined this to be so.

If this was true, it didn't matter how many common terms they might develop. The key was linking those terms to objects of importance. For instance, did they understand when Drur transmitted his name following his genome that *he* was the owner of that genome? Or were they simply repeating terms that were common between them?

Drur believed the latter was the case.

Every journey began with a single step and in this case, the step was the equivalent of a chasm. It was similar to the null space that existed between Drur and everyone else in the universe. The time had come to try and cross that chasm.

Drur repeated the transmission of his genome and name.

The response was the same.

He then transmitted the genome of Glenn, Velth, Kim, Selah, and Lawry, followed in each case with their name.

The response was the same.

He then transmitted the genomes of the entire crew, followed by the phrase "SET DEFINED AS CREW."

This time, there was a short pause before the entire transmission was repeated back to him followed by the phrase "SET EQUALS CREW."

"That's right, exactly," Drur said aloud.

He then transmitted his genome again, his name, and the phrase "MICHAEL DRUR EQUALS ELEMENT OF SET CREW."

The next response came immediately. "DEFINE RANSON VELTH."

"Now you're getting it," Drur said. He quickly transmitted Velth's genome, name, and the phrase "RANSON VELTH EQUALS ELEMENT OF SET CREW."

The next question was something of a head-scratcher. Two full genomes were sent, both followed by the name "Ranson Velth," followed by the word "DIFFERENTIATE."

Drur quickly compared the two genomes and found a number of new base pairs that had been added to Velth's original DNA. He responded by sending only the new base pairs along with the phrase "EVALUATION OF CURRENT INPUTS INDETERMINATE," his attempt to communicate that he did not understand the nature or value of the additions to Velth's genome.

This was greeted by a long string of bright flashes and no subspace equivalent.

"Don't get frustrated. This is hard," Drur said. "Stay with me."

He decided to try to change the subject. This time he transmitted the first alien genome he had received in response to his initial message, followed by the word "DEFINE."

The alien responded by sending the genome again and nothing else.

"Come on, you have to have a name," Drur said.

The truth was the alien didn't actually require a unique designation. His genome was perfectly accurate to differentiate him from the other Edrehmaia, just unwieldy. But if they were going to get anywhere, understanding the concept of a name was imperative.

Drur sent the same message again, this time adding the phrase "DEFINE ELEMENT."

Another pause that seemed to last forever. When the reply came, Drur could barely contain his excitement.

"CERTAINTY ADDED. DESIGNATE ELEMENT."

As best he could tell, that reply roughly translated to "I understand. You should give me my name." Drur thought long and hard. He finally settled on a name that was dear to him, that of his father's father and one not shared by any other member of *Galen*'s crew. He transmitted the alien's genome followed by the phrase "ELEMENT EQUALS FRED."

The response was unequivocal. Fred transmitted his entire genome back along with the phrase "ELEMENT EQUALS FRED. DEFINE SET FRED."

That one didn't require a lot of thought. Drur just hoped Fred wouldn't mind the designation the rest of the universe had adopted for his species.

"FRED ELEMENT OF SET EDREHMAIA."

Another long pause, followed by the largest transmission to date. It took a full five minutes for the computer to parse, even including the new algorithms installed to speed up that process. When it was done, it contained over eleven thousand discrete genomes followed by the phrase "SET EDREHMAIA."

"That's right," Drur said. "Hello, Fred."

When Harry Kim entered the quarters he had been assigned since he had become a de facto member of *Galen*'s crew, he found Conlon seated on the edge of the bed, her chin resting in her hands as she stared straight ahead.

"There you are," he greeted her. "I was just about to go down to engineering to see if you wanted to grab a quick rations pack."

She sat up as he entered, tilting her head toward him with a faint smile.

"How's Velth?" she asked.

"Doc is still working on him, but he seems like he's going to be okay." As he continued, he crossed past her to the quarter's 'fresher. "We have officially acquired some samples of Edrehmaia technology. They created things that allowed him to breathe and hydrate. They took him almost to the galactic barrier and he watched them create new stars. I'm not sure what it all means, but we'll figure it out." Popping his head back out after having removed his uniform jacket, he added, "And it sounds like Drur has made some progress. You should come to the bridge with me after we grab a bite."

"I'm not all that hungry," she said.

"Are you sure?"

"Yeah."

Kim paused to stare at her. She seemed only vaguely present, as if her mind were a thousand light-years away. He moved to sit beside her and, taking her hand in his, brought it to his lips.

"You all right?"

She inclined her head toward him. "I am. I will be. I just . . . I'm glad you came by. I have something for you."

"What?" he asked, wondering why she refused to turn and face him. She lifted her chin slightly, gesturing toward their small dining/worktable. Resting on its surface was a freshly replicated clarinet.

"Nancy," he said, shocked in a good way, but also confused. "We can't spare replicator rations for stuff like this."

"I used my rations for it. Trust me, I can spare them."

Kim crossed to take the clarinet in his hands. She had clearly used his personal database to create it: a perfect copy of the one he kept on *Voyager*. He brought it to his lips and played a few random notes. He was rusty, but it wouldn't take long to fix that.

"Thank you," he said. "I've really been missing mine."

"I know."

"I should play it for the baby, next time I can stop by for a bit. By the way, have you started thinking about names?"

She shook her head, a wistful expression on her face. "I honestly haven't. You?"

"Not really. Okay, maybe I have a short list forming in the back of my head, but, you know, it's totally up to you."

"No, it isn't," she said gently.

"How do you feel about Abigail, or Allison?"

"They're pretty, I guess."

"But not setting the world on fire for you, I can tell."

"There's plenty of time," she said.

He blew a few more notes. "I really can't thank you enough for this. I needed it, but I didn't want to, I mean, it seemed like an extravagance."

"I know it feels good to take care of everyone else, Harry, but sometimes, you need to take care of yourself too. Remember that, okay?"

"I will," he promised.

"Play something for me?"

"Any requests?"

"Whatever you feel like."

He thought for a moment and Debussy's suite drifted into his mind. "I was playing this one in my head the other night. Do you know it?"

He began to play, the music stirring deep wells of contentment he hadn't touched in too long. He closed his eyes as he continued, allowing himself to fall into the gentle, haunting lullaby of the moon. When he finished and opened his eyes again, tears were falling down Conlon's cheeks.

"Hey," he said, rushing to her side and taking both her hands in his. "What's wrong?"

She shook her head but still did not face him. "It's beautiful. That's all." Wiping her tears with the back of her hand, she added, "Thank you."

"For what?"

Finally, she turned her face to his. He noticed immediately that there was something different about her eyes, or more specifically, her gaze. She stared in his general direction, but not quite at him.

"It started a few hours ago," she began. "I was in the science lab, finalizing the specifications for our new benamite recrystallization matrix." She paused as new tears threatened, but she took a deep breath and continued.

As she did so, a heavy stone landed in the center of Kim's gut. "And?" he asked softly.

"I kept asking the computer to turn up the lights. It was hard to read the screen and I figured it was a short in the relay, but then the computer confirmed that the lights were at maximum. I didn't want to, I mean, I wanted to see you before I . . ."

"Nancy, what the hell has happened?"

She sighed, inhaled with a sniff, and said, "I need you to take me to sickbay, Harry. I can't see. I'm blind."

14

"Fifty percent of this is silicate—oxygen and silicon. The rest is metallic," Lieutenant Patel reported.

"I'm getting iron, nickel, palladium, and osmium over here," Paris said.

"That's the other fifty percent," Patel said.

"So, almost exactly like the other four asteroids we've searched today," Paris said. "I guess I was hoping for a little more variety."

Patel laughed lightly. "I was hoping for a little black box that said 'Property of the Edrehmaia' on it."

"And a button that said 'Push Here to Activate Quantum Entanglement'?" Paris teased.

"Doesn't seem like too much to ask."

"It's never that easy, Devi," Paris said. "They don't tell you in the brochures for Starfleet Academy, but at least seventy percent of what we do is figure out how to stave off boredom. And the other thirty percent is figuring out how to not die."

"Shall we do direct scans of the next sector or move on?" Patel asked.

Paris was as eager to get back to the ship as Patel, but he knew if he came home with nothing, B'Elanna was just going to send him back out again tomorrow.

"We're sure this is the cluster?" Paris asked.

"Scanners identified these fifteen asteroids as the ones from which most of the signals we detected emanated," Patel said. "Of course, we had to account for drift over the past week, but I'd be amazed if Lasren and Waters got their math wrong."

"Agreed. Let's move on to sector twelve and if nothing changes, we head back to the Flyer," Paris said.

Patel trudged ahead, her boots leaving little dusty prints on the surface of the rock. Paris left his tricorder's scanning function active but placed it back on his belt as he caught up with Patel and fell in line beside her.

"Do you think Seven's team is having better luck?" Patel asked.

"Hard to say," Paris replied. "We're due to collect her and Aubrey in an hour, so let's hope sector twelve lights up these tricorders like a dabo wheel."

"You play?"

"I was known, in my younger days, to frequent a number of establishments featuring games of chance."

"Were you any good?"

Paris laughed. "I was terrible. But that's the point. The house always wins. That's the way those games are designed."

"Do you miss it?"

"Not really. I mean, I still like a good game of pool now and again, but I wouldn't trade the life I have now for anything."

"Because you have children?"

"They're definitely part of it. Watching a human grow and develop and learn to do everything is kind of amazing. I missed a lot of the early days with Miral. I'm glad I get to see Michael's."

"It doesn't worry you, though?"

"I'm not sure what you're getting at, Lieutenant," Paris said. He tended to be a fairly open soul, especially with fellow crew members, but he couldn't recall Patel ever expressing the slightest interest in his personal life in the past. She kept to herself and he wasn't quite sure why she would suddenly be curious. Of course, she had recently nearly died and that might have ignited a desire on her part to expand her horizons a little. Or maybe eight hours into this mission, small talk was just out of the question.

"I beg your pardon, Commander," Patel said quickly. *"It was not my intention to pry."*

"No, it's not a problem."

"I do owe you an apology, don't I? I'm doing a lot of that lately," she added.

Paris paused. He wanted to keep his partner on this mission focused and in good spirits. They were trudging across an asteroid wearing the best environmental protection Starfleet had devised, but that didn't mean that one wrong move couldn't end in disaster. But conversations like this were better suited to the mess hall, or the holodeck, where tone and physical cues were easier to read. Shutting her down completely, however, was going to make the rest of the mission incredibly awkward. He proceeded with caution.

"I can't think of anything you've done that would require forgiveness from me, Devi," he said sincerely. "Making conversation isn't a crime."

"I was referring to the rescue mission you and Commander Torres undertook to save my team and the fact that I lied to you both during that mission. I am sorry. It placed both of you in danger. You have a family, and if something I did meant that your children no longer had parents, that would have been unforgivable."

Paris took a minute to think before responding. "I'm not going to lie to you. That was tough. And B'Elanna and I had a long talk afterward about the wisdom of joint away missions in the future. Full disclosure, I'm against them. She's not, depending on the circumstances. But the thing is, what you did is the only reason we have a hope in hell of finding the *Galen* now. So, while I'm not going to suggest that you make a habit of keeping decisions like that to yourself going forward, I acknowledge that I played a part in that decision. You asked us to keep the line open to transmit your data and I was against it. If I had listened better or given your opinion greater weight, it might have gone differently."

"It's kind of you to say so, sir," Patel said. *"Thank you."*

"I don't really think having Miral and Michael with us for this mission makes it more difficult," Paris continued, now that he better understood Patel's question. "I don't think of it as optional. My mom was content to raise my sisters and me while my father served in Starfleet. That was their choice. It is not one I would ever make.

Missing all of that time with my father was difficult. I won't do to them what he did to me.

"But are there moments, when we were staring down a few dozen ships outside the Confederacy's gateway, or when that Voth ship attacked, that I recognize the danger to them and wish like hell they were somewhere safer? Yes. Definitely. At which point B'Elanna usually reminds me that the alternative would be worse. Put it this way: As it stands right now, the rewards outweigh the risks. If that ever changes, our choice might have to change as well."

"I remember when I realized I was going to die in that cavern. All I knew was that terrible as that choice was, there was no better alternative. It's a line everyone has to find inside themselves and sometimes that only happens in the moment. You don't know how much you are willing to risk until the second you have to make that call," Patel said.

"Yeah. Personally, I could go the rest of my life without facing one of those seconds again."

"We've had more than our fair share this year, haven't we?" she asked.

"I blame the Delta Quadrant," Paris said lightly. "There just seems to be no end to the sheer tonnage of strange, messed-up—"

A loud beep from Paris's tricorder cut him off. He pulled it from his suit and checked the display as a similar alarm sounded from Patel's.

"Hydrogen?" they both said simultaneously.

Patel put some distance between herself and Paris as she began to scan what appeared to be a very shallow crater just a few meters wide and mere centimeters deep.

"How does hydrogen get here?" Paris asked.

Patel was tapping her tricorder, obviously altering its scanning configuration. After a few moments, she went to her knees, her hand playing over the fine dust that formed the asteroid's surface. *"There was water here, fairly recently,"* she said.

"Where did it come from?" Paris asked.

"We know that at least some of these asteroids contain the Edrehmaia base," Patel said. *"Until now, I have assumed that was a random occur-*

rence, the result of debris from the formation of the binary system leaving deposits out here that were originally part of another body."

"Have you changed your mind about that?"

"We will need to do deep scans of several of the other asteroids to make sure, but I think there might be another explanation."

"Don't keep me in suspense, Devi."

Patel rose and walked around the crater's edge, scanning as she went. "Do you remember how the water sources on SWOW were lined with silicon?" she asked.

"SWOW?"

"DK-1116."

"Oh, right. The lakes. Yeah, that was weird."

"It was intentional. The water had to be pure to function as a natural circuit breaker. But how did they come up with that? I mean, you solve problems by working with the elements that are readily available, but that's still a leap, isn't it?"

Paris studied his own readings and noted the presence of a band of silicon several meters down that could have been a natural deposit but was a little too regular in its size and shape. More important, there was a hollow space within the silicon formation for which almost nothing natural could account.

"The Edrehmaia did it first, and the others learned from them," he realized. "The species that studied DK-1116 must have also spent some time analyzing this asteroid field."

"That's right," Patel agreed. "What if the technology we're looking for is simply the Edrehmaia substance itself? They place a few cubic meters of the substance at the center of these asteroids and quantumly code it to become entangled with the other deposits as well as the planet."

"Then you wrap it in silicon to make sure it doesn't activate accidentally," Paris said.

"Or when someone digging for samples happens to strike too deep," Patel suggested, clearly thinking of Gwyn and Seven's earlier mission.

"And then you place a vein of frozen water within the silicon, pure water, that prevents unintentional reaction."

"The heat generated when the planet's energy is released warms the asteroids and the water, which melts and trickles up to the surface, forming this small crater with its residual hydrogen," Patel continued.

"Which allowed for the reaction of the Edrehmaia base that transmitted the energy waves to adjust the star's motion so it didn't destroy the rest of the system when it broke orbit," Paris concluded.

"The technology isn't on the asteroids," Patel said. *"It is the asteroids."*

"Let's go," Paris said. "We're going to pick up Seven's team a little early."

"What's the rush?" Patel asked.

"I just really want us to be the ones that figured this out before she did."

VESTA

Doctor Sal's workload once she had returned to duty hadn't been terribly strenuous. The most challenging problem she'd faced as part of the Full Circle Fleet had been Nancy Conlon's degenerative condition, and despite the fact that Conlon might well be dead already, Sal hated unfinished business on principle.

She had approached Conlon's illness the same way she did most problems—take what you know and build from there. Vega Nine's cure, while instructional, had not been a perfect fit. In that case, the introduction of an alien virus had been responsible and ultimately possible to unwind by introducing a new vector into the infected patients that restored the proper protein sequences. The problem with Conlon's illness was that it was impossible to determine the actual cause. Proximity to the alien possession that had preceded it suggested that the assault had to be connected. But the alien in question was gone and the few scans that existed of Conlon while possessed hadn't been thorough enough to show any definitive cause.

It did, however, suggest that the trauma had begun in her brain. This was further supported when the first serious damage it caused was also to her brain.

There was no reason for Sal to continue working this problem. Odds were good that even if they found the *Galen* with her crew still alive, Sal wouldn't be permitted to rejoin the team treating Conlon.

But that didn't mean that she couldn't keep thinking about it, and hell, if any of her new thoughts showed promise, a test or two, run on her own time and to satisfy her own curiosity, wouldn't be out of bounds.

All of her work up until this point—the Vega Nine vectors, the metamorphic cells—had been designed to treat the resulting damage to Conlon's DNA. Sal still believed that the metamorphic cells would have cured Conlon, but as she would never again be able to access them, it was another dead end.

Perhaps she needed to search for a new vector, something malleable enough to effect change in the damaged cells without activating their self-defense mechanisms.

Or, perhaps, she needed to start over. From the very top. She had far more experience than any other doctors in the fleet at treating syndromes like Conlon's. The other physicians on the case had deferred to her expertise, time and again, working to minimize the symptoms and buy Sal the time she needed to find a cure.

Had that been her mistake? She hated to think Regina had been right, but her primary complaint had been the secrecy with which Sal had pursued her goals. Had she shared her theories and plans with the others, they might have said no, but she hadn't bothered to ask.

Pride placed deep in her pocket, where it was most useful, Sal transmitted a message to *Voyager*'s sickbay. Soon, the wide, mottled face and warm eyes of Doctor Sharak appeared on her viewscreen.

"Doctor Sal, it is good to see you," he greeted her. *"I trust you are well?"*

"I have been better," Sal replied.

"I believe that is true of all of us and will be until we have found our sister ship."

"I cannot help but feel the call of unfinished business," Sal said.

"Do you require assistance?"

"I do. I have been going over the work I did on Lieutenant Conlon's case."

"I, too, believe we will find her, and while I hope the Doctor will have made progress, I do not think any efforts we might make on their behalf would be wasted."

"You identified the DNA damage repair syndrome first," Sal said. "In your initial diagnosis, did you spend much time attempting to locate the cause?"

"As I reported to you when we first discussed the case, I did not," Sharak replied. *"The progress of the disease was alarmingly brisk and my work in pure genetics is limited. Have you made any discoveries in that respect?"*

"I haven't," Sal admitted. "But that's largely because I didn't try. I assumed that it was a result of her possession by the Seriareen consciousness, but none of the scans made while he was still in control of her revealed any obvious injuries or mutations that could account for the changes to her DNA. Frankly, I was operating under the belief that her own immune system, reacting to the alien presence, attempted to respond and that resulted in the alterations to her DNA."

"A reasonable assumption," Sharak agreed. *"One we all shared."*

"I focused entirely on finding a way to help her DNA regain its damage repair functions . . ."

"While we monitored her for any new disease processes resulting from the damage to her DNA," Sharak finished for her.

"So, this is my question: Did we miss something?" Sal asked.

Sharak considered this for a moment, then said, *"You believe we acted precipitously?"*

"Given that this was a singular case, and none of our test results showed a possible cause, we dismissed the notion of searching for one," Sal said. "But maybe we shouldn't have?"

"None of her work-ups showed any evidence of an obvious infectious agent," Sharak reminded her. *"But that does not mean none was present."*

"Where would you even begin to look?" Sal asked.

Sharak shifted his gaze from the screen, sitting back. *"As an intellectual exercise, let us assume that the invasion of her consciousness was the cause of the damage to her DNA. This would suggest that the mechanism was introduced by the consciousness itself."*

"It's not like we have numerous, or really *any*, other examples to study," Sal said, "but from the point of view of the Seriareen consciousness, an entity that had evolved to infect multiple host bodies, it does seem possible that it also evolved a means to limit the host's ability to reject it."

"You believe it altered her DNA intentionally?"

"Maybe?"

Sharak nodded. *"Anything is possible. Without evidence, however, it is only an interesting supposition."*

"The attack was centered in her neural pathways," Sal said. "And most of the secondary disease processes we have treated were also neurological."

"The invading consciousness would have to target individual cells, effect the alteration to her DNA in such a way that would compromise her immune response, and suppress her normal repair mechanisms. Very specific knowledge of the host would be required to do so without also killing the host, and I would assume that evolution would select for modifications that did as little damage as possible."

"I don't know about that," Sal said. "I mean, they had the ability to jump to new hosts at will. Any old body would do. Maybe keeping their hosts alive indefinitely was never a priority or was secondary to preventing rejection."

"It is, forgive me, what is the term? Upside-down thinking?"

"Counterintuitive," Sal offered, remembering that Sharak's mother tongue was not Standard. "But only because we're not used to thinking like the Seriareen."

"A moment," Sharak requested, then began to work his data panel.

"What is it?"

"It occurs to me that while there are no other human patients to consider, we do have thorough scans in our database of three other individuals who were compromised by the Seriareen."

Sal was struck by the revelation. "I am an idiot."

"Not in my experience," Sharak retorted kindly as he continued to work.

"You're talking about the other three possessed individuals, ones we transported to our ships and detained," Sal said.

"Precisely," Sharak said. *"All were processed through sickbay prior to their incarceration. No infectious agents were detected, but the scans themselves might prove illuminating."* After a moment he added, *"I have transmitted the files to you. I suggest we begin a new analysis. Let us search these scans for any evidence of DNA damage to the other hosts, Emem, Tirrit, and Adaeze."*

"Do we have baselines for these species?"

"We do. You should have files in your database for the Devore, Turei, and Vaadwaur, respectively."

"Thank you, Doctor Sharak."

"It is nothing," he replied. "Niana at Rorestan."

"I apologize, Doctor. I don't understand that reference."

"Good hunting," Sharak said.

"To both of us," Sal agreed.

"So, the good news is that there are literally thousands of asteroids within the inner belt that could be used to attract the attention of the Edrehmaia," Admiral Janeway said. "And the bad news is that we have no way of creating the necessary conditions to activate them."

"It appears so," Seven replied.

As soon as the away teams had returned with this new intelligence, Janeway had called a late-night briefing with Seven, Patel, and Torres. The four sat in the admiral's office around a low table strewn with sandwiches, fruit, and mugs of tea and coffee. More casual than most official briefings, the gathering reminded Janeway of the many times she and her fellow cadets had pulled all-night study sessions in preparation for particularly difficult exams.

"How hard would it be to capture one of the smaller asteroids and bring it aboard?" the admiral asked.

"To what end?" Seven inquired.

"To access the inert Edrehmaia substance," Janeway replied.

"I would not suggest coming within arm's length of it," Seven said.

"Without proper containment, I agree with you," Janeway replied. "But Commander O'Donnell is working, as we speak, on a way to safely experiment with it."

"Clearly, it can be done," Patel said. "I expect he's using the metal fragments we found at Station One."

"Yes. And I have great faith in his persistence. I think he's taken personal offense at the notion that other species have already done so with apparent ease."

"It is absurd to base one's self-worth on comparisons with others," Seven noted.

Janeway turned to Seven with a quizzical smile. For a moment she was transported back in time to Seven's first days aboard *Voyager*. Even now, there remained occasional rare hints of the angry, superior, dismissive, and completely lost young woman Janeway had forcibly severed from the Collective. But she had come so far in eight years of exploring her humanity. Even this small insight would have been well beyond Seven once.

"The species that experimented on the planet had access to plenty of it, but I'm not sure that alone will be sufficient," Patel reminded them. "Simply interacting with it does not seem to interest the Edrehmaia."

"No, but it's still the key," Torres said.

"How so?" Janeway asked.

"The Edrehmaia base, wherever it is located, has the ability to act as a point of quantum entanglement. When the base within the asteroids was activated to create the field that adjusted the star's course, a quantum connection was established between here and wherever the Edrehmaia are located."

"We don't need to bring the Edrehmaia here," Janeway realized. "We need to create quantum sensors that can visualize both points of entanglement. Then, we simply calculate the coordinates that correspond to the Edrehmaia's location."

"The Borg applied principles of quantum entanglement in the maintenance of their transwarp network," Seven said. "The various apertures were too distant and the power requirements too vast to allow for constant activation. Ingress and egress points were brought into quantum synchronization once an aperture was activated. While the specifics of the Edrehmaia's systems will, of course, differ, the foundation should be the same, unless the Edrehmaia operate in domains or realities we have yet to discover."

"Let's hope they don't," Janeway said.

"How come this is the first I'm hearing of this?" Torres asked.

"It has only now become relevant," Seven replied.

"But we still need to activate the energy field generated by the asteroids," Patel said. "How do we do that?"

A faint smile flickered across Torres's lips. "The same way it was activated the first time. We move a star."

It was an absurd notion, but in her gut, Janeway also knew it was true.

"It took that planet thousands of years to store enough energy to affect the star's motion," Patel said. "Where are we going to get that kind of power?"

"We don't need anywhere near that much," Torres corrected her. "DK-1116 had to pull a star out of orbit. We just need to nudge it off course a little."

"How?" Patel asked.

"How *much* is the real issue," Seven noted.

"Deflectors can't do it," Janeway said. "Any beam powerful enough to impact the star would easily overload our arrays."

"Not to mention the extra energy required for shields, given how close we'd have to get to the star," Patel added.

"We don't touch the star," Torres said. "We alter the space around it."

"You are suggesting destabilizing the area of space along the star's current course?" Janeway asked.

"I am."

"How?"

"A stable quantum slipstream corridor alters the geometry of normal space as soon as it is formed," Torres said.

"But those alterations are projected forward along our intended course," Seven reminded her.

"And the wake dissipates within seconds. What we want to do is elongate the wake enough to intersect with the star's course," Torres continued.

"Without pulling the star into the slipstream itself," Janeway warned.

"So we would need two ships, *Vesta* and *Voyager*, to plot synchronous slipstream jumps. The first, most likely the *Vesta*, would bring the corridor within a few thousand kilometers of the star's course, and then *Voyager* would have to exit the slipstream seconds after the point of intersection," Torres finished.

Janeway began to visualize the plan along with the many, many ways it could go wrong. It definitely qualified as misuse of a Starfleet resource, but it was this kind of radical thinking that had brought *Voyager* across seventy thousand light-years in only seven years.

"Okay. Assuming we can make the math work, and assuming that altering the star's course reactivates the energy field within the asteroid belt, the quantum sensors would need to be in place prior to our synchronous jump," the admiral said.

"I'd like Seven to work with Bryce and Icheb on those sensors," Torres said.

"Of course," Seven agreed.

"Which still leaves us with one big problem left to solve," Janeway said.

"Once we locate the Edrehmaia, how do we communicate with them," Patel rightly surmised.

"How is Lasren coming along with his new language?" Torres inquired.

"Slowly. He has a number of interesting theories about terms we might use to establish and build a shared language. But until we can actually test them, it is impossible to know whether or not they will succeed," Janeway replied.

"Last he and I spoke, he was still trying to figure out the mathematical equivalent of the word *please*," Patel noted.

"I wonder if we should hedge that bet," Janeway said.

"How?" Torres asked.

"The interlocutors seem to be the functional transitional state between organic matter and the Edrehmaia base. That they recognized the creation of Devi's and its potential as a means of communication in their first transmissions to us leads me to believe that if we could re-create our own, it might make our conversations a great deal easier," Janeway mused.

"We do have scans of the technology that was present in the cavern," Patel said. "I admit, I haven't reviewed them yet with the intention of reverse engineering it."

"You have been otherwise occupied," Janeway said kindly.

"I can take a look at those systems and see about replicating them on one of our shuttles," Torres offered.

"It would require access to a significant quantity of the base, as well as a secure environment in which to test it," Patel said.

"That thought had occurred to me as well," Janeway noted. "The first problem is finding a source for the Edrehmaia base that we can safely extract and contain. The asteroids are still the most likely candidate."

"Not necessarily," Patel said. "Station One remains largely intact. Its architecture suggests that there were veins of the substance within some proximity, given the placement of the circuit-breaking pool. We should scan for deposits of silicon, similar to those in the asteroids, and consider excavating one. It's an environment that will be easier to control than the surface of an asteroid."

"It always comes back to—what did O'Donnell call it? SWOW?" Janeway asked.

"I implore you not to encourage Commander O'Donnell's flagrant whimsy," Seven pleaded, at which point Janeway, Torres, and Patel erupted in a fit of spontaneous laughter. All three were having difficulty breathing and wiping tears from their eyes before it passed, a sure sign of their mutual exhaustion.

Once they had departed, Janeway considered reviewing the many communiques and reports in her queue. She was falling well behind on her daily workload, as so much of her attention was consumed by the work of various departments to find the *Galen*.

She opted, instead, to see whether or not Chakotay was still awake. "Good evening, my love," he greeted her when his face appeared on her personal screen.

"How goes the battle?" she asked.

"It feels like we're getting closer by the minute to our next encounter with the Edrehmaia and the recovery of our people."

"I hope so," she agreed.

"The coordination between the various departments of the fleet is inspiring. Tom, Atlee, and Roach have been devising multiple retrieval scenarios and running drills. Aubrey, Url, and Denisov have selected incursion teams in the event it becomes necessary to board the *Galen*, and Hoch and Falto are taking the lead on both offensive and defensive flight patterns."

"You did design our assignments on DK-1116 for just that purpose: to allow the officers of our fleet to get to know one another better and start to think of themselves as one large crew. Whatever the outcome, that success is worth celebrating."

"You may be right," Chakotay said, "though it's hard to say that the price was worth it."

In the last several days, once she and the rest of the fleet had committed themselves to recovering *Galen*, Chakotay's initial anger had been transformed into laser-like focus on their task. She was relieved to see that he was no longer tormenting himself for having suggested this mission in the first place, but he could not hide the deep regret that would always color his memories of this part of their journey.

She longed to take him in her arms and remind him that she would always be his safe place, that his burdens were never his alone, they were always shared. But he was right. It was possible that within hours the fleet would be ready to set course to rescue their sister ship and he didn't need any distractions, however pleasant, right now.

She was suddenly struck by a random disquieting certainty. She and Chakotay had been through so much together, from their first days in the Delta Quadrant, the constant struggles of the seven years it took to return home, the years they had denied themselves the love and comfort of their absolute commitment to each other, and now, standing beside each other through the worst this mission could throw at them. If anything had been constant throughout, it was change and how often it came upon them unexpectedly.

As she stared into his eyes, she feared that more change was just beyond the horizon. She wondered if, when it came, she would regret wasting even one moment they might spend together.

"I'm about to turn in for a few hours," she said. "Join me?"

He hesitated, but only briefly.

"I'm on my way."

15

Nancy Conlon lay on a biobed, terrified. Now that the moment had come, all of the misgivings she should have already considered were at the forefront of her mind. It didn't help that there was a constant ringing in her ears and that even with her eyes open, the overhead light, which was surely set at maximum illumination, was little more than a grayish smudge in a field of black. Her body was collapsing around her, shutting down, one system at a time. That her mind could remain so clear and functional throughout this process was almost unfair. A little less clarity would have gone a long way right now toward numbing, or at least ratcheting down, the abject horror of her personal, slow-motion apocalypse.

She was freezing cold. The Doctor had already injected the first of the compounds that would slowly reduce her neurological functions and render her body comatose. She imagined the medicine moving through her veins and, as it did so, the cold spread to her extremities.

Gentle pressure squeezed her right hand. She assumed it was the Doctor. As soon as Kim had brought her to sickbay, the Doctor had kindly but firmly ordered him to return to his duties, assuring him that Conlon would be fine. He had protested until she had asked with a great deal more surety than she'd felt that he listen to the Doctor. She had not been able to see the fear and disappointment on his face, but it had not been hard to imagine. He had taken her hands in his, kissed her gently on the cheek, and promised her that he would be back as soon as the Doctor allowed it. She had told him not to worry and promised to see him soon.

She didn't know why she hadn't wished to discuss this choice with him. It might have been a desire to spare him both the attendant fears of anticipation and, if it should fail, any responsibility for the outcome. Once this was done, he would accept her choice as the only one possible. There was no reason to force him to endure the stress of the actual procedure. Soon enough, this would be over, one way or another.

"Nancy, squeeze my hand if you can hear me," the Doctor said calmly.

She did so, though her fingers ached with the herculean effort.

"I want you to prepare yourself. In a few moments, you will awaken in your holographic body. It might take time for you to acclimate. Don't be afraid. Reg and I are here."

She was conscious of a new sense of heaviness throughout her entire body, almost as if an incredibly warm blanket had been placed over her. She was tired. She had fought so hard and so long. It was difficult to remember what her life had been like before it was in danger of ending.

As she drifted away, she tried to remember the song Harry had played for her; the lovely, sad progression had taken her back to the moment Harry had shown her the holographic starfield. She imagined them there again, standing in the void, surrounded by countless stars, the freedom of it, the wonder. For a few minutes, she, Harry, and their daughter had been the only people who existed. All of her past fears had suddenly seemed insignificant, or perhaps they had just lost their power to induce paralyzing terror. In that moment, something had been returned to her, something she had tried to embrace. It was the will to choose her own destiny, to live however many days remaining to her on her own terms. She had chosen Harry. She had chosen their daughter. For a fleeting moment, that choice had seemed to fill her with a new sense of purpose.

Had it not been for the *Galen*'s disaster, that choice might have taken root. Given time to nurture it, she might have come to truly embrace it. But there had been no time, since then, to do that. And now, there never would be.

Nancy Conlon knew what she wanted. All that was required for her to attain it was release.

She could no longer feel the Doctor's hand holding hers. Her last thought as she drifted away was to wonder if she would ever actually feel the touch of anyone's hand on hers again.

Commander Glenn had remained by Lieutenant Velth's bedside as he slept, continuing to run tests and analyze results. His recovery from his extended sojourn with the Edrehmaia was coming along, slow and steady. Once returned to the ship's atmosphere and given intravenous fluids and nutrients, his body had begun to heal at what appeared to her to be an accelerated rate.

There were, however, a few causes for concern. Both his bronchial and nasal passages were inflamed. This could have resulted from the levels of oxygen and the specific method of filtering carbon dioxide used by the Edrehmaia to sustain him inside his EV suit. She had done several panels searching for any infectious agents and found a few anomalies, but nothing that was generating a typical immune response. She was tempted to write these symptoms off as a secondary infection or simple inflammation—tempted, but not yet content.

Further, his cellular metabolism had increased, even in the absence of ingested nutrients. He was periodically receiving synthesized compounds meant to slowly restore normal metabolic functions, but these seemed to have been sent into overdrive. As with the inflammation, there was no discernible cause.

Selah's analysis of the Edrehmaia's water-generating technology had been predictably inconclusive. The substance itself was composed of dozens of molecular compounds that were not identifiable by the ship's computers. Much like the *Sevenofninonium* that had brought the fleet to DK-1116, it seemed to be composed of synthetic elements and isotopes that were either as yet undiscovered or created by the Edrehmaia for purposes of their own. None of these were present in Velth's blood, but the long-term effects of his exposure to them remained to be seen.

She tried, as ever, not to allow fear of the unknown to create anxiety. For now, he seemed to be well into his recovery and within a few days could likely return to duty. That he had survived at all was a miracle, and she tried to focus on that unexpected blessing rather than unknowable consequences.

His return had also provided some new insight into their alien friends. It was interesting to her how quickly her perspective of them had shifted from aggressors, hostiles, or captors to benevolent, if inscrutable, entities. Their actions did seem to indicate curiosity and a desire to communicate, even if their language was conceptually limited. There was clearly more to this entire situation than she yet understood. In time, she hoped more clarity would be possible.

The sound of raised voices had briefly drawn her from Velth's room into the main bay. Lieutenant Kim had entered with Lieutenant Conlon and she had immediately become the focus of the Doctor's efforts. He had called for Lieutenant Barclay as an unspoken understanding had passed between her and the EMH. Clearly, the time to transfer Conlon's consciousness had come. She hoped the procedure would be effective. Conlon's last reports had indicated that they would soon be ready to attempt to recrystallize enough benamite to restore the slipstream drive and begin their journey back to the fleet. It now seemed possible that the Edrehmaia, their curiosity satisfied, might be willing to allow them to depart in peace.

Glenn had left the Doctor and Barclay to their work and returned to Velth's bedside, surprised to find him sitting up on the side of his biobed.

"How are you feeling?" she greeted him.

"Starving," he replied. "I need to eat."

Given his bloodwork, this wasn't surprising. In fact, it might be a good time to reintroduce solid food to his diet.

"Sickbay's replicators are notoriously limited, but let me see what we can do here," she replied. "How does chicken and rice sound?"

Velth shook his head. "Terrible."

"If you can keep it down, I promise your next meal will include cheese," Glenn offered.

Velth lifted his eyes to hers. Normally, they were a gentle hazel color. Now, both his pupils and the irises were jet black.

Glenn suddenly remembered the two different genomes that the Edrehmaia had used in reference to Velth. Wondering how vast the changes they had made to him were, she reached instinctively for a medical tricorder and began a new scan. It revealed even higher metabolic functions than she had previously observed and incredibly odd enzymatic levels. She had not yet lowered the tricorder when Velth slid off the bed and moved to the replicator.

"Stand down, Lieutenant Velth," Glenn said in a tone that was clearly an order as she moved to her instrument panel on the room's diagnostic station to retrieve a hypo and code it with a sedative.

He ignored her, his fingers tapping the replicator pad as he hastily searched through the available options.

"No, no, no," he said, growing more anxious by the second.

"Ranson, listen to me," Glenn said as she stepped cautiously toward him. There was something almost feral in his manner, clearly dangerous.

Velth slammed his fists into the replicator panel hard enough to send sparks flying. A low, guttural growl was followed by spasmodic, wet coughing.

She was only a step behind him when he turned, registered the hypo, and knocked her back with both hands, tossing her unceremoniously to the deck.

Glenn tapped her combadge. "Glenn to security. Emergency team to sickbay, immediately." Conscious of the danger to herself but far more concerned about the rest of the ship, she added, "Computer, seal this door until security override is provided." The computer responded with a pleasant chirp. As she tried to pull herself up, she felt a sharp pain just below her collarbone where he had struck her.

Velth was struggling to breathe, his wild eyes searching the room desperately. Finally, he turned back to the replicator, came to his knees before it, and with his bare hands began to tug at the panel beneath, bending the metal edges until he could rip it from its housing. This exposed a set of power relays and a conduit. He then reached for the conduit and ripped it free of the clasps that held it in place.

Glenn watched, both astonished and alarmed, as he grasped the conduit with both hands and the tips of his fingers seemed to melt into it. The panel lights immediately adjacent to it, as well as the room's interior lighting, began to flicker as Velth's savage hunger was sated by the power he was absorbing directly from the ship.

"What the holy hell?" Glenn said, horrified. She briefly considered reaching for the room's emergency storage and using a phaser to disable him and end this freakish spectacle but wondered just as quickly if the power released by a phaser would stun him or feed him.

There's really only one way to do this, she realized, and her window of opportunity was probably closing quickly.

Velth hugged the conduit to his body like a lifeline. Glenn raised the level of the sedative she had ordered to maximum, enough to subdue a being twice Velth's size and normal strength. Gathering her nerve, she shot forward, aiming for Velth's neck but making contact just below his right shoulder, and depressed the hypospray. His eyes opened and another growl died in his throat as the sedative took effect. The lights continued to dim as, even unconscious, his body continued to draw power from the ship.

By the time security began pounding on the door, she was standing over his inert form, studying the place where his fingers had merged with the power source, certain of one thing: whatever this was, it was no longer Ranson Velth.

The Doctor had waited patiently as Lieutenant Conlon drifted slowly into a comatose state. He paid close attention to her neurological functions displayed on the surgical arch, preparing to transfer her consciousness as soon as her engrammatic patterns had stabilized. As this was the second time he had performed this procedure, he was not unduly concerned. He and Barclay had tested the holographic interface, now running through his mobile emitter, several times and were certain of its stability. Unlike Danara Pel, Lieutenant Conlon had been thoroughly prepared for the procedure. He sensed her trepidation but knew it would pass as soon as she awoke in a body that was free of pain and fully functional.

Barclay stood by, monitoring the active holomatrix. "The engrammatic buffers are ready to receive, Doctor," he reported.

"Just another minute or two," the Doctor advised. "The neuroleptic has not entirely subdued her autonomic nervous—"

Before he could complete his thought, the lights in sickbay began to flicker. "What the . . . ?" the Doctor began as a series of automated alarms sounded from the interface regulating Conlon's procedure. The lights dimmed intermittently as the Doctor turned his attention to the display's main board. "Why are we losing power?" he demanded. "Computer, reroute power to this bio-station through emergency backups," he then added quickly.

"That's going to be a problem," Barclay informed him as Commander Glenn's voice sounded shipwide. *"Glenn to security. Emergency team to sickbay, immediately."*

The Doctor watched as Conlon's neurological functions began to dysregulate. He considered shutting down the chemical drip but knew that any interruption at this moment could have disastrous consequences. Never mind the consciousness transfer, he could lose Conlon before he even had the chance.

"What's wrong with the emergency backups?" the Doctor shouted as a pair of armed security ensigns burst into the main bay.

"Where is the captain, sir?" Ensign Borland asked.

"Commander Glenn is in observation room three," the Doctor reported. They hurried past him to respond to their captain's request. "Reg?"

Barclay had moved to the bay's main power console and was clearly working to restore full power to the bio-station now connected to Nancy Conlon. "We don't have battery backups right now. We used them all in the first thirty-six hours we were here, and no one has yet taken the time to replenish them," he said.

"Do I have to tell you that if we don't stabilize this station immediately . . . ?"

"No, you don't," Barclay cut him off. "There is an unexpected drain coming from an adjacent conduit. It looks like an overload or a breach. I'm going to reroute but I need a few more seconds."

"Hurry," the Doctor pleaded, watching in horror as Conlon's vitals began to show signs of distress. "Computer, silence alarms," he added. "I'm well aware there's a problem."

"There we go," Barclay finally said. "Is that better?"

It was. A little. Once the neuroleptic flow settled back into its prescribed, uninterrupted dosage, Conlon's neural functions began to revert to more normal patterns.

"Is the holomatrix still stable?" the Doctor asked.

"It is," Barclay replied.

"We have to begin the transfer now."

"Go ahead."

Even though the overhead lighting continued to blink, Barclay's quick work had segregated full power to Conlon's bio-station. Ignoring the shouting of the security team down the hall as they attempted to gain access to Glenn, the Doctor activated the transfer protocol and watched as the engrammatic transfer began.

"The buffers are receiving data," Barclay reported. "Transfer at sixteen percent and rising."

The Doctor kept his eyes glued to the display showing Conlon's neurological stability. There were troubling, intermittent spikes, but it was much too late to alter course now.

"Twenty-seven percent," Barclay said.

"Any signs of rejection?" the Doctor asked.

"No."

"Small mercies. What the hell is happening back there?" the Doctor asked.

"You don't want me to stop and check right now, do you?" Barclay asked.

"Of course not."

Lieutenant Kim rushed into sickbay. "Why did the captain call for . . . ?" he began but stopped short the minute his eyes found the hologram of Nancy Conlon that stood motionless beside the biobed on which her body lay.

"Is that . . . ?" he asked.

"Yes, Lieutenant," the Doctor said.

"The last time we talked about this, it was only a hypothetical eventuality," Kim said, clearly understanding what was happening.

"As you have no doubt surmised, it is now an actuality," the Doctor said. "The lieutenant agreed to the consciousness transfer but asked that we keep the matter confidential until it was complete. Given that we have managed to fail her quite spectacularly in that regard in the past, I felt obligated to honor her request."

"It's okay, Doc," Kim said, watching the hologram tensely. "I get it."

"We're holding at sixty-seven percent," Barclay interjected. "There seems to be a lag in the transfer."

"Is something wrong?" Kim demanded.

"I don't know," the Doctor said. "There was a brief power disruption right before we began. But it shouldn't have affected the transfer."

"The transfer rate has slowed significantly," Barclay said, "but the engrammatic buffers are still stable. I don't think the hologram is rejecting the transfer. I think the problem is on the other end."

Kim moved to the opposite side of the biobed and took Conlon's free hand in his. "Nancy, it's Harry. I'm here. Listen to my voice. I need you to come back to me. I need you. The baby needs you. Every person on this ship is counting on you to keep us alive out here. Don't be afraid."

To the Doctor's surprise, Barclay said, "Sixty-eight percent."

"Keep talking," the Doctor ordered Kim.

"Just listen to my voice, Nancy. You're almost there. Don't be afraid. Remember how it was when we were standing among the stars. Remember how we promised to be there for each other, no matter what. I'm here and I'm waiting for you to come back to me. I know you can do it."

"Seventy-five percent."

"Transfer rate has stabilized," the Doctor said, relieved.

"That's it, Nancy. You're doing great. Come on. Just a little further. I'm here. Find my voice," Kim said, his tone strong and certain.

"Ninety percent," Barclay reported. "Ninety-two. Ninety-five." And finally, with a deep sigh of relief, "Transfer complete."

The Doctor turned his attention toward the hologram. She had stood, throughout the procedure, with her eyes open but her face slack. Her eyes began to flutter rapidly. She looked to her left and right, searching the faces staring at her intently.

Kim still held Conlon's hand, but his eyes were on the hologram's face, filled with hope.

"Nancy?" he asked.

She turned to him and a faint smile crossed her lips.

"Hi there," she said softly.

Kim moved back to stand directly across from her. "Hello, beautiful," he said. "Are you okay?"

"I'm fine," she said, extending her arms before her and staring at the backs of her hands. She wriggled her fingers, considering them quizzically, then took a few unsteady steps forward. When she stopped, her attention shifted to her right arm, where the mobile emitter generating her body rested on a black band.

"Where am I?" she asked.

"You're in sickbay," the Doctor said gently. "The consciousness transfer was completed successfully. Take as much time as you need to acclimate yourself."

"The matrix is functioning well within normal parameters," Barclay said. "You should have access to all of your memory files now."

Conlon stood still, her focus clearly inward as she appeared to search those files for the first time. Finally, she said, "It worked. I'm here. I'm real."

"Of course you are," the Doctor said with a smile. "As real as any of us."

"I can see again. What's wrong with the lights?"

"A security issue," the Doctor said. "I am sure the captain has it well in hand by now."

She took a few more steps, now surefooted. "It's amazing. I can't remember ever feeling like this."

"What do you mean?" Kim asked.

"It's hard to explain," she replied. "But I feel like I could do absolutely anything. It's just hard to decide what to do first."

"First, you're going to take a seat and let me run a full diagnostic," Barclay said.

"Oh, all right," she said cheerfully, for the first time noticing her body lying on the biobed. Her face fell into concerned lines. "Am I okay?" she asked.

"You are," the Doctor said. "Your body will remain in this condition as we continue to work to heal it."

She nodded. "Good. Yes. That's good."

Kim crossed to stand opposite her. "Do you mind if I stick around?"

"Of course I don't," she said with a genuine smile, then asked, "Who are you?"

16

Captain Regina Farkas needed to turn in for the night. Gamma shift was already four hours old and no one was going to care how much sleep she had missed when alpha shift dawned bright and early. Apart from her typical duties—running a starship crewed by almost eight hundred souls was no picnic on a good day—her slipstream specialists were now working in conjunction with *Voyager's* to calculate a slipstream flyby of the rogue star that apparently had a better than average chance of turning both ships into salsa. Lieutenant Bryce and Seven were pulling all-nighters adding a few Borg-inspired components to some remote scanners to make sure that when the Edrehmaia took offense to altering the star's course, they would be able to identify their present location and, hopefully, *Galen's* along with it. Bryce had tried three times to explain the math to his captain before she had agreed to simply trust him, simultaneously assuring him that he would never see the inside of a starship again should any of those Borg parts begin to assimilate her ship.

Oh, and a good two-thirds of her engineers were busy excavating tunnels on DK-1116 in an effort to obtain some of the Edrehmaia substance because Commander Liam O'Donnell was constitutionally incapable of leaving well enough alone.

All of this, while her tactical and security teams were running hourly drills covering every conceivable scenario they could imagine for the rescue of *Galen* and the Edrehmaia's potential responses. Farkas could see how much her XO, Commander Malcolm Roach, was enjoying these activities, so she kept to herself her certainty that *nothing* could possibly prepare them for this encounter. It was all so much whistling in the dark until the two interested parties were capable of having the most basic conversation and, on that front, progress was dubious at best.

It was nights like this when she allowed herself five minutes to wonder why she hadn't taken Admiral Bivout up on his offer a few years back to retire from active duty and begin an illustrious teaching career at the Academy. She knew the reasons, and all of them had sounded so good at the time. Foremost among them was her general apprehension of young men and women of the age of most cadets. Sure, they were smart, but they were also emotional messes because their brains were not yet fully formed. Patience with nonsense had never been one of her many virtues, and if and when she did finally retire, she doubted seriously it would ever include adding a small group of lunatics hoping to learn the basics of command to her list of daily contacts.

She *belonged* here. This, she rarely doubted. She just wished that here would cut her a goddamned break once in a while instead of constantly testing her willingness to absorb shock, pain, and the great unknown.

She thought her ears were playing tricks on her when the chime at the door to her quarters sounded. Rising from the chair at her desk and tugging the end of her uniform undershirt down at the waist, she said, "Come."

Of course it was El'nor. *Who else would it be at this time of night unless the ship was under attack?*

"Are you up late, or early?" Farkas asked.

"Oh, I haven't slept since yesterday," Sal said, punctuating her response with a hearty yawn.

"Can I interest you in a bedtime story?"

Sal didn't respond immediately. Instead she crossed to the chair that sat opposite Farkas's desk and dropped into it, lifting her sock-clad feet to rest them on the front of said desk and placing her hands behind her head.

"Do make yourself comfortable," Farkas said. "I didn't realize it was 'optional footwear day' again already."

"You don't really mind," Sal insisted.

Farkas didn't. She was padding around her quarters barefoot, but in fairness, she did live here.

"I have good news," Sal said.

Farkas returned to her chair, placed her elbows on the desk, and rested her chin in both hands. "Hit me," she said. "I could use some of that about now."

"Doctor Sharak and I have figured out how to cure Nancy Conlon."

Farkas's spine stiffened. "I returned you to duty, El'nor. I didn't say you would ever come within arm's reach of the lieutenant again."

"Fine," Sal said. "It's not going to be a difficult procedure. Sharak can take all the credit. I don't give a damn."

"May I ask how you did that without access to the patient?"

"I think that might have been the key to *his* success," Sal replied pointedly.

"How so?"

"Turns out not being under the stress of watching a human being die right in front of you frees up all kinds of processing space in the brain. Together, we quite fearlessly abandoned all previous lines of inquiry and went looking for a snipe."

"Those don't exist."

"Neither should the cause of Conlon's illness, but here we are. Long story very short, when a Seriareen consciousness invades a new host body, the first thing it does is rewrite the DNA of a handful of neurological cells with a particularly annoying set of instructions. Those cells, which appear normal unless you know what you're looking for, inhibit the host's ability to reject the invading neural patterns. They destroy the ability of normal DNA to repair itself, causing a great deal of damage to the host over time, but in the short term, making sure that the Seriareen can take absolute control of its chosen body."

"That doesn't sound like a recipe for long-term survival," Farkas noted.

"An assumption with which both Sharak and I agreed until we

remembered that a compliant host was more important than one that could fight back. Once its current body began to degenerate severely, the Seriareen could just find a new host."

"Cheeky bastards," Farkas noted.

"Right?" Sal agreed, nodding. "It was sitting there in our damned databases all along. The bodies of the other three Seriareen were scanned before we put them in our brig and their genetic results allowed us to find the pattern."

"I've honestly never been a fan of irony," Farkas said.

"Me neither, but now that we know which cells are perpetuating the problem, removing them is as simple as a relatively minor surgery. Add to that some stem-cell therapy and the lieutenant will be good as new."

Farkas sat back in her chair. "You did it," she said. "Congratulations."

"Sharak did it," Sal reminded her with a wink.

"No, I'm going to cut you more slack than you deserve here. It's nice to have you back, my friend. I am damned proud of you right now."

"That's fine. You go ahead and enjoy the moment. I'm going to continue kicking myself for my stupidity until we find Conlon alive and are able to perform the necessary procedure. That's just me, though."

"I really like to live and let live, El'nor, but that doesn't sound like a great long-term plan."

"Peace of mind is for people who don't almost kill two patients out of arrogance and a desire for retribution," Sal said. "You were right about that. Nancy Conlon deserves to live, but I won't feel good about this, probably ever."

"You're not that bad."

"Sure I am."

"El'nor, I can think of at least three or four people I've met in this life who are worse than you."

"That many?"

"How much do you know about the DTI?"

"The Department of Temporal Investigations? Nothing. And I'd just as soon keep it that way."

"Too bad. It occurred to me after the last time we spoke that turning my career or the admiral's over to their tender mercies might not be the best idea without gaining a more thorough understanding of their policies and agendas."

Sal chuckled. "You've been calling in favors, haven't you?"

"Only about a dozen," Farkas admitted. "I still have enough friends at Command who are willing to speak freely that I have been able to cobble together a rather troubling dossier on our friendly local time police."

"If they don't already call themselves that, they should," Sal said. "That right there is good branding. Even I wouldn't mind a visit from my friendly local time cop."

"I confess, I have never before really considered the issue. I assumed that if you were part of the Federation government, you were probably going to be on the right side of most arguments."

"They're not?"

"We'll never really know," Farkas replied. "They are, to my knowledge, the only organization with the authority to commandeer Starfleet vessels and override the chain of command, even, when they deem it necessary, the C-in-C, without so much as a shred of oversight."

"That makes it sound like we all work for them," Sal said, troubled.

"Not on paper, but in practice, it appears so."

"Well, I don't know about you, but that's something I would definitely want to lodge a complaint with the management about."

"They don't even have to tell us why they are ordering us to proceed in whatever manner they see fit. In every instance where they have intervened with officers I know personally, officers who are then sworn to absolute silence, no matter how pear-shaped any of these missions go, Starfleet is required to defer to their authority. They may be experts in temporal mechanics, but none of them are trained in the finer points of command. Fear seems to drive every choice they make, and they are, essentially, a law unto themselves."

"Next time, I'm picking the bedtime story."

"Sorry."

"Have you heard from Dulmur again?"

"No. I scared him off. And I don't regret it. But I'm also willing to bet we haven't heard from them for the last time."

"I don't know our admiral as well as you do, but I can't see her bending to the will of a bunch of folks back home no matter what the regulations say."

"I can't either. Which means it won't be up to her. It will be up to me. I'm the next officer they will tap to follow their orders."

"You want a note from your doctor? *I regret to inform you that Regina Farkas is unable to captain today.*"

"Then it will fall to Roach. Or Tom Paris."

"They'll end up with a mutiny on their hands."

Farkas smiled ruefully. "But what if they're right? They don't have to tell us everything. They don't have to tell us anything other than where to go and what to do. And the oath I swore demands that I agree, no matter what. I hate it on principle, but what if they do know something we don't that makes my obstinance the worst possible choice?"

Sal did her the credit of seriously considering the question. "Here's the thing about people who are right, at least in my experience, and I'm including myself in this. They usually don't have a problem sharing the facts that support their argument. Folks who won't . . . those are the ones you need to worry about."

"Time will tell, I suppose."

"Oh, come on, Regina. You can do better than that."

VOYAGER

Ensign Aytar Gwyn was not sleeping well. She rarely managed more than a few hours each night and those were shallow and fraught. Her duties had been relatively simple the past few weeks. Counselor

Cambridge, with whom she had shared four unproductive sessions since he had confirmed her bond with Kim and Conlon's child, had restricted her from bridge duty. She didn't blame him. Waves of crippling anxiety washed over her regularly, definitely not optimal while flying a starship, even one that was essentially holding position. Running flight-control checks on *Voyager*'s shuttles and reviewing the conn reports of her fellow pilots comprised most of her waking hours.

It was good, in that it allowed her to spend at least half her day alone, focused on her connection to the child that had consumed her, a child that, by some reckonings, was hardly a person yet. Still largely a collection of very busy cells, this being's continued existence had become as essential to Gwyn's as her own. She wasn't sure what would happen should she ever open the door in her heart that was now bound to another by an invisible string of light and purpose and find that tie severed. It was terrifying to contemplate, which accounted for the constant anxiety as well as her default moods of cranky and pissed as hell.

At first, the bonding had been such a positive experience. It had focused her and revealed internal depths of strength and compassion she had never known. And had *Galen* not been taken, had Gwyn been able to observe on a daily basis, even from a distance, the child of her heart's continued growth and well-being, she might never have come to regret the choice she had made as powerfully as she did now. The state in which she found herself was simply unendurable. She was trapped in a relationship that should never have been formed, all because she had been so determined to rescue Devi Patel, she had never truly considered the consequences of her actions.

She had shared exactly none of this with the counselor. He hadn't pushed her, which seemed odd, given that normally, he had absolutely no problem speaking his mind. He had simply accepted her brisk lies in response to his inquiries about her general health and state of mind and otherwise left her to her own devices. *Why am I even continuing to see him?* she wondered.

Lasren had been a much better sounding board, given that he understood what psionic connections felt like. He had listened patiently as she spoke of her fears and reminded her that she might yet be responsible for saving the life that was so important to her. If not for her initial protests, who was to say that the fleet would have pursued the mystery of *Galen's* loss to the point of confirming their continued existence?

But Kenth's duties were onerous. She hated to demand too much from him and feared that his patience might be wearing thin.

For the first time in her life, the lack of deep personal relationships was becoming a problem and she could find no ready answer for it.

When her quarter's data panel alerted her to an incoming transmission, she assumed it was an intrafleet issue, *hoped* it was, in fact. It might force her to think about something else, at least for a few hours.

She was ill prepared for the shock of seeing the face of her mother, Vara Gwyn, when she opened the channel.

"Mom?" Gwyn asked, incredulous. "Is everything all right?"

"What have you done to your hair, Aytar?"

Gwyn struggled for a moment to remember the last time she'd colored it. *Oh, right . . . wild indigo.* But she had let it slide long enough that it was probably a mess of dark roots and faded purple by now. "I like it this way," she insisted.

The disappointment on Vara's face was only eclipsed by her obvious concern.

"Why are you calling me?" Gwyn demanded. "You never call me."

"I was contacted over a week ago by someone from your Starfleet indicating that you wished to speak. I gather it was difficult to arrange because of your location and involved a great deal of rerouting of their communication satellites. This suggested your concerns, whatever they may be, are serious. So, here I am."

Her mother was not normally this forthright. A great deal in the everyday communications of Kriosians was unsaid rather than plainly spoken. Their psionic abilities were partially responsible, but Gwyn had always sensed a deep well of secrecy and shame in that mix. It was one of the things she liked least about her people and one of the many reasons she had never felt at home among them.

"I didn't call you," Gwyn said. "I didn't even . . ." *Oh, wait.* Just before she had chosen to complete the *finiis'ral* she had wanted more than anything to speak with her mother. But the only person who heard that had been Icheb, and they hadn't shared so much as a "hello" since then. She doubted he could have arranged for this communication, even had he desired to do so.

"Does that matter now?" her mother asked. *"Are you all right?"*

"I'm fine."

Vara sighed. *"You want to try telling that to someone who hasn't known you since you first drew breath?"*

Lying was pointless with her mother, always had been. It was a byproduct of fear. However, her current crisis somehow made that fear seem less important.

"How come you never told me about Mayla? About what you did for her?"

Vara appeared taken aback but then a slow smile started to spread across her face. *"I did nothing for her that any Kriosian woman would not have done in my place. Mayla was my dearest friend long before you were born."*

"Was?" Gwyn asked tentatively.

Vara's smile vanished. *"She passed last year."*

"No," Gwyn said as tears that were never far from the surface formed and began to fall. "No, no, no, what happened?"

"She took ill. A virus she contracted in Gikhu Province. It was quick, if not painless. I was with her from the moment she came home until the end."

Gwyn felt her heart breaking anew as an overwhelming loneliness engulfed her. "How am I supposed to live without her?" she demanded petulantly.

"The same way we all do. You remember the good things, forget the

bad, and try to live as best you can when loss becomes one of your constant companions."

Mayla Fui, her *leedi*, said things like that often when Gwyn was younger. She rarely heard them from her mother. The resemblance between them that had eluded her until now suddenly struck her forcefully. She had always been at odds with her mother, always running to Mayla for a comforting ear.

"I am so sorry for your loss, Mother. And mine."

That small smile was back.

"*How did you come to know the truth about your* leedi?"

"It's a long story."

"*I like long stories.*"

"There were many things you never told me," Gwyn said bitterly, "things I needed to know."

"*My, that does sound serious,*" Vara said in the semi-mocking tone that always raised Gwyn's ire. "*Would you like me to inquire about finding you a new mother?*"

"Please, don't start."

"*There was nothing you needed to know from me that I didn't tell you once if not a thousand times before you left this house promising never to return.*"

"I didn't mean that."

"*I know you didn't. I'm your mother. Not that it hurt any less,*" she added.

This was news to Gwyn. "How did you know?"

"*You have always been a child of mercurial moods. Your storms blow the strongest just before they are about to pass. Life held lessons you could not learn here, but that didn't mean you wouldn't understand eventually.*"

If it weren't true, Gwyn would have been annoyed. As it was, she accepted it begrudgingly.

"I guess I understand why you kept the secret from me for so long, but how could she?"

"*You do understand the risk we took, and the consequences should we have been discovered. The authorities continue to believe that their ability to detect metamorphs in utero is perfect. They hate to be proven wrong."*

"You didn't trust me not to tell anyone?"

"No, I suppose I didn't. Was I wrong?"

The question hurt, but not as much as the answer.

"I'm not sure."

"What happened, Aytar?"

"There was an accident," Gwyn said. "When I woke up, I wasn't myself anymore. I was suddenly . . . incomplete."

"I understand," Vara said, the nature of her daughter's pain suddenly becoming clear. *"You should know that this was only ever a remote possibility. You are but half Kriosian and unlikely to carry the variation, even in a recessive form. I find it hard to believe . . ."*

The only thing worse than sharing this much with her mother would have been admitting that it only happened because of the procedure she underwent to help Nancy Conlon. She had rarely risked this much honesty with Vara. Their trust issues were mutual. "That doesn't matter now. What does . . ."

"Is your choice. Of course. But, it has been several days. Are you still . . . ?"

"The choice has been made. It is done. And for what it's worth, it felt right. It felt like the only thing I could do."

"You would not have otherwise survived."

The doctors had told Gwyn this. It had been their greatest fear when she was in the throes of the *finiis'ral.* Somehow in all of her anger at Devi, she had forgotten or, at the very least, seriously downplayed this unpleasant fact.

"It may seem difficult now, but I promise you that in time, it will become easier. Tell me about this man you have chosen."

Gwyn laughed aloud. "There is no man, Mother."

"Oh. This woman, then?"

"Try again."

"You don't mean . . . a child?"

"Yes."

"Do the parents understand?"

"They don't even know yet. She is only a few weeks old."

"Will they allow you to . . . ? Of course they won't. I assume they are human?"

"Can we do the judgmental part of this conversation the next time we speak and focus, please, Mom?"

"You must tell them."

"Why? Why can't I just love her, the way Mayla loved me?"

"What you shared with Mayla was only possible because I allowed it. Passing interest in the children of others is common, normal even. Her parents' ignorance will not change your needs and might make them suspect worse of you than the truth."

"I would never hurt her. I couldn't."

"What you feel, it won't go away. It won't diminish. It will continue to grow stronger with each passing day. It is an imperfect solution to a biological imperative because it is, by definition, a one-sided attachment. I nurtured your relationship with Mayla because I understood that no one, not even I, could love you as well as she did. I sacrificed my natural bond with you to spare her the necessity of losing herself to another. But without full understanding . . ."

"I wish I could take it back. I wish I'd never . . ."

"No, my love. No," Vara said as her eyes began to glisten. *"It is a gift, an opportunity to learn how to open your heart to another. Mayla spoke of it often. I envied her what she shared with you. And it gave me great joy to see you return her affection, to trust her so deeply."*

"She knew me," Gwyn said simply, "in a way no one else ever could."

"As you will come to know this child, whether her parents wish it or not."

"The child is gone. The vessel where she was incubating was taken from us. I know she is still alive. I feel it. But I can't get to her, and without her . . ."

"Physical separation is survivable. The day you left Krios Prime,

Mayla was broken. For months after, I worried every day that she might do herself harm. But over time, she learned to live within the bond, even from a distance. She never left you, no matter how far you wandered."

"She could have reached out to me. I would never have denied her," Gwyn protested.

"You still don't understand. The one you have chosen will always be free to follow her own heart. Your task is to bend to that reality and offer her the same freedom she has given you."

"But it hurts so much."

"Welcome to adulthood."

"Mom."

"No. You avoided it far too long. It comes for each of us in its own time and ways. But it was never optional, once the potential within you was unlocked. It hurts, because you continue to search for reasons to resist. Accept it. Build upon it. And never forget to be grateful to her. You live, because she does."

"So, what you're telling me is that I'm screwed."

"What I am trying to tell you is that your world just got bigger. What you do with it is entirely up to you."

"Is that what you did?"

"I was not like Mayla. I was never forced to make such a choice. Few of us are anymore. But when she came to me, saying that the elders were trying to force her to bond where she could not love, to a man that would remake her into someone she would despise . . . I had no choice. I always hoped that, at the very least, you would have done the same. As you grew older, became so defiant, so fiercely independent, so terrified of intimacy, I feared you might never know what it was to have friends for whom you would sacrifice anything. You shared it with Jerrik, but once that was broken . . ."

"Intimacy is not my problem, Mother."

"I'm not talking about sex. I'm talking about allowing others to see you as you truly are, embracing them in all of their imperfections without fear, and remaining true to them come what may. I'm talking about connections that run so deep, it no longer matters where you end and

they begin. Some find it in marital love, others in friendship. Both are *worth risking."*

And just like that, the last eight years of Aytar Gwyn's life snapped into sharp relief. It had been eight years since she had decided that her first love had been a mistake. Except . . . *it hadn't been.* It had been the love meant to show her who she really was and what she really wanted. And in that way, it had been a spectacular success. Its abrupt end hadn't been the fault of Jerrik or an indictment of what they had shared. It had been a moment of clarity—just like the one she had experienced when Devi Patel's voice echoed over a static-filled comm line and Gwyn had known that if she failed to act, it was the last time she would ever hear that voice. And for reasons still not entirely explicable, that had been completely unacceptable to Aytar Gwyn.

She hadn't chosen to bond with the baby because she feared that if she didn't she would die. That reality had remained a distant fear throughout her ordeal. She had chosen to bond with the baby because it was the easiest and only way to eliminate the obstacle standing between her and saving Patel's life.

Devi Patel had been her first true friend. *Her* Mayla Fui. No one else, not even those with whom she had shared her body, had ever gained access to her heart. No one had cared enough to argue with her about her choices, to push her toward greater self-awareness, or to annoy the hell out of her every time she refused to acknowledge her own gaping blind spots. She loved Devi like a sister. She needed Devi because she'd never had one of those before and though she had never acknowledged it, even to herself, having someone was good. It helped. And had this not been true, she would never have been so angry with Devi now. She also might have realized it sooner had she not wasted most of those eight years sleeping with anything with a pulse in search of something it turned out she would never find because it simply didn't exist. It required effort. It had to be created. And she wasn't sure she was ready to do that yet.

Adulthood.

Damn.

"I have to go, Mom."

Vara was clearly shocked by the abrupt dismissal. *"I'm not judging you, dear one . . ."* she began.

"No, I know," Gwyn insisted. "It's just . . . there's someone else I need to talk to. I'm glad you called. And I promise, I will talk to you soon. I'll let you know how all of this works out."

"I'll try not to worry."

"Love you, Mom."

SWOW (THE PLANET FORMERLY KNOWN AS DK-1116)

"Once we're done here, Lieutenant, I want you to think about a transfer to Demeter,*"* Commander O'Donnell said as he trudged along beside Patel through a newly excavated tunnel that terminated in the base they had discovered at Station One.

Patel felt her cheeks begin to burn. It could have been a failure of temperature optimization in her EV suit, or the fact that Liam O'Donnell was unlike anyone else she had ever met. His brilliance was only eclipsed by his deep and abiding self-interest. He reminded her of Gwyn in that way. Much as she had enjoyed working with him for the last several days, it was only their shared desire to untangle this mystery that bound them. As a mentor, he was likely to become a disappointment. "I appreciate that, sir, but *Voyager* keeps me busy enough these days."

On the admiral's orders, deep scans of Station One had revealed the presence of several previously excavated caverns adjacent to the primary area. Some had clearly collapsed when the planet's stored energy was released, but others, like this one, appeared to have been sealed off at some point in the period during which this station and its six siblings had been in regular use. It had taken two dozen of *Vesta*'s engineers less than a day to reopen it, and it contained multiple pockets of the Edrehmaia substance hidden within the walls, surrounded by the same silicon banding Patel and Paris had discovered on their mission in the asteroid field. Another three dozen engineers had worked to excavate the tunnel that led from the station to the surface where the shuttle that would be the home of the second stage of this experiment waited.

"How certain are you that your containment pod will function properly?" Patel asked.

"Garv Elkins is the smartest man I've ever met. He tested it, at least theoretically, and believes it will do the trick," O'Donnell replied.

"How did you convince him to take command of *Demeter*'s engine room for this mission?" Patel asked, genuinely curious. "Has he ever served outside a starbase?"

"He didn't come for me," O'Donnell said. *"He came for* her.*"*

"Her?"

"Demeter. *He designed her and wanted to make sure that my command didn't end up damaging his reputation."*

"Are you sure he just didn't want anyone else mucking about her innards?" Patel asked.

O'Donnell chuckled. *"I'm sure that was part of it."*

They approached the end of the tunnel, where two engineers clad in EV suits stood behind a force field generated by a portable unit. Their suits were covered in dust released into the enclosed space where they had slowly and diligently exposed a vein of silicon, beneath which O'Donnell and Patel's quarry rested.

One of the engineers, his face covered in sweat beneath his helmet, greeted them as they neared the force field. *"We're all set here, sirs."*

"Excellent work. Drop the force field and initiate transport," O'Donnell ordered.

Moments later, the field vanished along with the engineers. Lieutenant Elkins waited at the entrance to the tunnel for O'Donnell and Patel's return, but it had been decided that they alone would attempt to retrieve the Edrehmaia substance that would be used to create a second interlocutor. Another force field had been erected at the entrance to the tunnel to protect Elkins in the event O'Donnell's container failed.

After confirming that the engineers were safely back aboard *Vesta*, O'Donnell stepped toward the fissure in the cavern wall where the silicon was visible. He then retrieved from his rucksack a circular jar of metal, roughly the size of a deep petri dish.

"That's it?" Patel asked.

"I know it doesn't look like much," O'Donnell replied. *"The only matter from the sample we took here that didn't survive the transport contained trace molecules of the Edrehmaia base. We were able to replicate some of the required elements and isotopes. Three were handcrafted in our lab and six had to be forged by Vesta's chief, Lieutenant Bryce. This is as close as we can come to what our predecessors used to contain the base. If it doesn't work, we're done here and there will be no way to form your interlocutor."*

A small scaffold had been erected at the edge of the vein with a panel atop, where he proceeded to secure the dish. As soon as the vessel was filled, its top would iris closed, sealing the substance inside.

At least theoretically.

As O'Donnell tested the canister's lid one last time, Patel affixed a small chunk of chemical explosive to the exposed silicon. At its center was a time-delayed detonator.

O'Donnell placed the canister at the center of the scaffolding. Then, he and Patel stepped back. Patel tapped her combadge. "Patel to *Voyager*. We are about to begin the extraction."

"Good luck," the voice of Captain Chakotay sounded in reply. *"We have a lock on your coordinates and will transport you to safety should that be required. Comm lines will remain open."*

"Thank you, Captain," O'Donnell, said then turned to Patel. *"Ready?"*

Patel nodded. "Stand back, please." Stepping forward again, she activated the detonator, hurried to O'Donnell's side, and reactivated the force field.

One full minute passed before the detonator erupted with a pop and hiss, exposing a hole in the silicon.

"Come on," O'Donnell said softly.

What started as a trickle of water soon became a steady stream. Seconds later, that stream thickened as the viscous black substance began to drip into its container.

Five seconds later, the container emitted a burst of air that splattered the substance still dripping onto the rock face. It then sealed itself with a loud chirp. The panel atop the scaffolding holding the container instantly retracted and floated across the cavern toward the force field so as to avoid contaminating the outside of the container with any of the Edrehmaia base.

"Antigrav?" Patel asked.

"Elkins doesn't miss a trick," O'Donnell replied, noting that the Edrehmaia base resumed its flow down the wall of the cavern from the fissure in the silicon created by the explosive.

"Dropping the force field," Patel said as she raised her phaser and aimed it at the fissure.

"Go ahead."

The field dropped and O'Donnell raised his tricorder to scan the container as Patel directed her phaser at the fissure and fired it at maximum strength. Just as it had when Seven had fired upon the substance when it had first attacked Ensign Gwyn, the fluid began to solidify.

"We have containment," O'Donnell reported, ecstatic. He gave the antigrav a gentle shove in the direction of the tunnel's exit as Patel again raised the force field. Neither remained to observe her handiwork. Instead, they turned and ran for all they were worth, barely keeping pace with the floating canister in their bulky suits until they reached the tunnel's end.

There, Lieutenant Elkins greeted them from the far side of the secondary force field.

"Drop it!" O'Donnell shouted, gasping for air.

Elkins did so. As soon as O'Donnell, Patel, and the canister were safe in the main chamber, Elkins reactivated the field. Seconds later, a loud boom sounded behind them as explosives embedded in the tunnel walls only a few meters from the fissure were detonated, collapsing the end of the tunnel and sealing what remained of the substance they had released behind meters of solid rock.

Everyone paused to catch their breath, O'Donnell's, Patel's, and Elkins's eyes glued to the canister. A bright, steady green light that circled the lid confirmed for all of them that containment was still in effect.

Elkins approached the force field and completed a scan. *"Structural integrity confirmed,"* he reported. *"The main body of the cavern remains intact at ninety-nine percent of previous stability."*

At this, the entire group cheered.

"We did it," Elkins said, placing a hand on Patel's shoulder.

"Did you doubt it for a second?" Patel asked.

"Commander, report," Chakotay ordered over the comm.

Through ragged breaths, O'Donnell said, *"We successfully collapsed the tunnel and have retrieved a sample of the Edrehmaia substance that is safely contained."*

"Well done," Chakotay congratulated him as applause from *Voyager*'s bridge echoed over the open comm line. *"The* Okinawa *is in position on the surface. Start walking, folks. We'll expect you topside within the hour."*

"We're on our way, sir," Patel replied.

As the group began to move slowly toward their exit, the antigrav floating before them, O'Donnell said, *"How wrong is it that this is the only part of our mission I was truly dreading?"*

"You and me both, Captain," Elkins said.

"I don't understand," Patel said. "The hard part is over."

"I haven't hiked for more than three minutes in a decade, Lieutenant," O'Donnell said. *"For me, the hard part is just about to begin."*

17

Lieutenant Harry Kim vaguely remembered the last time he had felt this cold. It was within seconds of regaining consciousness following *Galen*'s transport by the Edrehmaia. He hadn't registered the change then because he had been unconscious. But the moment Conlon looked at him, her eyes bright, and calmly asked him to identify himself, an icy blast ripped through him.

"I'm Harry. I'm the, I'm *your*—"

"Lieutenant Kim, please don't panic," the Doctor interjected. "Let's run a full diagnostic. This might just be a processing lag."

Conlon's brow furrowed. It was a gesture Kim had seen a thousand times directed toward him. Clearly some, perhaps *most*, of Conlon's consciousness now animated this holomatrix. "What's wrong?" she demanded as Barclay began his scans.

"Doc, I don't understand," Kim began.

"Neither do I," he replied, "but I promise you, we will get to the bottom of this."

"Bridge to Lieutenant Kim," Drur's voice sounded over the comm.

Kim tapped his badge automatically. "It's not a great time, Mike," he said briskly, his voice cracking.

"Oh, um . . . okay? It's just . . ."

"Can it wait?" Kim demanded tensely.

"I'm sorry, sir, but I don't think so. I've been talking with Fred, and a few of his friends have shown up and I really think you should get up here before they—"

"Who the hell is Fred?"

This time, Drur's voice cracked as he replied, *"One of the Edrehmaia, sir."*

Kim felt his knees begin to buckle as Commander Glenn entered the main bay, her face ashen. As soon as her eyes locked with Kim's she said, "We have a problem."

Get in line rose immediately to mind, but some small shred of rational thinking urged Kim against direct insubordination.

They now had at least three pressing problems. Kim didn't know what the captain's was, so it was difficult to prioritize. Drur's sounded like his should top the list, but neither mattered as much to him at this moment as the possibility that he had just lost Nancy Conlon.

"What is it?" Kim asked anyway.

"Velth isn't Velth anymore," Glenn replied. "Whatever they did to him, they didn't just save his life. They changed him in ways that aren't readily apparent except for the fact that he now drinks straight from power conduits with his hands." Turning to the Doctor, she said, "He's unconscious for now, and he needs to stay that way until we can do a full work-up."

"Understood," the Doctor said.

"I can continue working with Conlon," Barclay offered, "if you need to . . ."

Conlon rose from the chair where she had rested. "If he has accessed our main power supply, I'm going to need to lock that down."

"I rerouted from here," Barclay said, "but the affected conduit remains open."

"We can't just bleed power," Conlon said. "We barely have enough to keep the ship operational as it is."

It destroyed Harry to see her so completely herself, yet not.

"Where is it?" Conlon asked.

"Observation room three," Glenn replied.

Turning to Barclay, Conlon said, "I'm fine. You can continue the diagnostic but I'm going in there to see just how much damage has been done."

Barclay glanced toward the Doctor, who said, "Very well. But bear in mind that the mobile emitter you are wearing is one of a kind. If anything happens to it, you . . ."

Conlon placed a protective hand over the emitter. "Understood."

"There are two security officers guarding the door," Glenn said. "If he regains consciousness, you are to evacuate immediately."

"I can make sure he remains sedated," the Doctor offered. "In this case, Lieutenant Conlon and I are probably the only members of this crew who should get within arm's length of Velth until we understand what's happening to him."

Glenn considered this for a moment, then nodded. "Do it," she said. "Mister Kim?"

Both Admiral Janeway and Captain Chakotay had often spoken of the calm that lay at the center of every storm a captain faced. It was the only place from which the most difficult decisions of a Starfleet commanding officer could be made. Kim could not locate that place within him. He stood buffeted by powerfully conflicting needs and life-threatening realities, unsure where to go or what to do.

Glenn seemed to realize how hard he was struggling. "Harry," she said more gently, "what's happened? Are you all right?"

"No," he replied. "I'm not all right. None of this is all right. The woman I love, *the mother of my child*," he continued, "doesn't remember who I am. There's a monster unconscious down the hall, and apparently, Drur has just made first contact with the most powerful and truly alien life-forms I've ever seen. It's, you know, a bit much to deal with all at once. I can't even . . ."

Glenn's eyes went wide. "What was that last thing?"

Drur has made contact with the Edrehmaia.

The center quite suddenly found Kim.

"We have to get to the bridge," Kim said.

Glenn nodded. "I agree. Doctor?"

"We've got this," he said. "Go. I'll report in as soon as we know more."

"It's called compartmentalizing," Glenn said as she and Harry stepped onto the turbolift. "Normally, I'm not a fan. It can lead to all sorts of psychological issues. But right now, we both have to let everything else go, and focus. The Doctor and Reg will take care of Conlon and Velth. Are you with me?"

Kim had remained silent as they had hurried through the corridors toward the lift. He nodded. His eyes had lost the frantic, panicked quality they'd held minutes earlier back in sickbay, but she couldn't tell just by looking if he was truly here, or a thousand light-years away.

"Harry," she said sharply.

His eyes snapped toward hers.

"Yes, Captain," he replied. "I'm with you."

Glenn still didn't know exactly what this man was made of, but she believed him. "Honestly, is this the worst day the Delta Quadrant has thrown at you?" she asked.

He didn't pause to ponder. "Right now, it is."

The doors to the lift opened and they stepped out together. Ensign Drur stood at his normal operations post but the main viewscreen displayed an unusual sight. Hanging in space, perhaps only a few kilometers from the ship, were five Edrehmaia. Four were solid black, but bright white flashes of light cascaded over the body of the fifth.

"What do you want to bet that's John, Paul, George, and Ringo?" Glenn asked.

"Who was the fifth one?" Kim asked. "Pete?"

"No, that's Fred," Drur said.

"Report, Ensign," Glenn ordered.

"I was attempting to enhance our ability to communicate with the Edrehmaia by adding to our shared vocabulary using mathematical terms and it worked," Drur said.

"Which terms?" Kim asked dubiously.

"We began by defining our sets. That led to the most important breakthrough. Fred was the first to understand that our words represent concepts. Since then, I thought we were making progress, but then these four showed up and Fred started talking about 'positive infinity,' and I'm not sure what to make of that."

Kim moved to the ops console. "Show me," he said. "Captain, keep an eye on our friends out there."

Glenn did more than that. Tapping her combadge she said, "All hands, this is the captain. Alpha shift bridge officers are to report immediately. Yellow alert."

As Kim reviewed Drur's work, Lawry and Selah hurried onto the bridge and took their helm and science stations. Both looked pleasantly surprised to have been summoned until they registered the image on the main viewscreen.

"Lieutenant Kim, I hate to ask you to multitask, but I may need you at tactical," Glenn said.

"I'm going to do my best to make that unnecessary, Captain," Kim replied.

"Understood. What have you got?"

"I need a minute," Kim said, then turned to Drur. "So, the last thing you and Fred were talking about was 'Deriving the function of Set: Edrehmaia.' What does that mean?"

"They don't think like we do. They process data, facts, quantifiable realities. The closest I can get to communicating concepts that are beyond that is by using basic mathematical functions. Fred understands himself to be an individual now."

"Fred?" Selah asked.

"His full name is billions of characters long. Fred asked for a designation that was the equivalent of our names and I gave him one," Drur replied hotly.

"You've done amazing work here, Mike," Kim said, as much for him as for the other officers present.

"Thank you, sir."

"Not a problem. What does it mean to take the derivative of the set? What were you asking him?"

"Deriving a function or differentiating is to understand how much a thing is changing over time."

"So, you were basically asking him what the Edrehmaia are trying to do out here," Kim confirmed.

"Yes, that's right."

"And you're sure Fred understood the question?"

"I think so."

"And his response is 'FUNCTION OF SET EDREHMAIA IS EQUAL TO POSITIVE INFINITY.'"

"Right. He just keeps repeating it."

"Okay. Let's try this. 'DEFINE POSITIVE INFINITY.'"

"Wait," Drur said. "You need to tell him you don't understand. First add the phrase 'CURRENT INPUT INDETERMINATE.'"

"Okay . . . done," Kim said.

In response, complex equations began to flash on the screen in what appeared to be a random order.

"Looks like we've graduated to calculus," Kim said. "Computer, can you analyze these equations and find any equivalent in our database?"

A moment later, an image appeared on Kim's panel.

"Huh," he said.

"That's the . . ." Drur began.

"The galactic barrier," Kim finished for him. "They took Velth there, among other places. It's important to them, clearly. If 'positive infinity' can be understood as their ultimate goal, maybe the barrier is that goal."

"A barrier isn't a goal, it's a given in any equation," Selah noted.

"The only thing you can really do with a barrier is break it," Glenn said.

Kim and Glenn locked eyes.

"They're building a bridge of stars," Glenn began. "They use radiant energy like we use oxygen. They create stars, they move stars, and right now they've lined a bunch of them up leading to the galactic barrier. Their goal could very well be to move beyond it, but it might be the only thing this incredibly powerful species *can't* do."

"They can't break through it," Kim mused. "We can't break through it either. I mean, some people have tried but it never ends well. And Starfleet hasn't spent much time finding ways to move beyond it because even slipstream won't get you very far across the void to the next nearest galaxy for months."

"Is it possible they believe *we* can?" Glenn asked.

Kim shrugged. "Anything is possible."

"Could that be why they brought us here?" It wasn't something Glenn could confirm, but her gut said that the actions of the Edrehmaia were purposeful. This was the first section of the puzzle that seemed to be coming into focus for her. "Let's assume for a second that this was the purpose behind their actions. They think we can help them solve this problem. But in order to understand why they believe that's true, we need more than educated guesses. Ensign Drur, you are to be commended for getting us this far, but we're not going to be able to do much more unless we can communicate more efficiently. What are our options?" Glenn asked.

"I have a feeling they may be ahead of us on this one," Kim said. "Mike, can you ask them to explain the changes they made to Lieutenant Velth?"

"What changes?"

"They'll understand. Ask them if there was a purpose to those changes."

Drur collected his thoughts, then asked the question. "SOLVE FOR DERIVATIVE OF FACTOR VELTH." He followed this transmission with the two genomes he had received that were related to Velth.

At this, Fred began to flash wildly, as did the fab four. Their colors were brighter, all over the spectrum, but Fred's were the most intense.

"There's that coffee klatch Ranson was talking about," Glenn said.

"Is this their version of excitement?" Selah asked. "Because it sure looks like it."

The response finally came through Drur's panel. "DIFFERENTIATION POSITIVE FOR ADDING CERTAINTY."

Kim stated the response aloud, then asked, "What does that mean?"

"I think they're telling us that if we want to understand the purpose for the changes they made, we need to ask Velth about them," Drur replied.

"Can you ask them to give us time for that?" Kim asked.

"Yes."

"Do it," Glenn ordered.

Two hours later, Conlon had managed to lock down the power conduit in Velth's room and the Doctor had completed his new physical examination. Glenn, Kim, and Barclay joined them in the main medical bay to discuss the results. Velth remained sedated for the time being, but it was impossible to know how long that would last.

"The alterations to his DNA weren't that extensive," the Doctor began. "It seems that they went out of their way to make sure he could survive once he was returned to the ship. Even now, I can't tell you how or why the additions work, but they have to be responsible for our findings."

"Which are?" Glenn asked.

"There are now two Velths," the Doctor replied. "But they occupy the same body. One is the man we all knew. The other . . ."

"Likes his energy straight from the most efficient source?" Conlon asked.

"Among other things, I imagine," the Doctor said. "While unconscious, he transitions freely between his two states. Scans taken shortly after he was sedated show quantum fluctuations in his matter that are unique. They explain his ability to merge with solid matter and absorb . . . let's call them *nutrients*. They also show significant changes in his cerebrum. Activity between the two hemispheres increases by more than two hundred percent. But the longer we keep him under, the more frequently he reverts to the completely normal scans we took when he first returned to us."

"They did this on purpose," Glenn said. "They understood the communication challenge that existed and while we were working the problem one way, they were busy remaking a man into their instrument. It's like for a hammer, everything looks like a nail. For the Edrehmaia, everything is about building bridges."

"But they did it in a way that did not completely destroy the person he was," Kim noted. "That's promising. It suggests that they recognize his value as an individual to us and were trying to honor that while still finding a way to communicate clearly."

"There is at least one other significant change to his respiratory system while in his alternate state," the Doctor added.

"Which is?"

"The alveoli in his lungs cease to process oxygen."

"How does that not kill him?" Glenn asked.

The Doctor shrugged. "In his normal state, it probably would, but in the new one . . ."

"He could walk in space without the EV suit," Barclay said.

"I wouldn't recommend it," the Doctor noted. "Right now, we have no way of knowing if Velth can control when and how he transitions."

"We need to wake him and see if we can communicate with the 'new' Velth," Conlon said. "If they intend him to speak for them, we need to know what they were trying to say."

"Agreed," Glenn said. "But how do we do that safely?"

"We can bring him back into the main medical bay and place him behind a level-ten force field," Barclay said.

"I'm not certain that will contain him," the Doctor advised.

"It's all we have."

"I would prefer we do this in a less sensitive area of the ship," Glenn said. "Let's erect a temporary holding area in the cargo bay. Can we transport him directly there?"

"I wouldn't," Kim said. "They have the ability to transport anything anywhere they want to. They could have transported Velth back onto the ship when they were done with him, but they didn't. They used the airlock. Let's follow their lead on this and move him the hard way."

"Agreed," Conlon said.

"What are our contingencies should he become unstable or hostile?" Glenn asked Kim pointedly.

"The cargo bay has an exterior door. If we only have the Doctor and Conlon present for questioning, they can render themselves permeable in an instant and we can decompress the bay."

"Which apparently wouldn't kill him, so that's good," Conlon said.

"It's not my favorite plan. It's just better than any other I can think of," Glenn said. "Let's get started."

As the group disbanded, Kim approached the Doctor. "I don't know if you've had a chance to . . . ?" he began uncertainly.

"Reg ran the diagnostics twice. The power fluctuations occurred before we initiated the transfer. The transfer itself, as you know, did not go entirely smoothly. There are no processing problems. Everything that was transferred has merged perfectly with the holomatrix. And as far as I can tell, the only absences in terms of her memory relate to you and to your child."

"She doesn't remember either of us?"

"No. And more important, she doesn't seem concerned about that absence. I have explained the nature of your relationship and took her to see the baby. Her response was to state quite calmly that she understands but can't remember the feelings that accompany these relationships. It is not inhibiting her ability to perform her duties or engage in normal social interactions in any way. It's as if you and the child were simply excised from her memories."

"And you don't know how or why?"

The Doctor sighed deeply. "I have a theory."

"Do I want to hear it?"

"I think *she* might have done it," the Doctor said, nodding toward Conlon's still body beneath the surgical arch that was keeping her alive and comatose, "although I'm not certain it was intentional."

"How is that possible? And why would she?"

"It *shouldn't* have been possible. I certainly never considered it as a potential outcome. But this is only the second time of which I am aware that anyone has ever had their consciousness transferred in this way, so a lot of this is simply uncharted territory. If the lag in the transfer was a problem on her end, if during the procedure she was afraid, even panicked and attempting to resist it, it is possible that these specific parts of her were somehow psychologically segregated. You were the one that helped her complete it. You were connected to her physical body at that time. You were holding her hand. That might have been enough to keep those parts of her rooted in her physical body."

"But if you're right, our relationship, what we are to each other and to our child—all of those memories—are still in her physical mind?"

"It's an oddly specific loss otherwise," the Doctor said. "The hope, of course, is that I will find a way to heal her body and that once her consciousness is reintegrated, she will remember everything."

"So, I shouldn't try to help her do that now?"

"I wouldn't. We do have slightly bigger challenges before us, though it might not feel that way to you, personally."

Kim nodded. "Even if I wanted to fix this, you don't condense a relationship over a year in the making into a few conversations. And if this is what she actually wanted, it would be both useless and disrespectful for me to try. I want to drop everything and simply *fix this*, but I can't. Everything is on fire. This, whatever it actually is, is just going to have to wait," he said miserably.

"I promise you, we are going to find a way to heal her," the Doctor said, placing a comforting hand on Kim's shoulder.

Kim stared at him for a long moment, then departed for the cargo bay.

Nancy Conlon was quickly becoming accustomed to her new form. Although it lacked certain physical sensations that she had taken for granted her entire life, the upsides were considerable. There was no pain, emotional or physical, of which she was aware. Not a twinge, an ache, a weary muscle or tension headache to distract her. Only now did she realize how many small discomforts she had come to think of as *normal* since her illness had first been diagnosed.

The illness, as well, was gone. She was acutely aware that her current form was to all intents and purposes *perfect*. She wasn't hungry. She wasn't tired. She felt at the top of her professional game. Her *mind*, such as it was, processed information with a clarity she had never experienced. It was a *wake-up-fresh-to-start-a-busy-day-ready-to-take-on-the-world* feeling that never seemed to abate, even when confronted with troubling realities at every turn.

She knew that the transfer had not been completed exactly as anticipated. The Doctor had taken her to see the child her body had created, and poor Lieutenant Kim could not look at her without a pain and longing she understood as a matter of fact but could not reciprocate. At some point she was going to have to interrogate that situation more thoroughly, but it was only one of many priorities before her and was easily shifted down on her to-do list without creating the slightest hint of anxiety.

To exist in this state was remarkable. She gave absolutely no thought to how it would necessarily change when her consciousness was returned to her body. For the moment, she didn't honestly care if that ever came to pass.

There was work to be done, work that she was uniquely able to perform. Her purpose was simple and clear.

She was ready.

Once the preparations were complete, Glenn, Kim, and Barclay stood outside the cargo bay around a display screen from which they could monitor the events unfolding within it. Velth's transfer from sickbay had gone off without incident, and he was resting on a biobed within a columnar force field that was the maximum the ship could generate.

Conlon and the Doctor stood outside the field and a dedicated comm line was opened between the interior and immediate exterior of the bay. Drur continued to update the Edrehmaia on the team's work and indicated that for the moment, they seemed content to continue waiting.

Just before they passed through the force field, the Doctor said, "His current scans show normal physical readings."

"But that could change quickly, so be ready," Glenn warned over the comm.

"Of course, Captain," the Doctor replied.

They passed through the field. Conlon kept as much distance as possible as the Doctor moved to Velth and placed a hypospray on his neck.

As soon as the stimulant hit his system, his eyes snapped open and turned immediately toward the Doctor.

"What happened? Where am I?" he asked.

"You don't remember?" the Doctor asked.

Velth blinked a few times, perhaps searching his recollections, then said, "I was hungry."

"Are you still hungry?"

"No. Not even a little."

Conlon stepped forward. As soon as he noticed her, he smiled as if surprised to see her there.

"Lieutenant. It's good to see you."

"You too," she said.

The Doctor's tricorder beeped: an alarm set to indicate shifts in Velth's quantum state.

"We have run a number of tests and you need to be aware that while you were with the Edrehmaia, they made certain changes to your DNA. Those changes have begun to manifest in unusual ways. But we believe that there was a purpose to them. The Edrehmaia have said that you can help us understand them better. Is that true?" the Doctor asked.

Velth clearly didn't comprehend the question. "I don't know what you're talking about. I already told you everything I saw out there. I think they tried to communicate with me, but I never understood them."

"It's okay," Conlon said. "There have been a lot of big changes around here lately. We're all doing the best we can to keep up. We think," she continued, "that their work out here is inhibited by the galactic barrier. We believe they want us to help them pass through it so they can leave our galaxy. I've given the matter some thought and the only solution I can come up with involves using our slipstream drive. Slipstream tunnels are created at the intersection of normal space and subspace. They are a bridge of sorts between these two dimensions. A properly calculated jump could take us through the barrier without breaking it, but even so, I'm not sure our ship or crew would survive passage."

"I don't really . . ." Velth began, but before he could finish that thought, his body began to tremble. Panic flashed briefly across his face before he seemed to stabilize.

"His state has begun to fluctuate," the Doctor noted.

"Be careful," Glenn ordered.

Both the Doctor and Conlon stepped back as Velth lifted himself up and stepped down from the biobed. He stood silently, ignoring the two holograms, and scanned the cargo bay.

"Get them out of there," Kim's voice came over the comm.

"Agreed," Glenn said. *"Step outside the force field."*

The Doctor and Conlon complied. Velth didn't seem to mind. He kept focusing on various cargo containers until, finally, his eyes fixed on a small set of crates. He walked toward them, passing through the force field as if it didn't exist.

"So much for that," Conlon said softly.

"We are ready to vent the bay," Glenn said.

"Wait," Conlon said as she realized exactly which cargo containers had attracted Velth's attention. "That's what's left of our benamite supply."

Velth crossed to the containers, opened the topmost, and gathered a handful of pulverized benamite in his palm. As Conlon watched, fascinated, he closed his hand around the tiny fragments. His hand began to glow with a bright, orange light. When he opened his hand, a solid chunk of benamite rested on his palm.

Conlon moved toward him. Velth turned to her, extended his hand, and passed the crystal to her. Even as she recognized the extraordinary nature of what he had just done, there was no accompanying sense of elation. Those feelings were apparently beyond her. Still, she understood that one huge problem she had been working on since they arrived had likely just been solved.

"I'll need to test its purity," she said.

"There is more to be done," Velth said, his voice low and toneless.

Conlon nodded. "How much more?"

"I require access to this vessel's propulsion systems."

18

Counselor Cambridge had been standing outside the door to Ensign Gwyn's quarters for the better part of half an hour when she emerged without warning and almost ran straight into him.

"Counselor?"

"Indeed."

"What are you . . . ?" she began, then paused. For a moment, she seemed to be attempting to solve a particularly vexing math problem. Finally, she lifted her eyes to his and said, "Icheb told you I wanted to speak to my mother. You arranged for the call, didn't you?"

"I did," he said, relieved she had worked that out on her own. "Did it go well?"

Gwyn stepped back and released a deep breath. "I think so, yeah."

"Oh, good. Mothers, daughters, you know it was possible for that to have gone wrong in so many ways, but . . ."

"Does this mean we have to have another session right now?" she asked, clearly hoping the answer would be no.

"I am very curious to hear what insights into your current situation your mother might have been able to offer. Was it helpful?"

"It was. She did," Gwyn said vehemently. "I'm fine. Thank you."

Cambridge considered her carefully. Whatever revelations had come from her discussion with her mother had obviously had a profound impact, but she'd had no time yet to process them.

"Would you be willing to come to my office for a few minutes to discuss that further?" he asked. "I don't generally conduct consultations in the corridor."

"Can we do this later?"

"I'm afraid not. It has been my experience during our relatively brief sessions that you are disinclined to engage in the therapeutic work that will enable you to integrate our current reality with the trauma you recently endured."

"I know. I'm a terrible patient. I'm sorry."

"It's my job to make sure you have begun that process before returning you to active duty, but as it happens, your services are required on the bridge. I have been charged with clearing you for that duty."

"What duty?" Gwyn asked.

"My office, please." Cambridge gestured for her to follow him and she did so, walking briskly to keep pace with his long strides. By the time they arrived there, Gwyn's impatience had clearly grown exponentially.

"Feel free to sit," Cambridge began.

"I don't have time for this right now," Gwyn said. "I'm fine. I understand now. I'm better. Can't we just leave it at that?"

"Better how?"

Gwyn exhaled a long, frustrated breath.

"I know this is difficult for you, Ensign. But you are about to be entrusted with the lives of a hundred and fifty people who need you to be at your best. Unless I am satisfied of that, I will not put them at risk."

"I was angry, okay?"

"Was?"

"It's terrible to be separated from her. Now I know that's normal. I know it's never going to change. And I guess, I know it's also survivable."

"That definitely sounds like progress."

"I was trying to find a way out—a loophole—anything I could do to take it all back. But I don't want that anymore. Whatever I'm needed for, I assume it has something to do with finding the *Galen*. I want that. I want to help. If I can be part of the solution to this problem, I promise I won't let you or anyone else down. Let me talk to the captain. I'm sure he'll agree with me."

Cambridge considered her vehemence. He wanted very much to believe her. Both Chakotay and Paris had pressed him to return Gwyn to duty, even temporarily. But he found it impossible, or at the very least improbable, that she was suddenly capable of managing the stress of her current predicament. Her desire to once again be close to the child with whom she had bonded could lead her to reckless acts that could jeopardize the mission and *Voyager*'s crew. The call to her mother had been a last-ditch attempt to help her face the magnitude of what she had done, and it seemed to have accomplished that. But his gut told him she was still telling him only what she knew he wanted to hear.

"I will speak to the captain," Cambridge said, knowing he would recommend Chakotay find another pilot if Gleez wasn't up to the task ahead.

"Wait," Gwyn said. "Please."

"I'm sorry, Ensign. This was premature."

"No, it wasn't. It isn't. Look, metamorphic bonding is probably going to turn out to be the best thing that ever happened to me. Because, for the first time in my life now, I'm more concerned about the needs of others, the child, my friends, you, everyone, than I am with my own. I've been selfish. I've been stupid. I've wallowed for too long in how this change has hurt me rather than remembering how much it's given me. My mother reminded me that had I not chosen to bond I would have died. That tiny little human saved my life. I'm asking you for the chance to return that favor. Let me save hers."

It wasn't everything Cambridge needed to hear. But it was enough to force him to reconsider.

"Can you at least tell me what the mission is?" Gwyn asked.

"My understanding is that *Voyager* and *Vesta* are about to set course to intercept the rogue star and engage in a slipstream maneuver meant to alter its course."

"That sounds challenging," Gwyn agreed. "But surely Commander Paris is more than capable."

"Commander Paris is unavailable," Cambridge advised her. "He is currently piloting one of our runabouts as part of an away mission led by Commander O'Donnell and Lieutenant Patel."

Panic rose in Gwyn's eyes. "Devi's doing what?"

"She and O'Donnell are currently on board a runabout that has been transformed into a temporary lab facility where they are interacting directly with the Edrehmaia substance sample they collected from DK-1116. Commander Paris is with them."

"Who has *our* helm right now?" Gwyn demanded.

"Ensign Gleez. However, the captain would prefer you take the conn once we move into position to alter the star's course."

"I violently agree with that assessment."

"As does he, but . . ."

"If you're not convinced that I'm ready to return to *Voyager*'s conn, you could transport me to the runabout and let Commander Paris take over for Gleez. Babysitting a small ship holding position for a science experiment is something I could do in my sleep."

It was an interesting request and an easier proposal to accept but for one huge red flag. "You aren't concerned with the proximity to the substance that was responsible for your current predicament?" Cambridge asked.

"If Devi thinks it's safe, it must be," Gwyn said simply. "And I'm sure someone will have transporter locks on all of us in case anything happens, right?"

"*Demeter* is monitoring the safety of the away team."

"Then do we have a deal? I know this isn't the last conversation you and I are going to need to have. I know that there is lots of hard work ahead of me. You're going to have to help me figure out how to tell Lieutenants Kim and Conlon what's happened and there's a chance they won't let me within a light-year of their daughter when I do. We're not done here. We're just getting started. But I made the choice I did because I didn't want to lose myself to someone else's idea of who I should be, and I am the best possible version of myself when I am at the helm of a starship. I know I can do this."

Much to his surprise, Cambridge agreed.

RUNABOUT *OKINAWA*

While the excavations at Station One had been underway, Commander Torres had overseen the transformation of the rear passenger section of *Okinawa's* primary compartment. Using the data taken from Patel's tricorder, a transparent cell had been created that duplicated the alcoves Devi had found beneath the planet containing interlocutors for the various species that had done research at Station Four. They had been hideous things, terrifying to behold. The worst part was, even hundreds or thousands of years after their creation, many of them showed signs of life—or the odd *life that wasn't life* that characterized so many things that had come into contact with the Edrehmaia substance.

The one temporarily created from Patel's DNA, via blood samples that had been required to access the station at each of its doors, had resembled her body in shape, but had been composed entirely of the tar-like sludge now safely contained in a small canister within the cell. An open vial of Patel's blood sat beside the canister.

Torres had re-created the cell's component parts, including a small portable reactor to power the system. It remained to be seen if this would be sufficient. It was possible that the station's library system had been linked to the cells in unknown ways and that no effort on their part to duplicate this technology would function properly. But given that the Edrehmaia had specifically singled out Devi Patel and her genome in their initial communication attempts, it was likely that the creation of a new interlocutor was significant, and this was their best hope for doing so.

Patel and O'Donnell stood outside the cell, running final checks on their equipment. The process shouldn't take more than a few minutes and Patel was anxious for it to be done. She remembered well how terrifying it had been the first time but found it easier to maintain a little detachment now.

O'Donnell worked methodically, almost reverently. This was his first opportunity to observe and study a reaction between normal matter and the Edrehmaia substance. Given that it might also be his last, he intended to make the most of it.

"How's it going back there?" Commander Tom Paris asked from the helm.

"Is there somewhere else you need to be?" O'Donnell asked.

"Only if this doesn't go as planned," Paris shot back. Patel then heard him say, "I'm sorry, repeat that, *Voyager*."

"Drop shields and prepare for incoming transport."

"Copy that. Dropping shields."

"Who's coming aboard?" Patel demanded. Every moment of this mission had been meticulously calculated. Last-minute alterations were unwelcome. Her stomach dropped as the form on the transporter pad resolved itself into that of Ensign Gwyn.

"Hey, everybody," Gwyn said, stepping off the pad. She gave the cell a curious glance as she passed it and nodded toward Patel as she hurried to the helm.

"What gives?" Paris asked.

"Slight change of plans," Gwyn replied, handing him a padd. "*Voyager* and *Vesta* are about to head out to intercept the rogue star and Captain Chakotay decided he'd rather have you at the helm for that maneuver than Gleez."

"I thought you were going to take *Voyager*'s conn," Paris said.

Gwyn shrugged. "I'm back on duty but I think the captain is trying to keep my assignments as stress free as possible."

Paris rose from his seat. "Understood. Commander Fife is maintaining your transporter lock. If anything goes wrong, *Demeter* is standing by."

"Sounds good," Gwyn said as she slid into the pilot's seat. "The gravimetric sheer coming off that star is going to be fierce. Watch your attitude."

Paris laughed. "Wait, you're saying I *shouldn't* allow *Voyager* to fall into the star's gravity well, thereby incinerating her along with all hands?"

"I mean, *I wouldn't*," Gwyn teased.

"Good to have you back, Ensign," Paris said as he headed toward the transporter pad. "Good luck," he added just before the transporter effect commenced.

Gwyn's sudden arrival took Patel completely by surprise. Her concentration faltered and she mis-keyed a test sequence.

"Hold on," O'Donnell said. "Why is there a fault in the—"

"That was me," Patel said quickly. "I'm fixing it now."

"Okay, that makes more sense," O'Donnell said. "Are you all right?"

There was no time to explain her recent history with Gwyn, nor would O'Donnell care at a moment like this. But she doubted her ability to ignore the pit of anxiety forming in her gut. "Can you give me just a second?" she asked.

O'Donnell turned his head and stared at her, incredulous.

"Seriously, one second."

"Take as many as you like but then I need you focused here, Devi."

"I understand. Thank you."

With that, Patel hurried toward the navigation station and slid into the empty seat next to Gwyn. Keeping her voice low, she asked, "What the hell are you doing here?"

"I was ordered to return to duty," Gwyn began, "but I requested this one because I wanted to tell you that I am sorry. I am an idiot. You are not responsible for my choices and there has been no excuse for my behavior toward you over the last several days."

Patel was stunned, not just by Gwyn's words, but more so by their obvious sincerity.

"Thank you," she replied.

"There was a reason," Gwyn continued. "But we don't have to talk about that now. I know you're busy. You do your job, I'll do mine, and when it's all done, we'll talk. Preferably over drinks."

Patel smiled as the knot in her stomach released.

"What *are* you doing, by the way?" Gwyn asked.

"We're trying to re-create an organic technology that will allow us to communicate with the Edrehmaia."

"Don't we have to find them first?"

"All of the Edrehmaia matter appears to have quantum-entangled properties. When we alter the star's course, we expect the energy field in the asteroid belt to activate again, and we have deployed special sensors that should be able to detect all of the entangled particles and their location. We're going to find *Galen* but when we do, we need to make sure we can make them understand that we mean them no harm and just want our ship back."

Gwyn nodded. "Sounds like a good plan."

"Honestly, it could go wrong in about fifty different ways."

"It won't," Gwyn assured her. "You've got this. You're brilliant, Devi, and I'm glad everybody knows that now."

Patel was seized by a sudden desire to put the mission on hold and continue this conversation but there was simply no time. "I want the *whole* story after this," she said.

"You'll get it. I promise."

The tension between them dispersed, Patel returned to O'Donnell's side. "I'm ready, Commander."

"You sure?"

"Absolutely."

"Very well. O'Donnell to *Demeter*."

"Go ahead, Commander," Fife replied.

"We are ready to initiate."

"Good luck, sir. We will be ready to transport you to safety should you require it."

"I have no doubt, Atlee. Stand by."

"Preparing to release containment," Patel said.

"Releasing containment on my mark. Three, two, one . . . mark."

Patel watched as the seal on the container snapped open. Countless tiny black particles were ejected with force and hung suspended in the air within the cell longer than gravity should have permitted. They began to slowly rain down and for a moment Patel wondered if they might all simply settle on the floor of the cell. A single droplet impacted the vial of Patel's blood and a shiver of recognition moved through the remaining particles. As if drawn by a magnet, they all reversed their course and darted toward the vial.

Patel was simultaneously monitoring the alcove's stability. It remained constant. O'Donnell was watching the cell's internal sensors as the reaction began.

"Detecting cellular breach. The base is targeting the DNA contained in the blood cells and beginning to alter it," he reported, unable to contain the joy in his voice.

"Is the base replicating itself?" Patel asked. Her biggest concern with this entire plan had been to wonder if they would be able to extract enough of the substance to create an entire interlocutor.

"It is," O'Donnell confirmed. "Activating alpha and beta wave generators."

Although Patel had not realized it at the time, all of the alcoves had contained unusually high levels of invisible radiation. The precise cocktail had been re-created to instigate the formation of the interlocutor. If they were to succeed, Patel knew that the next thing she would hear was a deafening scream.

The vial had been completely coated by a mass of undulating black fluid. The moment the radiant energy contacted the mass, it began to expand. As hoped, the Edrehmaia base was using the radiant energy to replicate itself.

"Mass has increased by sixty percent," Patel noted.

"It's going to need to get a lot higher than that," O'Donnell warned.

"It will," she promised.

The black sludge now resembled an orb. Patel watched, astonished, as orifices began to form on the surface. *Eyes, nostrils, and . . .*

As soon as a mouth began to open, the scream that had haunted Patel's dreams for weeks echoed throughout the small ship.

"Hello there," O'Donnell shouted over the din.

Patel quickly activated a sound-buffering program to silence the nightmarish scream.

"Much better. Thank you, Devi," O'Donnell said.

"Is that supposed to be happening?" Gwyn called from the conn.

Patel turned to see Gwyn staring in horror at the formation of the interlocutor.

"It is," Patel assured her. "Don't worry. It will be over soon."

"Not the face," Gwyn said. "*That*," she shouted, pointing to the base of the cell.

Patel looked down and saw a trail of the Edrehmaia base coursing along the bottom of the cell. It had flattened against the wall and moved over it as if it were seeking a way out.

"The original cellular DNA is replicating at impossible speeds," O'Donnell reported. "There are hundreds of new base pairs being added with each iteration."

But Patel couldn't focus on the version of her face that was in the process of coming into being. Instead, her heart began to pound feverishly as she observed the fluid at the alcove's base. Containment began to falter as the substance started to change the alcove at the molecular level.

"We're losing containment," Patel shouted.

"Get back," Gwyn said, approaching the pair, her phaser drawn.

O'Donnell finally tore his eyes from his scanner and took note of the troubling development. He and Patel both moved back a few steps as the orb that had formed threw itself forward, splatting against the interior wall and sliding down toward the deck.

"Don't fire," O'Donnell ordered Gwyn.

"We're done here," Gwyn said. "That stuff is looking for a way out and I promise you it will find one. Get to the transporter pad."

"No," he insisted, training his scanner on the alcove again.

"We have to abort," Patel said.

O'Donnell stepped in front of both of them. "You go," he said. "I'm staying right here."

"I've already seen how this story ends, Commander," Gwyn said. "We leave or we die."

O'Donnell turned to Patel. "It's okay," he said. "It can have me."

"That's insane. Why would you . . . ?"

"I told you, Devi. Each of the first species that came to SWOW sacrificed at least one individual to direct exposure to the base. In almost every instance, the individual survived. That was the beginning of the creation of the interlocutors. It took decades for them to figure out how to do the same using only blood samples. You saw yourself how the Borg drones were changed. It didn't kill them. It transformed them. I want to know, I *must know,* what they became."

"You knew this could happen?" Patel said, horrified.

"Honestly, part of me hoped it would," he said.

The fluid continued to advance. Containment would fail in minutes, perhaps less. And when it did, everyone on board the runabout would be at risk.

Suddenly, Devi Patel began to taste iron. She found herself standing alone in the massive cavern connected to Station Four. Lasren, Vincent, and Jepel had transported to safety and it was her turn to join them. At her feet, the tricorders the team had used to collect the data on everything they had found were linked together. She had already decided what she must do. All that remained was summoning the courage to do it. Some things were worth dying for. She knew that then.

And she knew it now.

"I'm sorry, Commander," she said. Turning to Gwyn she ordered, "Stun him. Now."

Gwyn did not hesitate. Patel ducked behind O'Donnell as Gwyn redirected her phaser and shot the commander. Shock and betrayal were etched on his face as he fell into Patel's arms.

"Transporter pad," Patel said as she laid him gently on the deck.

"The transporter lock is still stable," Gwyn reported as she studied the transporter controls. "I'll alert *Demeter* to initiate—"

"No," Patel interjected as she stepped onto the pad, "I'm not leaving. You're going to transport me inside the alcove and then you need to drag O'Donnell up here and signal *Demeter* to get you to safety."

"The hell I am," Gwyn replied.

"There's no time to explain. The Edrehmaia asked for me when they came here. They transmitted my genome and that of my interlocutor. They're expecting me. I don't know why or what will happen, but if O'Donnell believed he would survive exposure, my guess is he was right."

"Devi, no. You can't do this," Gwyn said. "I've already been attacked by that stuff once. I barely survived."

"The process was interrupted when Seven fired on the substance," Patel insisted as the sound of sensor alarms added to her growing anxiety. "It never actually touched you. I'm sorry, but I have to do this. There is no other way."

"This was not the plan."

"I know. But you need to trust me. This is what is supposed to happen. I just know."

Gwyn shook her head. "I can't lose you," she said simply. "That's one of the things I realized. You are my best friend. You're my sister. Please don't ask me to do this."

"There is literally no one else who can, Gwyn," Patel said. "This is the only chance we have of saving everyone."

"I don't like our odds."

Patel smiled faintly. "Unless we're talking about trajectories, you suck at math."

Tears began to stream down Gwyn's face. She took a deep breath and initiated transport. A second later, Patel appeared in a cascade of light inside the alcove.

The fluid was drawn to her instantly. Withdrawing from the walls, it pooled at her feet. The moment it touched her, she felt a painful surge shooting through every cell of her body.

Gwyn had returned to the front of the alcove. She stood there, watching, witnessing, and, in her way, honoring the sacrifice Patel had just made for all of them.

"I love you, Devi Patel," Gwyn said.

These were the last words Patel heard.

VOYAGER

The view of the rogue star on the astrometric lab's gigantic screen was majestic. Seven rarely found astrological phenomena extraordinary, but in this case, she was willing to make an exception.

The quantum sensors she, Bryce, and Icheb had constructed and deployed were functioning optimally. *Vesta* and *Voyager* were moving into position to execute the slipstream maneuver that would nudge the star off its present course.

Torres stood beside Seven, her display divided into a dozen segments showing each of the quantum sensors. *Voyager* would be exiting the slipstream corridor first and, assuming that went well, would be in position to track any response from the asteroid energy field. The moment they detected its activation, all quantum fluctuations would be visible. These readings would be used to extrapolate the location of the Edrehmaia and, ultimately, the *Galen*.

"Bryce, can you hear me?" Torres asked.

"Yes, Commander."

"Module Eight's calibration is fluctuating."

"It's attempting to compensate for the motion of the field. Give it a second."

"If it doesn't stabilize, we might have to call this party off."

"I'm seeing a point zero four deviation. Anything less than point zero five will be fine," Seven noted.

"Bridge to astrometrics. Are you guys ready? It's starting to get a little bumpy up here," Commander Paris called over the comm.

As if to punctuate his point, the deck beneath Seven's feet began to shudder.

"We should begin," Seven said.

"We're only going to get one shot at this," Torres reminded her.

"My recommendation remains the same," Seven said.

"B'Elanna, we need to go now or break off and recalculate our trajectories."

Torres locked eyes with Seven, who nodded.

"Fine. We're ready."

Admiral Janeway sat to the right of Captain Chakotay on the bridge she had called home for seven years. Commander Paris had resumed his former flight control station. Lieutenant Lasren stood at ops and Lieutenant Aubrey controlled tactical.

A thousand kilometers ahead, *Vesta* was standing by to open the slipstream corridor both ships would use to make the relatively short jump required to alter the star's course. *Voyager* would exit the corridor at the farthest distance for their long-range sensors and immediately reverse course at maximum warp in order to capture the quantum sensor data. It would take *Vesta* a little longer to rejoin them, as she would maintain the corridor's stability for the duration. At the near impossible speeds of slipstream travel, that would leave a distance of almost half a light-year between them when the maneuver was complete.

"*Vesta to* Voyager,*" Farkas's voice rang out over the comm. "*Mister Hoch assures me that our window is closing.*"

"We are ready," Captain Chakotay replied.

"*Very well. We'll see you on the other side.*"

"That you will, *Vesta. Voyager* out."

Chakotay turned to Janeway, offering her a wink and a tight smile. She nodded briskly.

"Mister Paris?"

"Would this be a bad time to mention that this constitutes a highly unadvisable use of our slipstream capabilities?" Paris asked.

"Look at it this way, Tom. You're about to make history," Chakotay replied.

"Yeah, that's never quite as thrilling as it sounds."

"It'll be over before you know it."

"Promises, promises."

Ahead, *Vesta*'s nacelles began to burn with the bright orange color unique to slipstream propulsion.

"Here we go," Paris said.

The ship shuddered gently as a roiling tunnel of churning light formed around them. Billions of kilometers ahead, a star was moving through space. Janeway imagined it, trailing radiant energy as it tore a streak of light through the darkness.

"Preparing to exit slipstream corridor in three, two, one . . ." Paris intoned.

Janeway had come to take for granted the relative ease with which her fleet's vessels traveled using the miraculous propulsion system first discovered by *Voyager* years earlier. As the ship eased out of the churning maelstrom, she wondered idly if Arturis, the alien responsible for bringing quantum-slipstream technology to her people, had found peace and release when the Caeliar had transformed the Borg. She hoped he had. He had come to *Voyager* seeking revenge and that design had been thwarted. But in the process, he had unlocked a new wave of exploratory capability for which she could not help but be grateful.

A loud cracking sound and the groan of metal resisting impossible forces sounded just before alarm klaxons began to wail. Janeway instinctively held tight to her chair as the inertial dampers strained to maintain normal gravity.

The slipstream corridor was replaced by a normal starfield, but the view was disorienting as *Voyager* spun wildly. The body of Lieutenant Aubrey hit the deck beside the admiral. Tom Paris, who had likely known something was wrong before the rest of them, held his seat, but just barely.

"Hang on," he shouted above the din as he struggled to regain control of the helm.

Circuits overloaded, shooting sparks into the air. Janeway felt her stomach lurch and the momentary uncomfortable press of gravity on her chest.

"Paris," Chakotay barely choked out.

Another sharp jolt rattled the bridge as the spinning mercifully began to slow. Janeway gulped for air as her body attempted to adjust to the rapidly shifting environmental conditions.

"Almost got it," Paris reported through gritted teeth.

The next twenty seconds seemed to last forever, but through them, Janeway could sense normalcy creeping toward her.

As soon as space had ceased to spin, Chakotay ordered the emergency klaxons silent. "Commander Paris, what's our status?"

"We are holding position roughly one-quarter of a light-year from our intended egress point," he replied. "I don't know what the hell happened, but that didn't go as planned."

"That much I figured," Chakotay said. "Lasren, can you locate the star and determine if its course has changed?"

"I've got it on long-range sensors, sir. Calculating."

Janeway waited breathlessly for the next words to fall from his lips.

"I'm sorry, sir," he said. "The star's course remains unchanged."

"How soon can we go to warp?" Chakotay asked.

"B'Elanna is on her way to main engineering as we speak," Paris replied. "She'll need a minute to run diagnostics."

"Do we know what *Vesta*'s status is?"

"Captain Farkas is reporting minimal damage. She advises that *Vesta* was able to exit the slipstream corridor before it dispersed of its own accord."

"How?" Chakotay and Janeway asked simultaneously.

"Seven to the bridge."

"Go ahead," Chakotay ordered.

"I can confirm that the energy field was activated, but until we are within range of the quantum sensors, we won't know if they detected the anticipated entanglement."

"Does that mean the star's course might have been altered?" Chakotay asked. "How do you know that the energy field was activated?"

"Because it targeted our slipstream corridor just prior to our anticipated pass. It prevented us from altering the star's course."

"Well, that explains that," Paris said bitterly.

"Gods damnit," Chakotay added.

Janeway shared his frustration, but at the same time was forced once again to marvel at the Edrehmaia and their obvious foresight. She could only hope that despite their failure, the activation of the field had at least given them the data they required.

Somehow, though, she doubted it.

DEMETER

Liam O'Donnell returned to consciousness with the assistance of a blinding white light above him. For a fraction of a second he wondered if the Edrehmaia substance had claimed him and he had actually died.

"Can you hear me, sir?" Atlee Fife asked, scuttling that thought.

"Someone shot me," O'Donnell said as the memory of the final seconds of which he had been aware returned to him.

"Yes, sir. Ensign Gwyn."

"I want her brought up on charges," O'Donnell said as he pushed himself up off the biobed and assumed a seated position.

Fife stared at him, his unusually large eyes radiating cold rage. Finally, he said, "No, sir."

"No what?"

"No, you will not bring charges against Ensign Gwyn for stunning you. I would have done the same in her place."

"Did I miss a meeting? Are we allowed to just shoot people now?"

"We are when they act in a way that endangers their lives or the lives of their fellow officers," Fife replied evenly.

"How do you know . . . ?" O'Donnell began.

"I have yet to receive a full report from Ensign Gwyn. She has her hands quite full at the moment. But our sensors were locked onto the shuttle throughout the experiment and clearly indicated the beginnings of a containment breach. My assumption is that you were going to allow it and that Gwyn's quick action was the only thing that prevented you from doing so."

O'Donnell swallowed both his anger and the first response that occurred to him. Atlee Fife was a man of considerable personal integrity. It was that quality more than any other that had steeled O'Donnell's resolve to make their unusual co-captaincy work. This was the first moment since they had left Persephone that he'd experienced the slightest hint of regret over that decision.

"They wouldn't have been harmed," O'Donnell offered weakly.

Fife's face clearly communicated his utter disbelief. When he replied, there was no mistaking the disappointment in his tone. "You are easily the most extraordinary human being I have ever known. You have challenged me every single day we have served together to think through every issue from multiple perspectives. In so doing, you have expanded my understanding of humanity, of the aliens we have encountered, and of myself. I have followed you without question wherever it has pleased you to lead me.

"But you are human. You are capable of making mistakes. For the first time in our acquaintance, your arrogance has blinded you to the reality that your first duty is not to your own savage curiosity, but to those you command. I don't care that you are willing, anxious in fact, to sacrifice your life on the altar of transcendence. I do care that you believe I will permit you to do so on my watch. Until you have demonstrated to my satisfaction that you are willing to act both rationally and safely in pursuit of the knowledge you seek, I am hereby relieving you from duty and ordering a full psychiatric evaluation. Until then, you are restricted to your quarters, Captain."

"Atlee?"

"Tell me I'm wrong," Fife said. "Tell me you wouldn't do the same were our places reversed."

O'Donnell wanted to, but he couldn't.

VESTA

"Bryce tells me that we're at least a day away from completing repairs to the slipstream drive. He'd like me to lay off the warp drive for the duration as well," Farkas reported.

Janeway sighed. "*Voyager* suffered more severe damage. Torres estimates four days before her repairs will be done."

"I'm afraid there's more bad news, Admiral. Before we met back up with you and *Voyager*, we took a little detour at Bryce's request to pick up the quantum sensor data. He figured you wouldn't be able to, so . . ."

"That was very thoughtful of him," Janeway said.

"According to our readings, the energy field showed no signs of quantum entanglement when it activated. He thinks it was an automated response to the threat our maneuver posed to the star. Even while inert, it clearly has some low-intensity scanning capabilities."

"It's not going to let us, or anything else, affect that star as long as it is in range of the field."

"That's his conclusion, yes, Admiral," Farkas said.

"*Demeter* has yet to check in."

"Let's hope that's a good thing."

Farkas had stood before Janeway's desk while making this report. The two women locked eyes, clearly making the same complicated calculations. Janeway crossed to her replicator and ordered a hot cup of coffee. After a fortifying sip she said, "I have a feeling this is the part where you tell me we've done all we can to attempt to locate the *Galen* and that it is time to put this tragedy behind us and resume our primary mission."

Farkas deserved that. She and Janeway hadn't spoken privately to discuss anything other than direct orders since Regina had let her mouth run without a filter in the hours following *Galen*'s loss.

"If you believe that, I've done a piss-poor job while serving under your command of showing you who I am," Farkas replied.

A single eyebrow was raised as the admiral took another swig of her coffee.

"As long as there is a chance the crew of the *Galen* is alive, *they are our primary mission*," Farkas said.

Janeway nodded. "I'm glad we agree about that. But the reality of this situation is that no matter how much we want to find them, it may not be possible, now or ever. It will take the better part of a decade for that star to move beyond the range of the asteroid field that is protecting it. Experimenting directly with the Edrehmaia substance in order to unlock its quantum nature will likely cost more lives and still might not yield the results we require."

"Isn't O'Donnell already in the process of doing just that?"

"It's a limited experiment with multiple safeguards in place. Frankly, it feels like a long shot, but you know how he is."

"I do," Farkas replied with a smile.

"And even if it succeeds, having functional translation technology isn't going to do us much good if we can't get the Edrehmaia on the other end of a transmission."

"It does begin to feel like if they don't want to be found, we might never find them," Farkas allowed.

"I know our engineering and science departments are already in the process of finding work-arounds and new hypotheses. Given enough time, they might come up with a few alternatives. It's just . . ."

Finally, Farkas understood the admiral's unique position. "How long did it take Starfleet to declare *Voyager* lost the first time you were out here?"

Janeway smiled bitterly. "Two years."

"And how much longer did it take for you to prove them wrong?"

"Another fourteen months."

"It hasn't been fourteen days yet, Admiral, since we were given good reason to believe that the ship survived."

"And if there were no other pressing matters on the horizon, we wouldn't be having this conversation."

"Admiral?"

"I've ignored four requests from the Department of Temporal Investigations to return to Krenim space and attempt to establish diplomatic relations," Janeway admitted. "They're not going to let me keep that up indefinitely."

"No, they aren't," Farkas agreed. "I know, because one of their directors reached out to me several weeks ago and asked that I do everything in my power to make sure you followed that order. In fact, it was made clear to me that should you refuse, you would be relieved of your command and I would be tasked with completing that mission."

The eyes that met Farkas's following this pronouncement were clear blue skies suddenly streaked with storm clouds.

"And how did you respond to the director in question?"

"I told him exactly where he could shove his threats. I don't like bullies, especially ones who want you to dance to a tune they won't even allow you to hear," Farkas replied. "And to be honest, in the absence of a great deal more information than I was given, I'm not at all sure anyone from the Federation should kick that hornets' nest again."

Janeway's relief was clear. "You and I have a great deal in common, Captain."

"I think that's why I'm so hard on you. I know for sure that on any given day, I could just as easily be the one writing letters of condolence to heartbroken families."

"There but for the grace of . . ."

"Something," Farkas finished for her. "Someone, actually."

"Doctor Sal?"

"Every captain should be lucky enough to have the same doctor for more than forty years."

"I will bear that in mind."

"The last time we spoke, I was angry. That's a luxury you are not afforded. And I only enjoy it because you are standing behind me, taking responsibility for the actions of everyone you command."

"Still, I appreciate your honesty."

"You will always have it."

"So how would you propose I answer the DTI?"

"Depends. Do you like being the admiral in charge of this fleet?"

"Very much."

"Then sooner or later you're going to have to follow that directive. I would be remiss in my duty if I didn't tell you I believe it is the single dumbest directive ever issued. We've used our temporal shielding often enough to know that whatever the Krenim are up to, they haven't made any alterations to the timeline since last we enjoyed their company. I'm inclined to believe that the only thing that might change that would be them picking up *Voyager*'s approach on their long-range sensors. I don't know what has the DTI so spooked, but I don't believe it's the Krenim and I would need a lot more than the word of some temporal bureaucrat to make me curious enough to leave thirty of our people at the mercy of an alien species.

"So, here's my promise to you, Admiral. The day Dulmur, Lucsly, or Admiral Akaar order me to take command of this fleet is the day I resign my commission. And if they think Chakotay, Paris, O'Donnell, or Fife would do any different, they don't know us at all."

"What if *I* ordered you to take *Vesta* back to Krenim space?"

"I'd lay in a course and do the best I could."

Janeway bowed her head and shook it gently. When she lifted her face again to Farkas's, her eyes were glistening.

"Thank you, Regina."

"Of course, Admiral."

"Chakotay to Admiral Janeway."

Janeway tapped her combadge. "Go ahead, Captain."

"I've just received a full report from Ensign Gwyn aboard the Okinawa. *Lieutenant Patel successfully created a new interlocutor. She is in communion with the Edrehmaia and has provided us with their coordinates."*

It only took the admiral a few seconds to recover from the shock of Chakotay's words. "That's wonderful. We'll lay in a course as soon as repairs are complete."

"Captain Chakotay, this is Farkas. When you say, 'in communion,' what exactly do you mean?"

"Those were Gwyn's words, Regina. And there is more to report."

Farkas didn't like the sound of that and she could see the dread creeping over the admiral's face as well.

"Lieutenant Patel was unable to complete the experiment as intended. She has merged at the molecular level with the Edrehmaia. According to Gwyn, Devi Patel died a few hours ago, the moment our interlocutor was created."

19

The mess hall had been cleared of all personnel save Commander Glenn; Lieutenants Kim, Conlon, and Barclay; and the Doctor. Glenn was aware that the transfer of Conlon's consciousness had not gone seamlessly, but in the two days she had spent with Velth, who in his quantum-agitated state did not require sleep, Conlon had performed her duties as chief engineer quite capably. Those duties had included preparations for several permanent alterations to the ship's slipstream drive as well as the creation by the Edrehmaia of substances meant to integrate with the deflector controls and to provide new shields. All of this had been completed, but not yet implemented.

It was time to make a decision and while Glenn knew that, ultimately, she would make the call, she would not do so without the input of her senior officers. Weeks ago, Velth and Benoit would have been in this meeting.

Things had changed.

"In the interest of clarity and making certain we are all on the same page, would you go over the Edrehmaia's proposal once more for the group, Lieutenant Conlon?"

"Yes, Commander," Conlon replied. "Our initial supposition was correct. The scans the Edrehmaia took of our fleet alerted them to the presence of our slipstream drive. This was of interest not because of the speed it provides our vessels, but because of the unique ways in which a slipstream corridor interacts with normal space and subspace. It is also not technology they can simply replicate. Their methods of propulsion are unlike ours. They are generated from their physiology using undiluted radiant energy. What we initially identified as a vessel was actually a large group of Edrehmaia clustered together."

"Our sensors are still unable to accurately render life signs, even when they approach as individuals," Kim noted.

"That problem will be corrected once the modifications under discussion have been made," Conlon said.

"Which are?"

"The Edrehmaia wish to leave our galaxy. They intend to travel into the void and beyond to the next nearest galaxy, Sagittarius Dwarf Elliptical. In order to do that, they must breach the galactic barrier with a single star in tow. They have attempted to do this several times without success. The last attempt was made by a group of several million Edrehmaia, all of whom perished in the attempt."

Glenn remembered well Velth's description of the large spherical Edrehmaia structure he had seen. It awed and saddened her to understand that it was, essentially, a massive grave marker.

"A properly constructed slipstream corridor will allow them to do this," Conlon continued. "Now that they have been given the molecular composition of benamite, they can provide us with an inexhaustible supply. They require our vessel, properly modified, to create and sustain the corridor."

"It's the part about towing a star into that corridor that has me worried," Glenn admitted.

"A number of individual Edrehmaia will act as a barrier between our ship and the star, which is actually quite small. They have the ability to manipulate stars at every moment of their life cycle and the most significant compensation required will be reinforcing the corridor to prevent the star's gravity from dispersing it."

"And you are satisfied that this is possible?" Glenn asked.

"I am," Conlon replied.

"And they are content to allow us to join them on this journey?" the Doctor asked.

"They are," she replied. "There is, however, an alternative."

"Which is?" Kim asked.

"They could modify each crew member as they have already

changed Lieutenant Velth. We would then be allowed to remain here to live out the rest of our lives."

"In open space?" Kim asked, incredulous.

"They don't know another way to live," Conlon said. "Just because we do doesn't make it a ridiculous suggestion, at least from their point of view."

"Are they open to discussing any counterproposals?" Glenn asked.

"Such as?"

"If they give us the benamite we require, we could use our slipstream drive to locate and rejoin the fleet. At that point we could take this proposal to Starfleet Command. I do not doubt they would be interested in working together to solve the Edrehmaia's problem. It would be a fantastic achievement for both our species and theirs."

"They will not allow us to do that," Conlon replied.

"Why not?" Kim demanded.

"When I asked to make contact with the rest of our fleet, they offered to bring the other ships here."

"No," Kim said. "They can't. We lost a dozen people the first time. There's no telling how many would die if they attempted another transport."

"They don't see that as much of a sacrifice," Conlon said. "They lost millions to their last attempt. We might be talking about a few hundred."

"It's not about the damn math, Nancy," Kim said, his voice rising.

"It is *only* about the math, at least to them," she replied. "Don't confuse our ability to exchange more than our names with clear communication, Lieutenant Kim. They don't think like we do. They don't prioritize individual life as we do. They aren't us. They don't share our values, and it is impossible for them to grasp the concept of our refusal, let alone our reasons."

"They left behind life-forms like ours billions of years ago. We are irrelevant to them," Kim realized.

"That's not entirely true," Glenn said. "Superior though they may be in many ways, we have the solution to their problem. That makes us very relevant."

"Could we take the benamite and calculate a jump back to the fleet's last-known coordinates without their knowledge?" Barclay asked. "I'm not saying we should. I just want to know if it's possible."

"Once we make the appropriate changes to the drive, it will be inadvisable to attempt a normal slipstream jump. Without the added mass of the star as part of the equation, the new corridor we form would crush the ship," Conlon replied.

"So, we are their prisoners and we have no choice," Kim said.

"Correction," the Doctor said. "The organic life-forms among us can choose to go with the Edrehmaia, or remain here in some eternal purgatory, transformed into a new state of being that, while alive, resembles in no way their normal way of living. I assume this option is not open to those among us who are holographic?"

"I would be required to remain with the ship no matter what," Conlon said. "You could choose deactivation or to remain here, but no, you could not survive transformation."

"What about the baby?" Kim asked. "She wouldn't survive transformation either, would she?"

"I would recommend leaving her on the ship and allowing her to continue to gestate. Once her maturation is complete, she could easily be cared for by the existing holographic crew members or any humans who chose to take the journey," Conlon replied.

"But what kind of life would that be for a child?" Kim demanded. "Human children have human needs."

"She would survive," Conlon argued.

"Only to face the most warped version of existence I can imagine," Kim shot back. Turning to the captain he said, "We can't do this. We can't allow them to do this to us."

"Then give me another alternative," Glenn said.

"We go down fighting," Kim replied. "We refuse and make sure they know that if they try to force us, we will take as many of them with us as possible before it's over."

Glenn shook her head. "You were the one counseling patience and understanding when all of this started."

"That's because I had no idea what they wanted. Now that I do know, I've reconsidered," Kim said.

"Setting aside the *going-down-in-a-blaze-of-glory* option," Glenn said, "can any of you think of an alternative?"

"We keep talking," the Doctor suggested. "While it is true that we can't presently make them understand our concerns, perhaps in time that could change. We have already come quite a way in terms of bridging the communication gap. Perhaps more progress would still be possible."

"I was barely able to buy us enough time to take this meeting," Conlon said. "Velth is waiting to begin the modifications and I don't think he will wait much longer."

"Let's put the best possible spin on this for a minute," Glenn suggested. "Say we choose to go with them. We would be agreeing to live the rest of our lives on this ship, limited to replicated food and the company of those who are now present. But we can survive quite well here. And we would be the first of our kind to explore the universe beyond our galaxy in this way. We would all learn a great deal."

"A great deal we could never communicate to the rest of humanity," Kim reminded her. "I agree, it isn't the worst life I could imagine, but let's not kid ourselves about it serving the interests of anyone but the Edrehmaia."

"Still, it does seem preferable to dying now or submitting to their version of transformation, doesn't it?" she asked.

Silence descended.

"I want another option," Kim said.

"I do too," Glenn agreed. "But there really isn't one, is there?"

When no one responded, Glenn said, "I'm going to take a few hours to think about this. I know the Edrehmaia are impatient to begin, but I need the time. We will reconvene at zero six hundred and I will issue orders."

Kim stared at her, aghast.

"Unless there is anything else, you are dismissed."

Harry Kim harbored no illusions about getting any sleep over the next few hours. An hour in his quarters alone had confirmed that. Taking his clarinet, he ventured to sickbay, intending to spend a few more minutes talking to his daughter. But when he arrived, the first thing he noted was that Nancy's body was no longer in the main bay.

"Doc?"

The Doctor materialized beside him immediately.

"Yes, Harry?"

"Where's Nancy?"

"I assume she has returned to main engineering to stall Velth."

"Not her."

"Oh, I moved Lieutenant Conlon's body to a private room. Four doors down on the right."

Kim entered the room where Conlon lay beneath a surgical arch. All of the diagnostic bars glowed a reassuring green. Beside her, the gestational incubator rested, his daughter floating peacefully, continuing to grow, utterly insensate of the universe into which she would someday awake.

He had allowed himself to dream that one day this would be his family. Their lives, like Tom's, B'Elanna's, Miral's, and Michael's, would go on, much like they always had before. There would be adventures, discoveries, and new challenges, to be sure. But there would also be lengthy stretches in between filled with conversations and holodeck stories and dinners and duty shifts, the boring things he had always taken for granted.

Standing here now, he finally understood that no matter what Glenn decided, that would not be his future. Whatever he was to become, he faced a new kind of darkness ahead. Only now was he forced to accept that no amount of wanting, working, problem solving, hoping, or striving would restore what had been lost. And no matter how far he stretched his imagination, he could not force into being, even in his mind, a picture of what would take its place.

In a few hours, Glenn would make her choice and the path before him would become clearer. This was his last chance to live with a dying dream, his last chance to share a moment with the woman he loved and the child they had created while he was still the Harry Kim who had begun this journey so full of hope and determination.

Kim moved back to the room's holographic control panel and initiated the program he and Nancy had shared what felt like a lifetime ago. The room fell away and was replaced by a starfield. Lifting his clarinet to his lips, he began to play the only song that had made sense to him all this time, the only song this instrument had ever known.

Tears fell from his eyes as the song of the moon filled the heavens.

Lieutenant Ranson Velth awoke standing beside the slipstream assembly in main engineering. Nancy Conlon was speaking.

". . . the variances are calculated automatically, but the range will have to be extended beyond . . ." she was saying.

"What?" Velth asked.

Conlon's brow furrowed. She lifted a tricorder and scanned him quickly.

"Oh, you're back," she said. "I haven't seen you in days."

"Where have I been? What the hell is going on here?"

"I don't understand why you've transitioned," Conlon said as if it should have made sense to him.

"Do you hear that?" he asked. In the distance, haunting, beautiful music could be heard.

"The music?" she asked. "Someone must have the volume control for their environmental entertainment set too high."

Velth shook his head. "No."

"Velth, listen to me. You've been shifting between versions of yourself. There are two of you. There's you, as you are now, and there's one that is somehow part of the Edrehmaia. They've been using you to communicate with us."

A sick pit opened in Velth's stomach. "That's impossible."

"I promise you it isn't. The *other* you has been showing me how to modify our slipstream drive so the Edrehmaia can use it to leave the galaxy."

"What happens to us when they do that?" Velth demanded.

"The captain hasn't decided yet. We'll know soon."

Velth needed to sit. He needed to think. He needed to *remember* something that was terribly important.

"Where the hell is that music coming from?"

Conlon looked up and thought for a minute. "Sickbay, maybe? One of the Doctor's operas, perhaps?"

"We all live in a yellow submarine," he said softly.

"What?"

"Come with me," Velth ordered.

Commander Glenn's quarters felt suffocating. She imagined spending the rest of her life here and instinctively rebelled at the thought. Rather than fight it, she decided to take a walk. Strolling through the corridors of each deck, she tried to resign herself to the possibility of allowing the Edrehmaia to use her ship as they intended. This, too, felt like a violation. Even if she ultimately came to accept it as the best choice for herself and her crew, this ship, which had once felt like a boundless place, a catalyst for discovery and a safe haven in an endless darkness, would inevitably become a prison, then a graveyard.

It was unfair. It was infuriating. It offended her to the core of her being.

And it was still better than any alternative that included the senseless death of any more of her crew.

Where there is life, there is hope.

She wanted to believe that. Perhaps, in time, she would.

Turning a corner, she realized she was heading toward sickbay. Lieutenant Conlon and Velth were approaching from the opposite end of the corridor. The sight of him wandering freely, this monster who had taken the form of her friend and most trusted companion, only served to intensify the sensation of injury with which she struggled. She considered turning back and retracing her steps when Velth called to her.

"Clarissa?"

"Ranson?"

She hurried toward him as he rushed to close the distance between them and take her in his arms. She accepted the hug but demanded an explanation from Conlon with her eyes.

"He's back," Conlon said simply. "I don't know for how long."

"Come with me," Velth said. "Something's happening I don't understand."

"There's a lot of that going around," Glenn said as she followed him into sickbay.

"Where is the music coming from?" Velth asked.

"This way," Conlon said, leading them toward the private rooms.

When they reached the door from which the song was clearly emanating, Velth pounded on the door.

The music stopped abruptly.

Seconds later, the door slid open, revealing Lieutenant Kim. His face was red, and his eyes were glistening. As soon as he saw Velth's face, his eyes hardened. Rage replaced the pain they had previously held.

"What do you want?" Kim demanded, taking note of Glenn and Conlon curiously.

"The music," Velth said. "What is it?"

" 'Clair de Lune'?" Kim asked.

"No, what *is* it?" Velth asked again.

Kim was clearly at a loss. "It was written in the late nineteenth century by Claude Debussy. It's a famous piece with both baroque and impressionistic influences. It was reworked several times before it was published, initially based on a piece of romantic poetry about taking a stroll and seeing birds take flight. Eventually it became part of a suite known as *Bergamasque*. Roughly translated it means 'moonlight.'"

Velth began to shudder. "Please," he said. "Please . . ."

Kim took a step back as Velth's eyes darkened.

"He's transitioning," Conlon warned.

"Play it again, Harry," Glenn said. "That's an order."

Kim reflexively lifted the clarinet to his lips and started to play. Velth stood motionless as the sound cascaded over him.

"Explain this," Velth said simply.

Glenn moved to stand between him and Kim, who continued to play. "It's called music," she said. "It's played on an instrument we call a clarinet. This particular piece was created by a human, one of us."

"What is its purpose?" Velth asked.

"It has no practical purpose," Glenn replied. "It is a thing of beauty. It is one of many ways we communicate feelings without words."

"You create this?"

"Among other things, yes."

"We understand its structure. Its expression is uncertain."

"You're saying it is a question that has no answer?" Glenn asked.

"And yet, it speaks to us," Velth said.

"It speaks to us too," Glenn said.

"You are builders," Velth said.

"I don't know what that means," Glenn said.

"You are like us."

"In some ways, yes. But in other ways, we are very different."

"Builders define what is."

"We, like all living species, grapple with our own existence, search for purpose and meaning, and are instruments of change," Glenn said.

"This creation is beyond our capacity."

"We have found many things in our travels that were, once, also beyond our capacity. That is part of our purpose. To learn new things."

The song ended. Kim lowered his clarinet. "The basis for music is mathematical. Rhythms and tones are ordered in original ways to evoke emotion and transcend space and time. We build music to understand ourselves and where we fit within the universe."

"Music as you define it is a bridge between what is and what cannot be expressed," Velth said. "We would know more."

"No," Kim said.

Clearly taken aback by Kim's refusal, Velth said, "Do you require more certainty?"

"No, we don't. We require freedom."

"You have not been limited."

"Yes, we have," Kim insisted. "You are limiting our existence. You are refusing to allow us to choose our own path. You want something from us, and you are taking it without our permission. You have given us no choice.

"We do not want to go with you. We do not want to explore beyond the barrier. We want to return to the company of those who were with us when you found our ship. We want to continue to explore on our own terms. We would welcome the chance to understand you better, but not like this."

"Builders exist to call into being that which sustains life. Life must be extended beyond this place. You, alone among all builders, can help us create positive infinity."

"Why?" Kim asked. "Why is it so damned important for you to move beyond the barrier?"

"This is the process by which we understand ourselves and our place in the universe."

"Will you allow us to help you, but in a way that does not violate our rights as builders? Will you accept that we are your peers and not force us to do that which limits us and our existence?" Kim asked.

"All builders are architects of their own infinity," Velth replied. "All builders live in a yellow submarine."

Kim looked to Glenn, who was smiling sadly.

"I think we finally understand each other," Glenn said.

Kim nodded.

"Bridge to Commander Glenn."

"Go ahead, Ensign Drur."

"We have incoming."

"Who?"

"The entire fleet has just emerged from a slipstream corridor. They are moving to intercept us."

"Tell them to hold position until we make further contact and to take no aggressive action."

"Aye, Captain."

Glenn placed a hand on Velth's arm. "Do not harm them."

"They, too, are builders?"

"Yes, they are."

20

Admiral Kathryn Janeway had seen more than her fair share of extraordinary days in the Delta Quadrant. Few of them compared to the last several.

The first hours following the fleet's arrival in the Edrehmaia's space had been spent in conversation with Commander Glenn and Lieutenant Kim, after which the transfer of supplies and personnel required to fully restore the *Galen* had begun. It would be the work of weeks but the relief on both sides buoyed the spirits of everyone involved.

Heartfelt reunions between crew members and officers were also proceeding apace. A celebratory feeling suffused the atmosphere. Many, including the admiral, marveled at the actions taken by Glenn's crew, not the least of which was establishing the first meaningful exchange of ideas with the Edrehmaia.

The Edrehmaia had retreated, allowing the newly arrived ships to tend to their own. The interlocutor created when Devi Patel merged with the Edrehmaia substance had remained within the alcove aboard the *Okinawa* when the runabout was returned to *Voyager* and throughout its slipstream journey to the coordinates it had provided. Ensign Gwyn had remained with her and shortly after they arrived had suggested that Patel be released to join the Edrehmaia. Janeway had agreed but to her surprise, had received a counterproposal from Velth, who initially continued to serve as the primary translator for the Edrehmaia. Patel's transformation had been a blow from a blunt instrument, whereas Velth's had been painstakingly orchestrated to create the desired result—clear communication—while minimizing the damage to his body. Both processes could be reversed. Thanks to the efforts of both Velth and Patel, the Edrehmaia no longer required interlocutors to communicate with relative ease. Detailed instructions were provided to the Doctor, who performed the procedures with the assistance of Doctor Sharak. Janeway had been relieved to learn that both Velth and Patel would make complete recoveries.

Although the language barrier had been broken, there were so many concepts that eluded the Edrehmaia. Still, a great deal had been revealed.

The Edrehmaia had existed for millions of years. Space-born life-forms, they had roamed the galaxy, evolving by the light of the stars and eventually using the raw materials present to continue to advance ever outward. They had been attempting to breach the galactic barrier for almost two millennia. They would continue in their efforts, with or without the assistance of the new race of "builders" they now considered peers.

As the fleet would be remaining in Edrehmaia space for another few weeks at least, Janeway had dispatched the *Vesta* to plot a series of targeted slipstream jumps to drop new communications relays that would create a continuous link to Starfleet. Once their time here had ended, Janeway sincerely hoped to continue to observe the Edrehmaia's work. They were utterly fascinating.

Chakotay had retired for the evening, but when she entered the quarters they shared when she was aboard *Voyager*, she was surprised to find him still awake, seated in the living area, staring out a port. He greeted her with a pensive smile when she entered but remained seated on the low sofa.

"You look like you could use some company," she said, crossing to sit with him. Placing her back against his chest, he wrapped his arms around her. They sat like that in companionable silence, staring out at the stellar nursery.

Finally, Chakotay said, "I had an interesting conversation today with Commander Fife."

At Fife's request, Counselor Cambridge had been dispatched to *Demeter* shortly after the fleet had regrouped to conduct a complete psychiatric evaluation of Captain O'Donnell. His final report indicated that while the captain harbored an unhealthy fascination with the Edrehmaia and that several sessions of cognitive therapy would likely provide the necessary perspective for him to return to duty, he had begun to come to grips with his lapses in judgment. Cambridge supported Fife's orders to restrict O'Donnell's activities until those sessions were complete.

"Really? What did Fife want?"

"He wants us to allow the Edrehmaia to make the alterations they had proposed for the *Galen* to the *Demeter* instead."

"*Fife* made that request?" Janeway asked in disbelief.

Chakotay nodded.

"Did O'Donnell pressure him to do so?"

"I don't think so. They are an interesting pair, those two. While I would never want to share command with another captain, it has become clear to me that in their case, it is an ideal situation. What O'Donnell lacks in leadership abilities he more than makes up for in vision."

"And Fife provides the necessary balance to O'Donnell's occasional excesses, while managing the day-to-day operations and offering the crew an accessible leader," Janeway added. "But I still find it hard to believe that Fife wants to do this."

"He's not asking for himself. He had Lieutenant Elkins thoroughly review the proposed modifications and only when he agreed they were both safe and possible did Atlee come to me. He understands O'Donnell's fascination with the Edrehmaia, and while he intends to ensure that their future interactions are conducted with the necessary safeguards in place, I think he believes it would be cruel to deny Liam this opportunity."

As Janeway considered the magnitude of Fife's proposal, Chakotay continued, "While he would grant transfers to any of his crew who requested it, he wants to remain with O'Donnell and the Edrehmaia, enable them to breach the barrier, and follow them as they continue to explore beyond the Milky Way."

Janeway sat up and turned to face Chakotay.

"How did you respond?"

"I told him I would pass his request along to you."

"Why didn't he come to me himself?"

"He said he had requested a meeting but that your schedule hadn't permitted it."

"I have been ridiculously busy," Janeway allowed.

"I think he didn't want to wait any longer to get this on your radar. It's not a small undertaking."

"No, it isn't."

"What do you think?" Chakotay asked.

Janeway shook her head. "I think it's . . ." she began, then faltered. "I don't honestly know what I think."

"I'll say this much. We're never going to have an opportunity like this again. We find ourselves in a unique moment in space and time. The knowledge that could be gained by such an effort makes our continued exploration of the Delta Quadrant seem rather pedestrian."

"That's not fair."

"Really? With a modified slipstream drive and the assistance of the Edrehmaia, we're maybe a few months away from another galaxy. You're not even curious?"

Janeway suddenly realized that he was already way ahead of her in considering the possibilities and was clearly leaning in an unexpected direction.

"*Demeter* is a tiny ship. I wouldn't send her on her own into unexplored space, let alone another galaxy."

"Neither would I," Chakotay agreed.

The penny dropped.

"You want to take *Voyager* out there, don't you?"

Chakotay smiled. "I think this ship has already done extraordinary things, but her best days are still ahead of her, if we have the courage to make it so."

"'We'?"

"Yes," Chakotay said simply.

"How many of our officers do you think would be willing to

join us on such a mission, assuming Starfleet Command signed off on it?" Janeway asked.

"I have no idea. But I do think we should ask."

"We would need at least a hundred and twenty."

"There are almost a thousand people serving the fleet now. I bet we could get at least that many."

"We would be extending *Voyager*'s mission. We've only got about a year and a half left as it is. And there are serious supply considerations."

"The Edrehmaia can provide us with all of the benamite we require. We could stockpile other hard-to-replicate parts and equipment. I'd say our previous experience makes us uniquely well qualified to undertake something like this."

"It actually does," Janeway realized. "We would be opening up an entirely new avenue of exploration for the Federation."

"And cementing an alliance with one of the most extraordinary species we have ever encountered. Little as we seem to have in common now, we do share an insatiable desire to learn and to grow beyond our current limits—and an appreciation for good music. The Edrehmaia have mastered manipulation of matter in ways we still don't even understand."

"We would be taking our first steps into a much bigger universe," she said, allowing the explorer who had always lived in her heart to take the reins of her imagination.

"Then we agree?"

Staring into his eyes, she realized that the thing that had brought them together and kept them united throughout all of the years they had served together, through hardship, fear, death, painful compromise, and horrific losses, was Chakotay's unerring ability to reach her deepest, truest self and continue to challenge her to heed its wisdom. He was more than her partner, her lover, or her dearest friend. He was the best part of her, and she honored that by returning the favor as often as possible.

"I have one condition," she replied.

GALEN

Lieutenant Conlon was surprised when she answered a summons from the Doctor to find Counselor Cambridge waiting as well in the Doctor's private office.

"Sirs?" she greeted them.

"I have good news, Lieutenant," the Doctor began. "While we were separated, Doctors Sal and Sharak were able to find the cause of your genetic syndrome."

"What was it?" she asked.

"A mutation designed to make it difficult for your body to resist the invading consciousness. The others invaded by the Seriareen shared the mutation. That's how they found it."

Discovering the answer to the puzzle that had overshadowed every moment of Conlon's life for months should have been accompanied by relief. Oddly, it wasn't.

"I see."

"Doctor Sharak and I successfully eliminated the genetic sequence and it is now possible for us to return your consciousness to your organic body."

"Of course," Conlon said. "It's just . . . we're in the middle of serious repairs and I am currently *Galen*'s chief engineer. Perhaps we should wait . . ."

"Once the transfer is complete, you should be able to resume your duties within a few days at most, Lieutenant," the Doctor advised.

Conlon hesitated.

"Is there a problem?" the counselor asked.

"No. I mean, the truth is, there are considerable advantages to this form I'd never really imagined. I'm *not hating it*, as much as I feared I might."

"You are well aware that this was never intended to be a permanent solution. It can't be," the Doctor insisted.

"Has there been any degradation to my matrix?" she asked.

"Minor," he replied, "but it will only increase the longer you remain as you are."

"I haven't been aware of any limitations or processing difficulties."

"Be that as it may, eventually, you will be. There is no reason to wait any longer," the Doctor said.

"What if I refuse?"

The Doctor recoiled, as if certain he hadn't heard her properly.

"Doctor, may we have the room?" Cambridge asked.

He clearly wished to refuse but declined to do so.

"Of course."

"I have reviewed the reports surrounding your consciousness transfer as well as your duty logs since you assumed this form," the counselor said.

"I don't think I've ever been as good at my job as I am now," Conlon said a little too defensively.

"That's because you have been given a gift no other human has ever experienced," Cambridge said gently. "For most of us, duty is only part of the equation. We are defined as much by those with whom we share our lives as our professional aspirations. Our emotional connections can interfere with our reason and ability to function, but they also enrich our experience of living."

"I know that."

"Do you?"

"Of course. I'm still *me*, Counselor, even if there are parts of my life I don't remember."

Cambridge settled himself on the front edge of the Doctor's desk. "The Doctor has reported that very specific memories of your past relationship with Lieutenant Kim as well as of your child were apparently lost in the transfer process. He believes that those memories remain in your organic body and will be reintegrated when you return to it."

"I know that too."

"He believes that the power disruption, coupled with Lieutenant Kim's presence during the transfer, something you explicitly requested *not happen* prior to undergoing the transfer, are responsible for the loss," Cambridge continued.

Conlon nodded.

"I have also spoken at length with Lieutenant Kim about the events that transpired just before and after the *Galen's* transport by the Edrehmaia."

"And?"

"And I have a different theory."

Conlon honestly didn't want to hear it.

"What's that?"

"For most people, the idea of assuming a new form, no matter how perfect, would be terrifying. But you embraced the notion almost as soon as it was presented to you."

"There were no other options."

"Your life has been unusually fraught of late, Lieutenant. You were assaulted and gravely injured. You unexpectedly became pregnant with a child you had every intention of terminating. That choice was taken from you by circumstances beyond your control. When you awoke and were advised of this, at least according to Lieutenant Kim, you immediately embraced this new, troubling development. You carried on, seemingly content to continue your relationship and raise the child together."

"So I have been told, but I don't remember . . ."

"Moments after you made this choice, you were rendered unconscious and as soon as you awoke, found yourself in the midst of an even greater crisis. Survival became your only priority. You rose to the occasion admirably even as your body's deterioration continued to progress rapidly."

"I remember those events perfectly," Conlon said.

"And according to Kim, your relationship flourished."

"I don't doubt his memories, I just don't share them."

"Because you didn't want to," Cambridge said simply.

"That's ridiculous."

"Is it?"

"Why would I . . . ?"

"You didn't even tell Lieutenant Kim, the person who by all accounts you were closest to in the universe, that you intended to accept a holographic form. That's a big choice and one that at the very least you might have consulted with your partner about."

"It wouldn't have made any difference. It had to be done."

"Nancy, you and I have been through a great deal of this journey together. You have suffered the torments of the damned, and no one, least of all me, would blame you for wanting a clean slate."

"What?"

"I'm not even sure you were willing to admit it to yourself. We all have secrets we refuse to face. But none of us are ever given a chance like the one presented to you, a chance to make them go away."

Sensations Conlon had not experienced since the transfer began to assault her. Feelings, in all their messy, frustrating fullness, began to force their way into her consciousness.

"Please don't do this," she pleaded.

"I'm not doing anything," Cambridge replied. "Memories are nothing more or less than connections between our senses and our experiences. Your memories are now divided into partitions within your matrix. You can choose whether or not to access them. The Doctor and I have done a great deal of work with his program addressing a similar situation. It was that work that enabled me to intuitively grasp your current condition."

"I don't want to remember," Conlon realized.

"And in this form, you don't have to. That's its gift and its curse. But without all of your memories, you will never be whole. You will never again be the woman you were before your consciousness was transferred."

"I don't think I ever want to be that woman again," Conlon said.

Cambridge paused, allowing her time to live a little with this realization.

"Because?" he finally asked.

"Because she was broken. Because her life was not dictated by her choices. Everything about her existence, except her desire to work as a Starfleet engineer, was forced upon her by circumstance. I didn't know until all of it was gone how much I didn't miss it. And I don't want to go back."

"Even if that means sacrificing your relationship with Harry and your child?" Cambridge asked softly, without judgment.

The counselor had spoken the truth when he said that in this form, memories were partitioned, but that wasn't unique to this form. Even in her organic life, she had practiced the same art of compartmentalization: difficult emotions were often set aside to be dealt with later.

But later rarely came.

Each partition contained an imaginary door. The memories the counselor was attempting to unearth were locked behind one such door. She had but to open it to remember all of the beautiful and painful memories she had segregated. But before she subjected herself to that, she needed to understand why she had locked them away in the first place.

"I don't . . . why would I have . . . I mean . . ."

"Did you love Harry Kim?"

"I thought I did. No," she said, "I thought that given enough time, I *would*."

"And how did that work out?"

Conlon shook her head. "I was afraid. I didn't want to do this alone."

"Facing death and the termination of your pregnancy?"

Conlon cracked the door open ever so slightly.

"I remember standing on the holodeck in a simulation of a hillside with beautiful trees. I needed to make a choice about the baby, using its cells to save my life. I didn't want to do that because I didn't want to raise the child. Not knowing how long I would live after that was part of it. But the biggest part was that I wasn't ready to live that life."

"And Harry?"

Conlon shook her head. "When does liking someone a lot, wanting to know them better, and enjoying their company become love?" she asked. "What I realized that day was that he was safe and comfortable and having him beside me while I fought this fight would make it easier for me. When I'm with him, it just feels like whatever he says, or wants, or thinks, is right. What I want is somehow never as important when he's there.

"But that day, on the hillside, I knew that even though all of that was true, it wasn't love. Not like what he felt. It was need. It was weakness. It wasn't my truth."

"And you intended to tell him that?"

Conlon nodded. The only reason she could access this information without the emotions connected to them overwhelming her was because she was able to control the information processed by her matrix. Sorting this out in her human body would have been impossible.

It *had been* impossible.

"But then I woke up and the baby had been born. And Harry was there and said all of the right things and I just didn't have the strength to fight it. Or him. I could take the pain. It wasn't going to last forever. And then, he'd be free and he'd have what he wanted."

"The child?"

"He wanted her in a way I never could. It didn't seem like too much to ask. And the longer we spent here, struggling together to survive, the more it felt like the right choice. I do care for him. He is the best person I have ever known. I was dying. I knew it. So why not make these last days as happy as we could? What was the harm?"

"It wasn't what you wanted," Cambridge replied.

"No, it wasn't," she agreed.

"The consciousness transfer was completed perfectly, exactly as you decided it would be, wasn't it?"

"Yes," Conlon admitted to him and to herself for the first time.

"You do understand that retaining this holographic body can't be the solution to your problem either."

Conlon nodded.

"We'll take all of this one step at a time," Cambridge assured her.

"Would you do me a favor?"

"If I can."

"I want to speak to Harry before we do the transfer. I don't know if I'll be able to . . ."

"I think that can be arranged," Cambridge replied.

DEMETER

Commander Atlee Fife's interactions with his captain had been limited since they had rejoined the fleet. Given the counselor's recommendations it was unlikely that O'Donnell would resume his position prior to the dissemination of their new orders, but Fife wanted to make sure that O'Donnell heard that from him.

The captain's personal quarters had never been kept in regulation order. Fife was astonished when he entered to find the usual disarray had been replaced by a spotless workspace, a freshly made rack, and a visible deck.

His surprise was clearly not lost on O'Donnell.

"Just because I choose not to do something doesn't mean I don't know how," O'Donnell said, correctly intuiting the reason for the shock on Fife's face.

Now that the moment had come, Fife found himself at a loss for words.

O'Donnell spared him. "I have spoken at great length with Counselor Cambridge. I never saw much use for a counselor, let alone on a starship. But I might reconsider that in the future, assuming I have one with Starfleet. He's given me a lot to think about."

"I am pleased to hear that, sir."

"I bet you are." It sounded like a dig, but O'Donnell added quickly, "I owe you an apology, Atlee."

332 ■ KIRSTEN BEYER

"For what?"

"I lost track of my responsibilities to you and to our ship."

"It happens."

"Clearly. But you deserve better than that from me."

"Thank you, sir."

An uncomfortable pause followed until O'Donnell said, "I hope when we're done here, we'll be able to put this behind us."

"That's not . . . what I mean to say is . . ." Fife floundered.

O'Donnell's face paled. "Unless you have other ideas?"

"Actually, I did. But it didn't quite work out the way I expected."

"What are we talking about?"

"Are you aware of the reason the Edrehmaia brought *Galen* out here?" Fife asked.

"I haven't seen or heard anything that didn't happen in this room in days," O'Donnell replied.

Fife shifted his weight from foot to foot uncertainly.

"Sit the hell down and spit it out, Atlee," O'Donnell said.

Fife moved to one of the two chairs that sat at a small table beside the suite's replicator. O'Donnell joined him there.

"The Edrehmaia intend to leave our galaxy. They needed our slipstream drive to break the galactic barrier," Fife reported.

Delight, confusion, awe, and wonder played simultaneously across O'Donnell's face. "I did not see that coming," he said.

"None of us did. While *Galen* is clearly not an appropriate ship for such an undertaking, it occurred to me that *Demeter* might be."

A slow smile began to form on O'Donnell's face. "Did it?"

Fife nodded. "Just because you went about it in the most egregiously incompetent manner possible, that does not mean your scientific curiosity about the Edrehmaia was entirely misplaced."

"I'll allow that because we're friends, Atlee, but don't push it."

Fife chuckled agreeably. "I spoke with Captain Chakotay and asked if he thought the admiral would consider allowing *Demeter* to undertake that mission."

"Why?"

"Because I knew that once you learned what the Edrehmaia wanted, you would do the same."

"I would have," O'Donnell agreed, "but never in a million years would I expect it from you."

Fife shrugged. "Elkins assured me it was safe. I saw no reason to deny you the ability to continue to pursue the answers to the questions you've spent your entire life searching for. And as long as I was willing to support it, I assumed the admiral would at least give it due consideration."

"I appreciate that. But you still haven't answered my question. Why would you do that for me?"

"I betrayed you once, sir. And your response to that betrayal was to trust more, to communicate better, and to help me become an officer worthy of my position here. I owe you everything. It felt like the least I could do."

O'Donnell bowed his head for a moment. Finally, he said, "Thank you, Atlee."

"Unfortunately, the admiral has denied my request."

"I see," O'Donnell said. "I guess it was a long shot at best. Still, I appreciate that you were willing . . ."

"She has decided to take *Voyager* beyond the barrier instead."

O'Donnell shot out of his chair. "Are you serious?"

"Always, sir."

"Can we . . . ? I have to speak with her."

"I have already been assured that a position in *Voyager*'s science department is yours for the taking, sir."

O'Donnell began to pace fretfully. "That's just . . . I can't believe . . . do you realize what you've done, Atlee?"

"I believe so, yes, sir," Fife said, rising.

O'Donnell came to an abrupt halt. "Wait. What does this mean for you?"

"I have been asked to remain with the fleet and continue on as *Demeter*'s captain," Fife replied.

Some of the light in O'Donnell's eyes dimmed.

"I see."

"I told the admiral I would not accept until I had spoken to you."

"You want my permission?"

"No, sir. I want you to make me one promise. Two, come to think of it."

"Go ahead."

"I want you to be careful. More careful than has become your custom of late."

"I think I can manage that," O'Donnell assured him.

"And I want you to come back. Someday, I want to receive a transmission from you, and I want to hear everything that you saw and did and learned while you were away."

O'Donnell closed the space between them. Although he had never been physically demonstrative, he raised his arms and embraced Fife warmly. When he pulled away, his eyes were glistening.

"I never had a son, Atlee," O'Donnell said softly. "I wanted one. Or a daughter, I suppose. I thought I'd lost that opportunity forever when Alana died. I was wrong."

"That's kind of you to say, sir."

"Call me 'sir' one more time, Atlee . . ." O'Donnell said.

Fife's throat tightened as he replied, "Take care of yourself, Liam."

VOYAGER

Aytar Gwyn had remained with Devi Patel since the moment of her transformation. She had spoken to the interlocutor Patel had become and found it to be the worst conversationalist she'd ever met, which was ironic given that its purpose was communication. Apart from the coordinates where the *Galen* could be found, it had spoken continuously about builders and architects and submarines and positive infinity, none of which meant anything to Gwyn. But she had let it speak, had asked it as many questions as she could think of, all in the hope that what had been done to Devi might somehow be undone. But for that to happen, this thing that had taken her friend had to remain alive.

And so, Gwyn had persisted.

She had stayed on the runabout even when it was recovered by *Voyager* and the determination was made that the interlocutor would remain contained there until they had reached the home of the Edrehmaia. She had been there while the interlocutor was questioned by the admiral and the captain and an endless stream of officers who were trying to figure out how to help the Edrehmaia. And she was there when she learned that the Doctor had been given the data required to reverse the process by which Patel had been transformed.

Gwyn had remained in sickbay throughout the procedure and Patel's convalescence. Seven had stopped by a few times, but Lasren was her most frequent companion. She had shared the entire series of events with him, but no one else. He had, of course, asked how Gwyn was doing now that she was assured of the child's well-being.

Much better, was the truth.

She continued to feel the presence of the child. That sense had grown stronger the moment *Voyager* had closed the distance between them. Gwyn had considered every possible way to share what she had done with Lieutenants Kim and Conlon but had not yet settled upon one.

It was weird. That was the bottom line. It was a relationship that made no sense to anyone who wasn't Kriosian and the only model Gwyn had to reference as a basis for comparison was useless. She barely knew Kim and didn't know Conlon at all beyond their professional interactions. The circle of those on the ship who knew Gwyn's truth was limited and she doubted any of them would reveal it to Kim or Conlon. As the days wore on, she began to wonder if she would ever reveal it herself. She expected Kim and Conlon to return to *Voyager* and to bring the child with them.

That might be enough. Perhaps the rest could wait until she was older. There was time.

These thoughts consumed her until the moment Devi Patel opened her eyes.

"Where am I?" was her first question.

Gwyn was on her feet in an instant. "You're home. You're on *Voyager*. You did it. You helped us find the *Galen*. Do you remember any of it?"

Patel thought for a moment. "I remember all of it," she said. "I remember the pain and I remember the moment it ended. I remember flying among the stars with the others who were like me. I remember being more than I have ever been and strange music. I remember speaking for them. But most of all, I remember you, always with me."

Gwyn smiled. "I promised the Doctor I would get him when you woke up. I should . . ."

"You were going to tell me a story," Patel said.

"It can wait."

"No. No more waiting."

"But . . ."

"You came back. You came to the runabout and you helped me and wait . . . you shot Commander O'Donnell."

"Because you ordered me to. Now are you convinced I know how to follow orders?"

"Is he okay?"

"He's fine."

"Good. That's good."

"For the last several days you have been one of the most important people on this ship, Devi. Everyone is going to want to talk to you and the Doctor needs to make sure you are okay. We have all the time in the world now," Gwyn insisted.

"I understand that. I've been here before, and I know how this works. As soon as people start walking through that door, they won't stop until I'm back on duty. What I still don't understand, the only piece of this puzzle I can't see, is how you went from being furious with me to shooting a superior officer just because I told you to. Let me be selfish for a minute, okay?"

"Okay," Gwyn said.

"Oh, and Aytar?" Patel said as Gwyn pulled her chair to the edge of the biobed and settled herself.

"Yes?"

"I love you, too."

Harry Kim was alone.

He had endured the endless debriefs and consultations and physical examinations and staff meetings stoically. When he was off duty it was worse. Damn near every single officer on *Voyager* had wanted to hear the story of *Galen*'s survival. To a man, they felt the need to share how much he had been missed and how glad they were to see him again. He had been commended repeatedly by Commander Glenn for his service to the *Galen*. He still received daily requests from Ensign Drur, who had worked tirelessly with Velth and Patel in expanding communication with the Edrehmaia. He had spent hours commiserating with the Doctor and several sessions with Counselor Cambridge, who had been incredibly blunt but also oddly helpful in helping him come to grips with his new reality.

And he had spent many hours with Tom and B'Elanna. Their reunion had been bittersweet. Of course, they had missed one another, but he found it difficult to look at them without thinking of all he would never have. They were struggling to make a decision regarding *Voyager*'s new mission. B'Elanna seemed inclined to continue on but Tom was putting up a hell of a fight. For him, exploring space with untested new modifications to the slipstream drive for an indeterminate amount of time was simply too dangerous to contemplate with the children. Bryce had offered to take *Voyager*'s engine room and last they had spoken, it seemed likely that both Parises would be transferring to the *Vesta* shortly.

The only person in the fleet, it seemed, who wanted nothing at all to do with him was Nancy Conlon.

Even now, days after she had called him to sickbay to tell him . . . her truth . . . it was still hard to believe. He thought he had done everything right. He had loved her, supported her, given all he had to offer, time and again. And still, it hadn't been enough. Sifting through his memories of every moment they had shared since she had fallen ill, he couldn't help but see the pattern. She had put distance between them. He had pulled her back. She had been afraid. He had insisted she set that aside. She had wanted things between them to be different and he had ignored that, certain he knew better.

He had been so very wrong.

How had he been so very wrong?

Again.

He wanted to hate her, but he couldn't hold on to that feeling for long. Every time he tried, he found the image of their child, floating in her little world, completely unaware that the two people responsible for creating her had come undone.

If he was being completely honest, part of him had felt it happening the last time he had stood among the holographic stars playing "Clair de Lune." He had begun to grieve the loss he hadn't yet been able to name. He would continue to grieve for a very long time.

But more important, he needed to think. He needed to make a decision. *Voyager* was about to embark on a new and incredibly dangerous mission. He, alone, was now responsible for the life of his daughter and he didn't know if it was right to expose her to that. Tom clearly wouldn't think so. But Tom had B'Elanna, Michael, and Miral. Kim had no one. He could not imagine spending the next several weeks, months, or years doing anything but the only job he had ever done, offering the admiral and the captain the best he had left to give, and learning to live again in the absence of Nancy Conlon. He had lost everything else. He couldn't lose *Voyager* or his daughter.

Nancy had been restored to her body. She was healed. And she had decided to remain aboard *Galen* for the duration of the fleet's mission. Their child now resided in *Voyager*'s sickbay, pending Kim's final notification to Captain Chakotay of his intentions.

He faced a future he didn't want, that he could hardly conceive. He had never in his life felt so desperate.

Or so alone.

21

VOYAGER

Commander Tom Paris was running late. It wasn't his fault. Michael hadn't slept well the previous night and truly didn't care that his parents were expected in the mess hall at eleven hundred hours in full dress uniforms. Miral had been up since zero six hundred, demanding to put on the white dress with the poofy skirt that had been replicated for her so that she could spin and twirl and leap, testing the skirt's buoyancy.

And B'Elanna still hadn't forgiven him.

It didn't help that watching her fasten the last of the buttons that secured her dress tunic only made him think of how nice it would be to help her undo them.

When she turned to face him, she had no trouble at all translating the look in his eyes.

"Don't even think about it."

"I wasn't."

"You were."

"I love you."

"We're late." Poking her head out of their bedroom she called, "Miral, if you rip that skirt one more time, you're not going to the wedding."

"I has to go, Mommy," she shouted back. "I am flower girl."

"You know, if there isn't already a superhero holoprogram with that name, I'm going to write one," Paris said.

"Yeah, well, you'll have plenty of free time to do that in a few days," Torres tossed back.

"Do we have to talk about this again?" he asked.

"What's to talk about? You've made your decision," Torres replied, stepping into the 'fresher to check her hair one last time.

"I thought we agreed."

"You said you would resign your commission and take the children back to Earth if I refused. That's blackmail. Not agreement."

"I needed you to know how seriously I feel about this," Paris insisted. "I wouldn't have actually done it."

"I know. I would have killed you first."

"B'Elanna, I get it. I really do. Together we can do anything and who's to say that the fleet won't encounter any number of dangerous things in the next year and a half that will make staying on *Voyager* for this trip seem like the better choice. But sometimes, you have to consider the odds."

"Janeway and Chakotay got this ship seventy thousand light-years in seven years," Torres reminded him. "We survived the Borg, Species 8472, the stupid Malon, and a bunch of other hostile species I can't even remember now. I think they can handle the interstellar void and a quick tour of Sagittarius Dwarf Elliptical."

"I agree. I think they'll do great out there. But that's a very different mission profile than the one you and I agreed to undertake when we decided to stay with the fleet."

"They need us," Torres insisted.

"I need us more," Paris replied. "I'm willing to risk a lot when it comes to Starfleet, but turns out, I've found my limit and this is it."

B'Elanna glided past him, heading into the living room. He caught her hand and lifted it gently to his lips.

"You were supposed to be in Chakotay's ready room ten minutes ago," she reminded him.

"He'll wait. He's not going anywhere without his best man."

"And doesn't that tell you anything?"

"He and I have already discussed this. He understands our choice."

"Your choice."

"B'Elanna, stop. Look at me."

She did so, lifting stormy eyes to meet his.

"Now look at them," he said.

Torres turned to see Miral springing off the sofa and landing on the deck with her skirt flying over her face. Michael lay in his bassinet, sleeping soundly.

"It's time," he said simply. "Miral needs a ship with children her age. One of the *Galaxy* classes maybe, with a proper school. And Michael needs us both. He's going to be walking before we know it."

"We can make do."

"I know we can, because we have for years now. But this isn't the time to take them deeper into the unknown. This is the time to give them the foundation they will build upon, and that foundation needs to be rock solid."

"You're talking about Earth?"

"I can think of worse places."

"And what are we supposed to do there?"

"Whatever you want."

"And our friends?"

"Will be back in a couple of years with some amazing stories to tell," he assured her.

"I don't know, Tom," she said. "It's such a big change. I like our lives the way they are now."

"I'll make you a deal. Come home with me. See what Starfleet can offer us, and if you hate it, as soon as *Voyager* gets back, we'll join them again."

"But . . ."

"Okay. I've never done this before, not in the entire history of our marriage. But I'm doing it now."

"Tom . . ."

"I need this. I need our lives to be just a little safer. I need a few less nights of worrying if we're going to live to see another day. I need to know that our jobs aren't putting our children's future at significant risk every moment of every day. We brought them into this universe and we owe it to them to be here as long as possible to help them grow.

"I need to give them what I never had."

Her eyes softened. "I wonder if that's the problem."

"What do you mean?"

"I never had that life either. I don't even know what it would feel like."

"Then can we please find out together?"

"It's not fair," Hugh Cambridge said miserably.

"You look fine," Seven assured him.

"I look like a prat and I can't breathe in this thing."

"Shall I tell the admiral and the captain you were unable to attend the ceremony because your collar was too tight?"

"Would you? I'd be ever so grateful."

Seven, who found the full-dress version of the mission specialist's uniform equally uncomfortable, had no pity for the counselor.

"You'll live."

"I don't suppose there's any way to get out of this, is there?"

"No."

"I wasn't actually talking about the day's festivities."

Seven paused, but before the word *explain* fell from her lips, she understood. "*Voyager* is going to lead the Edrehmaia beyond this galaxy. I will be with her. What you decide to do when she departs is entirely up to you."

"You don't mean that."

She didn't.

Seven lifted a single eyebrow.

Cambridge countered by slipping gracefully into her personal space and placing his hands on her hips.

"You would be lost without me. Every damn one of you. There has never in the history of Starfleet been a vessel whose need of a full-time counselor eclipsed *Voyager*'s."

"I believe the *Vesta*'s Counselor Bayi has expressed interest in a transfer," Seven noted.

"Bayi's a hack."

"Not true."

"No, it isn't, but that doesn't change the fact that . . ." Cambridge trailed off. "Oh, damn it all, Seven, would it kill you, just once, to acknowledge that this, what we share and will continue to share as long as you'll have me, is by far the most compelling, frustrating, yet worthwhile relationship you have ever known?"

Seven leaned in and kissed him lightly.

"So stipulated," she said. "But I do not believe anyone should join this mission who is not committed to it for their own reasons."

"I just told you my reasons."

"Our need of you is not *your* need."

"I'm not sure I see an appreciable difference anymore."

She did.

But she didn't care.

"Then I will see you shortly. I'll be the one up front, right next to the bride."

"Do what you can not to overshadow her. You will fail miserably, but make the effort anyway."

"You are horrible."

"Fine. Have it your way. Shine as brightly as the star we'll be dragging across the galactic barrier in a few days."

"The moment the admiral enters the room, no one will pay the slightest bit of attention to anyone other than her. Which is as it should be. This is her day, and the captain's. You will be on time, dressed appropriately, and you will engage with abandon in the festivities that follow the ceremony."

"I can't remember the last time I did anything with abandon."

"I can."

Captain Regina Farkas was about to depart *Vesta* to report to *Voyager* when she finally received the transmission she had been awaiting from Admiral James Akaar, commander-in-chief of Starfleet.

"Admiral," she greeted his stern visage as soon as it appeared on her viewscreen.

"I understand congratulations are in order for Admiral Janeway and Captain Chakotay," he said without preamble.

"I was just on my way to make it official," Farkas said.

"Give them my best, won't you?"

"Gladly, sir. *Voyager* will be departing tomorrow morning, first thing. I had planned to stick around, not that I think anything will go wrong, but . . ."

"A wise precaution. I will expect your report as soon as they successfully breach the barrier."

"We don't expect our long-range sensors to be of much use after that."

"No, they wouldn't be."

"We have dropped sufficient communications relays to ensure that when they return, Starfleet will be aware immediately."

"Have you received the new orders I issued?"

Farkas nodded. "I have."

"Excellent. Agent Lucsly will be in touch to—"

"Admiral, with all due respect, I am going to have to refuse your orders to return to Krenim space at the behest of the DTI."

It was clear from Akaar's face that he was unprepared and unaccustomed to hearing refusals. *"Captain Farkas?"*

"I have no doubt, Admiral, that this fleet's last encounter with the Krenim raised concerns among the Department of Temporal Investigations. And I have no way of knowing how they determine which concerns merit risking the provocation of the kinds of actions they are duty bound to prevent. But I do know that the Krenim, as of our last communication with them, perceive Starfleet as an existential threat. And I know that the last thing Admiral Janeway promised was that as long as we didn't detect further alterations to the timeline, which our temporal shielding would have alerted us to, we would not darken their door again."

"Would it change your calculations if you learned that despite your temporal shielding, evidence exists suggesting just that?" Akaar asked.

"No," Farkas replied.

"*I see.*"

"My understanding is that the DTI prefers surgical strikes in their attempts to correct temporal incursions. I know they must have ships of their own, and qualified officers staffing them. Joint missions with Starfleet usually only involve the ships responsible for or directly connected to the anomalies in question."

"*That is true.*"

"But I have seen firsthand what the Krenim are capable of and I am here to tell you that if they have decided to begin manipulating time again in order to expand their empire, one ship—hell, three ships—won't make a difference."

"*The Krenim need to know that we pose no threat to their sovereignty,*" Akaar said.

"If they are altering the timeline, I believe we will be required to pose such a threat," Farkas said. "And if they're not, they might seriously consider doing so if we go back."

The admiral's glare was piercing.

"I'm sure I'm not telling you anything Admiral Janeway hasn't. And I'm sorry if you assumed that granting her request to initiate an exploratory mission with the Edrehmaia meant you would be dealing with an officer more amenable to ignoring her instincts and falling in line. But my gut says that if we are going to face an all-out conflict with the Krenim, we'll need a lot more than the *Vesta* and two small special-mission ships to do it. You'd be sending us into a bloodbath and I've seen enough of those out here to last me a lifetime."

"*May I ask if . . .*" Akaar began, his face reddening, "*Hell, did Janeway put you up to this?*"

"She did not."

"*Because it sure sounds like her.*"

"I take that as a compliment, sir," Farkas said. "One of the directors of the DTI reached out to me personally a few weeks back. He asked me to see to it that Janeway followed the directive of the DTI and warned me that should she fail to do so, she would lose her command."

"I was unaware of that."

"I have followed Kathryn Janeway's orders for the last several months and while we haven't always seen eye to eye, she has never acted without great personal integrity, nor has she ever given me an order I found unconscionable. Director Dulmur did both of those things within the first five minutes of meeting me. You are asking me to risk the lives of hundreds of officers on the orders of individuals who clearly see us as pawns to be moved around on a board of temporal chess.

"I won't do it, Admiral."

Stony silence greeted this admission. Finally, Akaar said, *"Once* Voyager *departs, you will resume your previously planned exploration of the Delta Quadrant. Your reservations are noted and will be added to the information already provided to the DTI. And I will speak personally with Director Dulmur, was it?"*

"Yes, sir. Marion Dulmur."

"I can't go into details right now, but I can tell you that I am convinced by the evidence that I have seen that we may yet have need of your services out there. But if that should become necessary, you will do so with every bit of support Starfleet can provide."

"I would appreciate that, sir."

"Akaar out."

PERSONAL LOG: LIEUTENANT HARRY KIM

Hey there, little one.

How do you like your new room? You're on a ship called Voyager *now. She's a good ship. She's special to me because she's the first starship I ever served on and she's also the ship where I met your mom.*

Yeah. Your mom.

"Computer, delete . . ."

No, never mind. We have to talk about this at some point, so may as well start now. Your mom has been through a lot. She was pretty sick when you were born and even though it looks like she's going to be fine now, she has decided . . . well, we decided together but it was more her idea than mine . . . that the best thing for all of us is that she and I would no longer be in a relationship. She's still your mother. She'll always be that. Half of your DNA will always be hers. When you get a little older if you want to meet her or talk to her we can make that happen.

But for now, and probably forever, it's just going to be you and me. It might be a long time before you even realize that's unusual. Although it isn't, necessarily. Lots of children are raised by one parent, even if their parents are married. Some families have more than two parents in a relationship. The Andorians come to mind. Anyway, point is, families come in all kinds of shapes and sizes and for now, we are a family of two.

And I'm okay with that. From the moment I knew you existed, all I wanted was for you to be born and for us to meet and for you to know how much I already love you. You've already changed my life for the better. Not that that's your job, but you have. It's just a fact.

And it's important to both of us that you understand that what happened between me and your mom had nothing to do with you.

Remember when we were talking about communication? About how you can sometimes want to communicate clearly, but no matter how hard you try, it can be really hard? For a long time, your mom tried to tell me what she really needed from me. But I thought that what she really needed was different. I thought I knew better. She was right to tell me the truth. There's nothing more important than that, even if it's hard. I wish—

"Oh, I'm sorry."

"Computer, pause log."

Kim turned to see Ensign Gwyn standing in the doorway. "What are you doing here?" he asked.

"Why aren't you at the wedding?"

"It doesn't start for another half an hour."

"But aren't you one of the groomsmen? Shouldn't you be with the captain right now?"

"Gwyn?"

"Right. Sorry."

"What are you doing here?"

Gwyn was momentarily at a total loss for words. "I just wanted to see how she was doing," she finally admitted. "Doctor Sharak said it would be okay."

"I'm not sure Sharak is the one you should be asking," Kim suggested.

"I'm sorry. You're right. I'll go."

"No, hang on," Kim said. "Come in here."

Gwyn stepped forward warily.

"She's fine. She's about twelve weeks old, three inches long. Her face is fully formed. She's got thumbs," Kim said.

Gwyn smiled. "It's cool that you know that."

"I spend time with her every day if I can."

"Also, very cool."

"I guess."

"Does she have a name yet?"

Kim shook his head. "I was waiting, but, no. I haven't chosen one yet."

"There's plenty of time."

"Yeah. People keep saying that, but I don't know."

"And she's definitely coming with us when we go tomorrow?"

Kim nodded. "Yeah. I'm, she's . . ." he began. It was hard to say, but he was going to have to start getting used to it, so he added, "I'm going to be a single parent."

"I heard."

"Great," Kim said miserably.

"Nobody's happy about it," Gwyn said quickly.

"I just don't like the thought of people discussing my personal life."

"Come on. It's not like you have the weirdest personal story to tell these days. Your relationship didn't work out. My best friend was transformed by a bunch of black goo into a temporary universal translator a few weeks ago. Just, you know, keeping things in perspective."

Kim chuckled involuntarily. It had been a while since he'd done that. "My best friend once broke the warp-ten threshold and evolved into a salamander."

"Tom Paris?"

"Yep. He kidnapped Admiral Janeway, turned her into a sala-mander as well, and by the time we caught up with them, she had given birth to a little pack of salamander babies."

"Does Chakotay know?"

"He was there, Gwyn."

"Is that why it's impossible to push the drive past warp nine point nine? Is that the reason the fail-safe was installed?"

"Yep."

"But we travel at speeds well beyond maximum warp when we use the slipstream drive."

Kim shrugged. "Something about the geometry allows for that in a slipstream corridor. The problem with warp ten is that it is an impossible speed. It bends space to the point that you end up oc-cupying all points in the universe at the same time."

Gwyn considered this. "Okay, but were you *there* when Paris hyperevolved? Did you watch it happen? Because if you didn't, I've still got you beat."

"It's not a contest, Gwyn."

"Right, but if it was, I might still win."

Kim didn't really understand how he had suddenly found him-self in this bizarre conversation, but he wasn't exactly hating it. Still, it made little sense.

"Why are you so concerned about the baby?" he asked. "I re-member you saw her when she was on the *Galen*, but, and this isn't a judgment, you don't seem like the type of person who would care about any child, let alone this one."

"I know. I didn't used to be. But she's . . ."

"What?"

Gwyn shook her head. "Never mind. Enjoy the wedding. And for what it's worth, I think you're going to make a great dad."

It almost broke something in Kim to hear her say that. He hadn't realized until that moment how much he needed to hear someone say it.

"I don't know about that. I just know that ever since she was born, she became the most important person in the universe for me. I'd do anything for her. I don't know how not to. She saved my life already."

"Yeah, mine too," Gwyn said.

Kim found that understandably confusing. "Huh?"

Gwyn seemed to immediately regret that admission.

"I mean, you know . . ."

"No, I don't know. How did she save your life?"

Gwyn shook her head, appeared to consider fleeing, then consciously chose to stand her ground.

"It's a long story. But someday, when you have some time, I'd like to tell you about it."

Gwyn was not someone he considered a friend. She was a gifted and clearly complicated young woman. But on at least one recent occasion, she had been a source of unexpected wisdom. He had no idea how she had come to believe what she obviously sincerely did. But something in her eyes, a combination of hope and defiance he had never seen before, roused his curiosity.

"Let's talk when your duty shift ends," he suggested.

Gwyn nodded and smiled ruefully. "We can do that."

Once she had gone, Kim thought about completing the log entry, but thought better of it. Instead, he ordered the computer to delete all of the logs he had recorded for the baby thus far.

The past was the past. Someday, when he had a little more distance from it and perspective on it, he would figure out how to tell his daughter everything she needed to know about how she came into the universe.

For now, it was enough that she had. The rest, Harry Kim would figure out as he went along.

Despite the fact that several versions of the event had been considered in the last few days, it was finally decided that this should be a relatively intimate affair.

Voyager's mess hall had been rearranged, a few tables lining the rear wall and two dozen chairs lined up on either side of a small aisle. The bride carried a small bouquet of lilies of the valley, her flower girl a nosegay of purple dahlias.

The bride and groom wore full dress uniforms. Each was attended by two of those dearest to them, Seven and B'Elanna Torres for the bride, Tom Paris and Harry Kim for the groom.

The Doctor was the event's official holographer. Captain Regina Farkas served as its officiant. The witnesses included Captains Glenn and O'Donnell, Lieutenant Commander Fife, Lieutenants Patel, Lasren, Aubrey, Bryce, Barclay, and Elkins, as well as Ensign Icheb. Counselor Cambridge along with Doctors Sharak and Sal rounded out the small group. Lieutenant Conlon was the only officer invited who sent her regrets along with her best wishes for the bride and groom.

The ceremony was brief, the vows somewhat traditional. Admiral Kathryn Janeway and Captain Chakotay promised before the assembly to love and honor each other, to remember that each day contained the promise of new wisdom, that every challenge was a doorway to deeper understanding, and that the promise they had made would be remade again and again and fulfilled through every moment of the rest of their lives.

Their commitment was accompanied by the exchange of simple white-gold wedding bands and sealed with a gentle kiss.

After a brief reception, during which heartfelt congratulations were offered by all present and several toasts were made to the couple's continued health and happiness, the admiral and captain departed to spend the rest of the day alone. The guests returned to their regular duties.

Come alpha shift the following morning, a new journey would begin.

ACKNOWLEDGMENTS

Well, here we are.

Since this is the last time I'm going to write one of these for a while, I am a little overwhelmed by the gratitude I feel for the people in my life who loved and supported me long before I was a professional writer (Fred, Patricia, Matthew, Paul, David, and Heather); the people who have given me the opportunity to write these novels (Marco, Margaret, and Ed) and by so doing, gave me the experience I would need to pursue dreams beyond these novels; the people whose work on these books makes them better (Scott and John); the people whose work inspires me daily and pushes me to always try and do better (David, Dayton, Kevin, Christopher, Una, Dave, DRG, James, and Mike); the people who make sure I behave myself (Maura and Cheryl); the people whose love for *Trek* and these stories and whose thoughtful reading always gives me a lot to think about (Malcolm and Matt); and the people who are my lifeline as I do this work (David and Anorah).

Then there are the people I have been blessed to work with over the last few years as writing television became my primary focus and writing novels became my secret, solitary joy (Heather, Alex, Aaron, Akiva, Michael, Joe, Craig, Boey, Erika, Jenny, Jonathan, and, most recently, Ken, Terry, and Henry).

A few things you should know about this book. I would never have attempted it without Malcolm's help with the language of math. I would never have finished it without Ed insisting that I should and Margaret believing that I would. And John, to whom this book is dedicated and who has probably forgotten more about *Star Trek* than I will ever know, has always kept me on the straight and narrow, and I hope will always know how very dear he is to me and how much I appreciate everything he does.

I have never before thanked those actors who played the characters that have occupied an inordinate amount of space in my mind for the last fifteen years (Kate, Robert, Robbie, Bob, Roxann, Jeri, Tim, Garret, Ethan, and Jennifer), nor have I mentioned the writers and producers who created them (Rick, Michael, Jeri, Branon, Joe, Ken, Bryan, Ron, Lisa, and Mike). I owe the greatest imaginable debt to all of you.

But finally, it comes down to you. The people who have read these books since the beginning, waited patiently for me to finish the next one, argued with me on the TrekBBS, and kept me honest throughout. To each and every one of you, I can only say thank you for sharing this journey with me. Despite the fact that this was by far the most difficult novel I have ever written because it had to be written off and on over the course of two years (which is ridiculous, I know), at the end of the day I needed to finish my part of this story as much for you as for myself. I hope it was worth the wait.

Until we meet again. . . .

ABOUT THE AUTHOR

KIRSTEN BEYER is the *New York Times* bestselling author of eleven *Star Trek: Voyager* novels: *String Theory: Fusion, Full Circle, Unworthy, Children of the Storm, The Eternal Tide, Protectors, Acts of Contrition, Atonement, A Pocket Full of Lies, Architects of Infinity,* and *To Lose the Earth.* She wrote the *Buffy the Vampire Slayer* novel *One Thing or Your Mother* and the *Alias* APO novel *Once Lost.* She contributed the short story "Isabo's Shirt" to the *Star Trek: Distant Shores* anthology as well as the short story "Widow's Weeds" to *Space Grunts.* She has also written several articles for *Star Trek* magazine.

In 2016, she joined the writing staff of CBS All Access's *Star Trek: Discovery* series. She has worked on three seasons of *Discovery* as a staff writer, executive story editor, and co-producer. In 2017, she pitched a premise for a new series centered around one of *Star Trek*'s most beloved captains, Jean-Luc Picard, and became one of that series' co-creators along with Alex Kurtzman, Akiva Goldsman, and Michael Chabon. She served as supervising producer on the first season of *Picard* and is returning for the second season as a co-executive producer. A *Star Trek: Short Treks* work, "Children of Mars," which she co-wrote with Alex Kurtzman and Jenny Lumet, was released in January 2020.

In addition to her writing and producing responsibilities, Kirsten also serves as the resident *Star Trek* canon resource for the writers' rooms and production departments, as well as the liaison between the series and the tie-in licensors. In that capacity, she has overseen the creation of six *Discovery* novels and co-written numerous *Discovery* comic books with Mike Johnson, including the acclaimed

Light of Kahless, Succession, and *Aftermath*. She continues to oversee the creation of new ancillary stories for *Star Trek: Picard*, including the release of its bestselling first novel, *The Last Best Hope* by Una McCormack.

Kirsten received undergraduate degrees in English literature and theater arts, and an MFA degree from UCLA. She lives in Los Angeles with her husband and their daughter.